		DATE DUE		

TOO
HIGH

TOO HIGH

Corson Hirschfeld

A Tom Doherty Associates Book
New York

TOO HIGH

Copyright © 2001 by Corson Hirschfeld

This book is printed on acid-free paper.

A Forge Book
Published by Tom Doherty Associates, LLC
175 Fifth Avenue
New York, NY 10010

www.tor.com

Forge® is a registered trademark of Tom Doherty Associates, LLC.

Library of Congress Cataloging-in-Publication Data

Hirschfeld, Corson.
    Too high / Corson Hirschfeld.—1st ed.
      p. cm.
    "A Tom Doherty Associates book."
    ISBN 0-765-30011-7 (alk. paper)
    1. Archaeologists—Fiction. 2. Antiquities—Collection and preservation—Fiction. 3. Herpetologists—Fiction. 4. Rattlesnakes—Fiction. 5. Kentucky—Fiction. I. Title.

PS3558.I672 T66 2001
813'.54—dc21

2001033486

First Edition: September 2001

Printed in the United States of America

0 9 8 7 6 5 4 3 2 1

To Joseph T. Collins, king of the slinkies and of things that go hop in the night. During our high school and college years we collected reptiles and amphibians from one end of Kentucky to the other.

TOO
HIGH

PROLOGUE

J imbo glanced over his shoulder and spoke to his babies, jostling in the back of the shorty school bus. "Hang on, sweethearts. We're in the home stretch now."

No more than half a mile down the road, his chin bumped his chest and he bobbed awake. He white-knuckled the wheel, and shook his head, fast. "Coffee. What I need is coffee. And more beer."

Jimbo fired up a cigarette, nearly missed the pull-off to Big Earl's Truckers' Rest. Shifting a sluggish foot to the brake, he angled from the road onto gravel—a bit too abruptly, thanks to five hours of bleary-eyed, predawn driving and three quarts of drown-the-highway-blues beer sloshing under his loosened belt. He overcorrected, hit the pedal hard, and felt the bus slip into a four-wheel skid—"Oh, mama!"

In a cloud of dust and skittering pea gravel, the bus came to rest four feet from plate glass, eight from a hands-on-hips waitress with three breakfast specials soaking her once-white Easy Spirit sneakers.

Jimbo touched his safari hat with a friendly grin and shook the dregs of his third quart onto the seat to douse the dislodged tip of his smoke, fast burning a mean black hole in the vinyl. He eased away, drove to the blind side of the building, and wiped his forehead with the back of an arm. "Whew-ee, boy," he said to his reflection in the rearview mirror. "That was close."

The grin disappeared as Jimbo remembered his cargo. "Shee-it! My babies." He parted the heavy drapes behind the driver's seat, flew into the back to the sound of ten thousand strips of bacon crackling on a hell-hot griddle. "Calm down! Calm down, sweethearts." Waving the air. "No harm done."

A hundred built-in wooden cages with metal mesh doors lined the walls of the seatless bus. Inside the cages, none too happy, writhed Jungle Jimbo Bybee's babies: 436 fresh-caught timber rattlesnakes, *Crotalus horridus*.

"Ssshhh," said Jimbo. Not that his deaf charges heard him, not that he heard himself over the rattling, hissing, and, worse, thumping of scaly noses striking metal screen doors.

"Settle down, babies," Jimbo pleaded. And, gradually, they did. He moved slowly along the tiers of cages, counting noses, more accurately inspecting them, hopeful to see no damaged merchandise. Crimson marred a mere dozen battered reptilian prows. "Could be worse."

In pristine condition, his babies would bring from forty to sixty dollars apiece. This was Jimbo's first-of-the-season snake run to the serpent handlers in the cities to the north: Cincinnati, Dayton, Columbus, Cleveland, Detroit, Chicago. The parent churches in the mountains caught their own, but the clandestine, big-city, tiny but true-to-the-faith splinter cults depended upon Jungle Jimbo Bybee, looked to his arrival each spring like kids lusting for the first *ting-a-ling* of the Mister Softee truck.

Jimbo owned Jungle Jimbo Bybee's Serpentarium in Cave City, Kentucky, 150 miles to the west. He had left Cave City ten days ago on a buying route that took him through the lowlands of Alabama, Georgia, and South Carolina. Now he was headed north, through eastern Kentucky, Daniel Boone country. It had been a good circuit, promised to pay the major share of the behemoth four-by-four Jimbo had dreamt of all winter. The next trip, he'd mix in some economical copperheads (no cottonmouths or diamondback rattlers—too feisty for even the Lord's work), but Jimbo knew when he rolled into those snake-starved cities on his first visit with only high-ticket, off-the-ark-perfect, colorful, southern timber rattlers, he'd move every one.

Had he been transporting snakes for himself or reptile collectors, he would have carried them in tied-off gunny sacks, but Jimbo learned years ago that *seeing* all the merchandise at once, in a confined space, induced an electric, nigh-on sexual mania in the snake preachers. Thus the blacked-out windows, the cedar cages, the Heaven's Gold shag carpet, the boom box with the hymns, the royal blue paint, the Gothic script on the sides—"They shall take up serpents, and it shall not hurt them"—and the twin bumper stickers: MARK 16:18, and JOHN 3:3.

Jimbo fueled up, bought a cello-wrapped egg salad sandwich, a large coffee, and two more quarts of cold beer— enough to get him through the next three dry counties, Galloway, Bradford, and McAfee—and hit the road on the last leg to Cincinnati.

Eight miles inside the McAfee County line, winding through hilly country, a small town in a valley to his left, a forested ridge to his right, Jimbo cranked up the radio—Willie Nelson, singing "A Redheaded Stranger"—and took a long pull on the second quart. Feelin' good.

He recalled the warning from the cashier: "Keep that foot light on the pedal through McAfee County, friend. That's one tough county—has a hard-assed sheriff who loves his radar, keeps close company with the judge." Jimbo checked the speedometer—uh-oh—let off the gas, and scanned the road for cops.

"Whoa, Nellie!" Coming his way at sixty-five miles an hour: not a cop, but the unmistakable sinuous silhouette of a heavy-bodied serpent crossing the highway. A rattler, for sure. No chance of stopping in time or swerving, so Jimbo kept his eyes on the slowly undulating form and worked the wheel to center the snake safely between the bus's front tires. Yes! He watched it fly by below, unscathed. He tapped the brakes, already picturing the trot back, lifting the sassy timber with his snake hook, and adding an easy sixty bucks to the pot.

What Jimbo saw when he looked up, however, was— "*Yeow!*"—a hairpin curve, fence—*Kee-rack!*—and then open air.

The bus soared thirty feet, slowed as it swished through treetops, and—*Whack!*—stopped in the flick of an eye, wedged between two mammoth oaks. Jimbo, however, kept going, through the windshield and another forty feet before smacking into the gnarly trunk of an Indian cigar tree.

The late Jungle Jimbo Bybee's custom cedarwood cages ripped from the bus's crimped walls with the impact. Within minutes, well before the smoking engine ignited dripping fuel and sent a snick of crackling orange fire along the underbelly of the chassis toward the fractured fuel tank, 436 buzzing, shaken-up timber rattlesnakes crawled to the floor, dropped through the sprung doors to the ground, and headed for the hills, or the town, or the surrounding homes and farms of McAfee County, Kentucky, with freedom on their minds.

I

—

Digger Fitz twined his fingers through the stiff wire mesh two feet from his nose and shook the grid. Solid. He felt for the car's rear door handle, looked for the window crank. Missing.

"Damned cop." Mumbling. "Said he was taking me to see Edgar. Instead, he's got me caged in here like some animal."

A scared rodent thumped and bumped in his chest as the old cop fear took hold. He squinted through the glass. Where the hell did the man go? There—ten paces away, talking with a little guy in western boots and a black cowboy hat wide as his shoulders. The sheriff, I'll bet. Edgar's hurt, and these Kentucky good old boys are in no hurry at all.

With the air-conditioning off, the windows closed, and the morning sun baking the big Crown Victoria, the temperature rose fast. Digger wrinkled his nose at the traces of booze, sweat, and the deputy's fried chicken. Eight in the morning and the man was chowing down on it.

He waggled the mesh again and cursed, a touch of panic in his voice. "Edgar. Where are you Edgar?" He tugged at his once-reddish, now going-to-gray beard, scanned the interior, and saw, nearly hidden under the front seat, three inches from his white-socked, sandaled toes, a neatly wrapped joint, thick and long as his little finger.

Digger had a flashback of postgrad days, of Berkeley and redwoods, a droning sitar, ardent young women with ironed hair to their waists, peace rallies and ban-the-bomb placards. The good old days. With no thought and a furtive swoop, he snagged the joint and dropped it in his shirt pocket.

He sat bolt upright as the trunk lid opened, and then slammed. A swollen belly materialized at the window, curly black hairs matted to sweaty white skin bulging past a sprung button. Digger's hand flopped over his pocket as he caught sight of the king-size deputy, whose face, screwed up, had *Gotcha* written all over it.

The panic returned. Busted.

But no, the deputy was merely hacking up farm dust. He spit to the side, opened the front door and fished a chicken leg from a red-and-white paper bucket on the seat. "Sorry about the wait," he said, and, finally, let Digger out. He nodded to several of his cohorts. "In the black hat, near the shack—that's Coony McCoy, McAfee County Sheriff."

Digger climbed out with an uneasy glance at the cars: ominous with their blazing roof hardware and stars on the doors. He saw cops in khaki, wearing tan cowboy hats with guns at their hips. All popped out of the same mold. All trouble.

He took in his own flowery red aloha shirt over baggy shorts, and dry swallowed. Running a hand through his long, reddish, white-flecked hair, he took a reluctant step forward. Ever since his postgrad days, cops gave Digger Fitz the heebie-jeebies. Chill out, he told himself, they're not after me. They're here because Edgar's injured. Poor old Edgar. I come all this way to reconnect and look what happens. Hang on, cousin.

The sheriff met them halfway. Ignoring Digger, he slapped the chicken leg from the deputy's hand, apparently more out of habit than anger. "What did I say, Gabe? You need to snack, stay with the celery sticks and carrots. You're blowin' up so big you won't fit in the damn cruiser—have to haul you around in the bed of a pick-em-up truck."

The deputy scowled at the chicken leg still rolling in the dirt.

"Don't worry, you'll live till lunch," the sheriff said; then to Digger: "Appreciate your coming." The words rolled off his lips in a drawl as soft and sweet as fresh licorice, with plenty of twang. "We don't want to move him yet, and I thought, you being a doctor . . ."

Digger forgot his shirt pocket contraband, the cop heebie-jeebies, the soothing voice. "Me?" He felt his face flush with professorial indignation. "I'm a Ph.D., an archae-ologist, not a medical doctor. Damn it to hell, I hope you called an ambulance. How badly is Edgar hurt?"

"Hurt?" The sheriff cocked his head, apparently unsure what to make of that. "Birdie, down at the E-Z Zees Mo-tel, said you two knew one another, said somebody phoned, called you doctor. Look, your friend—your friend's dead."

"Edgar? *Dead?*"

"Dead?" repeated a gaunt, rawboned deputy with a wan-dering left eye. "I hope to hell he's dead."

The sheriff threw the deputy a withering stare. "Watch your lip, Ike."

"Edgar, dead," Digger said, half to himself. "So, I'm too late." He backed against a car. "The officer who picked me up said there'd been an accident. I had no idea . . . How did it happen?"

"Lead poisoning," answered the gaunt deputy, with a wry smile. That got him another evil eye from the sheriff.

"You mean Edgar was *shot?*"

"Not perzactly," said the sheriff.

Twenty feet away, blue lightning pops lit the building's dusty, web-spanned windows from inside. Half a minute later, a young deputy barely out of his teens stumbled from the building, latex gloves on his hands, a 35 mm camera with flash dangling from his neck. He ripped off the gloves, leaned forward, hands on knees, skin blanched, eyes wide, and took two deep breaths.

"Got you some good close-ups, did you, Johnny?" asked his raw-boned cohort.

"Dammit, Ike," said the sheriff. "Johnny's new at this, so cut him some slack."He turned to Digger. "Farmer's boy was hunting rabbits after dawn. If his dog hadn't a scratched open the door, it might have been—hell—a long time before anyone came by."

At the words "long time," Ike pinched his nose with one hand and waved the air with the other.

The sheriff let that one pass, instead gave Digger a once-, then twice-over, from his shoulder-length hair to his sandaled feet. "Tell you what," he said, "if you're up to it, a positive identification would help. We found the motel's card in his pocket with your room number"—a hint of accusation in his voice. "The man's an outsider, none of us has seen him before."

He opened a red-and-yellow pack of Juicy Fruit, slid out a foil-wrapped stick, and offered it to Digger. Digger shook his head. The sheriff folded the gum twice and popped it in his mouth, chewed for half a minute. "Why don't you tell me who you are, how you know the man, when you seen him last." He removed his cowboy hat, played with its Indian beaded band, looking not at Digger, but beyond a weed-filled swale to the rolling Kentucky hills.

Digger peered at the ominous, bare wood structure, the only building in sight. The roof, dark corrugated iron weeping red with rust, teetered near collapse. Brambles consumed nearly a third of it. A sharp farm scent of manure mingled with the cloying sweetness of the sheriff's gum. Woozy, he put his hand over his mouth and nose, spoke through his fingers. "I'm Harmon Fitz. Edgar Fitz and I are cousins."

"Bo didn't mention the same last name." The sheriff cocked an eye at a fourth deputy speaking into a radio, tall, fair-haired, muscular. "Sometimes it seems I'm the last to know what the hell's going on." Eyes back to Digger: "So, you're related."

"We hadn't seen each other for three years . . . until last night." Digger pressed his palms to his eyes. "Edgar, dead." He dropped his hands and blinked. "Edgar planned to take me float fishing, discuss some business. My niece Nikki is coming down from Cincinnati tomorrow. The three of us wanted to reconnect. We're the last of the Fitzes."

"Ah," said the sheriff, "you're a fishin' man."

"The fishing would have been more of an excuse to talk."

The sheriff nodded. "The two of you was about to do a business deal, and last night you was together." Chewing slowly, he watched a hawk glide across a fallow field; then he rolled the Juicy Fruit foil into a small tight ball and bounced it off the car roof into the weeds. "Go on."

"What happened to him? Was he robbed?"

Chewing, the sheriff prompted: "You seen him last night . . ."

"I flew into Lexington. He picked me up, we arrived about six. Edgar's from Ann Arbor. He's been living here a couple of months. We had dinner at the pancake house by the motel around seven, then a few beers up the road." He pointed at the sun, still low in the eastern sky.

"Drinking. McAfee County here's dry. County Line Inn? Next county over?"

"That sounds right. Was a real . . ." He was about to say redneck bar, thought better of it, and said, ". . . rough-looking place. We talked about this and that. Mostly archaeology. Edgar is . . . Edgar *was*, an archaeologist, too. He expected Nikki and me to stay at his house, but I got here a day early, and he wanted to clean it up first—not that it mattered. Anyway, he arranged for me to stay at the E-Z Zees, dropped me off around eleven."

"That's what Birdie at the motel said. And you and her husband, Tyler, drank bourbon and played cards. You lost." A chuckle. "The first time old Tyler's won in a blue moon."

"Yeah. The fates haven't been smiling on me lately."

"And you kept losing till—how late?"

"One, at least. I went to bed, called Edgar this morning. No answer, so I assumed he was on his way. Your deputy got me out of the shower."

"You flew into Lexington." The sheriff nodded at Digger's sandals. "Don't see many men dressed in those around here." The emphasis on the words *men* and *those* held implications. "Guess you wear colored socks with them things sometimes?"

Digger scowled. "No, I'm a white-sock man. Life's simpler that way. What's your point?"

"Short pants, that shirt—you're not from these parts."

"Honolulu, Hawaii."

"Huly-huly girls, huh?" The sheriff sly-winked. "How long you been out of the country?"

"Excuse me?"

"High-wah-yah. That's where you been living?"

Digger studied the man. For the first time, he noticed his large eyes: light blue with long lashes, set in a delicate face framed by thick black hair cropped short at the sides, and neatly side-parted with a small wave over his left eyebrow. A compressed ring from the cowboy hat ran around his hair, ear-high, continued as a red band across his forehead. Digger placed him in his late fifties, eight or nine years younger than himself. And shorter, several inches shorter than Digger's own modest five-eight. Trim. No doubt a popular man in this remote rural county where everyone knew everyone else.

But still a cop. Another look, and he concluded he didn't see much intelligence behind the blue eyes. "Hawaii's the fiftieth state," he said. "We're part of the USA."

"Do tell?" Grinning.

Digger looked away, wondered if the man had ever seen an ocean. Hell, had ever been out of Kentucky. He recalled the sheriff's word *outsider*, thinking, Edgar, they've written you off already. Whoever shot you will go scot-free. He's back in the hills already, your money in his pocket, your watch on his wrist.

Eager to be done with the pointless conversation, he said, "I've lived in Hawaii thirty-five years, okay? Look, I want to see Edgar."

"Why not? Follow me and stay close. Don't touch nothing."

At the shack, Digger reached for the knob, but jumped back. "Snake!" He jabbed a finger at the base of the door.

"No more," said the sheriff. "That's a shed skin." He nudged it with his boot toe. "Was a rattler, good size. Second one I've seen in as many days. Skin's still soft, so its owner must have been here not long ago, maybe saw our murderer. Somewhere out there now." He waved a hand across the fields, and then turned and took a long look at Digger. "If snakes could talk, huh?"

"Snakes give me the creeps." Fascinated in spite of himself with the translucent, grayish, faintly patterned and flattened skin, Digger pushed open the door, stepped wide over the snakeskin, and stumbled inside. He was momentarily disoriented by the dim interior lit only by two smudged windows, one darkened by brambles, the other casting a long trapezoid of white sunlight across faded, peeling linoleum. Somewhere ahead, in the cool, mold-ripe interior, he knew he'd find Edgar. Shot dead.

With a start, he made out a shadowy form sprawled on the floor, facing the back wall. Edgar: flesh pale as candle wax, a double handful of gumball-size dark spheres scattered around his head. Digger reeled. Only the sheriff's steadying hand at his elbow kept him on his feet. For several seconds he stared at the ceiling and then took a reluctant step closer. Though he couldn't make out the gunshot wound, eight feet past Edgar's head, he saw what he first took to be a splash of blood. He winced before making it out to be a red sock, the toe bulging. Near the sock lay a mammoth galvanized funnel.

"What's that around Edgar's head?"

"When Ike first seen that," the sheriff said, "he thought it was hard candy—that the man had done himself in with sugar, was maybe a diabetic, had overdosed. Ain't that right, Ike?"

"I said it before I seen him good," Ike said, a step behind. "Was just a theory right off, see?"

The sheriff patted Ike on the shoulder.

Digger edged closer to his dead cousin and looked at his face. It was then he saw the fishhook run through Edgar's lips, pinning them together, and the six-inch baby snake crawling out of his mouth.

2

Camo-clad Ben, Golden Leaf town barber, general in the Daniel Boone Rangers, gazed into the green valley below. A dapper sixty-five-year-old, Ben rolled the tips of his waxed, white handlebar mustache, removed his pillbox fatigue cap, and ran a long black comb through his still-immaculate pompadour, a metallic platinum gray. He slipped the comb into a custom pocket in his starched fatigue shirt and readjusted the aluminum foil lining his cap.

"The configuration of the cerebral cortex is distinctive," Ben explained in an aside to two militia recruits, "much like the whorls of a fingerprint. The FBI is able to identify and track an individual by satellite from the unique infrared emissions from the top of his head, then read his thoughts. Foil garbles their reception. When we get to the mess hall, I'll show you where we keep the Reynolds Wrap."

Ben replaced the cap, nodded to the Rangers' armorer, Luther, and reverently touched the cool metal of the newly arrived 106-millimeter recoilless rifle, an impressive eleven feet long, mounted on a heavy tripod with hand cranks for adjusting elevation and horizontal deflection.

Luther, a major, near Ben's age but more knowledgeable

than Ben in the ways of weapons and war, announced, "She's ready for action, sir. Although the scope and this .50 caliber spotting rifle mounted on the barrel for bore-sighting need calibration. It'll take some zeroing in to hit a target in the valley, but we've got plenty of ammo. Not to worry."

Ben nodded. "Excellent. Good-bye, sheriff, eh?" He pointed his riding crop at the horizon. "The north highway," he said. "That's the way the others will come. We'll take them out together."

"Who's that, sir?" asked a sergeant.

"Why, the aliens, of course. And it will be soon, what with all the abductions and sightings. They'll haul them in those silver tanker trucks. Frozen. From Wright Patterson Air Force Base in Ohio. Roswell clones grown from the pieces the army cut out at the autopsy. The powers-that-be plan to set them up in the Daniel Boone National Forest."

"Aliens," repeated B. G. Butz, nicknamed Big Butt, a forty-year-old colonel and proprietor of Big B's Tobacco City and Beer Drive-Thru, just over the McAfee County line. As memorable in silhouette as a 220-pound pear, Big Butt sported a close-cropped goatee, starched fatigues, and a military buzz haircut. He had achieved his elevated rank less through performance than the heavy discounts he gave the Rangers' off-base commander on his considerable purchases of Budweiser and smokes, but he was ever eager to justify his rank. "Ain't that something?" he said with a knowing air. "Not only this world but the whole universe is against us." He flipped open a gunmetal gray Zippo and lit a cigar, a ten-dollar Corona Testosterona. "So be it, but adversity builds character—right, fellas?"

Colonel Butz directed the question to neither Ben nor his cohorts, but to the half dozen boys trooping at his side, armed with .22 pistols and rifles: the Junior Rangers, eleven-to fifteen-year-olds, wearing full-length fatigues, and to the Scooter Shooters, ages six to ten, in camo shorts and olive drab T-shirts.

"There you go, lads," said General Ben, with reference to Big Butt's adversity homily. "Always look for the lesson. And how was your small arms training today?"

"We done good, *sir!*" said Junior Ranger Heck Herkle with a snapping salute. "We got two rabbits, three squirrels, a chipmunk, four doves, a redbird, and a Woody the Woodpecker."

"That's the lad." Ben ruffled young Heck's yellow hair. "With Colonel Butz in charge, I would have expected no less."

Big Butt exhaled a mighty plume of smoke and returned to the subject of extraterrestrials. "The trouble with aliens," he waved the air with the cigar, preparing another lesson for the boys, "is, they're like, out there, hard to get a grip on. Until they come, we'll keep an eye on the sheriff and make ourselves ready."

"Yes, it's all in the preparation," agreed General Ben with a pat on the recoilless rifle. "Good-bye sheriff, good-bye aliens." He turned, scowling, distracted by shouting from Corporal Jesus Bob, who was puffing up the hill from the tobacco barn arsenal.

"Heard the truck come an' go," Jesus Bob yelled, still twenty paces downhill. "Brung the big gun, huh?"

Despite a chronic case of the sniffles, Jesus Bob had a lumberjack's ruddy good looks, with light unkempt hair and the bulk of a bear. He removed a clear glass vial the size of a thumb from his shirt pocket. With a practiced twirl of the lid, a tap-tap over the back of his meaty hand and a noisy snort, he inhaled a sugar-packet-size cone of white powder. He massaged his upper lip with a tattooed knuckle and grinned. "Whooee, pardners, I am *cranked.*"

A disapproving Ben extracted a cigarette from a hard pack and tapped it assertively against the box for attention. Jesus Bob ignored him, so Ben lit it and blew discrete puffs of smoke directly at the irreverent Ranger, small clouds of discontent, enveloping Jesus Bob's head, but dissipating without effect. Ben barked a rebuke: "You have not been with us long, Corporal, but hear this: We do not countenance *drugs* here on the Reserve. Can't you see there are youngsters about?"

Jesus Bob pointed toward the rising sun. "Sheriff's headquarters is right about there. Load up, we'll wipe out the fucking law." He swiped a white crystalline fleck from his left nostril and sniffled. "Got me a score to settle with them bastards."

"Language!" Ben said, as another reminder of the youngsters. "We know the sheriff has gone over. Indeed, one of these shells has his name on it, but we must await the tankers with the aliens."

"What's that you say?" asked Jesus Bob.

"Aliens. Bald, with slanty black eyes that never close."

"Aliens?" Jesus Bob screwed up his face. "Man, I hate aliens. Almost as much as I hate snakes and the fucking law."

Ben observed Scooter Shooters and Junior Rangers looking from one elder to the next with disturbing grins on their young faces. "Language!" he said again.

Jesus Bob moved toward the big gun. "I say wipe out the law now."

Ben slapped his riding crop on the barrel of the recoilless rifle with a *thwank*. "Look here, Corporal—I am your general; B. G. Butz, your colonel. This is not a democracy. We wait till I give the order. Is that understood?"

"Yeah, sure."

"Yeah, sure, *sir*."

"Hey," Jesus Bob said, with another idea. "What say we send a shell into them cows first, look like ants down there, make some hamburger. Idiots in the valley'll think it's blasting from one of the strip mines."

A bit higher on the mountain, a dozen small white frame buildings clung to the base of the fringing forest. A large tin sign over the door of the first read BARRACKS #1. (Although it and the other structures looked less like military dormitories than church camp cabins—which, in fact, they had been in a previous incarnation.) Inside, Rita Rae lifted her cell phone and dialed a local number. At the hello on the other end, she kissed the mouthpiece with an audible *smooo-ch* and said, "I've upped the ante. You want in, it'll be a hundred and fifty thousand, cash up front."

"What!?" the voice said. "After all I've—"

She hung up, dialed again, long distance. She cooed, "It's me," then, "A nonrefundable cash deposit of a hundred fifty thou will keep you in the action." She held the phone a foot away until the cursing died. "Does that mean you're bowing out?" She drummed red nails on the table. "It really makes it easier . . . No?" She smiled, took a fast drag on her cigarette, flaring the tip. "I'll call with details." Then, "Au revoir, baby." She set the phone down, and at the washstand mirror, took a last, long pull on her smoke, flipped it in the toilet, and renewed her lipstick, Love's Blood Red.

She spray-shellacked wispy bangs into place under her bouffant doo perched high on her head like a golden shrub, and winked at her reflection. "Just the right touch of pink to the blond this time, honey. A perfect match for those baby blues and that luscious island tan." With a flip, twist, and a tuck, she tied the tails of a man's fatigue shirt into a square knot at her sternum and patted her bare, toast-brown stomach. "Not bad for forty-four. Still flat as prom night." She ran a hand across the taut fabric of her shorts, around her bottom, along a thigh. "Still firm, yes, indeed." After checking her cherry-red toe polish, she slipped her feet into the red Charles Jourdan pumps she had picked up at the Miami airport on the way north. "Bee-yoo-tee-ful, baby."

Half a hand taller now, nail file reworking the not-yet-perfect parabola at the end of her right forefinger, Rita Rae glanced out the window. "Wonder what those lunkheads are up to?"

*   *   *

"How's it go?" Jesus Bob broke into song, "And the cow-ow jumped over the moo-oon . . ."He moved toward the new gun, intent on sending a herd of slow-moving bossies into lunar orbit.

Cool Luther edged between Jesus Bob and the recoilless rifle, AK-47 gripped at his chest. "The general says back off, you back off, Corporal, or . . ."

Little Heck Herkle tugged at Big Butt's shirt. Big Butt followed his gaze and tapped Ben on the arm, nodding toward Barracks #1, the open door, and Rita Rae on the top step: Rita Rae, rumored to harbor the dried tip of an ex-lover's penis in the heart-shaped locket at her neck; Rita Rae of the wildfire temper, presently filing red talons, head cocked, scowling their way.

"Uh-oh," said Big Butt.

"A complication we do not need," agreed General Ben.

"It's her," said young Heck to his younger pals. "The witch."

"Say what?" said Jesus Bob, held for the moment at bay by Luther. He followed their gaze over his shoulder, and froze at the sight of the scarlet-accented blonde swivel-hipping toward him at a brisk pace, detouring only to avoid a puddle of oil from the troop's incontinent Humvee, currently on clandestine maneuvers in the Daniel Boone National Forest.

Rita Rae stopped two feet from Jesus Bob and sighed. With the speed of a striking snake, she slapped his face with one hand and, with the other, jabbed his genitals with the nail file.

Rangers, Junior Rangers, and Scooter Shooters formed a widening circle.

Raised on tippy-toes, Love's Blood Red lips at Jesus Bob's ear, Rita Rae spoke. "Now, baby brother, what did I say about getting into trouble? Didn't I tell you,"—she glanced to the others to be sure they understood her use of the plural you—"not to mess with that pop gun when it arrived until our business here was over?"

Body stiff, Jesus Bob grunted, nodded.

". . . because if this damn cannon goes off first, some-thing else is going off, too." Her left hand worked the file into the camo at his crotch. "Gonna slice it and dice it, fry it up for breakfast. Do I make myself clear?"

More nodding.

"What else did I tell you?"

Jesus Bob whispered, "Keep out of McAfee County 'cept up here unless you tell me otherwise. Don't mess with the law yet. Low profile."

"And—?"

"I don't remember."

"Hell you don't. Stay off the uppers, I said—you know how wild they make you. And the booze—you don't, you're gonna lose your liver. And go easy on the downers, too. What if I need you and can't wake your sorry butt up? Look at you, sun's barely up, and you're higher than a seven-foot whore in Denver."

"No, no. Just feeling good 'cause a the fresh air and all, these good old boys is such cheerful company . . ."

"I ought to dump your stash down the crapper."

"Not my medicine! I'd die up here without it."

She poked again at the vital, fabric-covered flesh. "Then behave."

"I will, Sis." Jesus Bob cast a sheepish eye at his com-rades.

Rita Rae blew in his ear and stepped back, focused now on shaping her forefinger nail. Satisfied with its point, she aimed it at the others. "Rest of you? No big booms yet—hmmm?—or it's geldings all around." She sliced the air with the file for emphasis. "And you little farts will end up as choir boys. Understand?"

"I don't get it," said a worried Scooter Shooter.

"She'll cut off our balls," said Junior Ranger Heck Herkle.

"Smart kid." Rita Rae patted him on the head, twiddled the locket with a sharp eye around the group, then spun on her heels and ambled back to Barracks #1.

Big Butt mouthed a long, "Sa-umm-bitch."

"Hear, hear," said General Ben. "No disrespect, Corporal Jesus Bob, her being a relation, but I swear, that female is the Devil's spawn."

Jesus Bob readjusted the contents of his Fruit of the Looms and stared at the ground, frowning, studying ants small as ground pepper heft grains of sand nearly as large as themselves from a tiny hole in the earth, carry it to the top of a frail mound and drop it on the outer slope. By the time a sand grain tumbled to the bottom, the ant had run into the hole for more.

"End of the world is a'coming," he said with a grim chortle, and ground the anthill under his boot. With a quick glance at Rita Rae, a safe fifty feet away, he wheeled to confront his compatriots. "Hear this, you bastards." He shook a fist, blurry tattoos running like bruises across his blocky knuckles. "The minute her business is done, we take out the McAfee sheriff and his goddamned deputies. Smoking hole in the ground—get it?

"That," he said to the nodding Rangers, "is one promise I aim to keep."

3

Digger ran from the shed and sank to the ground, swallowing to keep his stomach down.

Half a minute later, he became aware of a buzzing grasshopper, the screech of a jay, and he heard the sheriff's soft drawl. "So, the dead man's your cousin?"

"It's Edgar, all right." Digger's stomach fluttered. "Horrible, the hook, that snake crawling out of his mouth." He shuddered. "I hate snakes."

"Snake?" said the sheriff. "That ain't no snake. That's a Winky Worm. More perzactly, a Peppermint Twist Stinky Winky."

"A *what?*"

"And you said you was a fisherman! A Winky Worm. Scented fish bait. The factory's right here in McAfee County. Biggest employer we got. They been making Winky Worms here for thirty-three years. That was a Peppermint Twist model, garlic scented, so Johnny tells me. A Stinky Winky."

Digger changed the subject. "I didn't see the wound. Where was Edgar shot?"

"Didn't say he was shot."

"Then—?"

"Someone sapped him from behind with that red sock—it's weighted with half-ounce lead fishing sinkers. While he was down, they rammed that steel funnel in his mouth and must of crammed at least a double handful of the damned things down his gullet. That's what you seen scattered around his head. Then they hooked his lips together with the Winky Worm. Man would have been dead by then, of course."

Digger gaped.

"One thing more—there's enough dope scattered around in there to keep the Golden Leaf senior class happy for a three-day weekend."

His voice softened. "Why don't you tell me what your cousin was up to in McAfee County, old friend? Might make you feel better."

Long-buried memories surfaced. Digger concluded the sheriff was playing good cop, bad cop all by himself. "Up to?" he said. "Feel better? What would make me feel better is Edgar alive. How's that?"

"Easy there. Let's start with what the man was doing here."

"Edgar is an archaeologist. Retired from the University of Michigan, moved here a couple of months ago. He planned to consult."

"He needed money." The sheriff stopped chewing his Juicy Fruit, straightened his back, and stared at a metallic glint near the crest of one of the low mountains. Whatever it was faded into the forest, and his jaws resumed their rhythmic motion. "Your cousin needed money . . ."

"Not my point. The late grandmother of one of Edgar's grad students lived here. The family wanted to keep her land out of the hands of the coal people, and gave Edgar a good deal. Look," he fumbled in his pocket, "here's his map."

"Living right here in McAfee County? An archaeologist? Odd, I never seen him." The sheriff took the map, drawn on a scrap of paper, scratched his chin, and motioned over the tall deputy Digger had seen using the radio. He was in his early thirties, muscular, with neatly trimmed, light sandy hair; a soap opera version of a clean-cut country boy, though he walked with a limp. "Bo," said the sheriff, "call Amy Lou at McAfee Realty, have her track down this property."

Deputy Bo glanced at the map. "I know that place. Sits on a big hill backed up against the forest. Nice old lady lived there, then a bunch of bikers rented it four or five months ago. I'll check."

"Dr. Fitz," the sheriff looked him in the eyes, "here's how I read it."

Digger waited.

"It looks like a drug deal gone bad."

"Ridiculous." Although, Digger's indignation dropped to his stomach and turned sour when he remembered the contraband doobie over his heart. He could hear the sheriff's next words: What's that bulge in your shirt pocket? Digger did his best to keep a poker face, thinking: Stay on the offensive. "Have you considered the obvious? That someone robbed the poor man?"

"Credit cards and sixty-two dollars, still in his wallet. Dope in there. Your cousin, sir, was an outsider. If he was dealing with a local, I believe I would of heard about it, so I'd say it was an outsider what killed him—one into drugs."

Poker face. Poker face.

"I suppose you wouldn't know anything about such things? An old hippie like you?"

Here it comes. Cop jitters rising, Digger cleared his throat, looked for the fat deputy who set him up—and saw him, arms crossed, resting against a patrol car, watching, waiting, gnawing on another chicken leg.

Don't lose your cool. Remember the first time they hassled you? You were a teaching assistant. The law pulled you over that night for no reason at all, and you with a sky-high sophomore half in your lap, blouse unbuttoned, fat Baggie in the back seat under a blanket. Grilled you at the window, flashed a light around, but you bluffed your way through it.

Digger faked a chuckle. "I taught at Berkeley in the good

old days, may even have inhaled once or twice. Bet you did, too, back in the flower power days, huh?"

He stared at a straight face.

The sheriff was saying, "Maybe he got involved with the wrong crowd. We're not far from the pipeline north. Mayhaps he had contacts with bad boys from Florida, or the Mexes. Or High-wah-yans, huh? Maui Wowie, ain't that what you call it?"

"You're way off base." But Digger knew Edgar had made some bad investments and worried about supporting himself. That was the reason, he assumed, for downscaling from Ann Arbor to the middle of nowhere. "Consulting," Edgar had said. "You can pick up some easy money, too." But drugs? Edgar never so much as smoked a joint, even in college.

"You may as well tell me if the two of you was doing business," said the sheriff. "Cause I'll find out soon enough."

Digger wished he'd never seen the damned thing. Well, go ahead, Mr. Lawman. Pat me down, "discover" it.

But instead, the sheriff glanced back at the mountains, fiddled with the brim of his black hat, canted his head, off on a new tack. "There's other possibilities. Enemies—or"— he narrowed his eyes—"how much was your cousin worth?"

"Peanuts. Look, while you're jumping to conclusions, Edgar's murderer is getting away."

The sheriff patted the air. "Hang tight. You want to help? How's about we visit his house?" He cupped his hand to his mouth, yelled at the clean-cut deputy, still in his patrol car. "Bo? What's the scoop on that house?"

The deputy yelled back. "Amy Lou handled the deal herself. Mortgage is in the name of Edgar Allen Fitz, previous address, Ann Arbor, Michigan."

The sheriff retrieved the map. "Bo, take charge of the crime scene. Get Ike and Gabe back on the highway—someone's gotta pay the rent. Call Doc. When him and Johnny's through here, have Trask Mortuary pick up the body. Then you and Johnny come to the victim's house, hear?"

Bo gave him a two-fingered salute. "Yessir."

The sheriff nodded to a blue Pontiac Bonneville with a small gold star on the door, motioned Digger to get in—up front this time. He drove leisurely, elbow out the window, waving to approaching cars or to the occasional man or woman on foot.

The road wound though a narrow steep-sided valley, a coal-polluted stream on the left, strips of still-shadowed new tobacco, vegetable gardens, or thready cornfields on the right. Steep green mountains rose to either side, their peaks loped off like picked scabs, their shoulders girdled by strip mining. Every half mile or so, they passed a rickety frame house or a lonely trailer raised on blocks.

Digger stared out the window in grim silence, wondering if there was a curse on the Fitzes: the out-of-the-blue heart attack that took his brother, Nikki's father, three years before, his own recent run of incredibly rotten luck, and now, poor Edgar. Chewing his lip, he remembered the sheriff's words: "Business deal, hmmm?" "You wear colored socks?" "Ah, you're a fishing man." And, "You're next of kin." Glancing down at the cylindrical bulge under the red hibiscus on his shirt pocket, Digger thought of all the drug talk and moaned with the realization that the tiny sheriff in the black cowboy hat, the slow-talking son of a bitch, had pegged Edgar, "the outsider"—the straightest man Digger ever met—as a drug dealer, and was fast laying the groundwork to set up Digger himself as Edgar's killer. The sheriff had his man plant the marijuana joint on the floor of the cop car, knowing Digger would pick it up. And, of course, he had.

He cupped a palm over his eyes. It's me against the cops again, he thought. And at my age, I don't know if I'm up to it this time.

4

The sheriff left the highway, drove along a secondary road thick with woods, and up a winding gravel drive. Near the top, at the center of a half acre of grass, flanked by two thick maple trees and a farm pond, stood a small white Gothic cottage with a high peaked roof and a gingerbread-trimmed porch running around three sides. Bushy ferns hung at the corners. Hollyhocks, already waist-high, bordered the steps, and coffee cans with red and blue petunias sat along the porch rail. The surrounding mountains were unscathed by coaling, mantled in pristine green, feathered here and there by wisps of morning mist still clinging to cool western slopes.

A stout woman pushing fifty, with poufed, unnaturally bright orange hair fringing a pumpkin face, leaned against a pink El Dorado in the drive. Stickers on the rear bumpers read GOD'S LAST NAME ISN'T DAMMIT, IT'S THE ELEVENTH HOUR—DO YOU KNOW WHERE YOUR SOUL IS? and ASK ME ABOUT MARY KAY. She waved as they rolled to a stop.

"How-do, Amy Lou. Thanks for coming out."

Amy Lou, in a snug pink blazer, navy polyester slacks, and white, patent leather sandals, raised a pink-nailed finger and thumb dangling a house key. "Thought I'd better take a look at the place myself, Coony. See that you and your boys don't mess it up. I had to paint after the last tenants left. Kitchen was a shameful mess—must have been awful cooks. You should have seen that brown ceiling." She adjusted cat's-eye glasses, looked sharply at Digger's shorts and aloha shirt. "And this would be?"

"Harmon Fitz, ma'am. Edgar was my cousin."

"A shame. Bo told me about your loss. Seemed a good Christian gentleman—a godsend compared to the previous tenants." She cast the sheriff a condemning scowl. "Bikers, Coony. One didn't look so bad, leased the place, and then the others showed up. Stayed two months and skipped out." She turned to Digger, probing. "You have plans to stay? Your cousin made two mortgage payments."

"My niece is coming down from Cincinnati this afternoon. I suppose we'll stay until we sort things out."

"Good idea," said the sheriff.

"Don't leave town, eh?"

"Thought you'd want to be close if we turn up anything."

"Right." He turned to the real estate woman. "I'm from Hawaii, ma'am."

"Lord. I've always wanted to see that place. My sister's youngest married money, went to Waikiki on her honeymoon, said it was the closest thing to heaven she could imagine. Palm trees, rainbows, luaus with roast pigs, hula girls, brown boys with surfboards, colored drinks with umbrellas. She saw the Five-O headquarters, the Don Ho show. I don't suppose you ever met—"

The sheriff cut her off. "Amy Lou, the key?"

Inside, he warned, "Don't touch nothing. Tell me if you see anything strange."

"I've never been here," Digger reminded him.

"Contents still belong to the original owners," Amy Lou was saying, "The crystal and the collectibles? Nearly match my own in quality. I boxed all the figurines when those bikers moved in, but I put them back for your cousin." She waved a hand, wall to wall. "Single man like him, it being furnished suited him fine. Although I see he brought some of his own things, the rolltop desk and that file cabinet." She pointed to a gray four-drawer legal file. "And those ugly bookcases." Four six-foot, industrial, gray steel standing shelves full of books, lined one wall. "I see he took down the art," she said, with a scowl. "Look, there it is, laying against the wall."

Digger regarded painted velvet sailing ships under setting suns, framed in plastic faux barnwood; what appeared to be a large owl with coat-button eyes woven from colored yarn, and a two-foot oval log slice, bark-rimmed, with a shellacked print of the Last Supper on its face—and decided Edgar knew a thing or two about art.

In the kitchen, they found convenience food, the kind appealing to a bachelor engrossed in his work. The sheriff lifted a nearly full fifth of Jim Beam. "No more than a swallow out of this bottle. The man must of had willpower."

Amy Lou clucked her tongue. "A streamlet becomes a river, Coony. And a drink is the first step to drunkenness."

He set the bottle on the counter. "Words of wisdom, I'm sure, darlin.' "

They walked through the house. Sheriff McCoy lifted a leatherette bible from a side table.

"I left that there to console the man when he felt lonely," Amy Lou explained.

The sheriff blew dust from the cover.

Amy Lou huffed. "A dusty bible makes for a dirty life."

Digger felt a twinge of anger and realized how far he and Edgar had drifted apart. He knew no more about Edgar's life in recent years than Edgar knew of his.

In the bathroom, the sheriff studied a coffee mug on the sink holding a razor, toothbrush, and toothpaste. He lifted it by the handle, sniffed. "Hmmm. Take a whiff, tell me what you smell." He passed it to Digger, bowl first.

Digger gripped the mug with both hands and lifted it to his nose. "Toothpaste. That's all."

"Yeah, could be." The sheriff took it by the handle, returned it to the sink.

Amy Lou's hand shot to her mouth at sight of a *Playboy* on the floor beside the commode. The sheriff shifted through a small stack of magazines—two issues of *Time*, three *Scientific Americans*, a *Smithsonian*—and then lifted the *Playboy* and flipped out the centerfold. Amy Lou gasped. "Checking for clues," he said with a wink, and let Miss May unfurl to his knees.

Amy Lou squeezed her eyes shut and turned her back to him.

He rustled the paper behind her. "Never know where evidence might turn up, honey."

Digger smiled, and then shuffled with embarrassment at sneaking through his cousin's home with strangers. Edgar would no doubt have hidden the *Playboy* before he welcomed his relations. The embarrassment turned to anger: Edgar's murderer had robbed the poor man of his privacy as well as his life.

In the living room, Edgar's study, the sheriff asked Digger, "What's his books and papers tell you?"

Digger scanned titles and folder tabs. "Colonial and early U.S. history, primarily the Ohio Valley—Edgar's specialty. Prehistory. Scholarly journals. Books on pioneer weapons, artifact conservation, geology, a French dictionary, some paperback novels, auction catalogs. Nothing extraordinary. Although . . ." He looked around the room.

"Although?" the sheriff repeated. "Go on . . ."

"Last night, Edgar told me about his new computer. Superfast new Mac portable. Held all his new work. I don't see it anywhere."

The sheriff raised an eyebrow, told Digger and Amy Lou to stay put, and walked through the house alone. He returned five minutes later. "No computer for damn sure."

They checked the free-standing garage and Edgar's old-style VW beetle. The sheriff patted the bug on its rounded roof. "You being kin, I guess you're welcome to this car and to move in, but I want Johnny, our crime tech, to take some photos, and him and Bo give this place a careful look-see first."

Digger nodded, although inwardly he rolled his eyes at the thought of the baby-faced kid with the see-through mustache, Deputy Johnny, looking for clues. His first thought, of the murderer long gone, returned. He realized how tired he was. "Any reason I need to hang around?"

"Tough day, I guess. Amy Lou? You mind taking our High-wah-yan visitor back to the E-Z-Zees?"

"My pleasure, Coony, but watch your boys—some of those storybook figurines are priceless."

The sheriff patted her arm. "They'll treat 'em like they was their mama's own, honey." He dropped his smile. "Now listen, both of you. I don't know what Bo told you, Amy Lou, but what happened today is police business, hear? It's an isolated incident. We're on top of it. I don't want people in McAfee County getting scared, spreading rumors of drug-crazed, devil-worshipping fishermen or who knows what. Not a word to no one. No telephone chitchat. No talks with the newspaper. Hear?"

"Land sakes, Coony," she said. "You know you can count on me."

Digger shrugged an okay. Grateful, and surprised, not to have been patted down, eager for a hot shower and a nap, he settled back in Amy Lou's big Caddy, hopeful she would keep quiet and leave him to his thoughts.

"Something terrible happened, didn't it?" she asked before they were out of the drive. "Your cousin was murdered! Coony wouldn't be making such a fuss if it wasn't awful. You can tell me. Coony won't mind."

"Kiddo," Digger said. "I'd rather not talk about it, okay?" He looked out the window and let the once-again bleak landscape fly by out of focus.

Amy Lou remained silent for nearly a minute before speaking again. "Now, I want to hear all about where they filmed Elvis in *Blue Hawaii*. I've seen that movie a dozen times, and I've always wondered . . ."

5

Digger rented a beat-up Dodge for fifteen dollars a day from the motel manager and retreated to his room. Reluctantly, he dialed his niece in Cincinnati to head her off.

Her stepfather answered. "Nikki? Left over an hour ago. And you would be her uncle Harmon from Hawaii. Ahhemm. Look, Nikki's mother and I don't approve of this trip. Mountains of east Kentucky? A child her age? The girl's going through difficult times, trying to decide what to do with her life, and—"

Digger held the phone from his ear, decided this might not be the best time to mention her Uncle Edgar's murder by sadistic hillbillies. He crumpled an empty potato chip bag from the night table with one hand and spoke from three feet away, moving the phone in and out. ". . . orry, can't hear . . . something wrong with . . . connection." *Crumple, crumple.* "Good to speak with you, too, sir," and hung up.

He took a long hot shower, closed the shades, and lay on the bed, alternately lamenting Edgar's death and cursing the lame local law. He sat up and punched the pillow. "Cops!"

Which reminded him of the contraband joint. He rolled off the bed, rummaged through his aloha shirt, took two steps toward the toilet with thought of a de-incriminating flush, and then thought, Why not? It's been a good long while, and a miserable day. He opened the window, moistened the tip with his lips, and fired it up. A minute later, he was back to muttering. "Forgot how foul these things—" *Cough, cough.* "—tasted." *Cough, hack, hack.*

"I'm not the man I used to be," he admitted, and flushed the barely toked joint down the commode. Feeling sorry for himself, he flopped on the bed and fell into a fitful sleep.

The phone jolted him awake at—he checked glowing numbers. Two o'clock. His mouth tasted foul as a poker game ashtray, and he couldn't remember where he was, whether it was day or night. Then the morning's memories flooded over him like hot acid, and he moaned. Poor Edgar, murdered. Cops suspect me.

He put the phone to his ear. "Uncle Digger! It's me, Nikki. In the lobby."

Digger ran a hand through tangled hair. He and Nikki had been buddies since she had been old enough to read and ask questions, although with the passing years, they saw less and less of one another. He wondered what to say, whether they would still be able to make easy conversation, how Nikki would take Edgar's death.

He heard himself saying he would be right down, and stumbled into the same shirt and shorts he'd worn earlier. He walked to the head of the stairs, overlooking the lobby, recalling the last time he had seen Nikki, briefly, in Waikiki over a year ago. She had received her master's degree only months before, and had enrolled in the doctoral program at his alma mater, the University of Michigan.

She stood by the reception desk, holding a small suitcase and a backpack, dressed in jeans and sneakers, her slim, athletic body hidden under an oversize Cincinnati Reds sweatshirt hanging to midthigh, a brown ponytail bouncing from the back of a baseball cap. You did good, Nikki, he thought. You got the Fitz brains and spirit from my brother Warren, and your mother's looks.

She saw him, ran up the stairs two at a time, threw her arms around his neck. "Uncle Digger! I got a ride down with some U of Tennessee students. I can't wait to talk. Is Hawaii still as—?"

He patted her back.

She stepped away and looked him in the eyes. "What's wrong? Where's Uncle Edgar?"

"Honey." He motioned for her to sit on the top step. He sat beside her, stared at the dust-covered plastic plants in the lobby. "Edgar . . . Edgar is dead."

"What? When? How?"

Digger told her about his morning.

When he finished, Nikki repeated the salient highlights: "Red sock? Lead sinkers? Fishhook?"

"Don't forget the Peppermint Twist Stinky Winky. Sick, huh?"

"Uncle Edgar told me he'd taken up fishing. These bass fishing contests are serious business, big cash prizes. What if Edgar, a beginner, from Michigan, caught the biggest fish? On a nightcrawler instead of a fancy lure or one of those phony worms? With a bamboo pole in a rowboat—jealous pros all around in thirty-thousand-dollar bass boats with fish finders, watching Uncle Edgar haul in this humongous large-mouth. Do you have any idea how much winning means to some men?"

Digger recalled his stopover in Las Vegas and craps fever, the deadly dice, that perky blonde urging him on . . .

Nikki snapped her fingers. "I saw three cars in the lot here with chrome fish symbols on the back. You see them all over. Maybe it's some kind of secret fishing cult, and Edgar got on to them, maybe . . ."

He patted her arm. "Calm down, kiddo. Check in, wash up. I'll meet you for coffee, we'll talk this through."

Digger sat in the adjacent restaurant, Chez Pancakes, staring through the window at a garish, sixties red-neon CHEZ by the highway, twice the size of a preexisting painted PAN- CAKES mounted on a post below. Inside, rococo flock wall- paper and gilt curlicues competed with knotty pine, mounted bass on walnut plaques, and photo murals of fishing lakes. The discontinuities didn't do much to cheer him up, merely reminded him of how out of place he was here, how impotent to deal with this awful turn of events.

Twenty minutes later, Nikki gave him a long look across a plateful of silver dollar pancakes. "I'll bet they have a sus- pect. Some guy with stuffed fish all over his wall—like that." She waved at the trophies.

"They have a suspect all right." Digger tapped his chest.

"Get real! You don't even fish, do you?"

"Hardly their line of reasoning. They claim they found drugs. The sheriff figures an ex–flower child like me, a stranger . . . Well, you get the idea."

Nikki whistled. "Don't they know you're a professor?" She shook her finger at him. "I hope you told them you're not a fisherman, that you don't do drugs." She looked down at her plate, back up, squinting. "You know . . . anymore."

Digger squirmed, wondered if she could smell the pot.

She frowned. "Some reunion."

"I'm sorry, honey." He ran a hand through his long hair, pushed it behind his ears. It fell back as soon as his hands dropped to the table. "I'll have to stick it out for a while, but with a maniac on the loose down here, you should go home."

Nikki played with a paper napkin, tearing it into long strips, and then leaned across the table and touched his shoulder. "I'll stay, too. We'll cheer one another up—get you off the hook, and find out who really killed Uncle Edgar."

"Bad idea. This isn't Cincinnati or Hawaii. It's a danger- ous place, kiddo. We don't know a soul here, the cops are useless, if not dangerous themselves, and whoever killed Ed- gar is long gone. No, you're going home."

"Whatever you say, Unc." Another long look. "There's something else you're not telling me. Your health? What's wrong?"

"I've had some financial reverses, that's all. I'll squeak by."

She motioned for information with a crooked finger.

Digger played with his coffee cup and finally spoke. "I was watching a macaw for a friend visiting the mainland. The damned bird chewed up my mail—cute little trick of his—including the invoice from my car insurance company, *and* the past due notice. I missed the payment, found the shreds later behind his cage. Then, my car was stolen. Thieves totaled it. My first new car in twelve years."

"Bummer. What about that lady you met?"

"Had a great time. We're still good friends."

"Oh. Friends."

Digger nodded, recalling how he and his first flame in ten years had singed their share of thatched huts in Tahiti before reaching a reluctant but wise decision to be friends—only—when they realized they both had wandering eyes, were too set in their ways, and liked one another much too much to become jealous lovers. So here he was alone and broke and another year older. He sighed. "I always wanted to see Las Vegas, so I stopped there on the way here—*big* mistake. I don't know what came over me. I've always been so rational. I lost my shirt and can kiss my house good-bye soon enough. I'm down somewhere over sixty grand, counting the car."

"Oh, Unc. I'm sorry."

"Yeah. I tossed and turned most of last night wondering what I'll do when I get back. Then I awoke to find Edgar . . ." He worried a hank of his hair. "You know, you always think things will get better as time goes by. Sometimes it doesn't work out that way." He waved the air. "Change of subject: What's going on with you?"

"Herpetology is still my love."

"Brrr." He shuddered. "A perverse interest for a young

woman. Snakes. That's why I moved to Hawaii: serpent free."
"You're in snake country now. I'll change your mind."
"No, you won't." Another shudder. "Have you settled on a topic for your dissertation?"
"Still waffling. Molecular systematics, comparative ecology. Maybe I'll study a single kind of beast, *A* to *Z*. She snorted. "Speaking of beasts, Mother—oh, she ticks me off—wants me to can zoology, go into *business*. Marketing. My stepdad will pay for it. Can you see me as a brand manager in a suit, killing my feet in high heels, getting ulcers over widgets?"
"Honey, follow your heart, even if it involves slimy—"
"They're not slimy—you know that." Nikki tapped her coffee cup against Digger's. "Thanks. I knew you'd take my side. Mother has changed since Dad died. He was like you, quirky—"
"Thank you."
"Well, you're not exactly . . . conventional. My stepdad Biffer is a big-time CEO." More eye-rolling. "They have a monster house with huge fiberglass columns. They dress for dinner—at home. And both of them broaden their *a*s when they remember to do it—*Rawther*. It's too much. Mother wants me to take up golf. Golf. Me." She shielded her eyes from an imaginary sun. "I say, fore! Drat. A rough lie, that. Rawther a long pitch for a wedge." She knocked her forehead with the base of her palm. "And, shit, I'm living with them. Oops!" She shook a finger at herself. " 'Watch your language, young woman. And look at you. Do you think you should go out in public, dressed like a teenage boy? Where are those gray slacks from Saks, your low heels and that lovely silk blouse?' "
"You had a place of your own."
"Yeah, Ann Arbor. Gave it up for a man. True love." She batted her eyelashes. "Exchange prof from Australia. Marsupialogist. Wrote that non-fiction best-seller, *And the Opossum Shall Inherit the Earth*. I guess I fell for the fame, moved in with him, thought my whole life had come together." Her

voice caught; she blinked and stared at her hands. Seconds passed. Nikki looked away and back at her uncle with narrowed eyes. "I found he had a *wife* and *seven kids* in Hobart, Tasmania."

Digger raised his eyebrows.

"Revenge really *is* sweet. I didn't let on I knew about the family. He was due for a trip home. I helped him pack." She got a wicked gleam in her eye. "You know how they ask you at the airport if you pack your bags yourself?"

Digger nodded.

"Good advice. The afternoon he left, I reopened his suitcase, threw out his underwear, substituted some of my bras and panties, and wrapped a roadkill opossum in his suit. It must be a thirty-hour trip to Tasmania. They have stiff laws for importing animals, too. Hah! End of that love story." She shrugged. "The real downside is, I moved back home with Mother and Biffer, so I've really been looking forward to this trip." She sipped coffee. "Tell me more about you. How's the sex coming?"

He thought of the flirty Las Vegas blonde—something else that went nowhere—and blushed.

"Your *work*. Sex in the Pacific, right? What makes the islanders tick."

"Oh. Fine, fine. Four new papers last year."

The small talk petered out. They shifted in their seats, played with their food.

Nikki broke the silence and cut to the subject they had been avoiding. "Unc, what about Edgar?"

"I'll find an attorney to track his affairs. As far as what we do with his remains, I've been thinking along the lines of cremation, taking his ashes to a high hill unsullied by the twentieth century, and scattering them to the four winds."

"Uncle Edgar would have liked that."

She stared out the window, chewing her lip, and back at Digger. "Uncle Edgar and I both lived in Ann Arbor, but with my studies and then moving to Cincy, I hardly saw him. Now this. Makes you realize—"

Digger balled a fist and rapped his other palm. "Don't I know it! I should have stayed in better touch with him myself. It's just you and me, now, kiddo. We're the last of the Fitzes."

They sat silently for several minutes. Digger paid the bill while Nikki pretended to look at postcards.

Outside, she pinched the tail of his red flowered shirt and tugged. "Unc, it won't do us any good to mope—I've got an idea. You don't exactly blend in here. Did you bring any other clothes?"

"Sure, my good plaid slacks, my mainland blue oxford cloth shirt, and some clean running shoes in case I need to dress up, plus more aloha shirts and shorts."

"First thing on the agenda, then, is shopping."

He raised his hands in protest, and then did a double take at a white Ford with McAfee County and a star on the side, arcade lights across the top, cruising the parking lot.

"Damn, damn, damn," he said. "They've come for me already. Eyes front, kiddo. Stay with me, we'll head to the back of the building. If they can't find me, they can't arrest me."

6

Digger steered Nikki toward the rear of the pancake house. He heard the patrol car idle behind them, the motor shudder and die, a door open and slam.

"Hey—where you two going?" Deep voice, a bit less twang than the sheriff. Digger recognized it as belonging to Bo, the blond country boy cop with the limp.

Digger stopped five feet shy of a Dumpster and a long cyclone fence. Trapped. He squeezed Nikki's hand and turned to give himself up.

Nikki walked around him, straight for the casually confident cop leaning against the patrol car door. A short pace away, she halted and shook a finger in his face. "Listen! There's no way my uncle—"

The deputy touched his hat. "Excuse me, ma'am, but I don't think we met. Name's Bo Deaver. And you would be?"

"Nikki Fitz, same last name as my uncle, same name as the man the fisherman murdered. I swear, you make one move to arrest my uncle—"

"Well now, Nikki Fitz, the truth is I wasn't planning to arrest your uncle just yet. I was stopping by the Chez"—he said it with a hard *ch*, rhyming it with *fez*—"to pick up some coffee for the boys. I recognized that red flowered shirt and thought I'd give your uncle some news. But if you two have your minds set on rooting in that Dumpster? Well, that's A-okay with me." He got back in the car, slammed the door.

"No you don't!" She grabbed the door handle. "What did you find?"

"Truth is, now that I recall, Coony warned us to stay clear of you two, so I'd best pick up the coffee and get back." He started the engine, shifted into reverse.

She tugged at the handle. "C'mon, c'mon." The window was open, the door locked.

"Is that a hint of apology, ma'am?"

"Apology? You're the ones treating my uncle like a crook, who want—"

The deputy looked over his shoulder, began to back up.

"Okay. I'm sorry. Stop the damned car."

He touched the brake. "When Coony talks to you, you didn't hear this from me. There was drug activity at the house, too."

"Rubbish," Digger said, now a step behind Nikki.

"I don't believe it," she agreed.

The deputy lifted his hands from the wheel, palms up. "Forget I said it. Now, if you'd like to confess, sir, or if there's anything else I can help you with, ma'am, speak up, because I'll catch heck if I don't get back there with hot coffee."

Digger pulled Nikki back by the wrist and whispered. "Be nice. Get him to tell us more."

She looked at the car, forced a cheesy smile. "Okay," she said, chewing her lip. "Umm . . . We want to get some suitable clothes for my uncle here, see? Western, I think. I haven't seen any department stores, and—"

"Stay on the highway through Golden Leaf—keep your speed down. Eight miles past, on the left, you'll find Sandler's Tack. Big plastic stallion rearing up—high school kids painted it pink last week, can't miss it. You tell them Bo Deaver sent you, they'll take good care of you." He touched his hat. "See you around, huh?" The car backed again.

"Wait," she said. "The house. What did they find? Who did it? Was it a fisherman?"

The car backed, slowly. The deputy alternated between watching his rearview mirror and the Fitzes.

"C'mon." Nikki trotted alongside. "Tell us." Then, a reluctant, "Please."

The deputy braked, leaned out. "Sorry. Said more than I should have already. Ma'am, nice to meet you. Sir, they say confession cleanses the soul." He smiled, backed twenty feet, stopped, drove to the pancake house entrance, and went inside.

"Typical male ego," Nikki said, grumbling. "Made me plead—you saw it—then told me zip. One-way street."

Digger muttered back. "Drugs. At least he didn't arrest me. Yet."

"Forget him. We'll take a drive, cool off."

Digger fished the rent-a-car key from his pocket and tossed it to her. Nikki drove in silence for several minutes, and then yelled "*A-O-R!*" and hit the brakes.

Digger's forearm flew up to shield his face. Nothing ahead. He spun, stared at the road behind. "What? What is it?"

The car slid to a stop. Nikki backed to the first stretch of wide shoulder, flew out the door, and ran back another hundred feet. She bent over the asphalt and returned to the car, grinning.

By the time she reached Digger's open window, her hands were behind her back. "Go ahead, pick one," she said, waving her left elbow, and then her right.

"I've got a feeling," he said, still seated, "that either side is a loser."

"C'mon, be a sport."

Digger nodded to her right.

"Close your eyes. It won't bite."

"No way. If I know you, it's a bug of some kind. And if it's a slinky, put it back in the grass. And what's this A-O-R stuff?"

"A-O-R: Alive on Road." She stuck her right arm toward him. Digger shied away at sight of the coils at her wrist, a pen-thick body with orange blotches over a pale gray background, twining slowly through her fingers. A small head nosed his way.

"Uhng!"

"Go ahead touch him. It's a young milk snake, maybe a foot and a half. *Lampropeltis triangulum*. A real beauty."

"I don't like snakes. You *know* that." He looked away.

"This guy couldn't be more harmless. Didn't even strike when I picked him up." She turned her hand so the snake's head was hidden. "Touch. You don't have to hold him."

Digger shook his head. No.

Nikki nodded and held the snake in place. Heart racing, Digger extended a tentative finger.

"Courage, Unc. One touch."

His finger came within a quarter inch of the glossy scales and jerked away. He clutched the finger to his chest. "I'm sorry, honey. I really am. I just can't do it."

Nikki let the snake crawl one hand to the other. "I'll change your mind. You'll see."

"No, you won't. I pride myself on my rationality, but . . . even the thought of snakes gives me the cold sweats."

"My unc, the cowardly lion. This boy's cleaner than any mammal or bird. An evolutionary and engineering marvel. And you know what else? He's a lucky sign: the first herp of the trip, alive, waiting for us to drive by. I'm gonna keep him."

Digger was staring at his nearly contaminated fingertip. "I was half-raised by a country woman who read Bible stories to me. I remember a picture she'd show me of Eve and the Serpent in the Garden of Eden—a reproduction of some Renaissance oil. The snake had a human face, leering, with horns. She'd tell me Satan, the snake, would chew me up and eat me if I was bad."

"Unc, the Garden of Eden is about a patriarchy supplanting the Goddess. The serpent is Mother Nature, calling Eve back, see?"

"If you say so."

"I do. And, snakes don't chew up their prey, they swallow them whole."

"Thank you. I feel better already."

"Now that you remember who scared you as a kid and why, the fear's gone—right? Catharsis."

"Not at all."

"So much for Freud." She rubbed the slick scales against her cheek. "Finding this baby was fate. What should we call him?"

"How about Gone?"

"What's the name of that sheriff?"

"Coony McCoy."

"Uncle Digger, meet Coony II. Get it? Coony, *too*." She rummaged through her pack, retrieved a small black sequined purse on a long strap. "Mother gave me this. It has open-weave cloth under the sequins, a zipper under the flap. A perfect traveling snake-tainer, huh?" She coaxed the snake into it, zipped it shut, and set it on the backseat. The purse pulsed rhythmically.

Nikki patted it. "Mother always had exquisite taste."

7

In the shadow of the pink stallion, Nikki crooked a finger. "Makeover time."

Twenty minutes later, Digger emerged from a dressing room wearing jeans, a braided horsehair belt, and a fancy blue Saturday-night shirt with scalloped pockets and mother-of-pearl snaps. He kicked at the carpet with his new Lucchese boot heel, and pivoted before a mirror. "I don't know, kiddo. I feel more like Trigger's ass than Roy Rogers."

"Nonsense," said the owner at the register, tallying the rest of Digger's new wardrobe. "You look manly, sir. Manly."

The teenage clerk, refolding one of Digger's new shirts, stopped blowing a three-inch Double Bubble. Hands on hips, she stared at Digger a full ten seconds, and then turned to the owner. "Goll-ee, look at him good, Mr. Sandler—the beard, the hair. I swear, if he ain't the spittin' image of Willie Nelson!"

The owner walked around him twice. "Damned if you're not, sir."

"No need to bullshit me," Digger said. "You already have my credit card."

The owner slapped him on the shoulder. "It's the God's

truth, friend. Honey, get the Polaroid, take my picture with this gentleman—no one'll know it wasn't Willie hisself here at Sandlers."

Flash. The pale print came to life in the clerk's hands. She passed it to the owner, who rummaged through a drawer and retrieved a pointy felt-tip marker, "Sir, you sign this picture 'Hey Burl!—Your good friend, Willie,' and don't tell no one you wasn't him, and I'll throw in one of these German silver, flying-eagle buckles for the horsehair belt."

Outside, Nikki struck a starlet's pose against the hood of the beat-up Dodge, fluttered her eyelashes, and drawled, "My hero, Uncle Willie."

The Daniel Boone Rangers were lounging before the mess hall at day's end, drinking, eating fried chicken, cleaning weapons.

"Dwight David Eisenhower," said General Ben, busy picking the security threads from water-soaked, new currency bills to keep the FBI from tracking him. Tomorrow, as he did every morning at the traffic light by his barbershop, Ben would tape the previous day's harvest to the backs of out-of-state trucks.

"I remember that name from school," said skinny Private Purcell, a Winky Worm scent inspector, recently self-named Beast. Purcell sat atop the camp's five-foot-high, concrete Ten Commandments, cast remarkably like the ones Charlton Heston brought down from the mountain—only enlarged and in English rather than illegible Hebrew. The divine directives were identical in content as well, except for the one about THOU SHALT NOT KILL, which was amended parenthetically with (UNLESS CALLED FOR). Purcell beat a rhythm against the holy cement with his heels. "Eisenhower was a president," he said, "the one before Nixon. After Roosevelt."

Purcell noticed Big Butt shaking the nearly empty chicken tub. "Hey! Uh . . . sir—gimme that last wing."

Big Butt tossed him the bucket. "Eisenhower was a general. A real hero."

"Yes," said General Ben. "At first. Later, though, he turned traitor, not unlike our own sheriff. Eisenhower is the one who sold us out to the Godless aliens. Bet you didn't read that in your history books, did you, young Purcell?"

"Call me Beast, sir." Strained through a mouthful of chicken skin, the words came out garbled.

Jesus Bob was lying on his stomach in the grass, teasing a delegged grasshopper. "Call him Beast, is what he said, Mr. Barber. Go ahead, give the kid something to live up to."

Ben ignored them both, directing his observations instead to Big Butt. "Remember the UFO crash in Roswell, New Mexico, Colonel Butz? Nineteen forty-seven. Truman administration. They hushed that up fast, but negotiations followed. Eisenhower signed the accord in 1953 that gave the aliens the right to abduct us at will, and to mutilate cattle."

"Aliens," said Purcell. "Jeezle-Pete, you guys are into cool stuff. You mutilate cattle, too?" He flipped the wing bone into the weeds, opened a foil pouch, and bit off a plug of chewing tobacco.

"Dwight D. Eisenhower?" Big Butt finished the last of a beer and burped.

"That's the one," said Ben.

"Makes no sense why a hero like Ike would do a deal with aliens."

"I've wondered, too." Ever neat, Ben wiped grease from his fingers and lips with an olive drab bandanna. "Because up until then the man had an exemplary career. But who knows the powers aliens hold to corrupt men's souls?

"After the Roswell crash—weather balloon, hah!—" Ben spat (a symbolic gesture, no saliva left his lips) "—the military got nowhere analyzing the alien wonder metal, and Ike must have figured a mutilated cow here and there, or some farmer from Iowa with his guts turned inside-out was no skin off his nose if he had something to gain, so he threw in permission for the abductions and the rest."

Ben removed a cigarette from a crush-proof box, leisurely tapped it against the face of his watch before lighting up. He blew a thin stream of smoke toward Big Butt, coughed gently, and continued. "That, Colonel Butz, is why Eisenhower sold us out: lusting for the alien wonder metal, free energy, acid that eats through anything, antigravity, mind control, and invisibility."

"Jeezle," said Purcell. "Invisibility. Imagine. If you was invisible, could you see yourself in a mirror? Could you see the food you just ate? If you peed, would you pee yellow or invisible? If you poked a babe real sneaky, would she know it or just get a sly smile on her face?" Slack-jawed, mind wandering at the potential of invisible seduction, Purcell forgot the chaw in his cheek, swallowed, and gagged on tobacco juice.

Big Butt massaged his chin. "You know, now that I think of it, Eisenhower kind of looked like an alien. He had that bald, dome-shaped head, almost too big for a normal man. You ever look at his portrait on a silver dollar?"

"Did he have those black bug-eyes, too?" asked Jesus Bob, staring intently at the grasshopper's head. He dispatched the maimed insect with a rock and rustled through his ever-present aluminum suitcase—THIS SIDE UP was stenciled on one side with an arrow pointing to the clouds, THIS SIDE DOWN on the other, an arrow, pointing to the Kentucky clay. He retrieved a finger-thick doobie from THIS SIDE DOWN, and lit up. Jittery, coming off a crystal-meth high, his already raw nerves abraded by too much harsh camp coffee, Jesus Bob needed mellowing.

"Man, I get the shivers whenever I think of the pictures in that book you showed us." He waved the joint Ben's way, ignoring the general's disapproving scowl. "Bad dreams, too. Woke up the other night, saw that picture of Jesus on the wall with his eyes all glowing in the dark, and mistook him for one of them aliens. Sis hit me in the head with an ashtray when I screamed. Look here." He showed them a fiery red welt over his right eyebrow.

"Abduction is a frightening phenomenon," agreed Ben. "Fraught with danger."

"Pardon my ig-no-rance," said Jesus Bob, with an evil squint, "but you, Mr. know-it-all barber, using these ten-dollar words—ak-ords, eggs-emplary, in-pee-un-i-ty, frawt, fa-mom-a-mom. What the hell's a DUCK-SHON, anyway?"

Ben smiled, but, wary of Jesus Bob and his reputed temper, not too patronizingly. "Abduction is when they steal you away, my pharmacologically addled young friend. Kidnap you into space and experiment on you. Stick probes up your nose, steal your liver and other organs, then seal you up so no one knows the wiser before they drop you back on earth."

"Kind of like what God did in the Book of Guinness," added Purcell. "Took Adam's rib out of him and made a babe with it. Adam never knew no different, only that here was this babe all of a sudden wanting him to eat apples and stuff."

Ben ignored the Biblical analogy. "Or," he said with a leer, "they have been known to perform bizarre sexual experiments." He drew out the sex-u-al for emphasis.

Jesus Bob's eyes went wide. "Oh, man, like screw you? What do you think their dinguses look like? I'll bet they're big, with knobs and stuff. You ever seen a snake prick? They got two of them, side by side, inside the tail. No shit—I shot this monster rattlesnake yesterday then smashed it to a pulp with a rifle butt, and I seen em, weird-assed with thorns and hooks. Yu-uck, I hate snakes, even dead ones." He took a massive drag of pot, held it in for succor. When his face went red, he coughed it out with a shiver. "To be buggered by some dome-headed, green alien pervert with bug eyes!" He squeezed his own eyes shut and shuddered again. "Or worse, what if they made you stick yours into one of their females? Trick your mind—"

"Mind control," Ben interjected. "A common practice."

"Yeah—trick you into thinking it's some hot Earth babe you've got the grip on. I'll bet their nooks is ice cold, maybe with claws inside, so you can't get it out. Stuck face-to-face with a green-faced, bug-eyed, dome-headed, ice-cold, hook-nooked alien." Jesus Bob fell to his knees. "Man, I think I'm gonna throw up." And he did.

Over the sound of Jesus Bob's retching, Purcell said, "I wonder if a female alien could get knocked up by a human man?"

"Just what crossed my mind," said Big Butt. "In particular, I was thinking about the *mother* of General and President, Dwight David, Bald and Dome-headed Eisenhower."

"Oh, Lord," said Ben. "I never reasoned it through. That explains everything."

8

ikki and Digger spent the sunny spring afternoon on the shore of Lake Boone, a river dammed in the fifties, skipping stones, watching fishermen in slow-moving boats, and catching up. By unspoken agreement, they avoided mention of the murder, although Digger once again reminded Nikki she had agreed to return to Cincinnati.

"Soon enough, Unc. Don't press me," she said and changed the subject.

The next morning, they rendezvoused in the lobby of the E-Z Zees at a leisurely ten o'clock. Amy Lou, the real estate lady, was waiting for them, sitting on a baby-blue velvet Mediterranean sofa, a pink vinyl tackle box and a white bag at her side. "Good morning, sleepyheads. Dr. Fitz, and—?"

"Nikki Fitz." Nikki shook the warm pudgy hand. "Uncle Digger's niece."

Amy Lou transferred a smoldering cigarette to her left hand and stuck out her right. "You just call me Amy Lou, honey. And . . . it's Digger? You don't mind if I call you Digger?"

Digger shook his head.

"I came by with a key to the house." Amy Lou returned the cigarette to her mouth, eyes watering from the smoke, and fumbled in her purse. She handed Digger a key ring and a sheet of paper with directions.

"And look at you, Dr. Fitz—Digger. Fancy new wardrobe. I declare, you look nearly as good in those western clothes as Elvis looked in Hawaii in his flowered shirts. The sheriff's boys"—chattering fast—"haven't tracked mud inside or broken any of the collectibles—Coony knows I'd skin him if they did—although they got some kind of black dust all over. Johnny gave me a can of WD-40 to clean it off. It did the job, but now the place smells to high heaven. Coony says you can move in later. How about that? Your new home! Motel folks said you can check out late as supper, won't cost you a penny more." She turned to the sofa, lifted the white bag, and passed it to Nikki. "Here's a housewarming gift, a coffee cake. Baked it myself."

"That's really nice," Nikki said, looking to Digger for explanation of who this flouncy, fast-talking woman with the fire-ant-orange hair might be.

"Amy Lou handled the sale of the house to Edgar, kiddo. Remember, I told you how she met us?"

"Oh, yeah." Nikki gave Amy Lou a second take, trying to cast her in Digger's horror story.

Amy Lou tilted her head to the side and blew a cloud of smoke over her shoulder. "I want you folks to know you're welcome."

"I wish everyone felt that way," Digger said, frowning. "I'm afraid it's only a matter of time before your sheriff arrests me."

"Pish-tosh. I'm sure as soon as he gets word on your fingerprints, he'll—"

"Fingerprints? They didn't fingerprint me."

"I wouldn't know." She took a deep drag and looked Digger over, head to cowboy boots, before exhaling. "I may be of some help. When you're settled in, you give me a call—

there's some things we could do with that graying hair and beard that would make all the difference."

Digger looked confused.

"I'm with Mary Kay." She waved the cigarette at the pink tackle box on the sofa. "We do makeovers for men, too."

At the door, tackle box in hand, Amy Lou motioned Digger to her side and whispered. "That's a sweet child. Listen, I didn't want to touch it myself, but Coony left that smut in the bathroom. I don't even want to say the name—that magazine. Soon as you get there, you throw it out before the child sees it."

Digger gave assurances. She pressed a tiny, accordion-fold religious tract in his hand—PORNOGRAPHER: DOES HEAVEN OR HELL AWAIT THEE?—and walked to her pink Caddy. She started it up, leaned from the window, and shook a finger at him. "Throw it out, hear?"

At the alarm's safety buzz, 2:30 P.M., Digger jet-lag stumbled from his E-Z Zee's sway-backed bed after a much needed nap. He lifted a slip of paper from the orange and brown carpet by the door: *Unc. Went for a power walk. Meet you outside the pancake house at three—we'll check out and move to Edgar's. Love, N*

Thirty minutes later, he was waiting for her on the bench in front of Chez Pancakes.

A patrol car pulled into the lot. Digger's nemesis of the day before, Deputy Bo Deaver walked to the front door from the other side of the building, touched the brim of his hat in acknowledgment, and went inside. Three minutes later, he returned with two cardboard cups of coffee, handed one to Digger, and sat beside him.

"Lose your niece, sir?"

"You're not here to arrest me?"

"Not yet." He sipped coffee, watched the passing traffic.

Unsure of his game, Digger sipped warily. He tipped his

forehead toward the highway. "Exercise, be along any minute. Might be wise to get back to deputying. I'm not sure you're one of her favorite people after that business yesterday."

Bo grinned. "She's a hothead, huh?"

"You think it's funny? Finding Edgar murdered? Me, a suspect? Not knowing whether you people are doing anything to track his killer?"

Bo frowned at his coffee. "No, sir." Several seconds passed. He glanced up. "I apologize. That really wasn't my style. Something about your niece jumping on me like that . . . Anyway, we *are* working at it. I—"

Bo lost his train of thought as Nikki, wearing shorts, running shoes, and an oversize, sweat-soaked T-shirt, race-walked toward them with a fast, stiff-legged, hip-waggling stride.

Digger noticed Bo noticing Nikki's legs, scanning her body reflexively as she walked from the highway. Then Digger saw Nikki's blotchy face.

"You!" she said to Bo.

"I was just leaving, ma'am." He stood and edged away.

"You okay, kiddo?" Digger stood to get a better look at her face.

Her fists clenched. "Dammed rednecks!" She karate-kicked the bench.

Bo flinched. "What happened?"

She gave him a withering glare and turned. "How's this?" An irregular brown splotch stained the center of her back, five inches across, yellowish spatters to either side. Dribbles ran down her shirt.

Digger wondered how large birds grew in eastern Kentucky, and began to grin.

Nikki whipped around. "First one snickers, gets kicked in the balls. Got it?"

The grin evaporated.

"No, it wasn't birds. That's what you thought, wasn't it? It was a shit-kicker in a pickup truck. Crossed to my side of the road, drove behind me, two wheels on the shoulder. Made me walk in the weeds, yelled stuff"—her voice fell into an Appalachian twang—" 'City pussy, why you runnin' like a goose? You need straightenin' out by a real man? Show me your tits, baby.' Like that, and worse."

Bo and Digger shifted, avoided eye contact.

"I didn't answer, didn't look at him. I was afraid to stop." She swiped her wristband across her upper lip to wipe a sniffly nose. "Then he spit tobacco juice on me. Hot. I felt it slide down my back." Tears flowed, Nikki wiped her face, infuriated at crying.

Digger wrung his hands. "I knew something like this would happen."

Bo shushed Digger with a wave of the hand. "What did he look like?"

"Shit-kicker, like I said. Only saw the back of his head when he drove away. Sprayed gravel in my face. Probably one of your buddies."

Bo ignored the gibe. "Sit down. Breathe deep."

Nikki worked her hands over her face, rubbed her eyes. She inhaled, exhaled deliberately, three times, and sat.

"The truck." Bo said in a cop-serious voice. "Make, color?"

"I don't know. Dark. Green or blue. Blue, I think."

"Big? Small?"

"Huge."

"Kentucky plates? Did you see any numbers, the county?"

"No, it was over so fast. I was angry, scared. Yeah—" She paused, trying to remember. "Kentucky plates. I tried to see the numbers, but I was ducking gravel."

She stared at the ground, tears drying. "Don't remember the make. Bumper stickers." She closed her eyes, kneading her forehead. "One white with black letters, can't really re-member, the other red. Confederate flag! I yelled something about them losing the war when he drove off."

"Hmmm," Bo said. "That's not much to go on."

". . . but I don't think he heard me, because by then he

was pounding on the horn, his truck weaving all over the road on account of his one hand."

"His what?" Bo and Digger said it together.

She frowned. "Didn't I tell you? The bastard's left arm was missing. He must have been steering and honking with the right one. His left sleeve—one of those camouflage hunter's shirts—was pinned up to the shoulder. I got a good enough look at that. Didn't see his face, but I saw the shirt real clear."

"Well, well," said Bo, nodding, massaging his chin. "So, what we're looking for . . . is a one-armed man."

9

No sooner had Digger and Nikki checked out of the
E-Z Zees, than Digger spotted the sheriff himself in
his blue cruiser, swatting a newspaper on his thigh.
Digger peered over the roof of their rent-a-car.
"This may be it, kiddo. Looks like he's waiting for me."

The sheriff cocked his head their way, unsure if he recognized the head in the western hat. Evidently certain
enough, he approached with an arched eyebrow at Digger's
new look. He nodded to Nikki, "Ma'am," and spit out a "Sumbitch" at Digger. "You see this?" He spread the front page of
the Lexington newspaper on the hood.

It sizzled off the page: "Fiendish Murder in McAfee
County. 'The work of satanic fishing coven high on drugs,'
claims sheriff."

" 'Claims sheriff.' Says it all, what we found. That's not
the only one—Frankfort, Ashland, too. On the radio. By tomorrow morning, Cincinnati, Huntington, Louisville, papers
across the state will run it. The wire services'll pick it up next.
Satanic fishing coven. Sumbitch! Won't the bait dealers, the
boat rentals, the Winky Worm people love that!" He rolled
the paper up, slapped it on his thigh again. "Women'll be

afraid to leave their houses. One of them tabloids offered Johnny a thousand dollars for his photos. If he wasn't my nephew, knowed I'd shoot off his privates, he'd of done it."

"Uh-oh," Nikki said. "I didn't tell Mother."

The sheriff jabbed the rolled paper at Digger. "You called them, thought you'd light a fire under my ass for wanting to keep this under wraps, did you?"

Digger raised a hand. "You think I want people believing Edgar was mixed up in drugs? In devil worship? To know how he died? And—and, what's this about fingerprinting me?"

"Sumbitch. Who told you *that*?"

"News spreads fast."

"Don't it." The sheriff tucked the paper under an arm with a sigh. "Guess I knew it wasn't you, but I hoped." He noticed Nikki. "Sorry for the outburst, ma'am. Name's Coony McCoy, McAfee County sheriff. And you are?"

"Nikki Fitz. Digger's niece. Edgar was Digger's cousin. I'm not sure what that makes Edgar and me, but I always called him uncle, too."

"Digger?"

"That's what they call me," Digger said.

"Oh. They call me Coony," the sheriff replied absently. Fleeting emotions played over his face, he scowled, pursed his lips, wrinkled his nose. Then his face cleared, and he shook hands with both of them. "C'mon, I'll buy you a coffee, tell you the news."

Colonel B. J. Butz, aka Big Butt, adjusted his holster, slapped dust from his trouser cuffs and mirror-polished boots with the leather gloves he liked to wear draped over his belt. Dissatisfied with how the starched fatigue pants had ridden up above his tightly belted waist when he bent over—a perennial problem because of his prodigious, fabric-hungry behind—he retucked his shirt and set his midline right. A tug at each long-sleeve cuff, and he was satisfied his military bearing would well exceed the parameters of the inspection he and General Ben were about to spring on the men. Regarding himself in the full-length mirror in Barracks #5, he declared aloud, "You, my man, are one fine soldier."

He stepped outside and walked toward the milling troops. To a man, they would rather be running through the woods and shooting, he knew, but he was a colonel, and they would damn well be inspected. Only seven today—have to be one row. With one more man he could arrange them in two rows of four. Geometric, orderly. He could walk down one line, up the other. He grew angry at the thought of Jesus Bob, the eighth man, still sleeping in Barracks #1.

Jesus Bob. No discipline. No respect. Big Butt was proud of his ability to wipe smirks from happy faces with no more than a scream in the men's ears and a pinch of the short hairs at the back of their necks. He awed the troops, too, he knew, with accounts (embellished and theatrically presented) of his own exploits: the bombs, the sniping, the firing squad.

Discipline, respect, military bearing—all going to hell in a handbasket with the new man, Jesus Bob, in camp. He hated the lazy, nasty, drugged-out bastard. And his sister, the Blond Bitch from Hell, the only human Jesus Bob seemed to fear. Damn the sister's damnable long legs, too. No place for women in a military camp, no sir.

But the commander had said to put up with them, and the Reserve—every acre, tree, and cabin of it—belonged to the commander. So that was that.

"Jesus Bob." Big Butt snarled the name, and then swallowed with the realization that the loner Jesus Bob could instill more fear in a man—in Big Butt himself—with that squinty look of his, than the totality of Big Butt's own, mirror-practiced menacing. And—this was the part he really hated—there was no man who, truth be told, Big Butt would rather impress than the undisciplined, disrespectful, independent, and truly bad-assed Jesus Bob. Oh, to make Jesus

Bob say, "No shit, you did that?" or to make him belly-laugh, "You've got one hell of a sense of humor there, Big Butt!" But it wasn't apt to happen.

In troubled thought, he passed General Ben without comment.

"Not that I need a salute, Colonel Butz," said Ben. "But you might say hello."

Big Butt snapped to attention. "Sorry, sir." (Not "Sorry, Ben"—inspections always meant shelving familiarity.)

"I told them to assemble at fifteen hundred hours," Ben said. "They don't know about the inspection—wouldn't hurt for them to see us palavering, think we're discussing the shelling of the valley."

"Keep them on their toes? I like that," said Big Butt, the troublesome Jesus Bob forgotten.

"Tell me, Colonel," Ben said. "As I move around to face you, look over my shoulder and tell me if that odd, roundish cloud is moving our way."

Big Butt gave it a long look. "Hmm, hard to tell, sir."

"Don't stare, man! Keep your eyes on me, just glance now and again."

Big Butt returned his gaze to Ben. "Sir, uh, you gonna ask questions? Are you going to ask me anything?" He coughed. "I mean, I want to be sure I'll get it right in front of the men, and—"

Ben patted him on the arm. "Calm down, Colonel. You'll be fine."

"Sometimes I get the letters wrong. Those abbreviations."

"Acronyms. Once committed to memory, they will be like old friends. How about NATO, UN?"

"North Atlantic Treaty Organization, United Nations."

"Excellent. The cloud?"

"I'm pretty sure it's going the other way. Yeah, definitely smaller, headed east with the rest."

"Of course! They realize we're on to them." Ben gave Big Butt a sharp look. "But *never* underestimate them, do you hear?"

"Yes, sir."

"How about FBI, CIA, EPA, ATF, IRS, NEA?"

Translations of the hated acronyms rolled off Big Butt's lips with ease.

"UFO, LAW?"

"Unidentified Flying Object, Light Anti-tank Weapon."

"ZOG?"

Silence. Big Butt thought of *Dog* and *God*. Neither of which was correct, he knew.

General Ben explained: "Zionist Occupied Government."

"It's that word, *Zi-on-ist* that throws me. I always think of lions, but I know that's not it. It's a conspiracy I know, but—"

"Let me go over it for you, son. The Zionists are your big-nosed Jews. Their allies, the aliens, are helping them get into positions of power, see? Along with the Catholics, spearheaded by the spaghetti pope. There are far more of the Catholics, of course, they being the most populous creatures on earth, considering your Latins—more common even than beetles. But the Jews have the brains and the money, so it is probably the Jews—the international Zionists—who will ultimately pull the strings along with their alien cohorts.

"Establishing a federal tyranny is merely the first step. Coopting the local police follows—we've seen it here. They plan to install the New World Order, enslave the rag-heads, the mud races of Africa and Asia, and—this is the part you must never forget—to disenfranchise the good, hardworking white Christian men of this land, to take away our Bible and our arms, make homosexuals of our children, and rule by cabalistic fiat from across the ocean and from outer space. That is the ultimate conspiracy we oppose."

Big Butt blinked. Conspiracy registered. Jews and Catholics. Aliens, mud races. But lions kept popping into his head.

"We"—Ben tapped Big Butt and then himself on the chest—"are the bulwark against that evil scenario. The antagonists the Zionists fear. See?"

"Yes, sir."

"The Daniel Boone Rangers, my brave companions-in-arms, are at the vanguard, defending our mothers, wives, and children, the ideals we hold dear. No room for wavering. No room for doubt. You are a colonel in the Daniel Boone Rangers, an officer in the cause. You are a *hero*. Understand?"

"Yes, *sir!*" Big Butt saluted, clicked his heels, and, Jesus Bob and lions forgotten, marched proudly at Ben's side toward the unsuspecting troops.

10

The sheriff forced a smile at the Chez Pancakes cashier. "Rubella—table set apart, huh?"

The smoke rising from the butt-filled register ashtray prompted Digger to ask, "Do you smoke, Sheriff? Nikki and I . . . uh . . . don't."

Rubella, a fleshy forty and still growing, with puffy eyes and bleach-brittled hair, chuckled knowingly. "Except for the pipe at home," she said in a raspy voice, "he gave it up six months ago—along with certain other things—and no law says you have to, mister." She lifted her cigarette and airplaned it through the air, warbling *Twilight Zone* Doo-do-doo-dos.

The sheriff shot her a glare. "Enough, Rubella. No need to let the whole town know about my habits or the damn rumors, hear?"

Attentive, Digger and Nikki exchanged glances.

"Word gets around, Sheriff." Rubella's hand soared again, and then stopped in midzoom. She sucked smoke, exhaled it dragon-style through her nostrils, giving Digger a long look. "Say, don't I know you?"

A passing server said, "He's the one from Hawaii. You know, the *one*."

Rubella gave him a hard stare.

"He's one of them Baywatch stars," said the sheriff. "Duded up in western so the locals don't recognize him. Man wants privacy—so how about that table?"

"Yeah, we're in kind of a hurry," Nikki added.

Still studying Digger, the cashier jabbed the cigarette over her shoulder. "Take your pick, we're near empty."

A sparrow-skinny waitress barely out of her teens, with spiked hennaed hair and I LOVE JESUS tattooed on one arm, I LOVE JUDD on the other, brought a pot to the table. She filled the sheriff's cup automatically. When Nikki and Digger nodded to her, she poured them cups, too, and giggled. "How about some ham steak, Sheriff?"

"No thank you, Beth Ann."

She tittered again and busied herself rearranging flatware one table away.

"What's that all about?" Digger asked, his new white Stetson in hand, unsure what to do with it. The chair backs were round, there wasn't enough room on the table. The fourth chair had congealed blueberry syrup on the seat. He tried his lap, had to scoot his chair back. He scowled and put it back on.

"There you go," said the sheriff. He tapped his own hat, still on his head. Then, to the lingering waitress, "I believe you're needed in the kitchen, Beth Ann."

"That's right," Nikki said.

The girl frowned, took five steps away, turned and stuck her tongue out at Nikki's back, and retreated to the counter.

Digger pressed. "The hamsteak, the *Doo-do-Doo-dos?*"

"Passes for local humor. You wouldn't get it."

As soon as the waitress left, Nikki let loose. "Did you catch the murderer? He was a fisherman, wasn't he?"

"Darlin', be patient. Time will reveal all." Coony McCoy took a deep breath, adjusted his chair, lifted his cup to his nose, and sniffed. "The Chez—" again, the hard Ch, rhyming with fez—"has got the best damned coffee in three counties. Grind their own, you know."

"Come on, man," Digger said. "You intimated you knew who killed poor Edgar."

The sheriff set the cup down, cradled it between his palms. "Bikers."

"Bikers?" said Nikki. "Who are they? Did they confess?"

"We don't have them in custody, no names yet, not from around here."

Digger cocked a sarcastic eyebrow at Nikki. "Bikers. Drugs. Outsiders." He cast an uneasy look at the sheriff. "But I'm off your suspect list?"

The sheriff put the cup to his lips and sipped. "You seem to be who you say you are." He added a pregnant, "So far."

Digger blanched.

"What are you talking about?" Nikki said, confused. "You know darn well it wasn't Uncle Digger. How come bikers, not fishermen?"

"We went over the place with a fine-tooth comb. They was running a meth lab. Plenty of evidence—residues in the kitchen, trash in a ravine. Hardly a surprise the man who rented the place before your Edgar used a phony name, paid the rent cash in advance."

Digger was wiping his forehead with a napkin, staring at the table.

"And you think they came back and murdered Uncle Edgar?" Nikki asked.

The sheriff glanced indifferently at Digger, lifted his cup, rotated it in his palms, watching the brew. "They took him to that shack to throw suspicion off the house. Beyond that, there's several possibilities. One, your cousin was innocent of the whole deal."

"We knew that already," Nikki said.

A silencing finger rose. "He moves in, they come back for a stash, or, afraid they left something incriminating. Don't matter which—they do him in."

Digger regained his composure. "By cramming fishing

sinkers down his throat? Running a hook through his lips with that plastic snake?"

"Winky Worm. A cruel death, yes, but bikers are apt to be outcasts, mean and screwed up in the head. And methamphetamine turns addicts paranoid. Nutso."

"Could be, I guess," Digger said, partially deflated.

"The fishing angle?" The sheriff lifted his cup to his nose, eyes closed, set it down, and muttered, "Three cups a day." He looked at Digger. "Just about every man I know fishes and there aren't many fishermen around without a Winky Worm or three in their box, so that hardly narrows the field. It might have been a message: Here's what happens to men who don't keep their mouths shut."

Nikki screwed up her face. "Keep their mouths shut? That makes no sense."

The sheriff lifted the cup and took a full swallow. "It does if our second possibility pans out—that your Edgar was in on it."

"Here we go," warned Digger.

The sheriff motioned a *hold on*. "Maybe he moved the product up north. Ann Arbor's a college town, plenty of kids with money. Maybe he came here to hold the house, watch over inventory. They had a falling out—"

Nikki huffed. "No way."

"Okay. So we're left with our third and most likely see-nare-ee-o."

"Odds are," said Digger, "it's still outsiders and Edgar being a drug dealer."

"Not perzactly. Say he moves in, innocent, finds evidence of what was going on. He's a scientist, figures out the chemicals, the broken glassware in back."

"Edgar was an archaeologist."

"And archaeologists never study chemistry? Your Edgar dee-vines what's up and who's been doing it, suggests cash would keep him quiet. The man knows what he's dealing with, so he puts his proof where it would turn up if they hurt him—or claims he did. What's a couple thousand dollars a week for a healthy drug operation?"

Digger snorted. "A couple thousand dollars a week. Did you pull that out of your hat or from somewhere farther south?"

The sheriff gave him a short smile. "Touché. No, was like this: I figured if he's hiding evidence, there must be a safety deposit box and a bank account. My wife did some checking—"

"Your wife does police work for you?"

"Practically runs the department. If you got something against women in law enforcement, best not mention it to Etta."

"I didn't mean that, only—"

"As I was saying, Etta contacts her daddy, Judge Shirey, arranges to review your cousin's local bank dealings. When your cousin arrived six weeks ago he opened an account at Golden Leaf Savings with a check drawn on a Michigan bank for a thousand dollars."

"That's reasonable," said Nikki.

"Yep. No safety deposit box, but a week after your uncle arrives, he deposits two thousand dollars. Cash. One week later, another two thousand. And each week after that. Eight thousand bucks total. What's he doing here in McAfee County that nets him two thousand dollars a week in cash?"

Digger frowned, drummed his fingers on the tabletop. "Off hand, I don't know, but I'm sure Edgar wasn't involved in drugs."

"If he threatened to blow the whistle, the money and the murder make a whole lot of sense. Or, the money could of been his share of the profits."

The sheriff savored the next sip of coffee to let his reasoning sink in, and then reached into his back pocket for his wallet and removed four business cards. "Regardless, you folks got details to think about. Here's a card with the name of a reputable lawyer in Golden Leaf, my wife's brother. His

firm has served folks here for fifty years. I vouch for him."
He caught Digger's worried look. "For the *estate*, huh?" He
spread the other cards on the table, took a deep drink of
coffee, rolled it in his mouth before swallowing. "This one
with the willow tree is from Trask Mortuary. The pink one
is Amy Lou's."

"We saw her before," Nikki said. "She gave us a house
key and directions."

The sheriff nodded. "Keys to your Edgar's Volkswagen is
on the kitchen table—you may as well use it. This one"—he
tapped an embossed six-pointed gold star over navy type—
"is mine. You hear anything, call."

"Appreciate the cards," Digger said, "but the drug business is preposterous."

"Didn't mean to imply there aren't other suspects." The
sheriff looked over his cup, directly at Digger.

Digger swallowed and went silent.

"Oh, yeah," the sheriff added. "Before I forget, Etta wants
me to invite you two to supper. Tomorrow evening. With you
not knowing anyone hereabouts, we wouldn't want you to
think folks is inhospitable. Six o'clock? Directions and the
phone number is on my card."

Digger scooted his chair back. Hold on, he said to himself. I'm a suspect, Edgar's a drug dealer, and this cop's inviting us to his house for dinner? "Thanks," he said, "but we
wouldn't want to—"

"Dinner," Nikki said. "Nice. We'll be there."

"Dress casual." The sheriff took in Digger's new look. "Either that, or the High-wah-yan garb." He drank the last of
the coffee, and stood. "The invite is a might selfish." He
winked at Digger. "I got a surprise for you."

An hour after Nikki and Digger had checked out of the E-Z Zees, they were sitting in the front porch swing of Edgar's country cottage, watching swallows dip over a small farm pond at the edge of the yard. Digger pushed the swing forward and back with his feet. "That biker talk and the dinner invitation were diversions, kiddo. He wants me to let my guard down. I've seen them do it before."

"Chill out, Unc. We'll go, see what happens. Aren't you curious about his surprise?"

"Handcuffs after dessert, you'll see. Cop humor, like sending sweepstakes letters to suckers they plan to arrest—stop by for your big check. Back in the sixties, we knew better than to trust cops. You kids now are so naive." He noticed the smile. "Really, Nikki."

"Yeah, yeah. Meanwhile, let's go over this place ourselves. You might want to avoid the laundry tub by the way. That's Coony II's new bedroom."

*　　　*　　　*

Digger was at Edgar's desk, paging through stacked files. At his back, he heard, "Hey, Unc, check this out."

He swiveled the chair to see *Playboy's* Miss May dancing a foot away.

"Do men really like breasts this big?"

"Ummm . . . you're embarrassing me." Red-faced, he returned to the files, decided he should have listened to Amy Lou.

"Answer me. It may have a bearing on our investigation."

Nose down: "I suppose it depends upon whose they are, and, uh, circumstances."

"You should have been a politician." She refolded Miss May, but didn't speak.

Digger turned to face her, "All right, how do big breasts bear on our investigation?"

"I said 'may.'" She tossed the magazine on the desk. "I went through the rest of the house and the garage, found zip. I saw that stuff the cops found in the ravine. It could be what the sheriff said. You?"

Digger covered the *Playboy* with a file. "What I didn't find were Edgar's notes, a calendar, a bankbook, or his laptap."

"Pretty thorough bikers."

"What I thought, too. But I did find something disturbing. Edgar was an underliner—most of his books have colored highlights: blue, turquoise, pink, yellow, green. Unfortunately, he was one of those people who underline almost everything, so it's meaningless. However, this book on artifact conservation was lying at an angle, on top of the others, as if he had been referring to it. Only one section is underlined—in turquoise. His markers are in that cup—blue, pink, yellow, green. Look what was on the desk." He lifted the turquoise marker.

"What's that section about?"

Digger tapped the marker on the desk, stared at it for several seconds, and said: "Lead. As in fishing sinkers."

*   *   *

Digger pored over Edgar's books fruitlessly for two hours. He rubbed his eyes, lifted a pencil, made a notation—and broke the point at the scream. *Nikki!* Outside.

He shot to the porch, heard another screech up the hillside, in the woods. No motorcycles, no cars. Why the hell did she wander up there alone? Shouting. Adrenaline surging, he ran, heard her call his name, and picked up the pace. At the edge of the woods, breathless, he snatched a rock as a weapon and stepped cautiously into the shadows.

He saw her—silent, immobilized by fear, staring at the brush-shrouded ground, and realized she had found a *body.* Sheesh! "Easy, honey. Leave it alone. Come back by me."

Without turning, she said, "No, you come here." Excited, but hardly afraid. "You can talk, but don't stomp around."

He eased forward, the rock cradled in his palm. From ten feet away, he saw clearly through the undergrowth—not a body, but a snake. Unmoving, coiled round as a dinner plate with a blunt arrow-shaped head, black saddles circling a stout, tan, rough-scaled trunk. And at the tail? A buzzing, ten-button *rattle.* His heart thumped as he blurted it out: "Rattlesnake!"

"Bingo. *Crotalus horridus.* Man, what luck! A copperhead I might have expected, but a rattler? First time I walk up here. Isn't she a beauty?"

Angry: "Dammit, Nikki. I thought you'd been attacked or found a bod—" He caught himself, felt foolish—for no more than a second. A shiver ran up his spine. A rattlesnake! If there was one thing in the world that made his skin crawl, besides leeches—he cringed at memories of New Guinea—it was snakes. And this one was deadly. "Keep back!"

"I'm cool. She'll stay coiled—defensive posture."

The buzzing stopped, but a satiny tongue waved up and down, its tips trembling, tasting air.

Nikki lifted a section of dead but sturdy branch, about four feet long.

Digger surprised himself. "Don't kill it, kiddo. We'll leave it, go back to the house with a story to tell our friends."

"Kill it? I haven't played with a rattlesnake in three years."

"Play? Are you out of your mind?"

She was already extending the stick, ever so slowly. "She doesn't see this as threatening."

Digger did a shuffle step in place and whispered, "Keep your voice down."

Nikki was into a running description. ". . . by our standards, deaf . . . no ears, but do have vestigial middle ear bones . . . can pick up low frequencies. Fast movement will set them off, but working the branch this slow won't bother her in the—here we go." She wedged the branch tip below the coiled snake and lifted. The rattle buzzed, the snake unflexed a foot off the ground and began to crawl off the branch. Nikki leaned over and lightly gripped the tail to restrain it. "The secret's to barely hold them, see?" The serpent seemed not to mind her touch. "This girl's at least two and a half feet long."

"Sheesh! Careful. Be careful."

"See the eyes, the vertical pupils?"

He edged forward, marginally. "I see. Metallic, jewel-like. Evil."

"Animals aren't evil. People are evil."

"You know what I mean, no lids, no expression. Like that Bible picture."

"Forget the Bible picture. We're talking ID." She maneuvered the snake to face him. "Those pits between the eyes and the nostrils? Heat sensing. Around here, only poisonous snakes—timbers and copperheads—have pits and vertical pupils like that. Everything else is harmless. Here . . . you want to touch her?"

"Sure. How about I sling it around my neck, and you can take my picture? Put it down, kiddo, while you're ahead."

"Exactly what I plan to do." She eased the snake to the ground and it crawled lazily away, disappearing into the undergrowth.

Digger wiped his forehead. "Look—" He held his arm and palm straight out. "Trembling."

"Good. Gets the circulation up."

He backed away. "My knees are shaking. Really. I'm not a drinking man, but that bourbon of Edgar's is calling my name. I'm going back. Now."

Nikki hounded his heels, lecturing. ". . . can strike no more than half their body length, and even if they happen to crawl your way, which they won't, you can outwalk them. Timbers are shy. The only way you'd get bit is by reaching under the wrong rock or stepping on one—although don't always count on hearing a rattle first."

Over his shoulder: "And if you had been bit?"

"Oh, I'd be cursing a blue streak. It's a burning pain right off, like a hot poker. Swelling, yucky discoloration, tissue damage to follow. I wouldn't want to replay Cleopatra, or get bit on the nose—a body bite in the wrong place could do you in, although fatalities from snakebites in the U.S. are rare. Most bites are on hands or feet, although you could lose a chunk of flesh—or more—if you didn't get to a hospital with know-how and antivenom. Dry bites—no envenomation—happen, too. More snakebit people probably die from heart attacks than venom—they scare themselves to death."

"Comforting."

"Odds are, you'll never see another one this trip."

Digger grunted a "Good," and picked up the pace to the house and a double shot of Edgar's Jim Beam.

12

The two elm-shaded blocks east of the Golden Leaf town square held a dozen pristine Victorian houses, the abodes of attorneys and bankers, sellers of land, insurance, tobacco, and automobiles, the Winky Worm president, a mortician, two octogenarian spinster sisters, and one sheriff.

Nikki parked at the curb. "I guess this is the one," pointing to the two patrol cars in the drive; Coony McCoy's blue Bonneville and a white Ford, both with gold stars on the doors, the white one with a rack of roof lights.

Digger cast a suspicious eye at the three-story, white frame structure. "I've never been inside a cop's house before." A cone-topped tower crowned one corner, gables protruded asymmetrically from a dark slate roof, and a long porch ran along two sides. "Looks like some haunted house out of the movies, doesn't it?"

Nikki patted him on the shoulder. "More like a wedding cake. They're not from outer space, Unc. I suspect they eat and sleep like everybody else. You'll do fine. C'mon."

She twisted a brass crank in the seven-foot oak door,

ringing a bell on the other side. It swung open to reveal Deputy Bo Deaver, in jeans and a faded denim shirt.

Nikki backpedaled. "You!"

Bo took a short step back, himself. "Ma'am?"

"I guess we were expecting family only." Digger elbowed Nikki forward, a serves-you-right grin blooming.

"I've got no family," Bo said, holding the door open. "But Etta and Coony's near kin. I eat here three times a week: Tuesdays, Thursdays, and Saturdays, sometimes on Sunday. This is Saturday, so I'm here. Is there a problem, ma'am?"

"No," she said, "I was just, uh, surprised."

Bo turned to the interior, yelled, "Guests are here."

Nikki crossed her eyes at Digger.

"Finishing something, down in a minute," the sheriff shouted from an upper floor, his voice muffled. "Show them the parlor, Bo."

Bo motioned for them to follow. "No luck, so far, with your one-armed man, ma'am, but I've been on it."

"Good for you. And don't call me *ma'am*, okay? Just call me—"

Digger made a suggestion: "Ms. Fitz?"

She scowled at him. "No. Nikki will do."

Bo smiled. "Nikki. Yes, ma'am."

A fast-moving, boxy woman in her early fifties with prematurely white hair swept back in a duck tail, wearing a red apron over a UK sweatshirt, burst through a door at the back of the hall. "Well *hell*-o. I'm Etta." A cloud of home-cooking smells caught up with her, flooded the hall.

"And you must be Nikki." She wiped floury hands on the apron, took the bottle of apple juice Nikki had brought as a gift, smiled a thank-you, and shook Nikki's hand. "And here's our Hawaiian, Dr. Fitz." She clapped Digger on the shoulder hard enough to send him sideways. "You both know Bo. Bo, honey? Entertain them. I'm not together in the kitchen. Damned meringue won't set up." She disappeared the way she had come.

They followed Bo to a formal parlor, sat side by side on a brocade settee facing him. Stiff-backed in a wing chair, far less in command than he had been behind Chez Pancakes, Bo fiddled with his cuffs. The seconds ticked off, and the three smiled politely, at a loss for conversation, until a toilet flushed, noisily, upstairs.

"That would be Coony," Bo said unnecessarily.

Nikki snorted. Anticipating a snicker-fit, Digger knocked her knee with his and changed the subject. "Lots of antiques here, eh, Bo?"

"Lots. Old, too." Bo wriggled in the chair, ran a finger around the inside of his collar.

Nikki snorted again. Digger stared at the carpet.

"Glad you could join us," Coony McCoy said from the entryway, still adjusting his belt.

"Bo's been telling us about antiques," Digger said.

"Mostly heirlooms from Etta's family. Her granddaddy built this house. That medallion-backed sofa you're setting on dates from 1840. Walnut. Fine carving, huh? The mahogany shelf clock on the mantel is near as old."

He led them on a walk-through, winding up in the dining room. ". . . These Chippendale chairs are pre-Revolution, made in Philadelphia, brought across the mountains by a relative on Etta's momma's side. Could never afford them today—"

"Land sakes, Coony," his wife said from the kitchen doorway, "you'll bore them to tears. Show them the hall wash closet to clean up." To her guests, "I hope you like cottage ham and sauerkraut?"

"Yes, ma'am," Bo said. "You bet."

"Smells wonderful," Digger said diplomatically.

A minute later, Digger soaped his hands while Nikki dried hers. He whispered, "I've been a vegetarian for twenty-three years."

"Unc, in the country they eat meat three meals a day. How did you get by living with headhunters, acting like such a wuss?"

"You're right," he admitted. "Anthropologists' Code: Don't offend your hosts. I ate grubs in Australia, live fish in Tahiti, locusts in Mali. Even put away a bowl of missionary stew one time to please a chief."

"Cool!"

"Yeah. Nearly cracked a tooth on a brass crucifix, but the stew wasn't bad. Tasted like chicken à la king."

She screwed up her face. "Eeuw," then, "Wait a minute." She tugged at his sleeve on the way to the dining room, whispering, "I know you're bullshitting. For sure about the crucifix. You didn't really *eat* it, did you? Unc? Unc?"

When everyone had taken seats, Etta set a deep china platter in front of Digger with an encouraging, "Cottage ham over sauerkraut with green beans. No, don't be shy. Load up, but leave room for the stewed tomatoes and macaroni. Okra, too. And homemade cornbread."

Digger ladled a pile of the main course onto his plate while Etta added helpings of side dishes. He stared at stringy pink ham, globules of shiny white fat coating the kraut fibers and beans, melding with weeping tomatoes and flaccid macaroni, pooling around gelatinous okra, a slab of sand-dry cornbread on the edge of the dish. He lifted his fork, set it down again, lifted it, wishing there were a dog under the table.

He felt marginally better watching Nikki moving food around, looking a whole lot less cocky than during the wash-up.

Etta moved to the kitchen, returned with a white-and-blue Corningware bowl, and set it by her husband's plate. "Tofu and vegetable stir-fry for Coony. Eat up, dearie."

Coony caught Digger's stare. "No offense, I hope. I'm vegetarian. You all eat hearty."

Digger kicked Nikki hard enough in the ankle to make her drop a chunk of cornbread into her sauerkraut.

Etta took the seat between Coony and Nikki, filled her own plate. "It was our tenth anniversary," she said, prying apart cottage ham with knife and fork, "that Coony and I took our first real vacation—a present from my mama and daddy. Went to Waikiki, stayed at the Royal Hawaiian Hotel, that fancy pink one. Lord, I'll never forget it. Remember how disappointed you were to learn there was no such thing as Five-O, Coony?"

"Wait a minute, Sheriff." Digger set down his still-virgin fork. "When I told you where I lived, you weren't sure Hawaii was part of the United States."

Coony grinned at his tofu, spoke without looking up. "Sometimes you learn more from folks when they think you're half in the dark."

"Watch him," Etta said. "He's a slick one. And you—Digger," pointing her knife at his nose, "call the man by his first name." She noticed his plate. "Something wrong with the ham? Sometimes I cook it a little too long. Bo likes it chewy."

Digger took a reluctant bite. "Delicious. But I'm a little off feed today—a stomach virus . . . the traveling."

"Me, too," Nikki said, rubbing her stomach. "Must have caught it from him."

Etta clucked. "Poor dears. Better go easy till you settle in. We'll have you back. Always plenty to eat." She patted Digger on the arm. "Why don't you tell us about your archaeology?"

"Unc's specialty is sex."

Etta repeated the word. "Sex."

Coony set his fork down. "Do tell?"

Bo raised an eyebrow but kept chewing.

Digger blushed.

Etta poked him in the shoulder. "Well, come on. Out with it. Sounds like fun."

Still suffering from cop-a-phobia, Digger mumbled at his cornbread about Pacific cultures, but gradually segued into his specialty. As he ran over familiar ground, he loosened up, forgot his audience, and fell into a lecturing stride, relating his recent, alas solely academic, collaboration with the famous Dr. Van Tilburg, a sizzling young female archaeologist, who, as did Digger, saw sex in every standing stone or hole in the ground: ". . . have been studying the famous statues, *moai*, of Easter Island, metaphors for competitive ancestral power, their stony shafts thrusting to the heavens conjoining mortals with the gods." A finger pointed up for emphasis. "While the erections of some of the lesser polities were small—" he made bitty gestures with thumb and forefinger— "those of the more powerful Rapa Nui chiefs rose thirty feet in the air." He stood and stared at their imposing heads, straining skyward. "One monster, still lying on the volcano's flank, would have stretched to eighty feet if they had been able to get it up!" He spoke nonstop for ten minutes, finally concluded with, "Dr. Van Tilburg and I are calling our paper 'Bigger *is* better.' "

Nikki urged him into anecdotes of the weird things he had eaten in the field, hopeful he would reopen the kettle of missionary stew he had left unfinished in the hallway. Coony fired archaeological questions into dessert and, unlimbered, Digger answered him as if he were a student doing the asking and not the head cop. Silent, Bo wolfed whatever Etta put on his plate. Over lemon meringue pie, Etta asked what Nikki was studying to become.

"A herpetologist, ma'am."

"Say what?"

"A snake specialist." She described the snakes she had found.

"Bo," Coony set down his fork, "you ought to show her where old Brown got bit to death by the rattlesnake. He was swole up big as a dead cow and stunk twice as bad as I recall."

"Brown's wife made up the snake part," Bo said, still chewing. "As you well know. It was the boyfriend's knife blade that did Brown in, spread his ribs, punctured his lungs and sliced his heart, and five days in the ditch that did the swelling. I do remember his bloated black tongue, though, and Lord, the flies and maggots—"

"Enough shop talk at dinner," Etta said. "Eat your pie."

After the meal, Nikki offered to help Etta clean up in the kitchen. Bo tagged along.

"First time I've ever seen you offer to help with the dishes, Bo," Etta said. "Maybe we should invite these folks more often."

Coony crooked a finger at Digger. "How about the two of us go to my office—alone?"

13

arning flags unfurled as Digger remembered
the sheriff's promised surprise. He hung back
at the stairs, annoyed with himself for letting
his guard down at dinner.

"C'mon, man," Coony motioned him to follow. "Whadaya
think, I'm gonna arrest you?"

Digger had to grin at the gallows humor, thinking,
Damned if he's not toying with me. Resigned, he followed
him up the carpeted stairway into a dim hall.

Coony motioned him through a door. "Nothing but a re-
modeled bedroom," he said, flipping a light switch, "but it's
my small kingdom. Mind if I smoke a pipe?"

Digger shook his head, and circled the room. A pair of
flintlock muskets and two age-worn powder horns hung
above a Victorian faux-marble, cast iron fireplace. Frames
over an oak rolltop desk held Indian arrowheads mounted in
geometric designs. Floor-to-ceiling bookcases lined the opposite wall. He saw well-worn books on history, archaeology,
classics.

Coony sat in a crushed-velvet recliner, motioned Digger
to a leather armchair. He patted the recliner's arm. "I know

this ugly bastard don't fit in with the rest of the house, but it's comfortable. This is the only place in the house Etta'll let me light up. One pipe a day, the diet, three cups of coffee—little ticker problem a ways back. Love that woman, but she can be a bitch on wheels about some things. How about a drink? I get one a night."

At Digger's nod, he half filled two cut crystal tumblers with twelve-year-old bourbon from a side table. He held the glass just out of Digger's reach. "You sure you can handle it? A drink?"

Digger looked confused.

"With your stomach."

"My stomach?"

"That sudden flu." Coony slapped his leg and laughed, and then passed the glass. "Etta's the best damn deputy in the Commonwealth of Kentucky, runs our office like clockwork. I love her to death, but truth be told, she's not the greatest cook. Too much of a tomboy when she was little to spend time in the kitchen. Wouldn't dare mention it, of course, because she surely does try. I admit, I'm half thankful for this diet of mine, and that Bo will eat damn near anything on his plate that don't move."

"The meal smelled delicious."

Coony chuckled. "Cottage ham and sauerkraut? Woof! But her pork chops? Now, that's heaven's food, believe me." He sighed. "Alas, it's off-limits now."

The sheriff lit his pipe. "Some surprise to learn your cousin was an archaeologist," he said, sucking flame into the bowl, "him being a resident in the county for over a month, me not knowing nothing about it. See," he waved the pipe around the room, "archaeology's a bit of a hobby. I never stayed in school. My daddy gave me the collecting bug. Kentucky has a rich history. Settlers crossing the mountains, Indians. Plenty of stories." He blew a cloud of cherry-scented smoke and pointed to the bookcases. "I read near every one of those."

He stood, motioned Digger to a display-case coffee table,

lifted the glass top, and pointed to a shallow woven basket of flint arrowheads four to five inches long. "My pride and joy: turkey tail projectile points. This was a cache, a rare find. My daddy found all forty of them, digging a privy." He lifted one, passed it to Digger. "See the back? Notched like a wild turkey tail. Ceremonial, never used. Not burial pieces, neither. Makes you wonder who put so much care into knapping them, then hid them in the ground. What was they wishing for, huh?"

Digger held one under a lamp, acknowledged its beauty.

"Our boy knapped every one of these from a single Indiana hornstone nodule. Early Woodland culture, 500 to 1000 B.C. They used spear-throwers, atlatls, then. Bows and arrows hadn't been invented yet. Closer to the present—see those points in the frames?—they got sloppy, less concerned with perfection. Strictly utilitarian."

Digger pointed to two pale, remarkably thin and delicate flints with finely chipped edges and flutes running up the flat sides, looking more like petrified tropical fish than weapons. "Those are beauties. Paleo period. Eastern U.S.?"

"Might have speared a mastodon—imagine! Works of art, maybe a tribute to the spirit of the animal. One's from Kentucky, the other, Tennessee. Authentic, over ten thousand years old. I know the farmers who found them."

"You see many fakes?"

"Lord, yes. A good point like one of those is worth twelve hundred dollars. The Turkey Tail cache? Twenty thousand, easy. There's plenty of collectors and plenty of counterfeiters to supply them. I know 'em both. Yessir. Relics is big business."

He blew smoke, sipped bourbon. "I'm small potatoes, but most of what I've got is good. There's big collectors that could buy and sell me in an afternoon."

He aimed the stem of the pipe at the mantel. "That pale orange pot with the black overpainting is Hopi from the thirties, a wedding gift from the judge. The other two was handed down to me by my daddy. The plain gray one with the frog handles is Fort Ancient culture from northwest of here, maybe five hundred years old. It was pretty busted up before he restored it. The round one, the human head effigy with the slitty eyes, was supposed to be from Paducah, dating to the 1400s, but it's a fake. Somebody fooled the old man."

The sheriff talked, pointed, puffed, sipped, so into his collection that he drained a second, forbidden, bourbon. The alcohol made him more talkative.

With two bourbons under his belt on a nearly empty stomach, Digger loosened, his head buzzing, but still wondering where the conversation was leading.

Apparently nowhere. Forty minutes later Coony glanced at his watch. "Well hell, don't time fly? We best be getting back downstairs or Etta will scalp me."

At thought of Nikki in the kitchen, Digger paused at the head of the stairs. "Uh . . . Sheriff? Could be your boy Bo is taking a shine to my niece. You might want to warn him she's coming off a bad relationship. I doubt Nikki is interested."

Coony snorted. "Bo gets shot down, it's his problem. He hasn't been pestering her, taking advantage of his uniform, has he?"

"No, nothing like that."

"Wouldn't think so—for all his looks, especially out of uniform, the boy's shy around the ladies. I wouldn't worry, Bo's a good kid."

Digger nodded. "He told us he had no family, thinks of you as kin."

"Yep, Bo Deaver is family. Although what he said is a tad of a stretch." He leaned against the stair rail. "Bo's mama and daddy are dead, but he has an older brother and a half sister. Both bad news and far from here, I'm glad to say. The sister's daddy was a preacher, the spouting hell fire kind. Got caught in the wrong man's bed and was shotgunned to death, leaving Bo's mother and a little girl, Bo's half sister, behind. Wife remarried. This one, Bo's daddy, was a drunk, mean son of a bitch. Beat on the mama. She got into religion heavy toward the end, shouting Bible verses to passing cars at the intersection by the Chez. Took to snake handling, the religious kind—you know, to prove her faith. Thanks to the second husband, she got into booze, too, but a church rattlesnake took her away before the bottle. Bo's brother was at her side when she took the bite—gruesome scene—but there wasn't nothing he or no one else could do.

"Bo was the youngest. The mother named him Bo Regard, pretty much protected him from the old man. His brother, though, got into trouble early, was expelled from school for torturing young ones. In and out of detention. Drugs. I suspect he did in the old man."

"His own father?"

Coony sat on the top step, patted the carpet runner at his side.

Digger joined him.

"In a way," Coony said, "the mother set him up for it. Named the boy Judas Bob, might of been hoping he'd turn on the father. And sure enough, he did. We found the old man on the highway, run over. Hit and run. And run and hit—the car that did it struck him, backed over him, and took another pass to be sure. We suspected Judas Bob, but never had proof.

"His half sister, Rita Rae? She was some package. Took the new family name. Deaver. A hot number, that one. Got expelled for soliciting at her junior high prom. Must have falsified her records, because she got into a junior college on a scholarship. That girl was clever, a natural hustler. Came back to a job at the Winky Worm plant—until they caught her embezzling. Wound up in Pee Wee Valley."

"A whorehouse?"

"Kentucky Reformatory for Women. Got sent there for the Winky Worm till-dipping. Later, she got into trouble counterfeiting casino chips in Las Vegas. Rita Rae's been back to Golden Leaf once or twice over the years. Last I heard, she was running scams down south.

"Bo was the straight one. Went into law enforcement to make up for the others, does his best to avoid mention of them. McAfee County is happy enough to oblige him. Bo is the only Deaver we acknowledge."

"And the brother?"

"Judas Bob? About twelve years ago he tried to rob a new car wash here in the county. Drugged up, thought it was a drive-through bank. Held the clown hostage."

"Clown?"

"You know, the kind that motions cars in from the highway? Bo and I responded. Judas Bob holed up in one of the bays—shot the clown in the foot to show he meant business. Clown had on those big shoes, so he didn't really get hurt, but it scared the bejeezus out of him. He wiggled loose and ran, leaving Judas Bob with a handful of clown suit. Bo and Judas Bob faced off, guns drawn. I worked my way around back while Bo tried to talk him out. Bo set his own gun on the patrol car hood, raised his hands to calm Judas Bob, but the worthless bastard shot Bo in the leg. His own brother. I guess you noticed Bo's limp?"

Digger nodded.

"Bo was able to get his own gun, but still couldn't bring himself to shoot Judas Bob. Shot off the wash control box next to him instead. The bubble hose went crazy, filling the bay with suds thick as shaving cream. Judas Bob slipped and fell on his ass. By then I'd snuck in the back and thumped the bastard over the head.

"Judas Bob did time. A short stretch, he's seen longer since, but ever after, he's held Bo and me responsible for his miserable life, calls with a threat now and then. I try to follow his and the sister's paths without mention to Bo, and we both keep our eyes open against the day Judas Bob comes back. Last I heard, he'd changed his name and was living with Rita Rae in Florida."

Digger fumbled for a response, simply said, "Whoa." Some surprise, although he had been the one to bring up Bo, not the sheriff. Apparently the surprise had been the artifact collection. Digger took a deep breath of relief and followed his host down to the parlor.

During the after-dinner socializing, Digger did his best to avoid staring at Bo. Sitting across from Nikki, he also avoided the *wait till later* fire in her eyes. After good-byes, he scooted out the door ahead of her.

Nikki wouldn't unlock the car. "So, dear uncle, you retire with old Coony from the boonies and hit the booze—I can smell it—and leave me in the kitchen with the dishes and clodhopper Bo panting over my shoulder the whole time."

Digger raised a palm in defense. "Hold your fire, kiddo. Wait till you hear this. . . ."

14

At lunch the next day, Nikki announced an impromptu field trip: Cumberland Falls to see the moonbow, "one of the earth's wonders, like the pyramids of Giza, the Colossus of Rhodes, the Tower of Babel, or Las Vegas."

"Did that last one," Digger said. "And it did me, in fact. But a moonbow? You only live once."

They returned the old Dodge to the E-Z Zees manager. Nikki found Edgar's VW bug surprisingly snappy. Five miles out of Golden Leaf, she glanced at the rearview mirror. "Oh, no. A cop just pulled out. Look, I'm not speeding. Barely fifty." She tapped the brakes anyway, slowed to forty-five. "He's following me."

"They told me not to leave town," Digger said. "They must have been watching us. So much for the friendly dinner."

"Maybe it's a taillight out."

The cruiser tailgated. A half mile later, it flashed its lights.

They spoke at the same time: "Act like nothing's wrong," from Digger, "I don't believe this!" from Nikki. She pulled over, grumbling. Anticipating the license and registration routine, Nikki fished for her wallet while Digger fumbled in the glove box for the registration. He found it behind the frayed and yellowing operator's manual, handed it to Nikki, and shielded his face. Through spread fingers, he watched the khaki torso of a county cop walk to the side of the car. "License and registration, ma'am," said the torso, following the script.

Digger made himself small to Nikki's right. She passed the documents. "What's the problem, officer?"

"Speeding, ma'am. Fifty-seven in a thirty-five zone. We take speeding serious in McAfee County. Could be kids on the road."

"Well, what do you know?" Digger muttered. "Speeding. Wasn't me at all."

"What? Kids? In the middle of nowhere? Get real."

Digger patted her wrist to go easy.

"Maybe," said the cop, "you didn't see the sign when you entered McAfee County: 'Thirty-five unless otherwise posted.' We watch out for the little ones."

"Right. Little ones." Nikki drummed her fingers on the wheel.

Digger lowered his head to offer a mollifying smile and recognized the family-minded lecturer as Ike, the gaunt deputy with the wandering eye who had mouthed off at the murder scene.

The deputy pushed his hat higher on his forehead with a ballpoint pen, gave Nikki a stock smile, and flipped pages in his citation book. "See you're from Michigan. Fine for speeding is five dollars per mile over the limit, unless you want to post bond and hang around for trial. That might be a while. Then the judge adds court costs, seventy-five bucks. Being you're from out of state, best you follow me back. Take care of it now—cash or credit card—and you can be on your way. Hmmm. Registration's in another first name." He leaned down to check out the passenger. "Don't I know you?"

"My cousin Edgar was the man murdered."

"Sure. You're the one with the short pants. Fitz." He tapped the license in recognition, looked with greater interest at Nikki. "You, then, would be the niece?"

"That's right." Staring straight ahead, biting her lip. "The niece."

"Every bit as pretty and spunky as Bo said. Well, now," he returned the documents. "Sorry to trouble you, darlin'. Keep your foot easy on the pedal, especially at the bottom of that hill, because one of us usually hangs out behind those trees by the bridge." He touched his hat, rapped the car roof, and stepped back.

"I'd hate not to be recognized," she said, face glowing red, knuckles white on the wheel.

Digger added a "Thank you, officer."

As she pulled onto the pavement, she snarled, "What do you think of that?"

"Don't blame the man, kiddo: rattlesnakes rattle, cops hassle. Look on the bright side, it had nothing to do with me, and Bo saved us over a hundred bucks."

" 'Bo's little friend? Spunky?' What else do you think Bo said? Clodhopper! Thirty-five-mile-an-hour speed limit on a highway in the middle of East Jesus, not even a cow in sight."

As soon as she cleared the next hill, Nikki hunched over the wheel, took the bug to a whining seventy, and held it there to the county line. Conversation ran thin.

"D-O-R!" Nikki braked to a hard stop.

Digger lurched awake. "Sheesh! What is it?!"

She stared out her window at the pavement, shrugged her shoulders, and crept on at thirty mph.

"D-O-R? What's that?"

"You already know A-O-R. Remember Coony II? You're the professor."

"Great: Dead on Road. Dragged out of a fine nap to brake for slinky corpses."

"D-O-Rs give us morphological and distributional data. That was an eastern rat snake. Common. I've already passed an eastern racer and half a dozen squashed toads."

Digger rubbed his eyes, looked around. "Where are we? Where's the highway?"

"Back road. We're ahead of schedule. Moonbow doesn't show till dark."

Twenty minutes passed, three stops, and then another shout: "Hold on!" She hit the brake, shifted to reverse, backed along the center line, stopped, opened her door, and leaned out, head nearly to the asphalt.

"Throwing up from all the starting and stopping?"

She ignored him, set the brake, dropped to the pavement, reached under the car, and stood, holding a slender, brilliant but lifeless, foot-and-a-half snake by the tail, its middle mashed flat. She handed it to Digger through the open door. "Check this out."

He sat on his hands. "Rings of red, black and yellow. Squashed." The pattern registered. "Watch out! I've seen those in Central America. That's a coral snake. Deadly. May have enough life left to bite."

"No, he's kaput. Not to worry: red to yellow, kill a fellow."

"Say again?"

"Red to black, venom lack—the rhyme, how you tell coral snakes from harmless ones in the U.S., which bands touch which. And, no black head, see? No coral snakes this far north, anyway. This is a scarlet king snake, *Lampropeltis triangulum elapsoides*. Only three ever reported in Kentucky. We have one heck of a find." She climbed behind the wheel, tossed the snake onto Digger's lap, and drove to the shoulder.

"Yeowk!" Digger flipped the limp carcass onto the floor with a pencil.

"Write this down: two, three, five point two. Last digits of the odometer. As you guys in archaeology say, provenance is everything. When we get to an intersection, we'll take the mileage again." She leaned over the seat, rooted in her pack, and passed a quart mason jar of clear liquid to Digger. "Formalin: formaldehyde pickling juice. Here—Edgar had an atlas under the seat."

She embalmed the snake through its flat belly scales with a syringe and lifted it by the tail, twirled the limp body with the finesse of a pretzel maker into the jar, neatly coiled. "Man, this is a sure article in a scientific pub. How about you drive while I figure out where we are?"

Digger took the wheel while Nikki thumbed through the atlas.

"Intersection ahead," he said. "U.S. 27. Flat Rock and Whitley City to the south."

Nikki confirmed it on the map. "We're on route 1045. Yeah, runs south of Parker's Lake to Honeybee, then the park road." She lifted the jar, held it to the light like a glass of Château Lafite. "Boy, oh, boy—a scarlet king snake!"

"Unc?" She was studying the atlas.

"Kiddo?"

"Uncle Edgar made notes here. Like code. Colored circles, initials, and numbers." She paged. "Marks in New York, Pennsylvania, West Virginia, Kentucky, and Ohio. Cincinnati's circled, so is Golden Leaf. There's a dollar sign, a star, and a blue seven and a red number one by Golden Leaf. And letters. *S. M.*"

"A dollar sign," Digger repeated. "And a *star* at Golden Leaf? *S. M.?*"

They looked at one another, said the words in sync: "Sheriff McCoy."

"Could be somebody else," she said.

"Yeah, but how many wear a gold star?" He drove in silence, thinking. "Nikki? When Coony took me to his study, it wasn't only to drink. I knew he had an agenda, I just couldn't figure it out. I kept waiting for his surprise—not the Bo news. I brought that up. Apparently the surprise was his artifact collection. He made a point of telling me how valuable some of his pieces are, thousands of dollars, how counterfeiting is big business, how people who don't know what they're buying can be stung. I wonder if he was testing me."

"How so?"

"Let me work this through." The car slowed as his mind worked. "Okay. Coony said he didn't know Edgar. But what if he did, and they were doing some kind of deal? I don't like it, but it could account for those cash deposits and the dollar sign on your map. Edgar would never get involved with drugs, but what if he was tantalized by easy money misrepresenting phony antiquities? A useful rationalization if he thought real artifacts would be spared by selling phony ones to collectors. Edgar was a big believer in museum conservation."

"Speedometer."

"Huh?"

"You're going fifteen miles an hour."

"Oh." He took it to forty. "Where was I? Yeah, Coony told me he knew counterfeiters. He and Edgar would be a convincing pair. A sheriff, law and order man, tells a collector he knows a farmer with this fancy prehistoric object, see? He introduces them, vouches for the farmer. The scam is, the farmer's supposed to have discovered a major Indian burial site, not something he wants the world to know about, so he's selling objects on the sly. The sheriff mentions there's a famous archaeologist nearby. Why not let him have a look at it? Edgar studies the counterfeit, says 'It looks good.' Doesn't exactly lie, but ices the cake. Maybe Edgar urges they donate it a museum—that would clinch it. The object is sold, Coony pays the farmer a fee and kicks back a big chunk to Edgar, calls it a *grant* to soothe Edgar's conscience."

"Uncle Edgar, a con man?"

"I don't like it, but what about those cash deposits? And the McCoy's house—McAfee may be a poor county, but he's no pauper."

"Wife's money."

"Maybe. But a scenario like that would explain Edgar's moving here. He needed money. He didn't elaborate, but the night before he was killed, Edgar said he thought we might pick up some easy money if I hung around. *Consulting*—that was his word. Maybe he met Coony at an artifact show or even a scientific meeting. Maybe Coony lured Edgar to Golden Leaf, made his con sound like a minor transgression hurting no one but private collectors."

He slapped the wheel. "As sly as our sheriff is, I bet he was feeling me out to see what Edgar told me. It adds up."

Digger thought about it for a minute and raised a more ominous question. "What if he murdered Edgar? He seemed awfully eager to lay blame on anonymous bikers. Maybe Edgar had second thoughts, planned to tell a buyer he had been ripped off. Maybe the hook through Edgar's lips was indeed a message: Here's what happens to people who mess with the man in McAfee County."

"More likely," Nikki said, "the bikers were real, killed Edgar, and left the sheriff without an authority. Edgar didn't say anything about being afraid, did he?"

"No."

"Maybe Coony's been feeling you out to become his new partner. Maybe he has a big deal cooking, needs a Ph.D. to give it a seal of approval."

"Hypotheses." He sighed. "But damned unsettling ones."

"The real question is: What now?"

"I knew there was something odd from the start, how surprised Coony was when he heard I was a Ph.D. and not a medical doctor, then how he got me talking about archaeology over dinner, how eager he was to show me his collection."

"Plan of action?" Nikki said. "See what we can make of this atlas, then confront him."

"Risky, kiddo. He's a law unto himself in his county."

"Contact the Kentucky State Police."

"I thought of that the day of the murder, but they would have bought the bikers and drugs story. And cops are reluctant to tread on one another's turf."

"FBI?"

"Same-same, and there'd have to be federal laws broken."

"How's this? I'll put everything we suspect along with a copy of Edgar's atlas notes in an envelope and mail it to myself at mother's. She made me swear to call because she thinks I'm in questionable company, and she's probably throwing a hissy if she heard about Edgar. If she doesn't hear from me, she'll open the letter, and, believe me, between mother and Biffer, they'd have half the police in the Midwest as well as the FBI and the Pinkertons looking for us. When we get back, we'll draw Coony out. Not accuse him, but play dumb, hint around, see how he responds."

"Not bad. You put it together tonight, use the lodge's copy machine. We'll mail it tomorrow morning, and when we get back, we'll confront the fox in his den—turn the tables on Sheriff Coony McCoy."

Digger placed a nervous call to the McAfee Sheriff's department from Cumberland Falls. Coony would be unavailable most of tomorrow, Etta told him, but she would have him meet Nikki and Digger after supper if it was important.

"How about before?" Digger asked, worried about an after-dark meeting and wanting plenty of witnesses, "at Chez Pancakes?"

"We eat at six," Etta said. "I'll have him there at five, how's that?"

Digger said "Perfect."

"What's the scoop?" she asked.

"Oh, nothing," he said, fumbling. "I mean, we, uh, want to talk over some things with him."

"Things," she said. A pregnant silence followed. Etta spoke first, said they had confirmed that Edgar had died around two A.M., "and the house was definitely used to brew methamphetamine. Does look like drugs were behind the murder."

Digger relayed the conversation to Nikki. "The long and short of it is, the official conclusion is going to be 'drug-related homicide.' Case closed."

That night, they walked to the river and saw the ghostly moonbow floating in the mist over the falls.

"Eerily beautiful," said Digger. "But a rainbow at night? Disturbing."

A blanket of clouds rolled over the face of the man in the moon, and the moonbow winked out. Digger squeezed Nikki's hand. "That's an omen, kiddo. We'd damn well better watch our backs, jousting with the law in the hills of east Kentucky."

15

Anticipating the payoff, finally impressing the stand-offish Jesus Bob, Big Butt snickered, remembering how he'd nearly wet himself laughing before the mirror in Barracks #5. The one thing that seemed to get through to the bad-ass corporal was Ben's alien stories, and this would do the trick. He set a case of beer in the weeds, wedged the ends of half a dozen Winky Worms between his upper lip and front teeth, and moved forward stealthily, so as not to prematurely awaken his recumbent victim, snoring in the shade of a pine.

Carried away by the grand humor, Big Butt leaned over the twitching man's face, Winky Worms dangling from his mouth, jiggling past his chin like multicolored tentacles. He screwed black checkers into his eye sockets, lolled his head side to side, grimaced, and jabbed Jesus Bob in the ribs with a ferocious "Grrroower!"

Surrounded by gray aliens, strapped as he was to a wonder metal free-form gurney, Jesus Bob struggled. Nearly blinded by the sun-bright surgical lights, he counted six of the bastards, looking remarkably like the ones in General Ben's abduction stories, buggy black grasshopper eyes and all, crouching with horrific barbed probes in their hands. He writhed under the restraining straps, felt foul hot alien breath on his face. He heard the alien captain growl, saw the thrust of a silvery probe as the monster split his side, going for his liver.

Blinking awake from the sharp pain, he saw the tentacles, the sadistic grimace, the lifeless black eyes ten inches from his face, and screamed. *"Yeeoow!"* Mousetrap fast, he jackknifed from the waist. Forehead met nose with an audible crack, and Big Butt keeled backward into the weeds.

Jesus Bob staggered to his feet, screamed again, until the familiar forest, the absence of aliens, registered. Had they gotten his liver? Dumped him back on earth, like General Ben said? He felt his side. Intact. Ben was right about that, too: sealed up with nary a sign. He wondered how a man would get by with no liver in him.

Then he saw the soles of Big Butt's combat boots, and the moaning man beyond. He stood, shakily, and looked closer. Blood pulsed freely from Big Butt's nose, coating the remaining Winky Worms, his chin and throat a sickening scarlet.

"Goddamn!" said Jesus Bob. "They got him, too. Must have sucked the poor bastard's brains out his nose."

He threw up in the weeds, as much from the pharmacological cocktail polluting his innards as from the shock of the abduction. He swiped a sleeve across his mouth and kicked Big Butt in the shoulder, wondering if a man with no brains could speak.

"Easy, pardner. They got us both, but we're back. Can you talk?"

Big Butt groaned, "Ohhhaaa," and sat upright. Both hands rose to his face and felt for damage, dislodging the bloody Winky Worms (slivers of brains to Jesus Bob's anxious eyes). Checkers long gone, eyes open, dizzy, Big Butt stared at his crimson hands, his soaked fatigue shirt. "Lordy. What happened?"

Comforted that Big Butt could speak (maybe they hadn't gotten all his brains), Jesus Bob explained.

As consciousness and recollection returned, Big Butt concluded the abduction story made better sense than revealing his own little joke to the volatile Jesus Bob. When his nosebleed slowed to a gelatinous trickle, he recovered the beers, and the two men set to drinking.

"We're survivors, man," said Jesus Bob, into his eighth can.

"Right on," said Big Butt, swilling the last of his ninth.

They were cresting the bragging phase of their drunk, coasting into the confessional waters where friendships are forged.

Big Butt flipped an empty into the woods. "You know how I told you about that clinic I blew up in Georgia?"

"Sure do."

"Weren't exactly so."

Jesus Bob was past accusation or resentment. Bonded in abduction and drink, the two had become blood brothers. "What went wrong? Bad explosives? Timer?"

"What went wrong was the address. I blew up the wrong building. Wrong side of the street. A VFW hall."

"Tough."

"Yeah. Was in the middle of the day, see? I would've taught them filthy bitches a lesson, you know, but, hell, it wasn't like I told you. At eleven in the A.M. there was no one at all in the VFW. I didn't kill nobody. Not a one."

Jesus Bob punched him lightly on the shoulder. "Hey, shit happens. VFW, that's kinda like feds, ain't it? You blew up a building, so you did the bomb right. And you didn't get caught, neither. Hell, that's batting five hundred at least."

"I guess." Big Butt looked Jesus Bob square in the face, eager to confess all. "Full truth is, those other stories, the ones I tell little guys? The sniping? That firing squad? Hell, I never killed nobody. Not then, not ever. Not like you."

Jesus Bob nodded, committed to a confession of his own.

"Listen, that lawman I told you I crippled after I shot the clown in the foot?"

"Yeah?"

"And the Yo-boy two cells down I said I choked with the cord from his boom box for keeping me awake, made it look like he offed himself? That gas station raghead I told you I cut his little finger off for short-changing me? That bastard kid who whipped a stone at my truck in West Virginia, the one I said I dangled over the high bridge by his ankle? And that skinny biker in Texas, the one whose arm I said I broke before I borrowed his Harley?"

"Yeah?"

"I done them, and there's been others, too." Jesus Bob sucked beer. "But the full truth is, I never flayed the skin off that Jethro with my bowie knife and made a vest out of it like I told the bunch at breakfast the other day. I just stuck him and left him squealing behind the bar. God's honest truth, pardner. That was all."

Jesus Bob looked Big Butt in the eyes, postconfessionally. "I done the ones I done 'cause they needed doing. But, here's what I really want to say: What you and your buddies here has got, and I don't, is *ideals*. Keeping track of who all's after us. Shee-it, I never did nobody or nothing for noble cause, and that's a fact."

Big Butt sucked at his tenth can, tears welling from the bared emotion. "Before I leave this earth, I want to kill a man. I want to feel what it's like. What kind of pussy soldier am I, what kind of a leader for those boys, if I never do nobody?"

"Tell you what, pardner." Jesus Bob punched Big Butt in the shoulder again, a short affectionate jab. "You stick close to me, and you'll get your kill in. Not some pussy fee-male neither. A real man. A lawman, huh? Make that a whole department of em." He took a long last pull on the can and crushed it. "And that's a promise."

Big Butt knuckled away the tears flowing freely, shame-lessly. He sniffled, extended a hand. "Friends?"

They shook.

"Damned straight, pardner. Friends to the end."

16

Nikki and Digger were at the Chez by 4:15 P.M., shifting uneasily in their chairs, picking at pancake dinners, the incriminating atlas lying closed on the table. Nikki had mailed her just-in-case, call-out-the-Marines letter before they left the Falls.

"You do the talking, Unc, show Coony the atlas. I'll watch his face."

"You bet. Turn the tables on him."

"There he is," she said at ten to five, looking past Digger's shoulder to the door. "Act natural, but take control. Don't let him smooth-talk his way out of this."

"Don't worry about me." Digger turned to see, dragged an elbow across his syrupy plate. He was still peeling shreds of paper napkin from his elbow when the sheriff reached his side.

Coony squeezed his shoulder. "Nice shirt. Don't worry, a little lemon and water'll take it right out. Bought it at Sandlers?"

"How'd you know we went to Sanders?" Digger said it a little too fast.

"There's not much goes on in McAfee County I don't

know about—plus, it's the only tack shop in three counties."
Coony made cup-lifting motions to the waitress. When coffee
arrived, he took a slow sip, eyes closed, muttering, "Didn't
really finish number three, so this makes two and a half." He
set the cup down, all smiles, relaxed. "How was the Falls?
Still a falling?"

"Very impressive." Digger's voice was half an octave too
high. As a diversion, he reached for the fork on his plate to
busy himself with pancakes and hit the tines with the base
of his palm. The fork flipped six feet onto the carpet, spraying
drops of syrup across the tablecloth, Digger's shirt and face.

"We saw the moonbow," Nikki said, scowling at Digger's
loss of cool. "Romantic, wasn't it, Unc?"

Uncertain whether to retrieve the fork, but fast resigning
to losing another round with the law, Digger merely nodded.

"Darlin'," Coony said, "If you told Bo you spent a romantic night under the stars watching the moonbow without
him, he'd pine for a week."

"Wha—?" She aimed her own fork at Coony and shook
it. "Hey, I've done nothing to encourage your deputy."

Digger dabbed at syrup, thinking, The little bastard isn't
worried at all. He's toying with us.

"That just makes 'em more eager, don't it, Digger?"
Coony raised his chin to the ceiling tiles and coyote-howled,
"Owooooo!"

Enough was enough for Nikki. She forked Digger in the
shoulder. "Ask him. Go ahead. Do it."

Coony waved the air. "Just having a little fun. Etta filled
you in on the investigation, so I figure you got me here to
press me about your one-armed man, right?" He raised his
eyebrows rhetorically. "Sorry to disappoint, but I fear the
sole one-armed man I know of hereabouts is Witticus Pink-
ley, and Witticus has got only one foot as well, and that one's
nearly in the grave, because Witticus is ninety-seven and has
near drunk hisself to death. I'm sorry to say, your fella is still
at large."

"Um. Yeah . . . but that's not it. Unc?" No response. "Unc!"

"Coony—" Digger cleared his throat. "We found some, uh, evidence." He began fiddling with a packet of saltines. "Notes. Sort of." He tried to open the cellophane, ripped at it, got nowhere. Suddenly it vaporized in a blur of crumbs, spraying all three of them with white confetti.

Nikki sputtered. "That's *right*," she said, but not loud enough to undo the saltine trick. "We have *evidence*."

"Do tell?" Coony brushed crumbs from his shirt, crossed his hands on the table.

"We found Edgar's atlas," Digger said. "Right here." He tapped the eleven-by-fourteen book. "With notes. Circles, initials, numbers." He opened it to Kentucky.

Coony bent over it, eyes active.

Nikki snapped her fingers for Digger to hit Coony with the incriminating *S. M.*, star and dollar sign.

Digger gave her an acknowledging nod. "Look here at Golden Leaf." He tapped the map. "A circle with a *star*, a *money sign*, and the letters *S. M.*"

Coony scowled, ran his hand across the map, and leaned back in his chair to stare at the ceiling tile. He massaged his chin, said nothing for thirty seconds.

Nikki raised an eyebrow at Digger, mouthed a silent *Got him*.

Without warning, the sheriff rocked forward and slapped the table. Cups rattled. Nikki and Digger jumped. Heads turned. "That old bastard! I should have known."

Digger shied away, concluding, too late, they had miscalculated. Nikki's insurance letter meant zip. All he has to do, he realized, is arrest us—whoosh—and we're disappeared. Nikki's people will raise a stink, but too late.

Nikki pressed on. "You thought there was no record of what you two were up to, huh, Sheriff? Thought you destroyed all his notes?"

"Huh? Sorry, I didn't catch that. I was thinking this through."

"I said—"

Digger gripped her arm to slow her down, but then thought, What the hell, we've dealt the cards, we may as well play our hand. He swallowed and dived in. "It's not hard to fathom. The initials speak for themselves. The star and the dollar sign are obvious." There. But he felt his momentary courage dissipate like the steam over Coony's cooling coffee.

Coony finally spoke. "The dollar sign," he said, "signifies the money."

"Aha!" said Nikki.

"The star at Golden Leaf, probably marks your Edgar's home."

"Home?" Digger said. "Hmmm. Could be, I guess."

"What?" Nikki glared at both of them.

Coony nodded, took an appraising look at Nikki, then at Digger. "You found out about Smoot by yourselves? I *am* impressed."

"Smoot?" They said it together.

"Smoot Mudd, the old goat," Coony said. "I fault myself for not thinking of him sooner. Etta said she looked into whether your cousin had been consulting hereabouts. I thought along those lines, too, but let it go. Two thousand bucks a week cash from some teachers college, county historical society, or highway project? But Smoot? Hot damn!"

Coony scanned the restaurant to see who may have heard. "Mostly pass-throughs," he muttered. "But I oughta watch my temper and my mouth." He scrutinized nearby faces. "Never know who knows who. Listen, I'll take the atlas, finish my coffee on the front porch, and think. You two eat up, we'll talk outside."

As soon as he was out the door, Nikki said, "You think he made up that name?"

"He's quick on his feet. He may want us outside so he can arrest us away from people. Could be destroying the atlas or calling his deputies as we speak."

"You worry too much."

"And you're naive, kiddo."

"If he tries anything funny, we'll tell him about our letter."

"We could be dead meat by the time your mother gets that letter."

"He wouldn't dare. I'm gonna peek through that window."

"I'm coming with you."

While Digger paid, Nikki parted the gingham curtains and peered out. "Sitting on a bench, studying the atlas. That's all."

Digger shrugged. "All right. Let's go. But if he wants us to get in his car, run back inside, fast."

Coony saw them at the window and patted the bench.

Nikki sat at one end, Digger at the far edge of the other.

"I can tell you're eager," Coony said. "So, here it is: Smoot Mudd, old as stone, one of the biggest artifact collectors in Kentucky. Lives here in Golden Leaf. Since I didn't know your Edgar was an archaeologist, I didn't expect Smoot would know either. Hell, he must of been the one brought him here. To inventory or appraise his collection. Smoot's too afraid of thieves to let anyone in Kentucky mess with it. He probably figured he could trust your Edgar, being from Michigan and a professor."

"And this Smoot could have paid Edgar that much money?"

"Smoot's tighter than bark on a beech tree, but he's loaded. Coal money from way back. Smoot and his daddy bled their fortune from the hills of Kentucky and the backs of its sons. Smoot still holds the controlling interest in Wesvaky Coal."

"And you think he murdered Edgar?" Nikki asked.

"Darlin', I'd love to pin that on old Smoot. I confess, I don't like the sumbitch. My own daddy died from the black lung, daddy's brother in a cave-in." He rubbed his eyes, stared at the sky. "But hell, that's water over the dam, so Etta keeps telling me. Coal's changed, it's mostly strip, still dirty, fewer jobs, not so deadly. The business is way down now with cheaper, cleaner coal out West.

"Shrewd Smoot, though, saw that coming, got into tobacco as a hedge. Golden Leaf Tobacco Company? Smoot's. Sold it to Globalsmoke a few years back. Still a director on the national board, and he pulls some mighty big strings in the industry. He owns a good portion of the county, too, so I've got to watch my tongue."

He took a tiny sip of coffee and set the cup on the bench between his knees. "What I'd like to know is, if your uncle was working for Smoot, why didn't the old coot come forward when he learned your Edgar was murdered?"

"It occurred to us," Digger said, with a side-glance to Nikki, "that Edgar might have been asked to fudge on the authenticity or value of artifacts."

Nikki gave him a congratulatory grin. "Edgar," she said, "could have been working with this Smoot—or someone else."

Coony chewed his lip. "Maybe Smoot's got a theft planned. He has a larcenous enough heart. Maybe your Edgar got cold feet, was going to spill the beans to the insurance people."

"Go on."

"Smoot's a big supporter of one of Kentucky's militias."

Digger looked confused. "Militias?"

Nikki frowned. "One of?"

"The Daniel Boone Rangers. Smoot owns four hundred acres abutting the national forest, calls it the Reserve. Used to be an old church camp up there. Today, it's the Rangers' HQ."

Digger arched his eyebrows. "They're armed?"

"To the teeth, including a mother lode of explosives and ammo last time I heard. Word is, Smoot bought them a Humvee a month back."

Nikki went wide-eyed. "And this doesn't upset you?"

"The Humvee?" Coony chuckled. "They're paying for the

gas, not me. The Rangers boys figure they're flexing their constitutional rights. Hell, I don't know. The fact is, I'm in no position to stop them. There's maybe twenty of 'em, no more, but my boys would be outmanned and outgunned for damn sure. Worse, I'd never be reelected if I tried." He grinned. "And, I can tell you this with authority: Since the Daniel Boone Rangers has been running through the woods and fields of McAfee County, there's yet to be an invasion of A-rabs in sheets, Russian Mafia peddling vodka in bourbon bottles, the blue-helmeted UN releasing doves, or the EPA bearing trees and spring water."

Digger gave him a hard look. "You're truly not worried?"

Coony set his cup under the bench, removed his hat, and ran his fingers around the brim slowly. "Because they like to dress up, run through the woods, and shoot?" After a long pause, he said, "Yeah, I have my concerns." He fell silent, pursed his lips. "Damned if I don't. I worry about someone poking a stick in that hive. Especially after our falling out."

"Uh-oh."

Coony played with his beaded hatband. "Look, this don't go no further?"

Nikki and Digger shook their heads, edged closer.

"Once," Coony said, voice low, "was a time we talked. Then I went to this conference in Washington, D.C., on a federal grant the county got—rural law enforcement officers from across the country. An honor. Well, the Rangers got it in their minds I'd gone federal, and stopped talking to me. *Shun*, I believe the word is.

"Then it got worse."

Nikki drew her knees to her chin, hugged her shins. "Worse?"

"I got me this ticker problem." Coony tapped his chest. "Ventricular arrhythmia. Coupla bouts. Doctor here sent me to Louisville. Etta and me kept it to family and the deputies, said I'd gone fishing. No one wants a sick sheriff, see?" He looked both ways, unbuttoned the top three buttons of his shirt and pulled it open. "They put this thingy inside me."

He rubbed a three-inch scar over a slight rise in the skin on his chest. "They say the next time my heart goes tippety-tap, I get zapped, my hair stands on end—but the ticker gets set straight."

"Eeuuw."

Digger pressed a reassuring hand to his own chest. "Really sorry to hear about the heart problem, but I'm not sure I see the connection."

"Neither did I, and they wasn't talking to me by then. But my deputy, Ike, gets a haircut, finds out roundabout from old Ben, the head Ranger honcho. Ben's the town barber, been boring the men of Golden Leaf with his ten-dollar words and crazy ideas for four decades. Few years ago, Ben gets his big break. Ben has cut Smoot's hair forever, and is near about the only man Smoot trusts, so Smoot put him in charge of the Rangers. Ben's not just a barber now, see? Ben's a general.

"Ben, by the way, will still cut my hair but he won't talk to me. I have to sit there, read my *Field and Stream* while he barbers, all stiff and mum. And every time, the bastard manages to snip the back of my ear with his shears—damn that hurts!" He twisted his head and pulled his ears forward to show them three scabbed V-shaped cuts. "But I don't yell out like some coward in the chair, and it wouldn't sit well with the folks here if the sheriff went to another county for a haircut.

"Back to my story—Ike finds out that when I was gone so mysterious, Ben decided I was abducted by aliens."

Coony caught the look on their faces. "You know, from outer space." He pointed skyward.

Digger glanced at empty sky and took a hard look at Coony. "You're kidding!"

"Wait a minute," said Nikki. "Aliens?"

Digger hummed: "Doo do *Doo* do. Remember? Rubella, the cashier?"

Coony nodded. "Damned gossip. Her husband, Shep Grundy, is a Ranger."

Nikki said it again, "Aliens?"

"It's a conspiracy thing, darlin'. Aliens and federals and Jews are after them, see? Ben is nutso, suspicious, jumps real fast to the wrong conclusions."

Digger and Nikki exchanged guilty glances.

"I'd gone federal already, if you recall, and now the aliens got me on top of that. Then I went fishing at the lake last August—was fishing a Green Ghoul Stinky Winky on a silver spoon, as I recall. I took my shirt off, and one of the Rangers saw my scar, the bump. He told Ben, who put two and two together and got five: proof I'd been not only abducted, but probed and hot-wired by extraterrestrials.

Shee-it!" He swatted the hat with the back of his hand. "See what lying gets you? Anyways, I got reelected, but as far as the Rangers go, I'm a wired federal alien spy."

"Whoa!"

"Yeah. I don't know if Smoot buys into the alien business, but he had to be behind the secession."

"Succession? Like change of command?"

"*Sess*-session, not suk-session. A while back, the mayor found a declaration of independence nailed to the courthouse doors. The Rangers had seceded from the Commonwealth of Kentucky, from the U. S. of A., declaring themselves the Independent and Sovereign Nation of Boone.

"They holed up at Smoot's Reserve and waited for me to come after them. If not me, the state boys. If not them, the feds. Idea was, there'd be a firefight, martyrs—not Ben if I know him—national media attention, and then this whole part of the country would revolt in sympathy. Problem was, I never came calling. Neither did no one else. They finally got hungry or horny—pardon me, ma'am—and came down off the mountain to their jobs and families. Ben never forgave me. I suspect Smoot saw it as his lost claim to fame. Smoot Mudd, first President of the Republic of Boone, see?

"Smoot sees himself as a patriarch, like in the Bible. Wants to be loved. Given his daddy's past, he yearns for it.

"Some years back, he paid this genealogist woman a bundle. Guess what?" Coony snapped his fingers. "She came through, told Smoot his family went back to the first Virginians crossing the Alleghenies in the French and Indian times, that Daniel Boone was a direct ancestor."

He winked. "Half the people in the state, of course, claim old Daniel as kin. Back in the 1700s when the savages," he winked again, "got bent out of shape at the civilized white folks settling on their hunting grounds, trouble broke out. Sniping, scalping, burning, torture on both sides. Settlers of means built fortified cabins, sometimes actual forts. When raiding was in the wind, women and children, men, dogs and hogs would hightail it inside. Ones that didn't make it—especially women and young boys—was sometimes captured instead of killed. Then the settlers would organize the able-bodied men into a militia—there was no standing army west of the mountains. They'd track the Indians, shoot 'em up if they could, and do their damnedest to recapture any unfortunates who was kidnapped."

Coony sipped more coffee, whispering, "That's three." He looked up. "Where was I? Oh, yeah—Smoot. Smoot visions himself a leader of such a militia, Commander-in-Chief of the Daniel Boone Rangers; modern-day pioneers defending their homesteads against marauding savages."

He picked up the coffee cup and sloshed the dregs. "And there you got Smoot Mudd in a nutshell."

"So, what now?" Nikki asked.

Coony set the cup down and stood, atlas under his arm. "I'll study these maps over supper and get one of my boys to check to be sure Smoot's home. Unless you hear from me, I'll pick you up here at eight-thirty, and we'll pay Commander Smoot Mudd a surprise visit. How's that grab you?"

17

Digger handed Nikki a cardboard cup of hot chocolate and sat beside her on the bench outside Chez Pancakes. The sky glowed magenta. Mercury vapor lights flickered on, staining the asphalt an acid green. Passing cars whooshing into the east and growing darkness turned on headlights. In the fields beyond the highway, fireflies winked and katydids chirped.

Digger was feeling his age, and then some. And, worse, guilty. He looked at Nikki, hunched against the evening chill, thinking: Why didn't I send her home? Why? Because I'm selfish, a lonely old man, and wanted company. And now? Edgar murdered, rattlesnakes, armed militias, running off into the night, alone, with—

Nikki looked up at him. "I miss Uncle Edgar."

Digger felt queasy in the pit of his stomach, tried to speak, and choked. Poor kid.

She gave him a sharp punch on the arm. "But this is so-oo cool! What a trip. A scarlet kingsnake, a lucky milk snake, a timber rattlesnake right by the house, and we're on the track of murderers, working with a real sheriff. Cool!" She punched him again, stood up, and squinted along the high-way, toward town. "Where is that little shrimp? C'mon, c'mon, I want to meet this Smoot.

"By the way," she said over her shoulder. "I called mother while you were in the shower. You'll love this. She and Biffer were in a near-panic over Uncle Edgar. I got the five-minute lecture: Are you dispossessed of your senses, young woman? You come home this instant—yakity, yakity, bikers, drugs, Kentucky, your subversive Uncle Harmon, yakity, yakity—"

"Subversive?"

"Oh, yeah, then: 'What are you doing down there, any-way?' I say, 'Hunting poisonous snakes and other stuff you don't want to know about.' "

"You didn't."

"Sure. I wanted to rile her up, see? If we need the elev-enth hour cavalry, be sure mother and Biffer are primed. There's more. Mother huffs, demands to know what I mean by 'other stuff.' I tell her how handsome you look as a cow-boy—the very image of Willie himself—then casually men-tion that incest is as common as holding hands down here."

Digger groaned.

"Look! Here he comes." She waved from the curb.

The sheriff's blue Bonneville flashed its lights and rolled to a stop. Coony McCoy, chewing gum, dressed in civie jeans and boots, stepped out, bowed theatrically to Nikki, and opened the door. "Digger, you mind riding in back?"

Digger mouthed a *No*, but the moment the door slammed and he saw the wire barrier, smelled the cloying odor of Juicy Fruit, he sucked air, squeezed his eyes shut, and gripped his knees. He nearly gagged, recalling the sick-sweet smells of the deputy's car and the farm where Edgar was murdered: sweat, booze, manure, and fried chicken.

Coony spoke to the mirror. "You hanging in back there?"

Digger stared at the inquiring eyes in the glass and forced himself to breathe. Slowly, the odors of the murder evapo-rated, to rematerialize as mere chewing gum and—what?—

Coony's aftershave? He looked at the mirror again, saw a flat, happy-faced cardboard skunk swinging below it. "Yeah." He grinned. "I'm okay. Fine."

"Smoot lives a piece out of town," Coony was saying. "When we get there, you two play dumb, don't go talking out of turn, regardless of what you see, hear?"

Digger nodded. Nikki chirped a "Whatever you say, Sheriff."

Recalling his sister's threats, as occasionally he did, Jesus Bob resisted the urge to "up." Instead, following a dinner of microwaved burritos and beer in the mess hall, he swallowed three Mexican dreamtime zonkers.

While his compatriots settled in before a John Wayne video, Jesus Bob strolled outside and down the hill, drawn eventually to the setting sun and the rust-toned palette of the tobacco barn arsenal's gigantic barnsiding billboard. The board's heroic teenage couple, shown from the waist up, stood arm-in-arm, eyes fixed high, overlooking the valley and the highway far below. They posed before a sunrise, or perhaps a sunset—she, freckled and pigtailed, he, blond and rosy-cheeked. Bold block type proclaimed, YOUTH OF KENTUCKY! TOBACCO IS IN YOUR FUTURE.

In a mood for marveling, Jesus Bob gaped at the sheer size of the couple's ten-foot heads, the lettering too large to read. In a fleeting epiphany, he felt the immensity of the universe, his own insignificance. Then he looked down and became distracted by his feet. He lifted one, then the other, and tumbled to the ground. He waved his arms, marveling at how the air had liquefied. Feather light, he felt his body drift, float to the treetops, on to the moon. Branches swayed, danced languidly with puffy animate clouds, their tops still tinted orange from the sunset afterglow. Like flaming fish, fireflies swam through the quickening twilight, swirls of light tracing their paths. Jesus Bob reached for one, smiled as a hundred swarmed around his outstretched hand.

Fireflies forgotten, he felt the urge to urinate, scrambled to his feet, reflexively unzipped, and peed against the barn in playful swoops. He reached again for his zipper, but forgot why. Slumping against the rough wood, he felt his legs turn rubbery. He took a breath of the honeyed air and let gravity draw him once more to the velvety earth. Arms and legs akimbo, stomach to the sky, he counted stars.

Jesus Bob's lids grew heavy, his jaw gaped, his head lolled to the side.

Since her escape from Jungle Jimbo Bybee's bus, the three-foot timber rattlesnake had wandered, disoriented. Where were the familiar southern Georgia canebrakes, the fallen live oak log with the split side, the warm grassy sand, her retreat hole in the burned-out stump?

Her body had grown since she emerged from her cool-weather hibernaculum earlier this spring, and the subsequent two months had been generous—except for the terror of the capture, and that, she had survived. Regained her freedom.

This large wooden structure along whose perimeter she now crawled held promise. Confirmed by the heat-sensing pits between her eye and nostril, her flickering tongue caught molecules of a passing mouse. Normally such would stir her to pursuit and ambush. But this was not the time to hunt, but to seek refuge, for her first-of-the-year shed approached, a time of vulnerability. Her eyes were milkily opaque, temporarily blurring her vision. Her outermost layer of skin, its pattern dulled, felt stiff, ever more confining. Spurred by an evening chill, she probed the wall for a way inside, for warmth and safety until the time of release from the old skin.

She stopped, raised the forward quarter of her body, forked tongue active, waving in the evening air. She smell-tasted leather, picked up weak traces of rat and a stronger odor she associated with the capture.

Her wary, side-to-side probing, however, assured her the

territory ahead was still and secure; moreover, that considerable warmth and a dark concealing retreat lay before her. She slipped into a loose cloth tunnel, crawled as far as she could, and coiled at the fork of Jesus Bob's legs, cradled by his genitals. And slept.

The next morning, she awakened early, well before her unmoving host. She stretched tentatively, and felt her outer integument begin to part from the new skin beneath. She nosed flesh, and then fabric, seeking something rough on which to snag the loosening skin fraying at her lips. Ah— small strips of jagged metal. She rubbed, worried her chin and nose against the teeth of Jesus Bob's zipper, felt the old skin catch, begin to pull away. With a side-to-side writhing, she inched forward, and, like drawing a glove from a hand, inside-out, crawled entirely from her old skin, leaving the moist shed intact, its head at Jesus Bob's opened zipper, the tip at his neck.

Sight restored, fresh skin supple and brilliant, and with a new segment at the tip of her rattle, the renewed serpent glided over Jesus Bob's face, and away.

Ten minutes of full sun brought Jesus Bob around. He rubbed his eyes, feeling stiff but well-rested. He squinted at the tobacco barn arsenal, at the looming billboard, and then up the hill at the white cabins at the edge of the forest, and remembered, more or less, who and where he was. He took a deep breath of Kentucky morning, rose to his feet, reached down to initiate his morning pee, and felt moist parchment. Huh?

He glanced waistward, focused on: a snakeskin tie stuck to his shirt, its tail tickling his chin, its flattened neck in his fingers, its mouth open at his crotch.

Jesus Bob's screams rocked the thin walls of Barracks #1 through 10. In the distant valley, the wailing brought frightened farmers to their porches waving shotguns, fearful for their children and livestock. At the epicenter, however, in the tobacco barn arsenal, the recently shed timber rattlesnake, her sight restored but deaf and thus indifferent to the banshee yells, homed in on a noise-frozen rat, hunkering at the base of a kielbasa-stained crate of Polish hand grenades.

18

Coony turned onto a narrow gravel drive winding through deep shadows up a wooded hillside. He ignored the PRIVATE DRIVE, DO NOT ENTER warning nailed to a thick elm, and around the next bend, an ENGLISH ONLY SPOKE HERE sign. Fifty yards beyond, he passed STOP. BACK DOWN NOW, and, near the top of the hill, a final, YOUR ASS IS SHOT, IF YOU AIN'T BEEN INVITED.

"I had Johnny sneak through the woods earlier, take a peek, out of sight. Smoot's home," Coony said to Nikki at his right and to Digger behind the wire grid in the back. "He'll know someone's paying him a visit, because he's got a pressure hose under the gravel, tells him a car's a-coming."

The drive ended in a closed-loop circle at the front of a blocky house, fast falling to silhouette with the dying light.

Really more of an oversize cabin or lodge, Digger decided, built of thick logs, but, odd, running vertically, not longwise. No, on second thought, not a lodge, really more of a—

"Wow," Nikki said. "It looks like one of those forts in the cowboy and Indian movies. Only those two slitty windows alongside the door. Look how the second floor overhangs, has, like towers at the corners. It's even got those notches at the top."

"Crenelations," said Digger. "Those couldn't be real cannons up there."

They blinked as spotlights bathed the car and yard with brilliant white light.

Coony shielded his eyes. "You betcha. Four of them, one on each corner: Civil War twelve-pounders, naval howitzers. This is Smoot's idea of the pioneer forts built during the French and Indian times. The settlers would have enjoyed Smoot's improvements: the cannons, the front porch, the video cameras watching us there and there"—he pointed—"the spotlights, and that satellite dish." He thumped the wheel. "Okay, troops, let's let the commander know who's come a-calling."

They stood before a massive oak door with a bellybutton-high peep-hole lens. Coony raised and dropped a heavy, iron horseshoe knocker. The peephole went dark as an eye on the other side studied them.

Coony whispered from the side of his mouth, "Remember: smile, and keep quiet. Let me do the talking."

"Whatever you say," said Nikki. Digger mouthed an *okay*, rapped a fist against the logs, decided they were solid, not facing.

The heavy door opened only four inches, restrained by two thick iron chains on the inside. Yellow light spilled onto the porch. A backlit head appeared behind the crack, so low, Digger wondered if its owner was crouching.

A scratchy, apprehensive voice asked, "Who is it? What do you want?"

"Smoot, it's Coony McCoy, as you must know from the car. I've come for a visit."

"Who's that with you? What do you mean, *visit*?"

"Two friends from out of town. History buffs. I was telling them over supper that McAfee County had one of the country's leading collections of pioneer artifacts, and—"

"One of?"

"And they asked me so danged many questions. Couldn't be such a wonderful collection in east Kentucky, could there? 'Put your money where your mouth is, Coony,' they said, so—"

"All right. Come in." Chains rattled and the door swung open.

Digger followed Nikki and Coony inside. He looked left and right, then down, at a thin, slightly humpbacked, octogenarian gnome, hawk-nosed, a crisscross bandage on his forehead and another on his cheek. He stood no more than five feet tall, making Coony, at five-six, look large, and Digger at five-eight, a giant. At first glance the man appeared bald. A mere trace of eyebrows. A second look revealed white stubble—a shaved head—and, at the very back, a scrawny white ponytail, tied with blue ribbon, colonial-style. Dressed in leather moccasins and fringed buckskins with a cluster of gold stars on each shoulder, he leaned on a walker with two bomb-shaped bottles attached to the frame, one blue, one red. The red one, apparently a fire extinguisher, had a trigger grip and nozzle, while a clear plastic hose snaked from a regulator on the blue bottle to a breathing cup, hooked to the walker.

The gnome's right hand clutched a revolver nearly as long as his forearm. As soon as they were inside, he put his shoulder to the door, shut and rechained it.

"What's the gun for, Smoot?" Coony asked.

"Colt .45, Peacemaker, 1873."

"I know *what* it is. What's it *for*?"

"Why, protection, of course. A man's got to be careful. My collection's priceless." His voice wavered, his eyes darted side to side. Without warning he shouted, "Bolt! Where the hell are you, boy? Get your ass out here!"

Three seconds later, a six-foot, barrel-chested wildman jumped with a shout into the hallway, brandishing a mate to Smoot's revolver. Bare from the waist up, his head was crested with a flame of half-red, half-white hair. A wicked, inch-wide ivory scar, bordered by red flesh to either side, wound in a broad candy-cane spiral across his forehead, face and neck, around his chest and stomach, and into his buckskin trousers.

Nikki screamed. Digger moved to the door.

Coony stood his ground. "Why, it's my old friend Bolt."

"You all right, Commander?" the wildman asked. Without waiting for assurance, he moved between the old man and the intruders, and rocked, foot to moccasined foot.

"Where was you, boy?" Smoot said. "I coulda been scalped! Why wasn't you watching the monitors?"

Eyes forward, Bolt spoke over his shoulder. "Sorry, Commander. I was into *Last of the Mohicans*. Had it up good and loud—the part where the Indians ambush the British retreating through the woods, where—"

"Damned savages. Nearly piss my pants every time I see that part. Betrayed by the Frenchies and their redskin allies. It goes to show, if you're not on your toes, what can happen. Hell, put the gun down. If they wanted me dead, I'd be lying in a pool of blood. You know the sheriff. I don't know the other ones."

Smoot scooted the walker around Bolt to face the sheriff. "Haven't seen you in nine months, Coony. You might have called instead of coming by uninvited. What happened to your manners?"

"Why so edgy, Smoot?"

"Not edgy, careful," he spit back, fast. "Well, what do you want? Who are these people? You're not after Bolt again, are you?"

"Far as I know, Bolt's been a good boy lately. Right son? No fighting? No sniping at fishermen like the last time?"

Bolt glowered, fingered his revolver.

"You can put the armament away," Coony said. "This is a social call. I'd like you to meet my friends Nikki and Digger. They'd surely appreciate a peek at your collection, just to prove old Coony's no liar—then we'll be on our way."

Smoot squinted at the long-haired, bearded man and the slender young woman with the ponytail. "All right, a quick look-see. Don't touch nothing." He holstered the long gun. "Bolt, keep an eye on them. And give me a cee-gar. I've earned it."

Bolt slipped his revolver into a bandolier holster, pulled an aluminum cylinder from a buckskin waist pouch, removed a fat brown torpedo, clipped the end, and handed it to Smoot. Bolt held a lighter but didn't strike it. "Only a few puffs, Commander. Wait." He screwed tight the knob at the top of the blue cylinder, lifted the red one with the nozzle.

Smoot took the cigar, wet it between his lips. "Damned things can be bad for your health."

Nikki agreed. "If you don't mind my saying so, sir, then why do you smoke them?"

Smoot scowled at her. "Not the cigar, young woman, this damnable oxygen. You light up too near it, you go up like a torch. Whoosh! One would think that's obvious. See the scorch on the wall over there? I used to have eyebrows—you suppose I wear these Band-Aids for decoration?"

Standing clear, his arm extended, Bolt flicked a butane lighter.

Coony, Nikki, and Digger gave him room.

"Cowards. All of you." Smoot took six puffs on the cigar before his skin turned the shade of watered milk. He gasped. Bolt retrieved the cigar, knocked off the lit ash, put the shaft back in the silver tube, and twisted the oxygen regulator to high. He put the cup to Smoot's face, held him by the arm until the old man recovered.

Smoot shook off Bolt's grip and scuttled on his own power into a hallway, softly coughing and wheezing, leading the pack.

Nikki skidded to a stop. "Wow!" she said, at sight of a ninety-gallon aquarium filled with live plants and huge frogs, sitting on rocks or paddling in the water. "Are you into herps, sir? She tapped at the glass. "Most of them are *Rana catesbeiana*, bullfrogs, but those two are big green frogs, *Rana clamitans*. Bullfrogs lack that ridge of skin the green frogs have—see?—that runs from the eye down the side of the back. Nice, healthy specimens."

"Catch them myself," Bolt said. "Cook one up every morning for the commander's breakfast."

"Yuck! I don't see how anybody could—*ouch!*"

Coony gave her ponytail a quick tug and whispered by her ear. "I told you to button that lip, Miss Fitz. Leave the talking to me, hear?"

Bolt chuckled, continued with what must have been an inside joke. "The commander's got it in for frogs."

Smoot, at the head on the line, cackled. "Damn straight, boy. A hop-frog a day keeps the froggies at bay. Ha!"

Whatever the humor, Nikki didn't appreciate it. She cast a woeful eye at the aquarium as the group passed.

Smoot scuttled to the right, down a long corridor. Eight-foot-high curio cabinets with glass shelves, internally lit with pin-spots, lined the walls for forty feet.

"Wow!" Nikki said for the second time, frogs, at the moment, forgotten. "Beer cans. I've never seen so many in my life."

She reached to pick up a Budweiser can—the whole cabinet, in fact, all the cabinets, held tightly packed Bud cans—to see what was distinctive about them. Successive label designs? Misprints? Autographed by championship bowlers, demolition derby winners, famous duck hunters, wrestling superstars?

"Don't touch!" Bolt said.

Nikki dropped her hand. "The sheriff said you had a wonderful collection, sir," she said to Smoot, anxious to please, "but I had no idea—"

Coony elbowed her in the arm to shut her up.

"Twit," Smoot said. "That's not my collection, it's Bolt's."

Bolt puffed out his chest. "Drank every one myself."

Smoot hobbled on. "My collection's through the door at the end of the hall."

At the end of the passage, he turned a key in a hand-size

padlock and unlatched a wrought-iron reinforced wooden door. It opened into a baronial, high-ceilinged room paneled in varnished knotty pine, glowing like gold under three massive brass chandeliers.

Nikki and Digger stumbled to a stop, confronted at the center of the room by a head-high bull buffalo, head lowered, ready to charge.

"Buffalo Bill won't hurt you," said Smoot, with a hoarse cackle. He patted its stuffed, moth-eaten head and scuttled past.

A gilt gesso framed painting of a Rubenesque nude hung above a ten-by-ten-foot fieldstone fireplace at the far end of the room. Flintlock rifles, muskets and powder horns, fringed buckskins and leggings, frayed linsey-woolsey shirts, pistols, saddles, old leather bags, and iron tools covered the walls.

Smoot led them around glass-fronted display cases and dude-ranch-style brass-studded leather and log furniture.

"Molesworthy," Smoot said, of the furniture. "Good, like everything I own. That painting, the nude? An authentic Sharp. The Remington bronzes? No sloppy knock-offs. Those pioneer clothes?" He waved to the right. "That's what my ancestors donned when Kentucky was the frontier. They was heroes. Indian fighters. Survivors. Right, Bolt?"

"That's it, sir."

"Wonderful," said Nikki. "Like pages out of a history book." She side-glanced at Coony with a *How's that?* look.

Smoot gave her a pinched smile. "Yes. That's what I do. Preserve history. My ancestors live on in this room. You appreciate history, do you, young woman?"

"Oh, yes, sir. Where would we be without history?"

"We'd be savages," Smoot said. "Savages have no history." He pointed to the wall. "See how small those outfits are? People was little in the frontier days, like me. Not the leviathans they are today. Economical, built for running through the woods, living on less food. Those old boys and I share the same blood."

"The flintlock muskets?" Voice warming. "British and

American Revolutionary army issue. The real prizes, the ones to that side, are Kentucky rifles. Graceful, light. A tad slower firing, but much more accurate. Hit their marks at three and four hundred yards.

"The rifles to the left date from the mid-1700s. We fought the froggies and their redskin allies with those during the French and Indian War. Bastards gave us hell at first, but we finally drove the froggies out for good. Yessir. Sealed and signed at the Treaty of Paris in 1763. Right, Coony?"

Coony nodded.

"Let your eyes feast on that Kentucky rifle to the right." Smoot pointed. "Ain't that the prettiest tiger stripe maple you've ever seen? Made in east Pennsylvania about 1800. Octagon barrel, fifty caliber, forty-three and a half inches long, relief-carved stock sleek as a thirteen-year-old farmer's daughter, curving butt plate, curlicue brass patchbox, silver inlays. One of the Good Lord's wonders.

"Now, that big baby, that's a 1878 target model of a concealed hammer, Sharps-Borchardt single-shot buffalo rifle, set up with a vernier rear-sight."

"Great," Nikki said, ignoring Coony's growing scowl. "Perfect for killing animals like that stuffed one."

"That animal, young woman," said Smoot, "before it got its ass shot, was the last buffalo living in the wild, east of the Mississippi."

She dodged Coony's fingers, which were going for her ponytail. "I suppose you shot her with your buffalo rifle?"

Coony moved closer to give her a poke in the back instead.

"Not me. I'm not that old, young woman. But—yes, indeed—that rifle done him in, all right. My great great granddaddy bought that beast from a Wild West show, let it run up at the Reserve—although it was pretty old by then, limp along was more like it. He shot it one boring day with that very Sharps."

Digger saw Nikki's face redden, and spoke before she could answer. "You ever fire those Kentucky rifles?"

"Don't shoot much myself anymore," Smoot said, "but I lend one now and then to one of the Rangers to fire up at the Reserve. Kids now get spoiled with all the automatic weapons. Too easy. Did you know the best of the old frontiersmen used to load and fire a Kentucky rifle on the run? Hell—now they just pop in a preloaded magazine and pull the trigger. What's the fun in killing without finesse, I ask you?"

He scuttled to the mantle, his earlier anxiety forgotten. "Look, over the fireplace. Not the fanciest, but—oh, my— what a treasure. That Kentucky rifle belonged to Jesse Bryan Boone, Daniel's favorite son. We're related you know. Jesse Bryan and Daniel was my ancestors. Proof of it's on that gee-nee-oh-logical chart framed over there. Ain't that right, Coony?"

"I guess everyone in the county knows about you and Daniel Boone."

Digger leaned over a horizontal glass-topped display case. "Nice medals and some fine banded-slate Archaic bannerstones here."

"Those medals was given to redskin chiefs when they visited Washington," Smoot said. "Dazzled their breechclouts off, I daresay. Bannerstones? Those three are among the finest. Made up to eight thousand years ago, before the Europeans discovered America. Savages was healthier way back— bet you didn't know that. So, you recognize those as bannerstones? You have an interest in archaeology, sir?"

"Dr. Fitz, here, is an archaeologist," Coony said.

"Fitz? Did you say Fitz?" Smoot wheeled to face Coony, then Digger. His face went pale.

"Oh," Coony said. "I guess I forgot to mention my friends' full names. They're Digger and Nikki Fitz. Like in Edgar Fitz."

Smoot dropped into a studded, red leather chair. He hunched over. His lower lip trembled. Bolt stepped to his side, fists balling.

"You want to tell me about it, Smoot?" Coony said,

velvet-voiced, ignoring the ominous, hovering Bolt. "We know all about the two thousand dollars a week Fitz deposited in the bank." He walked to the chair and set his hand on Smoot's small shoulder, covering the cluster of gold stars. "Why'd you kill the man?"

Smoot ran arthritic fingers across his shaved head. He covered his eyes and slumped. "Me? Lord, no. It wasn't me." He looked back up, fearful. "It was the Frenchman, Coony. The Frenchman done it. And I'm next."

19

The Frenchman?" Nikki looked from Smoot to Coony. "Who's the Fr—?"

Coony flashed her a *zip your lip* with thumb and forefinger across his mouth, and then swung his head to Smoot. "Are you sure it wasn't one of your Ranger boys, after Edgar Fitz for the way he fancy talked? Maybe he said something untoward about somebody's favorite gun? Or, they were hitting the booze, got carried away—"

Bolt cut in. "No. Not the Rangers. The doctor was never up there. What the commander says is true—the Frenchman done it."

Coony continued the press. "Why didn't you come to me right away when you learned Fitz was dead?"

Smoot whimpered. "I was afraid. All that bikers and drug-dealer talk. I didn't want them coming after me if they thought I knew Fitz."

"If it was the Frenchman, it couldn't have been bikers. The game's over." He let it sink in, watched Smoot writhe. He held up a hand to keep Bolt away, and leaned close, cajoling. "Tell us about it, old fella, it'll make you feel better."

The all-too-familiar, hot-cold third degree made Digger's

stomach roil, his palms sweat. A primal voice said run, but instead, he found himself rooted to the floor like a witness to a hanging, waiting for the clack of the trap door.

Smoot's voice caught in his throat. "I—I figured out later the Frenchman done it. If he could get to Edgar, he could get to me."

Bolt said, "I'd never of let it happen, Commander."

Smoot shot him a glare. "Hell, Bolt. If that had been the Frenchman tonight instead of the law, he'd be waving my bloody scalp in his hands."

Coony raised a shushing hand. "I don't buy fear kept you from calling, Smoot. Maybe I'd have caught the Frenchman, gotten him off your back once and for all. Fess up."

"If I'd told you it was the Frenchman, you'd of laughed, like when he's come for me before. And what if it *was* bikers? You sure as hell haven't caught *them*."

"Make up your mind, Smoot. Bikers or the Frenchman. Why would the Frenchman murder Edgar Fitz?"

"To scare me. Because he's jealous. Because he hates me."

"You have to do better than that. Why Edgar Fitz?"

Smoot shrugged. He glanced at the case Digger had peered into two minutes back and chewed his lip, ruminating. He slapped the arm of his chair. "I have something the bastard wants, bad." He shuffled to the case, pointed to a seven-by-eleven-inch sheet of dull whitish-gray metal inscribed with block serif, capitalized letters in French. "You ever heard of Captain Pierre Joseph Céloron de Blainville, the Frenchie?"

Nikki shook her head. Digger said, "Sounds familiar."

Coony nodded. "Led the expedition sent by the governor of Canada—New France then—to cement the French claim to central North America west of the Alleghenies, to link the Saint Lawrence with Louisiana and close the land to the British."

Smoot cackled. "Ha! Coony McCoy knows his history, whatever else they say about him." Fists to his temples, he wiggled his little fingers like feelers at his forehead to underscore the "whatever else they say," and laughed a staccato "heh, heh, heh."

He lost his breath, snuffed oxygen. "Yes!" he said, agitated. "Make it all French, drive out the British. In June of 1749, Céloron sailed up the Saint Lawrence to Fort Frontenac, then along Lake Ontario to Fort Niagara, and south, portaging till he reached the big river, what we call the Allegheny and Ohio. With him was a Jesuit mathematician map-maker, thirty Frenchie officers and soldiers, close to two hundred Canadians, and another fifty-five redskins. Their goal? Lay claim to the heartland for Louis the Fifteenth and set the savages against the British."

Smoot snapped his bent fingers and tapped them against his lips: cigar. Bolt handed it to him, although he didn't offer, and Smoot didn't command, a light. Instead, for several seconds Smoot sucked on it with infantile nipple-slurps. Energized, he withdrew the soggy tip from his lips, kissed the shaft affectionately, and aimed it like a brown bomber at the dull metal plate in the case.

"The frogs carried a series of cast metal plaques like that one, pre-inscribed with French fancy talk claiming the land. At streams along the way, they did a froggie claiming ceremony, tacked the royal arms to a tree, filled in the blanks on one of the plates as to when and where they was; then buried it."

Digger bent over the case and read aloud, *"L'an 1749 du règne de Louis XV Roy de France, nous Céloron, Commandant d'un détachément envoié par monsieur le mis de la Galissoniere, Commandant General de la Nouvelle France pour rétablir la tranquillité dans quelques villages sauvages de ces cantons, avons enterré cette plaque . . ."*

"Damnit, man," Smoot said, "you read that wah-wah talk good. You ain't a French froggie are you?"

"I'm Scots-Irish like Edgar. The French is from eight seasons of digs in French Polynesia in the South Pacific."

"Thank the Good Lord. There's never been a French frog

crossed the threshold of this house and never there will be, right, Bolt?"

"Not a live one, sir." Bolt hovered behind Smoot, a protective shadow.

"In the inscription," Digger explained, "Céloron is giving his credentials and the rationalization for the expedition, establishing peace with the Indians and reinforcing the French claim."

"Frog puffery," said Smoot. "They left spaces blank for the dates and places where they buried them, see? This one's filled in."

Digger read, ". . . *a la rive gauche de la Rivière la Roche ce trente et un âout 1749, par la rive droite de la Rivière Oyo, autrement belle rivière . . .*" He translated, ". . . on the left bank of the Rocky River this thirty-first of August 1749, by the right bank of the Ohio River, also known as the beautiful river—"

"Buried for centuries before I got it," Smoot said. "Ha!" He raised the cigar to his lips, remoistened the end with lapping flicks of his pale pink tongue, sucked half its body into his mouth, corkscrewed it out with forefinger and thumb, sucked on it again, and began to chew the glutinous end.

Nikki caught Digger's eye, nodded at the cigar show, and dry-gagged. "What happened to the expedition?" she asked with a straight face.

"Patience, young lady," Smoot said, still licking, sucking. "A month earlier, the redskins, Senecas or Cayugas, stole the first plate Céloron was about to bury, or dug it up right off, took it to the British, asked them what the writing meant. The British, no dummies, told them it said the frogs was planning to steal their land and hunting grounds. Set those redskins in a tizzy, you may be sure. They sent belts of wampum south and west to their brothers, pronto, to warn 'em.

"The stolen plate was sent by Governor George Clinton of the Colony of New York to the Lords of Trade in London as evidence of French intentions. It's the only one the English saw, and it set the stage for counterclaims by the British that led down the pike to the French and Indian War."

"Wow!" Nikki said for the third time, duly impressed.

"Yes, young woman. *Wow* is the word. That first plate and Céloron's expedition led to the French and Indian War. Unfortunately, that momentous artifact disappeared from history." He drew the cigar from his lips fast, with a watery smack.

Smoot grinned. "Hell of a story, ain't it? The froggies headed southwest down the Ohio and buried six more, each with a different date and place name. At the end of August, Céloron reached the Great Miami near Cincinnati, their River la Roche. He figured he'd gone far enough and the redskins wasn't putting out the welcome mat, so he buried the last plate—this very one—and then hotfooted it back north along the Miami to Detroit, and back across the Great Lakes to Montreal.

"Only two other plates has been recovered, one of them incomplete. Both in museums. Four more, as far as the world knows, is still in the ground—but make that *three*, in fact, because one of them is here before your eyes. The *only* one in private hands. Hah!" Smoot clapped, scattering tatters of wet tobacco. "What do you think of them apples?"

"You're in a class of one," Coony said.

Smoot grinned, took it as a compliment. "I did my research, determined the last plate was buried on land owned by the gas and electric utility in Cincinnati. It was a long shot, but I got a man working on it, sneaky-like. He let it be known on the q.t. there was big money for the man who discovered it. A crewman laying pipe came across it. Lucky bastard. Naturally, because of the reward, he kept it mum until he found my man. But here's the best: six months before, the Frenchman made a big ta-doo about financing a dig not a hundred yards away to look for—get this—a Fort Ancient redskin village. Hah! Oh, the Frenchman's devious, all right.

"Edgar confirmed my plate was the real thing. I promised

Edgar when the paper came out, I'd consider donating it to a museum. That made *him* happy. The crewman? He got a seventy-foot houseboat. And me? I one-upped the Frenchman—snatched this wonder right out from under his long froggie nose."

Digger repeated, " 'Donate it to a museum.' Yes, that's the thing to do."

"I'm a man of my word," Smoot said. "When Edgar's paper comes out, I'll *consider* it. Heh, heh, heh."

"Good old Smoot," Coony said. "How much is this thingy worth?"

Smoot shook the disintegrating cigar at him. "Don't you get no ideas. Anyone causes trouble, this plate could disappear. Get me? Value?" Smoot pursed his lips, "I don't make it a habit to tell people what my collection's worth, but you may be sure it would be five, maybe six figures if I was to sell it. A pretty penny for a slab of lead."

"Lead?" said Digger.

Nikki echoed it. "Lead!"

"Sure," Smoot said. "Lead don't rust. And lead never worked up the treasure hunters like gold or silver. The Frenchies used lead to stake their claims all over—LaSalle buried lead plates to claim the middle of this continent for the French throne in 1682. Little did old Céloron guess a descendant of one of his enemies would pay a small fortune for this one, two hundred and fifty years later, huh?"

He caught the anguished looks on Nikki's and Digger's faces. "Oh, I see—lead. How Edgar died, huh? Well, sure, the Frenchman done him in like that as a double message to me: one, I could damn well choke on my own lead, and, two, if he could get to Edgar, he could get to me."

Smoot spit a shred of tobacco on the glass case. "Hell, I don't give a tinker's dam that the Frenchman found out. I got it. My, oh, my, how it must gall him."

He raised the cigar hand from his walker, waved it at each of his guests like a papal anointing. "You three and Edgar are among the lucky few to have seen the Smoot Mudd plate since it was buried over two centuries ago!"

"Let me get this straight," Digger said. "You're calling Edgar *lucky?*"

"You bet. Probably the most exciting thing to happen in his dull life. Edgar was thrilled to be the one I chose to publish it. Too bad he's dead, but I'll bet the man went out with a smile on his face."

"You son of a bitch!" Digger stepped toward him, shaking his fist. But before Digger's foot touched the carpet, a slab of a hand gripped the back of his shoulder and wrenched him off his feet.

Coony shouted, "Enough of that!"

Bolt grinned, and in one swift motion, swung Digger in an arm-span's arc to set him down five feet away. He bowed theatrically and dusted off Digger with a smirk.

"Don't press it, Bolt," Coony said, "or you'll be on jail rations and no Budweiser, fast." He turned to Smoot: "Tell me how you got Edgar Fitz involved."

Smoot winked at Bolt. "Fitz? I read about him speaking to this archaeological meet, got hold of him, and hired him to research my collection, the same way a museum would. I wanted him to document my Céloron plate ear-re-futably.

"A fancy Ph.D. working full-time on the Smoot Mudd collection in McAfee County, Kentucky. How's that? I was gonna have him go over my whole collection, write papers about it. Would have kept him so busy he wanted to bring in someone else to help." Smoot nodded at Digger. "Hah! Might have been you! Well, your cousin Edgar had a tight mouth. He didn't give a hoot about owning anything himself—not like most of those thieves out there. Believe this or not, Edgar never once asked what things was worth. No, I trusted Edgar. All he wanted was to work with my collection. That, and the money I paid him, of course. He held out for top dollar, I'll give him that, said that's what it would take to bring a famous archaeologist like him to Golden Leaf." Smoot spit. "So what? I'm worth plenty. My collection's worth it."

"Why cash?" Coony asked.

"I believe in a cash economy," Smoot said. "And to give him the chance to avoid taxes. Poor bugger wasn't worth a pot to piss in. All those years in science, and nothing to show for it. He deposited the money in a bank. For all his smarts, Edgar wasn't bright enough to hide the income."

"Maybe Uncle Edgar was just honest," Nikki said.

Smoot shrugged. "I have no reason to think he cheated me."

"If this was so hush-hush," Coony said, "how did the Frenchman find out about it? And why murder Edgar Fitz?"

"The Frenchman's got spies. He murdered Edgar because he could get to him and not to me. And because he's jealous. And, to screw up my plans to publish the Smoot Mudd plate in a scientific journal and rock the world. And, to scare me— which he damned well accomplished."

"Smoot," Coony shook his head. "It don't add up."

Smoot wheezed. Bolt adjusted the oxygen regulator, raised the mask. Ten long seconds later, Smoot spoke again. "Well, there is one thing more—"

"Commander," Bolt said, "don't tell him. They'll screw it up. Let me throw them out."

Coony walked to within a foot of Bolt's chest and glared up at him. "Let's get something clear. There's been a murder. If you two know more than you've said, you tell me about it now, or regrets will be the sentiment of the day. I've got a cold cell with your name on it, Bolt, and then Smoot here can fend for himself whilst you count cracks in the concrete."

Smoot patted Bolt on the arm. "Coony can keep a confidence, can't you, Coony? An elected official? One beholden to his friends?"

"Out with it, Smoot."

"Another Céloron plate turned up." He watched their faces and cackled. "Not just *any* one, but the very *first* one, the one the redskins stole. The Lords of Trade plate! An auction's planned. Private, between me and the Frenchman. A chance for me to own two plates, or for the Frenchman to catch up, put us on equal ground. The people who found it have good documentation, let both the Frenchman and me, and our experts examine it—separately, of course. It's as legitimate as the one you see here. Oh, the Frenchman wants it bad. And I want him not to have it even badder. So, Edgar's murder *was* a message. The Frenchman murdered him to scare me away from the auction."

"And did the message get through?" Coony asked.

"Hell, no!" Smoot said. "Bolt and me is on our toes. Ain't we, boy?"

"Yes, sir." Bolt fingered the revolver in his bandolier holster.

"Now that all the beans is spilled," Smoot said, all smiles. "Let me ask you something—Mickey, Digger is it?—you folks being, I gather, Edgar's kin."

"And that would be?" Digger asked.

"Edgar's records, the research he done. Inasmuch as I paid for it, you'll pass it along to me, huh?"

"So-ooo sorry," Coony said. "That ain't possible."

"What? Why not? It's mine. Mine!"

"Because whoever killed Edgar Fitz," Coony explained with a satisfying smile, "stole his computer and every sign of his work since he arrived in McAfee County."

Smoot coughed and hacked, and then spit a pinkish glob on the floor. He pinched the damp remains of the cigar so hard it bent in two. He glared at it, threw it onto the braided rope rug and ground it to shreds with the heel of his moccasin.

Bolt moved to his side, stroked Smoot's shaved head to calm him.

In gratitude, Smoot lifted the walker and banged it onto Bolt's foot.

"Edgar's work is gone all right," Digger said, emphasizing the *gone*. "I searched the house myself."

Nikki added, "Guess you're the one out of luck now, Mr. Commander."

"You twit!" Smoot tried to spit on her, but managed only

to choke. "Goddamn that Frenchman! Wasn't enough to kill my man. He stole his work—my work." Red-faced, Smoot twisted, stomped, tipped over the walker. Bolt righted it, chased Smoot with the oxygen mask. Smoot kicked at Bolt's shins, pounded his shoulders. "Oh, shh—" Without the air to finish, he gasped. Bolt gripped the back of his head like a basketball and strapped on the mask. Smoot wheezed and snorted, still whining. He ripped the mask off. "Now he's got an inventory of everything I own. Shit! Shit! Shit! And the eight thousand I gave Edgar? Down the tubes! Goddamnit, Coony, you're the sheriff. You nail that guilty son of a bitch, you hear?"

Coony tipped his hat to Smoot, then Bolt. "Never fear," he said. "Nailing guilty sons of bitches is what I do best."

20

As soon as the spotlights on Smoot's fort winked out, Nikki asked, for the second time, "Who's the Frenchman?"

Digger added, "And what's the story on Bolt?"

"If you two got the dime, I got the time. How about we stop at the Chez?" He glanced right, at Nikki, and into the rearview mirror at Digger. "One thing: You keep what was said tonight and whatever we may talk about later under your hats, hear?"

Digger nodded.

Nikki added, "Whatever you say, Sheriff."

Ten minutes later, they were back at the Chez. Coony asked Rubella for a table by the rear. She responded with *Twilight Zone* Doo-do-doo-dos.

A plump, slow-moving, older waitress, hair in a net, ketchup stains on her dress, waddled to the table. "Coony, sir," she said. "Rubella told me to say we still got plenty of pork chops, bacon, and country ham, but we run out of kosher tonight."

"Darlin'?" He cocked an eye at her. "You know, there's lots of Jews eat pork."

"But not you, huh, Coony, sir?"

"Tell me, do have any idea what kosher is?"

She kicked at a cigarette butt on the floor, shifted from one foot to the other. "Not exactly. Ain't on the menu. But I watch the *Star Trek* reruns regular, and I got a good mind it's what your kind eats, like—"

"Criminy! Pour the coffees, okay? And tell Rubella to button her lip."

When the waitress had left, Digger said, "You're *Jewish*! Not that . . . I mean . . ."

"With a name like McCoy," Nikki said. "I wouldn't have . . ."

Coony swatted the air. "I'm *not* Jewish, okay?"

"Fine, fine," said Digger. "None of our business anyway."

"Fine with me, too," said Nikki. "Either way, really."

Coony sipped coffee in grim silence for a long half-minute, and then clanged the cup on the saucer with a huff. "Here it is: The Jewish business is another of our barber Ben's cockamamie ideas. Remember what I said about aliens, and feds, and who-knows-what-else is after them? Well, Jews is a big part of it. With this diet of mine, no country ham steak or bacon in the mornings like I used to eat, no pork chops at night—they got in mind I'm a Jew, too. On top of a hot-wired alien fed."

Silence.

"Oh, yeah. Then six months ago, we got new emblems for the cars, stationery, package deal from this outfit in Frankfort. Good price, but the stars have six points like some of the old marshal badges, not five. Six, see? That clinched it.

"So now, I got to put up with this crap!" He blubbered air through his lips like a horse whinny. "Enough of that. Back to the Frenchman. His name's Alphonse LeCoup, lives in Cincinnati."

"Cincy?" Nikki said. "I live in Cincy. I never heard of Alphonse LeCoup."

"There's what, a million people there? Never met him

myself, but I've heard a good bit from Smoot over the years. LeCoup's a hotshot businessman, loaded."

He rocked the chair slowly on its rear legs. "Smoot and the Frenchman was once boo–sum buddies. Collectors of midwestern Americana. Went to the flea markets and auctions arm-in-arm, but eager to one-up each other, too."

When the waitress shuffled back with more coffee, Coony segued, without missing a beat, to kids knocking over mailboxes, and then shifted seamlessly back to Smoot and the Frenchman when she left. "They got into history—one of the pleasures of collecting. But these two took it more and more serious. Began acting it out. One of them, Smoot, I gather, got the idea of hiring a genealogist, thought if he skipped over his old man, he might find gold.

"Better than gold. The woman said Smoot was a son of the pioneers, descended from Daniel Boone himself."

"That's what he said at the house."

"Yep. Meanwhiles, the Frenchman was doing the same thing. His big-money genealogist told him his ancestors was New World French, out of Montreal. One, none other than the explorer La Salle, who discovered the Mississippi. Then there was a trapper, married a Huron—so there's Indian blood in his veins. Was a time, a man like LeCoup would have kept mum about that, but it's fashionable now, especially for a collector of Indian artifacts. This genealogist turned up not only Indians, but—surprise—chiefs, lots of them. The Frenchman is real proud of his Native American heritage since it puts his folks on this continent before his good buddy, Smoot.

"The Frenchman's ancestors fought in the French and Indian War, and Smoot's kin, from south of the Ohio River, fought on the side of the British Colonials. The more these boys hear about all this BS, the more their imaginations take hold. Pretty soon, they're reliving old skirmishes. Calling their ancestors by first names, dressing the parts. Guess you noticed Smoot and Bolt's get-up?"

"Davy Crockett," said Digger, "and his dress-up bear."

"Close: Davy's Tennessee, Daniel's Kentucky. Our boys find Bibles, letters, journals they decide are the ancestors', with first person accounts of battles, kidnappings, tortures, scalpings. Those rifles on Smoot's wall wasn't just collectibles anymore, they shot his kin's enemies. And Alphonse's tomahawks?—one of his specialties—they scalped British Colonials, or Virginians, later Kentuckians.

"One story is this Shawnee ancestor of Alphonse forms a war party, captures one of Smoot's ancestors' wives. Rape and good times in the woods. The offended husband takes chase but gets himself caught north of the Ohio. He's forced to run the gauntlet in Shawnee villages—two long lines of Indians, women and men with sticks, stones, and such, beating the hell out of him while he runs between. Then they scalp him and tie him to a stake with just enough line to dance around while they poke at him with pointed sticks and torches. That's before he's roasted alive.

"Ouch," Nikki said.

"Smoot didn't care for it, neither. You can be sure the Frenchman has stories about Kentuckians crossing the Ohio River where they don't belong, using LeCoup's ancestors for target practice.

"Soon, it's no longer a lark, it's a battle. Smoot and the Frenchman haven't spoken for years. They bad-talk each other to collectors and dealers, fight it out over choice artifacts. They nearly dueled. Smoot's a dead shot, and the Frenchman is hell with the saber—they say he studied in Europe. In a duel, the challenged gets to choose the weapons, so you see the difficulty.

"Once or twice a year, Smoot comes to me, convinced Alphonse has made a scalping pass at him—I guess you noticed he shaves his head. If it wasn't for Bolt and Smoot's Rangers, he'd of died of fright years ago."

"Bolt," Nikki said. "What's his story?"

Coony savored his coffee, letting the suspense build. "They say when Smoot's momma was full with him, she near got struck by lightning during a bodacious storm and gave birth premature—why Smoot's such a runt. He's been scared of lightning all his life. Fifteen years ago he was overseeing a mining operation up on Bald Knob, so-called after Wesvaky coal stripped the top of it off—flat and high, see? Mother of a storm comes up, booming thunder. No trees left, coupla dozers and the men was the highest things in sight.

"Lightning hits a dozer. It explodes. Smoot tries to run, but with his short legs and bad lungs, he gets nowhere before the jagged flashes are zapping all around. Men are running to save their asses or sprawled out low. All except one, taking his good old time, walking tall, no fear. 'I'm in the grace of the Lord, brother,' he says to this miner I know who was flat on the ground, quaking, ten feet away. Smoot pleads for help. 'Only the Lord can save your soul, brother,' says the guy, 'but I'll do what I can for your mortal body.' He—Bolt as they later call him—raises his arms, says, 'Merciful Lord, save this sinner at my feet for redemption!' and the Good Lord does— of a sorts.

"What happens is: *Zap!* This monster streak of lightning crackles out of the black heavens and hits, not Smoot, but Bolt, lights his hair on fire, spins him like a top and melts his soles to the ground. Guess you noticed the scars?"

They nodded.

"The storm passes. Smoot gets up, thrilled to be alive. Bolt's smoking, still standing, life in him, but barely. It put him in a coma for six weeks.

"One night, Smoot visits him, Bolt's lying there uncon- scious, a nurse checking his tubes and such, and Smoot, feel- ing uncharacteristically guilty, mutters he'd give Bolt anything he wants if only the man would come back to life. As if he'd been waiting for those very words, Bolt sits straight up, eyes wide—I heard this from the nurse herself—and shouts 'Three squares a day, never have to see no coal again, and all the beer I can drink!'

"That being a modest enough request, Smoot assented. He made Bolt his body guard and delivered on the beer drinking wish, too. Hell, you seen Bolt's collection. After the zapping, howsomever, Bolt lost his taste for religion. Never forgave the Good Lord for his bad aim.

"Bolt"—Coony rubbed his chin—"is high on my list of suspects."

"Bolt?"—Nikki asked. "You don't think the Frenchman killed Uncle Edgar?"

"Oh, the Frenchman's near the top."

"And bikers, still?"

"Them, too. Not as high. Right after the Rangers."

"But I'm off it?" Digger asked.

"You're pretty low down it at the moment," Coony said.

Digger frowned. "I don't see how—"

"Near the bottom. That make you feel better?"

Nikki pressed her question: "But why Bolt?"

"Bolt has always took care of Smoot's collection. Mayhaps he's in line for Smoot's fortune, there being no heirs. Then your uncle appears on the scene. Takes over the collection. Maybe Bolt worried about his place in Smoot's fortress, in his heart. And Bolt's a mean drunk."

Coony studied his cup, rotated it on the table with both hands, making circles with spilt coffee. "Still, this lead plate business points to the Frenchman. It's an angle needs checking out, but, hell, Cincinnati's not only out of my county, it's out of my state. Big city police up there—what are they gonna do if I call and raise suspicions about one of their rich citizens?"

"May I introduce," Nikki said, standing, bowing. "Fitz and Fitz, PIs."

"Hold on, young woman." Raising a hand. "Bad idea. If the man is our murderer, he's plenty dangerous, and the McAfee County Sheriff won't be worth a pile of beans to you in Cincinnati, Ohio."

"No—good idea. You admitted there isn't anything you can do. I'll call Biffer, my stepfather. Biffer's a big CEO, knows all those business guys. They play golf together, sit on one another's boards, have secret handshakes and stuff. I'll bet he knows the Frenchman."

"How's this?" said Digger. "We play it like we did tonight. Nikki calls this LeCoup, mentions Biffer's name, tells him her uncle is in town all the way from Hawaii and loves archaeology. Says her uncle heard about this wonderful collection. She avoids mentioning our last names until we're at his house—then we see how he reacts to the name Fitz."

Coony reminded him what happened to his cousin Edgar.

Digger gnawed his lip, looked suitably worried, but Nikki beamed.

Coony shook a finger at her. "You hear me? Dangerous. Don't do it."

"Sure, Sheriff." Grinning. "Whatever you say."

Bolt dialed the phone for Smoot, passed him the receiver. A man answered. Skipping the hellos, Smoot said, "Give me your sister, boy."

Rita Rae opened the conversation with kissy sounds.

"Enough of that. Guess who was here? Our busybody sheriff. With a smart-assed girl and an archaeologist, Edgar's relatives. Here in McAfee County and asking all the wrong questions."

"Cool down, honey. What did you tell them?"

He repeated most of what he remembered.

"You didn't mention the auction?"

"Uh, not me. But . . . they know about it. Dammit, Rita Rae, why didn't you sell the Lords of Trade plate to me flat out?"

"Because I know how close Smootikins is with his money. I still treasure the jewelry you gave me for bouncing on your lap back in my good old high school and golden rule days—the one-size-fits-all mood ring, the phony turquoise earrings."

"If you'd of stayed with me—"

"Sure. And if I'd sold the Lords of Trade plate to you outright, I suppose you'd have given me what it's worth, huh?

We poor ladies being so helpless when it comes to fi-*nan*-cial matters, you can't blame a girl for thinking about her future, can you?"

"Your future? You've got Sheriff Coony McCoy on your tail, now, so you'd best watch out. If Coony and Bo knew you and your crazy brother was in town—a damn good thing for you I fixed you up to stay up at the Reserve, out of sight, Rangers all around."

"Oh, yes. *Lov*-e-ly accommodations. Five star. And, lively conversationalists, these Rangers, so in touch with their inner selves."

"Listen to me, Rita Rae, you swore the auction would be here in McAfee County, I damn well won't go—"

"Right here, baby. Make the Frenchman come to us so you can trounce his butt once and for all, send him back to Cincinnati with his uppity tail between his legs."

Smoot grunted.

She smooched the phone again and hung up.

Rita Rae looked at the four names she had written on the back of a Victoria's Secret catalog: *Coony McCoy, Bo Deaver, Digger Fitz, Nikki Fitz.*

She lifted it to her Love's Blood red lips and planted a glossy lip print at the list's center. "Keep messing with Rita Rae," she said, "and you can kiss your meddling asses goodbye. Yes, indeed."

21

and over the phone, Nikki whispered, "He's getting on the line."

"Be respectful. Don't tick him off like you do your mother."

"I know how to handle Biffer." She dropped her hand. "Biffer? Hi! It's Nikki. Yeah, still in Kentucky . . . I already called her. . . . Oh, mother worries too much. . . . She said *what*? . . . Yuck! Of course we sleep in separate rooms. . . . Eeuuw, he's not only my uncle, but old. A real fossil."

Digger mouthed a silent *Fossil*?

"Biffer, you know better than to believe mother. It's her analyst—'verbalize your neuroses' and all that . . . No, an absolute gentleman, I promise. . . . The reason I called, is, Uncle Harmon—Digger—and I are coming up to Cincy tonight. We'll stay at the house, but you work so late and leave so early, we won't get much of a chance to talk, and Unc's really been looking forward to meeting you. He wants to visit the museums, and since we'll be downtown, I told him what a cool office you have, and about your art collection"—She bugged her eyes at Digger—"so he asked me if there was a chance we could come by, and I wanted to talk to you about the possibility of a future in business . . ."

Digger mimed heavy shoveling.

"Lunch? At the Pinnacle Club? Wow! Yeah, I know. Dress code, sure. Noon? Great. We'll see you at your office at eleven-thirty." She hung up.

"Kiddo, your mother's right. You were born for sales."

"I didn't want to ask him right out about the Frenchman or he'd get suspicious, start wondering if we would embarrass him. I guarantee, though, if this LeCoup is a businessman, in the bucks like Coony says, Biffer will know all about him. And if they're not crossing swords over some deal, I'll call LeCoup with, 'Hi, I'm Biffer's stepdaughter. My old uncle from Hawaii?—you know, like we said."

"My sweet niece. Such a bullshitter."

A horn honked. Nikki parted the chintz curtains at the front window. "Oh, no. It's Bo. Tell him I'm in town, shopping. Anything." She pushed Digger to the door.

Digger stepped onto the porch, left the door ajar. "Hey, Bo. What's up?"

Bo shook hands, looked over Digger's shoulder, inside. "Don't know if you've noticed, sir, but Coony's been having us keep an eye on your house. We drive by regular—being sure no one bothers you. I was on duty, thought I'd stop in and, you know, say hello."

"Patrolling?" Digger scanned the gravel road, three hundred feet away, and realized how vulnerable they were.

"I, uh, was wondering if your niece might be home."

Digger made a mental note to be more watchful and raised his voice to the open door. "Nikki? Where are you, kiddo? We've got company."

No answer. He called again, louder. "She's here, all right. Probably in the bathroom. Come in, we'll have a look."

Nikki appeared at the door, stepped onto the porch via Digger's right foot. "Sorry, Unc."

Digger winced, but kept the music in his voice. "Why

don't you two have a seat in the porch swing? I'll rustle you up some lemonade."

Bo moved to the swing. Nikki glowered.

Ten feet into the parlor, Digger stopped to listen, but the porch conversation was too muffled to hear. "That's for the incest talk to your mother," he said to the door. "Lemonade? I'm afraid that may take a while."

Ten minutes later, he poured three glasses of lemonade from a waxed carton, set them on a Dollywood souvenir tray, and returned to the porch. "Made some up fresh," he said, and passed out the glasses.

Bo downed his in four quick swallows. "Nothing like fresh lemonade." He stood, brushed the rim of his hat with his forefinger. "See you when you get back, huh?" He walked to the patrol car, tooted the siren with a single *whoop*, and drove away, trailing dust.

Nikki emptied her glass over the porch rail. "I'll get you for this."

"Payback for the incest comment, kiddo. What did Bo want?"

"What do you think? He asked me out."

"And?"

"I agreed to dinner when we got back from Cincy. It was the only way to get rid of him."

"A free dinner. Nothing wrong with that. I'd push for that corn-dog place, the other side of town."

"Old people are slow," she said.

"What's that supposed to mean?"

She crouched, wheeled and jabbed two fast air punches within three inches of his nose before he reacted. "See?"

A half second too late, Digger held up a hand to fend her off. "But we're smart," he said. "Follow me."

He led her to the desk. "The cryptic markings in Edgar's atlas? I guess we agree now that the *S. M.*, the star, and the dollar sign at Golden Leaf represent Smoot Mudd. Smoot said there were six lead plates buried by the French, plus one, the first, stolen by the Indians and sent to England. Total:

seven. There's a blue seven just west of Cincinnati, where Céloron buried the last one, and a red seven at Golden Leaf: the same one, recovered, now owned by Smoot Mudd. You see?"

"So far, but there's lots more numbers."

"But hardly random. Sequential, one through seven in blue, running southwest along the Allegheny and Ohio river valleys. Chautauqua, New York, number one; Warren, Pennsylvania, two; Franklin, Pennsylvania, three; Wheeling, West Virginia, four; Marietta, Ohio, five; Point Pleasant, West Virginia, six; and Cincinnati, Ohio, Smoot's seven. Blue stands for the sites where Céloron buried his plaques.

"We have three numbers in red, which must represent the present location of found plates: a five in Massachusetts, a six at Morehead, Kentucky, and here, at Golden Leaf, Smoot's seven. There's a one in the margin with a question mark—that first plate about to be auctioned. Smoot mentioned museums—I plan to check on our numbers five and six.

"This hatchet at Cincinnati? Smoot's nemesis the Frenchman. Coony said he collected tomahawks—or, maybe Edgar meant it as a danger sign."

He gave Nikki a worried look. "With Smoot Mudd and this Frenchman about to do battle over that first plate, we could be looking at the French and Indian War all over again, kiddo."

Nikki pulled off the Lexington beltway. "Discount department store ahead."

"So?"

"There's a dress code at Biffer's club. I'm sure the Frenchman follows the same rules, clothing-wise. Cincinnati Business Proper."

"Oh, no."

" 'Fraid so. Cincinnati's a pretty place—pretty uptight. They don't call it Little Singapore On The Ohio for nothing.

No loud colors or naughty magazines, no fast music or whistling on Sundays. And proper men like Biffer and the Frenchman dress in town, even on casual Fridays. When in Rome . . ." She held her hand out for Digger's beleaguered credit card. "Time for another makeover."

Back on I-75, forty minutes later, Digger said, "These khaki pants feel stiff."

"Wonder of modern chemistry, Unc. Never wrinkle, won't stain, wash them out in the shower. Jacket, too."

"The cuffs barely cover my ankles."

"High water pants are the style in Cincy. Believe me, you'll fit right in as the poor but making-the-effort professor from out of town."

Digger raised a foot to the dash. "Why do they put tassels on shoes?" He flipped the fringed leather back and forth, and then held out his green, Kentucky Derby winners horsehead tie. "All my life I've mistrusted the suits—now I am one."

"Lovely tie," said mom, an hour and a half later, with a frosty smile for Digger. She led him to a guest room one story up and a long hallway hike from Nikki's bedroom.

The next day, at high noon in the reception lounge of Superplastics, Inc., Digger straightened his horsehead tie and tugged at his buttoned collar.

"You'll be fine," Nikki said, black clutch purse in hand, dressed Jackie Kennedy prim, in a gray knee-length skirt, lace-rimmed blouse, and sensible black, low-heeled shoes. "Look Biffer in the eye, give him a firm handshake, and compliment his art—he'll take it from there. Biffer loves to hear himself talk."

"Well, well, well!" A stocky man, Digger's height, bearing more than a passing resemblance to Teddy Roosevelt down to the brush mustache and wire-rimmed glasses, jogged toward them, hand outstretched. "Biffer Billingsley here! And you're the uncle, nickname of Digger."

Digger squeezed the hand, met Biffer's gaze, said, "Digger it is. Pleasure to meet you at last. Been admiring your artwork. History in oils."

"Bully!" said Biffer, evidently aware of the Teddy Roosevelt resemblance. "Makes your heart race to stand before it, doesn't it?"

Digger looked at wild-eyed Indians chasing a runaway stage coach, the driver pincushioned with arrows, horses galloping for a red-rock chasm. "Makes you wonder if they'll get away with their skins intact."

"Yes, bully! Exactly what it says to me."

"And that one," Digger pointed. "The man shooting the mountain lion going after the wagon train girl's puppy—striking how much he looks like John Wayne."

"Incisive!" said Biffer. "Not everyone catches it. Now, walk back and forth, see how the little girl's eyes follow you."

Digger paced. "Spooky."

Biffer clapped Digger on the back. "My kind of man." He lifted a pocket watch and tapped the face. "Enough art talk. They're holding a table for us."

Ten minutes later, they stepped from a rosewood-paneled elevator into the posh penthouse Pinnacle Club.

A crisp hostess greeted them. "Ah, Mr. Billingsley. We have a table by the window for you and your guests. Fine view of Fountain Square."

Biffer stood at the plate glass, motioning for Digger to join him. "You know, whenever I watch the masses milling like ants on the plaza with their brown bags, I realize those Calvinists were right on the money."

Digger gave him a quizzical look.

"Them down there, me up here. That predestination business, eh? Industry, nose to the grindstone, the big payoff. Right on the money."

"In other words," said Digger, "you folks way up here in the Pinnacle Club are halfway to heaven already."

Biffer clapped him on the back for the second time. "Bully, sir. Bully!"

The waiter bowed slightly at the table, slid chairs out, dropped starched napkins on their laps. "The Dover sole looks excellent today, Mr. Billingsley."

"Sole's fine with me. You two order whatever you wish. Anything."

Digger asked for mahi mahi, settled for the sole. Nikki me-tooed.

"Nikki," Biffer said. He patted the back of her hand. "You can't imagine how pleased I am to hear you're contemplating a career in business. I have one word to say to you. Pay heed."

An inquisitive look from Nikki: "Biffer?"

Digger spoke for him: "Plastics!"

Biffer thumped the tablecloth. "I was about to say MBA." He thumped again. "But 'plastics'? Why, bully for you, sir!"

Digger was on a roll. "And how are they, Biffer? Plastics, I mean. Up, down?"

Biffer flashed him a perfected set of bleached teeth, not as prominent as T. R.'s but brighter, much brighter. "Super, Digger. Simply super. My company, Superplastics, is the leader in illuminated food, lodging, and oil company signs, exterior and interior. It's a Superplastics Supersign that hauls them in off the interstate two times out of five.

"This autumn? Superplastics debuts our DigiVid living billboards. Merely sit there at the side of the highway? Nossir. DigiVids will flash such brilliant, complementary colors, so fast, that drivers traveling at eighty, even ninety miles an hour—not hyperbole, that's by independent testing—won't be able to take their eyes off them. DigiVid'll knock the socks off the competition. Third quarter will put us five more points ahead of the pack or my name's not Biffer Billingsley."

"Amazing," said Digger.

Nikki elbowed him. "Didn't I tell you?"

By the end of the salads, Biffer turned to Nikki and patted her hand again. "Soon as you say good-bye to the bugs and get yourself through a good MBA program, be assured there'll be a place for you at Superplastics. Work your way up from the bottom—shipping, order clerk, installation—the way I did. That's that ticket."

"Whatever you say, Biffer."

Upon arrival of the sole, Nikki popped the big question. "Uh, Biffer. Do you happen to know a man named Alphonse LeCoup?"

"LeCoup?" He held his fork midair, turned from Nikki to Digger and back. "Nikki—how should I put this?—I can't blame you for shopping. But believe me, a career with Superplastics would be difficult to match. Good Lord, I hope you aren't thinking of joining LeCoup."

"Why do you say that, Biffer?"

"Because the man is deadly. Murderous."

Nikki and Digger stopped chewing. Nikki swallowed. "A murderer!"

"Well, he doesn't *kill* them, exactly. Corporate murder is what I meant. Spring Grove Cemetery is full of managers and line workers cut down by Alphonse LeCoup. Plenty of emasculated CEOs put out to pasture by the man as well. Oh, I admire him as a businessman. Eminently successful. Makes millions."

"What, exactly, does he do?" Digger asked.

Biffer set down his silverware, brushed his mustache with his napkin. He mentioned several of the recent deals LeCoup had put together, looking to Digger and Nikki for recognition. When it wasn't forthcoming, he explained. "Alphonse LeCoup is a shark. He moves in on a rotten performer, but with potential. Right-sizes. Puts the remaining salarieds on sixty-, seventy-hour workweeks, moves or threatens to move plants to the sticks or overseas. Whoever's left is grateful for a paycheck, even a thin one. He kills advertising, research, capital investment. Squeeze, squeeze, squeeze. Not a pretty picture, long range—as if anyone thinks long range anymore. But short term? The company's soon well in the black, the analysts take note, the stock soars, and LeCoup walks away with a hefty profit.

"Or, his target could be a cash cow. Shark bait. Woos the shareholders—hostile takeover. CEOs like me live in constant fear of him. Were it not for golden parachutes, it would be hard to face the dawn each morning." Biffer glanced out the window at the still-shining sun for reassurance.

"Or, maybe he spots a poor performer with hidden assets. He snatches it cheap, siphons off the cream he saw there all along, hands out the pink slips, chains the gates, and walks away with a bundle.

"Oh, LeCoup is good all right."

"Eeuuw."

"There, there." Another hand pat. "You're idealistic, dear. Fine trait in someone your age. Great to be concerned with the little people, the whales and the birds—but that's why we have charities and the government dole." Biffer took a sip of water and added, "If you're entering business, remember those two magic words."

"Number One, as in 'Watch out for'?" she asked.

"Well, that, too, of course." Biffer winked. "What I had in mind was Shareholder Value. Keep that stock rising, and you'll protect your haunches from the Terminator."

"The Terminator?"

"Alphonse LeCoup. Take my advice, dear. Particularly with those ideals of yours. Stay clear of Alphonse LeCoup."

Nikki gave her stepfather an innocent smile. "Of course, Biffer. Whatever you say."

"Speak of the devil!" Biffer nearly dropped his cut-crystal water glass.

Nikki and Digger followed his gaze. Sharing a table with a striking, deeply tanned woman in her early thirties wearing a turquoise suit with straight black hair flowing to her waist, sat a thin, perhaps seventy-year-old man with a high forehead and a long, narrow nose with a hawk's crook, the variety connoting nobility in nineteenth-century painted portraits. He was dressed impeccably in a three-piece navy suit, burgundy tie, and French cuffs. Coal-black hair, slicked back and center-parted ran to diplomatic gray at the temples. A Van Dyke beard emphasized an already pointed chin.

"That's Alphonse LeCoup, all right," Biffer said. "Eats here regularly. Could have been cast as the ingenue's father in a Fred Astaire romance, what? But don't be misled. See how none of the other members makes eye contact with him? No one knows who his next target will be."

"Who's the woman?" Digger asked. "A fair number of your members seem to be looking her way."

"I should say so." Biffer sighed. "Raven Buckhunter. Junior partner in Coup de Grace Investments. They say she's a full-blooded Indian. Lord, look at her. Makes Phoebe who works for me look like some sort of barnyard fowl. Rumor has it, this Raven and LeCoup do the—" Biffer glanced at Nikki and blushed furiously. "I'm sorry, honey. I forgot for a moment you were with us. How's that sole?"

"Sole's good. Go on with your boy talk. I want to hear this." She waved her hand. "No, no. It's okay. I promise I won't tell mother. Not a word."

Biffer cleared his throat.

"Cross my heart." She opened her jacket and crisscrossed her starched white blouse. "I'm a big girl. I can keep a secret."

"Well . . ." He leaned over the table and lowered his voice. "They say LeCoup and this Raven take turns tying one another to a big stake set up in his house. You know—like, play Indian games. Light fires under one another, so to speak." He cleared his throat again. "Locker room talk. I'm sorry I brought it up."

Nikki shook her head. "Shameful."

"Indeed," said Biffer Billingsley, eyes down, chasing the last lone flake of sole across his plate with fork and fish knife. "Alphonse LeCoup is not a nice man."

22

ello? Mr. LeCoup?" Nikki waggled the receiver, motioned a thumbs-up at Digger. "This is Biffer Billingsley's stepdaughter."

"Biffer Billingsley? Superplastics." Speaking
with a French accent right out of the movies: *Su-pair-plahs-
teeks.* "Yes, yes. I've had my eye on Biffer and his company
for some while. Working for him are you? Concerned about
your future?"

"Oh, no, sir. Strictly a social call. My uncle—he's from
Hawaii—and I are in Cincinnati for a short while. He's an
archaeologist, and we're both just crazy about North American history. The people at Bishop Museum in Honolulu told
Uncle Harmon if he was ever in this part of the country he
should make a point of seeing your collection, and we were
wondering if there was any chance—"

"Bishop Museum in Honolulu. Really?" LeCoup said it
ray-ah-lee.

"Yes. Uncle Harmon said the curator there told him it
was a match for many a museum collection, and—"

"As a rule, I don't open my collection to strangers. You're

Biffer's stepdaughter? Hawaii, eh? How long are you in town?"

"Not long, I'm afraid. If there're any way—"

"Hmmm. I am leaving the cee-tay tomorrow. You are free this evening? Seven o'clock?"

"We'll make a point of it." She flashed a circled thumb and forefinger A-okay to Digger.

"Biffer lives in Indian Hill, so you are no more than fifteen minutes away. I'm off Teepee Trail on Chief's Circle. It runs behind the country club. White château. Can't miss it."

"Yes, sir. We'll find it."

"Seven. Be on time. Just the two of you. No cameras."

"Boy, oh, boy! Thank you, sir."

Nikki parked behind a silver Peugeot with T R M N A T R license plates. Still in their Cincinnati-respectable clothes, they walked over crushed marble, around a ten-foot-high cast iron fountain gurgling at the center of a round, formal entry garden with a topiary perimeter, toward a looming white château clone.

Nikki straightened Digger's tie and dusted his lapels. "Very presentable." She pressed the doorbell and the first ten notes of "Alouette" chimed inside.

"I'm worried," said Digger. "If this is the man who—"

The door opened.

Le Coup appeared: LeCoup, sans his navy power suit—sans, in fact, much in the way of clothing at all. He wore only beaded moccasins, a buckskin breechclout with fringed flaps over his crotch and rear end, and a red-and-white porcupine quilled and beaded leather vest. Bars, dots, and zigzags of white, yellow and black paint streaked his face and bare chest.

Nikki and Digger took two quick steps back.

"No, no. Please, enter," said LeCoup. "I dress like my ancestors out of respect. I wouldn't consider entering the collection room in, well, like that." He waved disdainful fingers at Digger's blazer, tie, khakis, and tasseled shoes.

Digger wrinkled his nose.

A stiff, black-suited butler appeared at LeCoup's side and asked in Queen's English, "Miss, sir? Beverage?"

"Water's fine," Nikki said. Digger nodded water, too.

The butler left the entry hall through a side door. LeCoup winked. "English butler—the real thing. I call him Jeeves. Love the idea of an Englishman serving me." He turned a flapping posterior to them and walked into a candy box of a room encrusted with gilt, crystal, beveled mirrors, marble, inlaid wood, and gold, gesso-framed oil portraits of dyspeptic men in white wigs. Cherubs frolicked on a domed ceiling.

"Beautiful home," Nikki said to LeCoup's back. She faced Digger, opened her mouth, and mimed gagging.

"The furniture is authentic Louis Quinze—that's Louis the Fifteenth," LeCoup explained over his shoulder. He flipped up the back flap of his breechclout, sat on a curliqued settee, and motioned them to sit across from him in a pair of padded, cream lacquered armchairs. "My ancestors were aristocracy."

"From your dress," said Digger, "I thought—"

"Ah, yes. That, too. I'm part Shawnee and a good bit Huron. My European ancestors came over in the 1600s. Some from the royal line, others more humble—trappers and traders who knew the lay of this land long before there were good maps in Europe. René-Robert Cavelier, sieur de La Salle was one of my forebears." He acknowledged Digger's raised eyebrows. "*Mais, oui.* Genealogically documented. Best known for exploring the Mississippi to the Gulf of Mexico and establishing the French claim to the heartland." He closed his eyes. "Oh, to have been alive then."

The butler brought a silver tray with two bottles of Perrier, a French enamel ice bucket, silver tongs, and two cut crystal goblets. He set it on the table at Nikki's side. "Will that be all, sir?"

"*Oui, ça suffit*, Jeeves." LeCoup turned to Nikki. "You know, young lady, you mentioned your stepfather Biffer Billingsley, but I don't think I caught your names."

"Uh . . ." Reluctant to drop the Fitz bomb prematurely, Nikki glanced at the green bottles on the silver tray. "Perrier," she said. "I'm Nikki Perrier and this is my uncle, Harmon Perrier."

LeCoup's thin, thus far rigid, lips curved into a smile. "French ancestry? *Très bon!* I didn't realize." He stood, bowed from the waist, and kissed the back of Nikki's hand, shook Digger's. "Please, make yourselves com-for-tab-lah."

"*Merci*," said Digger, no slouch on the uptake. "*Vous êtes très gentil.*"

"And you speak *la langue belle? Mon dieu!*"

"French Polynesia," Digger said. "*Je suis archéologue. J'habitais à Papeete pour quatre ans, et je dirigais recherche à Bora Bora, et . . .*"

"*Je regrette*," said LeCoup, scowling, "*Je ne comprends pas entiérement.*" He spoke slowly, enunciating each syllable. *Pourriez vous parler plus lentement, s'il vous plait. Je*—shit! What the hell's that verb?" He snatched at the air. "Sorry, sorry." The accent vanished. "I've been studying at Berlitz for three years," he said in Midwest neutral, "and I still get flustered when someone talks so damned fast."

"Quite all right," Digger assured him, with a side-glance to Nikki. "I said I'm an archaeologist. I lived for a while in Papeete and conducted digs in Bora Bora. That's where I picked it up."

"I know exactly how frustrating that is when Uncle Harmon zips along like that," Nikki said. "My own French is terrible. If you both spoke English, it would be easier on me."

"*Pour la mademoiselle*," said LeCoup, relieved, with another bow. "We will speak English for the young woman." Miraculously, as swiftly as it had departed, his accent returned.

"Please, my guests, take your drinks. It's the collection you want to see, not this fusty European claptrap." He padded into the entryway and back a long, crystal chandelier-lit corridor to a stainless-steel door with a combination lock at the center.

LeCoup spoke as he worked the dial. "This is my real heritage. It is the French trappers and Indians whose blood flows strongest in me, Alphonse Henri Pouncing Eagle Le-Coup."

"Excuse me, sir," said Jeeves from their backs. "But what shall I do with the rattlesnakes?"

"*Rattlesnakes*? You keep herps, Mr. LeCoup?"

Here we go again, thought Digger. The butler fries them up for breakfast.

"Herps?" said LeCoup. "Sorry, I don't understand." To Jeeves: "Let the Rangers dispose of them."

Digger repeated the word, "Rangers?" thinking, This one has a militia, too?

Jeeves clarified: "Indian Hill Rangers. The police. Very efficient. They'll shoot them, I suspect."

"No!" from Nikki. "Let me see them. *Please*."

LeCoup cocked his head. "Why not? Everyone enjoys a spectacle, eh?" He fluttered his fingers at Jeeves to lead the way.

They followed him to a restaurant-size kitchen, replete with copper pots and pans hanging over banks of Viking ranges and Sub Zero refrigerators. Nikki chattered along the way. "They must have escaped from a collector. . . ."

"My niece's hobby," Digger explained.

Jeeves pointed to a Rubbermaid garbage can. Nikki lifted the lid.

Digger hung back a safe fifteen feet.

"Careful, miss," said Jeeves. "I dropped the open box in there, so they're loose. Two large ones."

"Holy moly! Somebody Scotch-taped their tails."

"So we couldn't hear them rattle before we opened the box," LeCoup said. "*Diabolique*. Left it gift-wrapped on the doorstep and rang the bell. Fortunately, Jeeves here has quick reflexes. Got the lid closed before they bit him. Someone's sick idea of a joke."

Nikki looked over her shoulder at Digger, reading his mind. "Someone. I'll bet they're from Kentucky."

"Kentucky?" LeCoup said, alarmed. "Why would you say Kentucky?"

She recovered fast. "Rattlesnakes aren't found in Cincy, but they're common down there."

"Yes, Kentucky," LeCoup agreed. "A wicked state. Snakes, incest, cockfighting, an economy based on alcohol, tobacco, and marijuana."

"Wait." Nikki leaned into the can. "These are canebrake variants, not the northern timber pattern. Same species, but—the orange-red stripe, the gray-pink ground color? No, these animals are a different geographic variant. They're from the deep south, not Kentucky."

LeCoup and Jeeves exchanged looks. "I suspect you are wrong there," said LeCoup. "Not that it matters. Deadly enough either way. You wanted to see the collection? Leave the snakes to the Rangers."

"No," she said. "I know the curator at the zoo. Uncle Harmon and I will take them. Please?"

LeCoup shrugged. "Suit yourself. But," offended, "I thought you had an interest in antiquities."

"*Certainement*," Digger said. "Nikki can pick up the snakes when we leave. *S'il vous plait, monsieur*, do show us this marvelous collection that awes even Bishop Museum in Honolulu."

23

eCoup swung open a heavy steel door to what appeared to be the inside of a dimly lit round barn, every bit as large as Smoot Mudd's collection room, the walls covered with cedar shakes and animal hides. Instead of Smoot's fireplace, however, at the center, a boulder-rimmed campfire burned on a low clay mound. Smoke curled to a conical, log-rimmed roof, and out a hole at the top.

Digger bumped Nikki with an elbow, nodded past the campfire at an eight-foot vertical stake, a tree trunk stripped of bark with truncated branches, rising from the floor with leather wrist restraints bolted to either side, waist-high.

Nikki whispered, "Ooo-lah-lah."

LeCoup walked to the campfire and sat cross-legged. "Please. Join me for a smoke. Kinnikinnick: Indian tobacco." He lifted a long, brass-studded pipe made of red stone and wood, with a carved animal for the bowl. He poked the glowing end of a stick from the fire into an aperture at the animal's back and puffed until swirling clouds of blue smoke rose toward the roof hole.

Nikki and Digger sat across from him.

"Cool pipe," Nikki said. "The bowl's shaped like a pig, huh?"

LeCoup cleared his throat. "Uh, no, Mademoiselle Perrier. It is a beaver, symbol of the fur trade that initially brought wealth to my people and later led to so much misery. Made of catlinite. The inlaid stem is very old, although I carved the beaver myself."

He set the pipe on a flat rock.

"The beaver bowl is beautiful," Digger said, with a *Real cute* look for Nikki.

"I excel at whatever I do," LeCoup responded, matter-of-factly. He passed the pipe to Digger, who inhaled—and doubled over hacking.

"Takes some getting used to," said their host. "Just puff."

Still wheezing, Digger passed the pipe to Nikki, who puffed tentatively, and stifled a cough by holding her breath.

"My specialty . . ." LeCoup ignored Nikki's watering eyes and red face, "is Native American weapons and attire." He took the pipe from Nikki, placed it on a rock, and waved a hand around the room.

Their shadows, cast by the flickering campfire, danced on the dim walls. Nikki squinted to see.

"Sorry," LeCoup said. "Much as I like the fire-lit atmosphere, you'll need more light for this." He clapped his hands hard, and spotlights mounted on the ceiling threw brilliant beams on tomahawks, knifes, rifles, buckskin bags, rattles, beaded vests, leggings, and moccasins. "Now you see it," he said with a smile. Another clap, and the lights went out. "Now you don't. I love it! An engineering marvel, eh?"

Another clap and the lights came on again. He stood, motioned the Perriers up, and walked around the now-bright walls. "Wooden masks up there with the big eye holes? Cherokee booger masks. The twisted one? Iroquois false face mask. Over there—a buffalo robe. These Plains shields? Kiowa, Mandan, Crow, Cheyenne. Cost a pretty penny. That's an original Lakota eagle feather headdress, by the way. Not a word to anyone that I own it, please—eagle feathers are a no-no. All across there, the bags with the floral designs? Great Lakes cultures."

He stopped at the weapons. "Flintlock muskets and rifles. I collect only those I can trace to Indians or the North American French, which makes these rare. Tomahawks are up there."

They saw dozens, in brass, steel, and nickel-plate, with studded and inlaid wooden hafts, hatchet-faced on one side, often with wicked spikes, or sometimes pipe bowls, on the other. Ball-ended, skull-bashing, studded war clubs hung among them.

"The metal," LeCoup explained, "was cast in New France—Canada—or Europe as trade goods. The tomahawk was used not only by the Indians, but also by their oppressors, the British colonists and early Americans. A brave with a tomahawk in one hand, flintlock rifle in the other, and a scalping knife at his waist was a formidable enemy, believe me. One whack in the head, and it's good-bye Kentuckian, or Virginian, or whatever paleface is on the receiving end."

"Eeuuw."

"Yes, brutal. But those were brutal times, the 1700s. Interlopers stealing the natives' land. Today, I do my part to right the wrongs of the past."

Digger asked: "You support a foundation?"

LeCoup ignored him, asked back, "You know your history? How the French traders befriended and supplied the Indians in the mid-1700s and helped them defend their homelands against the invading British colonists pouring over the Alleghenies? And later, when the French were driven back by the British in the French and Indian Wars, how the valiant native peoples fought on?"

LeCoup rubbed his hands together with excitement, and then frowned. "The colonial women had a dozen or more offspring. Bang-bang, knock-'em-up with whatever male relation was handy, pop out another baby, bang-bang again, and so on. Benjamin Franklin, for instance, was one of seventeen siblings. It's no wonder the colonials streamed out of the east like lemmings. You've heard the name Boone?" His lip curled into a sneer. "Bred like rabbits. The land south of here teemed with that incestuous frontier rabble. You see, the palefaces failed to live with nature like my native ancestors. Killed everything in their gun sights. Bison exterminated, along with most of the indigenes. Americans have always been into blind conquest.

"Back to history—the Americans moved from the headwaters of the Ohio into the Indians' Kentucky hunting grounds, and then into the Ohio country, off-limits to the whites, according to the very treaties the whites drafted. But you know all about the broken treaties, I am sure."

Agitated, he plucked a tomahawk from the wall and began to finger the blade. "Treaties? Hah! My people fought back. Raided, took hostages, scalps. Defeated two American armies before that bastard Mad Anthony Wayne overwhelmed them. Fought on farther and farther west, but fate and numbers were against them."

He waved the tomahawk through the air. "I, Alphonse Henri Pouncing Eagle LeCoup, keep up the good fight today." Without warning, he puffed his chest, leaned back and whooped at the ceiling, a blood-chilling war cry. "*Heeeow!*"

Nikki and Digger hunkered, squinted through the smoky room at the door.

"No, no, my friends, not to worry. You Perriers have good French blood flowing through your veins. It's the *Americans* I fight. I settle old scores."

Nikki squeezed Digger's arm.

"*How*, you ask?" Wildfire burned in his eyes. He shouted the answer: "*Mergers and acquisitions!*"

He whooped again. "I, LeCoup, beat them at their own game. I take their companies by the balls and squeeze"—he raised his left palm and wrenched his fingers into a fist—"then give their sorry asses the hatchet!" The tomahawk sliced the air. "Do you have any idea how many of them are on the streets because of me?"

"I can't imagine," Nikki said, edging away.

"This last year alone . . ." LeCoup's voice rose to a shout, "five thousand, seven hundred and sixty-one! There's no more than a handful of profit-conscious CEOs in the tri-state who can count half that many to their credit."

"After lunch, yesterday," Nikki said in a small voice, her eye on the hatchet, "Biffer told us about that HMO deal you put together."

"His eyes green with envy, no doubt," LeCoup made chop-chop motions with the tomahawk, "because it was masterful in every way. I cut the payroll by twenty-two percent. V-Ps?—slashed—then managers, and down the line. Cut the promotional budget—less competition, why waste your money advertising, eh? Kept a bigger slice of the premium dollar, denied even more claims, sliced thirty percent of the member physicians and reduced the remaining capitation allowances by fifteen percent." He wheeled toward the Perriers. "You see the beauty in that? Set the doctors and patients against one another! Deflect their antagonism.

"Strictly out of meanness, you think?" He winked. "Well, a little, to be sure, but highly profitable."

He looked at an angering Nikki. "Ah. From your expression, I see you are thinking Yes, but won't there be whining for health care reform, necessitating costly PACs to assure the loyalty of our friends the legislators? And you are right. But should the politicos forget for a moment which side their bread is buttered on?" He smiled wickedly. "I merely mention those dreaded letters: S and M."

"S and M?" Nikki said. "Sadomasochism? Like, you blackmail them, huh?"

LeCoup chuckled, "Seldom necessary, Mademoiselle Perrier. What I meant was: Socialized Medicine! Slaps them back to reality fast. Next thing you know they're sending me Congressional commendations for my entrepreneurial spirit.

"*Spirit!*" With a scream, he turned and threw the tomahawk at the stake. The weapon tumbled end over end to land blade first, head-high, with a loud *Thunk!*

LeCoup yelled at the top of his lungs, *"Heeah!"* and clapped his hands.

The lights went out.

Nikki screamed.

LeCoup clapped again, the room lit. *"Excusez-moi,"* he said softly, with a bow. "I tend to get carried away. Come, I'll show you more."

He walked past exhibition cases like Smoot Mudd's, here and there pointed to an artifact, urging them toward a tall cherry armoire. "Something I know you two will enjoy." He opened twin doors.

"Wigs," Nikki said, of the twenty or so hairpieces of varying shades and colors, hanging from pegs inside.

Digger remembered lunch with Biffer, and smiled with the thought of Indian games. He tried to imagine LeCoup's partner, Raven, disguised in one of the pale blond wigs, wearing one of the beaded buckskin dresses hanging on the wall.

He frowned with a disturbing thought: LeCoup had said Something you *two* will enjoy . . . Surely the man wasn't suggesting he and Nikki join him at the stake in a frontier *ménage à trois?*

Then his lip curled, and he pulled Nikki away by the wrist.

"What is it, Unc?"

"Aha," said LeCoup. "Our archaeologist recognizes my artifacts! *N'es-ce pas?*"

Digger whispered it to Nikki: "Scalps."

"Eeuuw!"

"Difficult to find," said LeCoup, "with moths and sensibilities what they are." He lifted a reddish gray hank from its hook. "Skin stretched over a hoop, see? The way it worked was—a quick circular slash with a scalping knife, a firm tug, shake the blood off, and voilà!"

"Oh, yuck!"

"By no means fatal in itself," LeCoup said. "If you weren't dead already, you may have lived to enthrall your grandchildren with the experience. And, while these, as you can see, are from palefaces, the whites took Indian scalps just as readily."

"Perhaps we should look elsewhere," Digger said. He moved to one of the cases, tugging Nikki—still staring at the hair in LeCoup's hands.

"Whoa. What's this?" Digger bent over a case.

Smiling at the effect of his trophies on his visitors, LeCoup replaced the scalp, closed the armoire doors, and walked to the case. He peered through the glass, under Digger's pointing finger. "That? Nothing really. A lead plaque. Base metal."

Digger read, *"l'an 1749 du règne de Louis XV Roi de France, nous Céloron, commandant d'un . . ."*

Nikki looked at Digger, wide-eyed.

" . . . a l'entree de la Rivière Chinodahichetha le 18 août, près de la Rivière Oyo . . ." He cocked his head at LeCoup. "That's the explorer Céloron, his expedition down the Ohio?"

"Yes, yes," said LeCoup, frowning. "It's only a copy, one of my few replicas. But, since Céloron's journey was of such significance to French claims in the New World—well, I keep it as a reminder. Some day, perhaps, I shall own an original."

Nikki tapped Digger's ankle with her foot. He tapped back.

LeCoup glanced at the watch on his bare wrist. "I fear it is growing late."

"Yes," Digger said. "We should be on our way. You've been very kind to show us your marvelous collection."

"My pleasure, entirely," LeCoup said, with an aristocratic bow. He led them out of the wilderness collection room into rococo splendor.

Nikki clutched the box of repackaged rattlesnakes and paused at the front door. "Mr. LeCoup, we heard about another collection. It's out of our way, but it's been highly recommended. Perhaps you could tell us if it's worth a side trip."

"Rowe here in town? Ross in Indianapolis?"

"No. Kentucky. A town called Golden Leaf, I think."

"Smoot Mudd!" LeCoup spit out the name like cheap wine.

"Yes, that's it. Do you know him? His collection?"

"A hillbilly. Half of what he owns is fake. Definitely not worth your while—and I warned you about Kentucky. How did you hear about Mudd?"

"I knew a man who was working for him," Digger said. "Edgar Fitz."

The Perriers studied LeCoup's face.

"I heard it on the news," Le Coup said, unflustered. "Murdered. Awful. Although . . ."

"Yes?" Digger raised his eyebrows.

"If this Fitz was working for Smoot Mudd, I'd venture a guess it wasn't satanic fishermen drug dealers that did him in like they say, but Mudd himself."

"Why would you say that?"

"Terrible reputation. Predisposed to violence. Genetic, you see. The man's a demented, inbred dwarf. Jealous. Mudd threatened me on more than one occasion.

"He supports one of those revolutionary mountain militias. If your man argued, fell out of grace with Mudd over money—Mudd is tight as wallpaper—or made disparaging remarks about Mudd's illiteracy or size—he's small as a shrew—or, insulted his storm troopers—*merde*, it could have been anything. No, my friends. It wouldn't surprise me one bit if Mudd or his henchmen killed the poor man."

LeCoup shook a long finger at them. "Here's some good advice. Stay north of the Ohio River. Stay clear of Smoot Mudd."

"*Mais, oui*, Monsieur LeCoup," Nikki said. "Whatever you say."

When they left, LeCoup dialed a string of numbers. "See here," he said to the woman who answered. "That madman

Mudd just tried to kill me. Put a box of *rattlesnakes* on my doorstep. Delivered, no doubt, by that barbarian flunky of his. If you think I'm going to Golden Leaf, Kentucky, for this auction, you're—"

"Alphonse, honey, keep your moccasins on. I understand how you feel, I do. We know how dangerous Smoot Mudd can be, and I sure don't want anything happening to *you*. But I promised Mudd I'd auction the item in Golden Leaf, and I'm a woman of my word. Poor old fella probably wouldn't survive a trip to Cincinnati."

"I'd pay his bus fare if I thought that was true."

"I should tell you, Mudd doubled his last offer to me if I'd sell the Lords of Trade plate to him outright. But I told *him*, I had promised *you* an opportunity to bid, so you see, I'm being fair to both of you. But unless you want to bow out . . ."

"*Merde*, woman. This is a matter of honor." He blew a burst of air against the mouthpiece in frustration. "Something else . . . two people, the Perriers, came by—good people, French ancestry, but they noticed the Jacob Cuppy plate, showed knowledge of Céloron, *and*, they wanted to visit Mudd. If he finds out . . ."

"Describe them."

He did.

"I'll take care of business down here—you watch your back."

24

$\int$ urrounded by ceiling-high bookshelves of virgin, leather-bound classics in Biffer's walnut-lined study, Digger crouched over a heavy Victorian library table, sorting through the notes he'd made that afternoon at the Cincinnati Museum Center.

Nikki raced in with a diet soda in one hand, a Cincinnati Zoo brochure in the other. "Success with the rattlesnakes. The curator's a neat guy, said he'd work them into a new exhibit—if they survive. Get this: Smoot or Bolt cut their fangs off! They can grow new ones, but if they're too traumatized, they could die.

"Not that Smoot cares about that—but he doesn't know much about snakes, because if LeCoup or his butler had been bit, there would still be a good chance of envenomation from teeth or the fang remnants."

Digger rubbed his bare arms and shuddered. "Smoot may know more than you give him credit for. He may not have wanted to murder LeCoup, but losing a finger? Seeing his butler writhing in pain?"

"Hmmm . . . could be. Here's something else. Remember how I said the rattlesnakes looked like deep southern animals? The curator and I did scale counts, and those said south, too. I was right on. Smoot must have imported them from Georgia or Alabama to divert suspicion."

Digger worried his beard, considering. "I'm not sure that adds up. What's the likelihood Smoot Mudd knows anything about snake morphology? Or LeCoup? I think Smoot would *want* LeCoup to think they were from Kentucky."

"You're right. It doesn't make sense, does it?"

"While you were at the zoo giving the slinkies oral exams, I was reading. Here's a twist." He tapped an age-worn buckram-bound book. "These are the journals of Christopher Gist, a frontiersman and associate of George Washington in the Ohio country. Remember Smoot telling us how the governor of the New York colony told the Indians who recovered Céloron's first plate that the French inscription meant France was stealing their land? Well, turnabout's fair play—seems there was a respected half–French Canadian, half-Indian woman, a Madame Montour, who listened to a Moravian Bishop preach in the colonies about Jesus. She told him she had been raised around French Jesuits who had a different version: Christ, they had explained to the Indians, was French, and had been crucified by Englishmen!"

"Ha! Eighteenth-century spin doctors."

"Thought you'd get a chuckle out of that. I also checked on Mr. Céloron. Look here." He spread notes, photocopies and maps across the mahogany table. "Both Céloron and his Jesuit navigator, a Father Bonnecamps, kept journals.

"LeCoup's replica was dated the thirty-first of August, 1749, which means the original is what historians call the Jacob Cuppy plate. Cuppy lived in the 1760s in today's West Virginia near the confluence of the Kenawa River with the Ohio. Cuppy must have found it eroded out of the riverbank, here," he pointed to Bonnecamps' surprisingly accurate map, "and kept it as a curiosity. Later, he floated on a flatboat down the Ohio with his wife, her brother, and nine children, and made his way up the Licking River deep into Kentucky, where he put down roots.

"Three generations later, a great grandson rifled through an old chest of Cuppy's and discovered his lead souvenir. It's now in the Folk Museum of Eastern Kentucky, in Morehead."

"The first plate to reach a museum is in Massachusetts. Kids found that one in 1798 near Marietta, Ohio, at the mouth of the Muskingum River—melted a good bit of it down for bullets. Add Smoot's and the Lords of Trade plates, you have four found, three still in the ground."

Nikki traced a finger across Bonnecamps' map of the Ohio Valley. "So?"

"They must bear on Edgar's murder—the lead sinkers, Edgar's underlining that lead article, Smoot's and LeCoup's rivalry, this auction. I'm thinking I'd like to take a leisurely look at one close-up. The Cuppy plate in Morehead is mere counties away from Golden Leaf. We have our Kentucky clothes. What say we drive to Morehead tomorrow? We'll be back in Golden Leaf by evening."

"You bet. That'll get me home late enough to blow off dinner with Bo."

"No—do the dinner. We'll make it back by five. Consider it part of our investigation. I'll see if Coony can get out. We'll each learn what we can about their investigation, whether I'm still really a suspect."

" 'Do the dinner, Nikki, find out whether I'm a suspect'— that's all you really care about, isn't it?"

She hopped off the table, fumed for ten seconds over Digger's protests, and then, resigned, changed the subject. "What did you think of LeCoup's stake? I'd say Biffer had it nailed. Hot times around the old campfire for fair maiden Raven and Chief Alphonse."

"I wonder if they applaud good performances?"

"Ha!" She clapped. "Let there be light!"

Digger frowned. "We laugh, but what if LeCoup murdered Edgar? Or had him murdered? Edgar was an 'American' after all—not like us Perriers—and he worked for Smoot—who owns an original Céloron plate.

"Although," he ran a hand through his long hair, "much of what LeCoup said about Smoot Mudd makes sense, too. His paranoia, disposition, that militia. And remember? When we mentioned Edgar's name, LeCoup didn't so much as blink. If he killed Edgar, he's a good actor."

"He does megamillion-buck deals—you think he doesn't have a poker face?"

"Yes, could be. There's Coony's biker scenario, too. And Bolt."

"All freaks. Tomahawks, swords, guns, scalps. Scalps! Yuck."

"Damned redskin frog. Get me my tobacco papers, Bolt."

Bolt carried a large cardboard box from the closet, placed the contents, a series of files and binders on Smoot's desk, many red-stamped CONFIDENTIAL, or SECURITY BAND THREE AND ABOVE, or READ AND DESTROY.

Smoot rooted through a SHRED AFTER READING file. "Never throw anything out, Bolt. You never know when it can come in handy." He set it down, retrieved another, a report with a BAND TWO AND ABOVE warning over the title, PROPOSED FIELD TEST OF EX2571. "This is the baby I remember," he said, flipping to the inside page bearing a subtitle REMORAS: EXPERIMENTAL ENHANCED TAR AND NICOTINE CIGARETTES. He pointed to a name and telephone number. "Get me this man on the line, boy."

While Bolt dialed, Smoot searched for another folder, this one with a mild PROPRIETARY DATA warning and the full title in plain text on the cover: GLOBALSMOKE TEST MARKETS, EASTERN NORTH AMERICA. Inside were a series of maps with checkerboard cross-hatching, polka dots, and shading.

Bolt held the receiver out, indicated he had the intended party on the line.

"Ziakowski?" Smoot tapped the speaker switch so Bolt could hear.

"Yes? You're calling from outside the company, who is this?"

"Smoot Mudd. Globalsmoke Board of Directors."

Pause. "Board of Directors? You want Milton Ziakowski?"

"You're my boy, all right. Lab X-23, New Product Development."

"I don't understand."

"Nice work on the Remoras, son."

"Thank you, sir. But . . . that's a classified project. May I have your current authorization code?"

Smoot frowned, read from the card Bolt held before him. Another pause, evidently looking it up, and then a perplexed, "Yes, sir, Mr. Mudd. What may I do for you?"

"I'm looking at this request you made to test market your Remoras. Looks like it didn't go no place."

"No, sir." Heavy with disappointment. "I had high hopes, put two years of my life into those sweethearts. Even thought up the ad slogan myself: 'Remoras—they'll never leave your side.' Unfortunately, we had a problem with the animal testing. Hyperaccelerated mortality."

"Hell, boy, everything dies."

"Yes, sir, my point exactly. Uh, sir, are you on a secure line?"

"Hell, yes," Smoot lied. He had no time for another man's paranoia.

"Our test animals," pause, "went belly-up pretty fast. But they sure loved those Remoras. Preferred them over food, water, even sex. I've been giving them to my lab assistant, and, believe me, there isn't a thing she won't do for . . . but that's hardly scientific. I wanted broader human testing, get the actuary folks involved. The company, though, turned me down, said diminished longevity would offset assured brand loyalty. Fewer NSYs—net smoker years, see? But how can you really know until you get the product out there? Give *people* a shot at it?"

"Good point, Ziakowski. I'm impressed, and I think your stuff's worth a real trial. I gather you pick a test market, mislabel your product as a regular brand, pull the real thing off the shelves, give it a few years, and see how performance stacks up with the straight brand somewheres else?"

"Exactly, sir. Run matched demographic controls with statistical analysis of comparative mortality. Now, if we had people dropping like the animals right out in the open, or people didn't stick with the Remoras—not a snowball's chance of that, let me assure you—then I'd be the first to admit it's back to the drawing board. But, like I say, how do you know until you field-test?"

"I'm with you, boy. I'm looking at two markets in Globalsmoke publication TM-01-2: NC-24, and SE-17."

"Give me a moment, sir." He set the phone down. Smoot heard footsteps, papers rustling, and then, "City of Quebec and the Cherokee Indian Reservation, North Carolina. Yes, sir."

"Those big enough for your trials?"

"Nice size, contrasting demographics. Oh, yes, sir."

"Go to it, boy. Choose your own controls. No futzin' around, I want those Remoras on the shelves ASAP, sweet-faced girlies passing out the free samples. Anyone gives you a hard time, you tell them I authorized it. You got my name?"

"Yes, *sir*, Mr. Mudd. If I may say so, I never realized people at the top followed our work. Makes me proud to be part of the Globalsmoke team. Truly proud, sir."

Jesus Bob was field testing his third modified fast-draw holster, drawing his .357 Magnum and shooting at unsuspecting doves foolish enough to fly his way. He had yet to see a satisfying, confirming confetti of silvery feathers, but that barely diminished the challenge.

Coo-oo. Slap. Draw. *Blam!* "Damn!" Another miss.

Big Butt watched from fifty feet away, shielded from the

action by a massive oak. "Hey, Jesus Bob!" he yelled, and ducked behind the trunk.

"Who the hell is it?"

"It's me. B. G. Butz. Okay if I come over?"

"Hell, yes, pardner. What's up?" Jesus Bob sheathed the Magnum.

"I use a .22 rifle with shot to pop doves," Big Butt said. "They say there's a little scoop a meat in 'em too, if you're into cleaning and cooking, though that seems like too much fuss to me. I say if God put doves on this earth for eating and not plinking, he'd of made 'em fat as turkeys."

"You keep your girlie rifle. If I hit them with this, there's fireworks in the sky. Know what I mean?" Jesus Bob fluttered his fingers.

"I guess." Tempted to stare at the bruisy-blue letters on Jesus Bob's knuckles, Big Butt kicked at the earth. "You said there was a chance your sister had an 'assignment,' you know . . ."

"A chance to carve that first notch, huh? Rita Rae's hinting around at it, and when it comes, you'll be by my side, pardner, don't you worry. Come out with some gold stars as souvenirs, if you know what I mean." Jesus Bob's hand went to his chest, fingering an imaginary badge.

Big Butt grinned at his new friend, found his eyes slipping inadvertently, dangerously, to Jesus Bob's hand at his chest and those blurry knuckle tattoos. Whenever curious eyes fell to those fists, Jesus Bob hid his hands and flashed back a deadly warning stare.

"Checking out my tatts, huh?"

"No, no, was only—"

Jesus Bob held both hands out, fingers spread. "Go ahead, get a good look. We're pardners, right?"

Big Butt made out L I F E S A B I T H. He scowled a *Huh*?

"I'll tell you once, cause we survived the abduction together. But you don't repeat it, or it's back to me being a pardner of one. Unnerstood?"

Big Butt nodded.

"Had this cellie, Rudie, a wonnerful artist, pudgy little pink fella with curly blond hair, looked like one of them kids' dolls. Rudie was—whoa, I know what you're thinking, and don't take that road no farther, pardner,'cause it weren't like that at all."

"Like what?"

"*Nevermind*. Point is, getting your knuck tatts is a once in a lifetime thing, like your first piece of ass, or your first kill." He jabbed Big Butt in the shoulder. "But you wouldn't know about that, huh? Anyways, I wasn't gonna screw up and do it myself like so many of those shitheads do, so I ask Rudie to do it. I tell him what I want. He says 'What an honor.' I ain't much of a speller, but Rudie wore these specs thick as the bottoms of bar glasses, so you know he was smart, huh?"

Jesus Bob chewed his lip, arriving at the sore point of his story. "The problem was, Wudie talked wike thith, thee?

"So my tatts come out *like this, see?*" He shook an angry A B I T H fist six inches from Big Butt's nose. "Either nobody else spelled good enough to know better, or if they did they didn't have the guts to say nothing. Wasn't till I got out I learned he fucked it up, or I'da twisted the little pussy's head off.

"The day after they spring me, I go to my favorite bar in Corpus, say a Hello-how-do-you-do to my old buddies and buy a round of drinks. I go to pay, and the goddamned bartender says real loud, so every one of them bastards hears, 'Hey bud, what's a bith?' 'What the hell you mean, a bith?' I says, looking at my knucks—It's bitch, asshole.' Then he spells *bitch* for me, and the whole goddamn bar laughs their asses off. At me! So I parted the bastard's hair with a beer bottle and got the hell out of that place. But ever since, if anyone looks cross-eyed at my—"

Big Butt backed up, palms waving the air. "Easy, friend, I would of never asked."

"Yeah, well now you don't got to, so keep your trap shut if we're to stay pards and you want your big wish granted."

25

Welcome to the Folk Museum of Eastern Kentucky." A plump woman in a blue gingham dress and matching bonnet greeted Nikki and Digger, smiling, smiling, smiling. "Free admission today, folks. Plenty to see and do. There's a tour of Daniel Boone's cabin in five minutes, and a broom-making demonstration in fifteen—"

"The Jacob Cuppy Plate," Digger said. "We heard it's on exhibition."

"Hmmm. Yes. Although I fear you'll find it disappointing. If I may suggest something more exciting—do you enjoy clogging?"

"Love to clog," said Digger, "but it's not what we had in mind today."

"Very well, if your heart's set, I'll show you. The case is easy to miss." She led them past frontier ceramics, whirligigs, weathervanes, butter churns. "Here we are. Don't say I didn't warn you."

She was right. It didn't look like much: lusterless gray, the size of a sheet of typing paper, thinner than a magazine, with an incised inscription, sitting on flyspecked blue velvet, under a two-by-two-foot Plexiglas box.

Digger read, "*L'an 1749 du règne de Louis XV roi de . . .*"

"My, you speak like a regular foreigner," said the woman in the sunbonnet. "We don't often hear French spoken here. Let me guess. You're a teacher?"

"Archaeologist."

"Ah. Then you know how the French expedition claimed this land for France, leading eventually to the French and Indian War. Oh, yes—I know the story. When things are slow in the gift shop, I wander around, read labels. Let me see, the name of the expedition leader was . . ." She bent to read the label.

"Céloron," said Nikki.

"And you're this gentleman's student, I'll bet. So many people come through this museum, go right to the action exhibits like the broom-making. It's the museum's fault this poor thing is ignored. It's dull as dirt—made of lead, you know. They were supposed to erect an interpretive panel with a map and buttons you'd push with colored lights to mark the route of the French expedition, but after the theft, I guess they put the money into alarms. There was some embarrassment over the robbery, and—"

Digger interrupted. "Robbery?"

"Broke in last year, ran off with everything in this room. They think it was college kids. Had a happy ending, though. They must have been afraid to sell their loot, so they sent a ransom note. The insurance company made a deal, and here it is. We got a new security system, and haven't had a lick of trouble since. They check for sounds or movement—see that little speaker up there?" She nodded at it with her head. "There are cameras, too, where you'd least expect. See that ventilation grate?"

"Mrs. McKinney!" A tall, balding, frowning stick-insect of a man in his fifties, with gray, plastic-rim glasses, in a loose suit and tie twenty years out of style walked to her side. "You're needed in the gift shop."

"Yes, sir." She hurried off, with an, "Enjoy your visit," over her shoulder.

"Fouts," said the man. "Clarence Fouts, director. McKinney knows better than to talk about security. I don't know what else she told you."

"About the theft," Digger said.

Fouts raised an eyebrow.

"And the ransom," said Nikki.

"Ransom? McKinney's a part-timer. Got her wires crossed. We did have a break-in, fraternity prank. Certainly no *ransom*. Kids wrapped up some things in those quilts, and ran off while the guard was on rounds upstairs. Easy pickings, I'm sorry to say, before we installed the new alarms. Then the fear of expulsion from school or a stint in the slammer got to our young thieves. We got it all back within a week." He shook his head, managed a thin smile. "You're enjoying our museum? You've seen the Daniel Boone cabin? Real logs, not an inch of plastic."

"Impressive," Digger said. "But I'm interested in the French explorer Céloron, and his lead plate. I wonder if there's a chance of examining it out of the case? I'm an archaeologist from Hawaii, Harmon Fitz." He fished a card from his wallet. "This is my niece, Nikki Fitz, grad student, University of Michigan."

Fouts removed his glasses and studied the card six inches from his nose. He replaced his glasses, and nodded to Nikki. "You're far afield. Won't find any hula-hula here, but we do have clogging every day on the even hour." He chuckled, a brittle, high-pitched, "Hee, hee, hee."

"No hula-hula, but clogging. Get it, Unc?" Nikki elbowed Digger in the ribs.

Digger smiled politely for Fouts.

The director cleared his throat. "Ahum, yes. We're honored to have you visit. Do sign the register." He frowned. "But examine the Jacob Cuppy plate? No, I'm sorry. There would be paperwork. Our preparator is the only one authorized to open a case, and he comes by infrequently. I'm sure you understand, being an academic?"

"Yes, of course." Digger pursed his lips. "I should have written. It's circumstantial that we're in Kentucky. Ohio Valley history interests me, though, and I had hoped, as an archaeologist, there might be a possibility . . ."

"Wouldn't see any more up close," said Fouts. "Only the name of the man who cast it on the back. It's lead. The French may have lost most of this continent, but they weren't stupid. They chose lead markers for the metal's durability."

"Not too much chalky stuff on it," Nikki said, with Smoot's plate in mind. "Do you polish it?"

Fouts scowled at her. "Certainly not! The fools who found it burnished away the patina—lead oxide and carbonate, formed from contact with groundwater. It had been buried for nearly a hundred years when Cuppy dug it up."

"Are copies for sale in the gift shop?" Nikki asked. "I'd love to take one home as a gift for my mother."

Digger kept a straight face.

"Copies? No, no, young woman. A humble artifact like this means nothing to your average museum-goer. Most of them have minuscule attention spans, spend their time glued to the TV. Seven seconds is about the most a static historic exhibit can expect to hold them. Now, the showy stuff? Quilts? Whirligigs? Toys like the Breckenridge County rocking horse? Our viewers take to those, spend up to twelve seconds with them. Those, we reproduce. Half the little boys in town chase their sisters with our miniature tomahawks. Big sellers. But replicas of base metal with inscriptions no one can read?"

Digger cocked his head. "So, the Cuppy Plate has never been reproduced?"

"What did I say? Absolutely not." Fouts scowled. His thin lips curled into a sliver of a smile. "Perhaps I could provide a photo of it if you wish, for a nominal charge." He glanced again at Digger's card and waved the air with it. "Forget the charge. It was featured in an old newsletter. If I can find a copy I'll send it to you, compliments of the Folk Museum of Eastern Kentucky. May take two or three weeks, but I'll see to it."

"How generous." Digger ran a finger over the locked case. "Tell you what—you look like a man of the world . . ." He cut a swift side-glance to Nikki. "I'll reciprocate with a reprint of one of my papers: 'Men are from Mangareva, Women are from Vanuatu: gender differentiated sexual manipulation among onanastic Tuamotuans.' May give you ideas for one of your action exhibits."

"Mmm, yes, I'm sure," Fouts said in monotone while studying his watch. "I guess that about covers it, then." He shook Digger's hand, a stiff jerk up and down. "I'm nearly late for an appointment with an influential patron." He turned, took three steps, and spoke over his shoulder. "Sorry if McKinney misled you."

The Fitzes watched him round the corner.

Digger twitched his nose, rabbitlike. "Something smell funny here, kiddo?"

"I suppose the woman in the bonnet was a little ditzy," Nikki said. "But we both saw the Frenchman's copy with the same date—no doubt of that."

Digger bent over the case, strained to get a better look at the thin slab of gray metal. "Says here, the Cuppy plate was donated to the Museum by heirs. Maybe LeCoup had his copy made before that."

An announcement boomed through the museum, "Clogging at four . . ."

Digger glanced at his wrist. "Sorry to drag you along, kiddo. I didn't learn much. I know you'd like to stay for the clogging, but if we don't get a move on, you won't have time to primp."

Nikki shook her head. "Call Bo. Tell him we're running late."

"You'd pass on free opossum quiche, squirrel brains, and scrapple pie?" Digger rubbed his stomach. "Or, perchance— information?"

"Pandering your own niece."

Digger waved the air. "Heaven forbid. Free dinner, an open ear, no more."

Clarence Fouts closed the door to his office and peered at the small black-and-white monitors, at the nosy old hippie with the long hair in his cowboy get-up, with the flippant young woman at his side, walking through the Shaker room, past Daniel Boone's cabin, by the gift shop toward the front door. He moved from the monitors to the window, parted the blinds, and watched them cross the parking lot to their car, a small white VW, parked no more than thirty feet away.

He wrote the license plate number on an envelope, ran a hand through thinning hair and stared at the telephone, lifted the receiver, set it down, lifted it again and dialed. He squeezed his eyes shut while it rang, waiting for the voice that would send steam pumping through his cold bony frame.

The ringing stopped. A low, gravelly female voice mumbled, "Whoozit?"

"It's me. Clarence." Fouts licked his lips, framed his words, and then blurted out, "Two people came by, asking about the Céloron plate."

"You're all worked up aren't you, sweetie? Who were they? History buffs?"

"No, no. More. Much more."

"Go on."

Fouts fingered the card. "Harmon Fitz—you recognize the name? Fitz? Same as the murdered man. He's an *archaeologist* from Hawaii. Young woman with him, just left. White VW bug, Michigan plates." He read the number.

"You played it cool, I hope."

"Give me some credit, Rita Rae. Fitz asked to see the damned thing. I told him it was impossible because of policy."

"And then what?"

"They left."

"You're worked up over that? They *asked* about it, and *left?*"

"Isn't that enough? Edgar Fitz came to see me, wanted to examine the plate, next thing he turns up dead. Choked on lead! You know damned well LeCoup murdered the man as a warning for me to keep my mouth shut. I'm scared, Rita Rae. Of LeCoup, of prison."

"Murder? LeCoup is dangerous. But hurt you? Not in his interest. Chill out, keep your mouth shut, and no one'll be the wiser."

Fouts mumbled, half to himself. "Why did I go along with it? God, I'm so stupid. How could I have believed LeCoup gave us all that money just to hold the damned thing in his hands for a week? That he'd *return* it to me? The bastard kept the original, gave me back a *copy.* He skunked us."

"Why would you think that?"

"He pulled a switch, all right." Fouts lifted a pencil, wrote F-A-K-E and J-A-I-L on a notepad, and broke the lead scratching out the words. "I was stupid not to suspect from the start. I never paid much attention to the thing, but the more I look at it, the surer I am. It was never sampled metallurgically, so analysis would tell us nothing. LeCoup knew I couldn't prove he gave us back a phony. And if I could—what? Sue him for breach of contract?"

"Clarence, think about it. Even if you're guessing right, if you're not sure yourself, how is anyone else gonna tell?"

He wedged the receiver between chin and shoulder and kneaded his throbbing temples. "I'm only a folklorist, Rita Rae. But an archeologist?"

"From Hawaii? You worry too much."

"You know what else I worry about? Us. 'Getaway money,' you said. 'margaritas on the beach. New life.' Now that our sordid business is done, I wonder if it will ever happen. It's been weeks since we've spoken."

"Poor babykins, has Wita been ignoring wittle Cwarence?" Kissy sounds squeaked through the line. "Soon as she finishes this big deal, mama'll make up for lost time. You may not be the fanciest rooster in the yard, sugar, but a girl doesn't meet a man as smart or chock-full of hormones as you every day.

"Cwarence? I'll bet your butt's settled in that big, soft vinyl office chair right now, legs tucked under that king-size desk of yours—right?—the desk the night the money came through, you flopped me back-down onto and banged the bejeezus out of me. You remember, sugar pie?"

Fouts pulled the handkerchief, the one with his initials, from his breast pocket and wiped his forehead. He remembered. How Rita Rae had shed her panties right in front of him, grabbed him by the necktie, lifted her skirts and pulled him onto her, swept the desktop clear with one swipe of an arm on the way down. He stared at the desk, papers again stacked neatly, edge to edge, and guiltily recalled the photograph of his Ruth bouncing off the wall, glass shattering, how he had stuffed it in the rear of the bottom drawer when Rita Rae had finished with him. He hadn't opened the drawer since. Fouts sighed, thought of his dried-up wife in her flannel nightgown, hair in rollers, making him turn out the lights the last Saturday of the month, his day to "have his way with her." Even in the dark of their bedroom, Ruth made him pull the covers over their heads, and, he knew by touch, squeezed her eyes shut the whole time.

Rita Rae—Whew!—Rita Rae had not only done it on his desk, but with the flourescents blaring like spotlights overhead so he could see everything.

She smooched the phone again. "What a bang! Took me two days to get my knees together. You were wearing that brown suit, babycakes, the one matches those big eyes of yours. Bet you have it on now, don't you?"

Fouts couldn't remember which one he had on today, both his suits were brown. He swallowed, oonched in the chair, knowing what was coming next.

"Why don't you settle back, slip your hand into your

pants, and I'll tell you what I'm going to do to you the next time I visit. You ready, baby?"

Fouts couldn't speak. He nodded, closed his eyes, felt his hand inching under his loosened belt as ordered, the murderous Alphonse LeCoup and prison far from his mind.

26

Nikki slalomed the VW onto Edgar's long gravel drive. The rear wheels broke loose, and the car slid a foot sideways.

Digger grabbed the dash. "Easy, kiddo."

"Racing turn, Unc." She tapped the accelerator, spun a fantail of dust and stones. "I'm ticked, you know. Making me a Mata Hari. And while I'm fending off the fair-haired country boy, you'll be drinking with Coony. Boys' night out. Strippers, booze."

"Nothing like that. I'll work *him* for information."

"Sure." She tapped the brakes. "Uh-oh. Pink Caddy in the drive."

"Yep. Amy Lou, dead ahead. In the porch swing, little pink suitcase at her feet. You don't suppose she's planning to move in, do you?"

Watching the porch, Amy Lou waved them up the stairs. "Land sakes, I thought you'd never get here. Let's see. First, that's a plate of chocolate chip cookies, still warm, top of the rail." Digger was already picking at clingy plastic. "Let myself in, hope you don't mind. I put some real lemonade in the fridge—I threw out that grocery stuff. Front door and the kitchen window are open, airing the place out.

"Second, Morton Trask says the remains of your relative are ready at the funeral parlor. He's been calling, needs to talk to you about arrangements, wonders if you could stop by in the morning."

"Arrangements?" Digger said over his shoulder. "Cremation—that was the *arrangements*."

Amy Lou held her palms up, defensively. "Don't look at me. I think it has to do with the service, selection of the urn, a repository."

Wiping crumbs from his lips, "We have something simpler in mind. Tupperware, a pleasant drive in the mountains, a stiff breeze and a personal farewell. We don't need *arrangements* to remember Edgar, do we, kiddo?"

Nikki shook her head.

Amy huffed. "If that's what you want—the man was your kin." She glanced at her watch and gave Nikki an eager look. "Honey? It's already past five. Bo said he'd be by at six. That gives us less than an hour."

"Us?" Nikki turned to Digger for an explanation, but he had judiciously turned his back at mention of Bo.

"I brought my kit," Amy Lou said. "I'll give you a makeover, dear, the full treatment, makeup, lipstick, eye shadow, put your hair up and all, and I don't want a penny. You ought to look your very best on your first date."

"First *what?*" Lips pinched. "I don't wear makeup. *If* I dress up, I *may* use mascara, light lipstick, but I'm not, *not*, dressing up *tonight*, and I'm wearing my hair like this, in a ponytail, and, how do you know about my going to dinner with Bo, anyway? And, it's not a *date*."

Amy Lou laughed. "Honey, everyone knows about your date. Bo's taking you to Curly's Pork-a-Que in Union City, next county over, fancy place. Now, an appropriate base, a touch of blush, one of those luscious new shades of—"

Nikki ran inside. The screen door slammed.

Amy Lou turned to Digger, chuckling. "Kids! Don't you

just love them? Poor child has the first-date jitters. Why don't you have a chat with her, set her mind at ease?"

Digger grunted, pointed to a mouthful of cookie.

Amy Lou walked to his side, selected a cookie herself. "I mentioned it once before," She gave him a coy smile. "I do makeovers for men, too."

Jesus Bob rummaged through THIS SIDE UP, finally settling on a see-through cellophane envelope the size of a sugar packet. He tore the edge away with his teeth, peeled back one side and lifted a tiny square of gelatin from the center with his fingertip and held it face-high. With his other hand, he pried open his right eyelid and pressed the magical, translucent flake to his eye.

"Lord," said Purcell. "I'd rather wear glasses than use them things. How can you stand to touch your eyeball like that?"

"I don't think that's no contact lens," said Big Butt.

"If you don't go blind," Jesus Bob said, "it's good shit. You boys want some, I'll share. Speak up fast, 'cause I'm going to another planet soon enough."

Big Butt said he didn't think so and lit up a cheroot with his gunmetal Zippo. Purcell said, "I don't get it."

Big Butt explained: "LSD. Bad business, Purcell. Kids get hold of it cheap, use it more than I'd like to see." He took a drag and shook his head in disapproval. "Like I said, real bad for business. They get high on that crap, and you think they give a damn about beer and smokes anymore? It's no wonder LSD's illegal. I warn the Scooter Shooters . . ."

While Big Butt lectured, Jesus Bob smiled at the blue sky. It wasn't long before the sunflower sun began growing larger and yellower. "Whoa!" he said as it filled half the sky, a pinwheel of heat and sparking fire. "Whoa!" he said again, as he watched his compatriots shimmer under the raining sunlight. Yellow drops pelted their heads, drenched them in butter. Jesus Bob smelled hotcakes, giggled at how much Big

Butt looked like Mrs. Butterworth. He watched Mrs. Butterworth, a fatigue hat on her head instead of that yellow cap she usually wore, and butter-soaked Purcell melt before his eyes, pool at his feet in tiger stripes of camo green, brown, and yellow. Mrs. Butterworth's fatigue cap floated for several seconds (or was it three minutes, or three years?) before transforming into a turtle. The turtle's long tail gave Jesus Bob a start as it sprouted rattles and grew into a—*no way!* He willed it into a fried chicken tree.

Purcell's voice pierced the mist. "Watch out for that tree!"

Bonk.

Jesus Bob felt grass at his fingertips, saw a sci-fi sky of streaking pinpoint suns overhead. The grass turned rubbery. He rocked this way and that, backfloating on the sea of lime Jell-O to a rollicking chorus of *Yellow Submarine. Yellow Submarine?* He tried to switch channels, tune in some Lynyrd Skynyrd.

"Uh-oh," sounded from somewhere high in the clouds.

"You two stay put." A daunting, familiar voice.

Jesus Bob felt his ankle tickle, raised his head, saw a Woody the Woodpecker like the one the Junior Rangers had bagged, pecking like crazy at his ankle. Persistent. *Ha-ha-ha-HAH-ha!* Woody turned into a hissing red blowtorch. "Ouch!" The red blowtorch became a four-inch Charles Jourdan high heel. Peck, Peck, Pick, Kick, Kick.

"Is this pitiful, or what? I told you Boy Scouts to watch him. I turn my back and what—"

"I'm sorry ma'am. He kinda snuck away and—"

"Carry his worthless carcass to the cabin. I'll bring the damned aluminum case."

Swaying in bourbon rapids down a booze and hot-wings-scented canyon, Jesus Bob heard himself singing "Row, row, row your boat . . ." in a voice sweet as a choir girl's. He tried to look up the choir girl's robe, catch some choir girl beaver, but saw, instead—oh-oh—Rita Rae, none too pleased. He closed his eyes, dived back into the amber sea.

"Drop him over there. Take that rope, hobble his feet, tie his arms to the legs of the bunk. I don't want him wandering off, and it's looking like I may need him sooner than I thought."

27

I t don't weigh much, Bolt." Smoot Mudd shook the brown paper–wrapped package the size of a shirt box at his ear, and reread the return address on the baby blue, lavender-scented envelope. "Miss Emily Boone, number five Front Street, Rabbit Hash, Boone County, Kentucky. Says, 'Please read letter before opening box.' I never heard of the woman, but, you caught the Boone?"

"Yes, sir." To compensate for the commander's enervating arm-curl of the package, Bolt raised the oxygen mask.

Smoot leaned into it, sucked up what he could manage, and pushed it away. "All right, Emily. You got my attention." He ripped at the envelope and removed two sheets of the same blue paper. For a moment, the scent of lavender nearly overpowered the wet tobacco smell of his chewed cigar. "See that penmanship, boy? Like they used to write a hundred years ago. Writ with a fountain pen, too, not some damn cheapo ballpoint. Bet she's an old gal." Smoot flipped the cigar into the fireplace, adjusted the reading glasses on the bridge of his nose, and read aloud:

Dear Commander Mudd,

Allow me to introduce myself. I am Emily Boone, retired now, seventeen years from Boone County High School, where I served as librarian for more years than I care to count. You and I, sir, though we never met, are related, both scions of the Commonwealth's most famous son, Daniel Boone.

"A Boone relative!" Trembling, Smoot pressed the letter against the top rung of his walker to hold it still. A bony finger traced the words.

I am certain you must be as proud of Daniel's blood pumping through your veins as am I.

"Damn straight!"

Do pardon my imposition—me, a stranger coming into your day with the postman, out of the blue. Dear sir, I have spent nearly every spare minute for decades researching Daniel's life and descendants. I know of your illustrious father's role in developing Kentucky's coal industry, and your success in founding the Golden Leaf Tobacco Company.

I have heard (yes, I have my sources!) that you are also a student of the life and times of our great ancestor. And a collector, as am I.

While my meager accomplishments pale, I am sure, against those of a wealthy and clever man like yourself, through my correspondence and diligence (allow me to crow a bit), I have managed over the years to acquire a few modest fragments of the Kentucky pioneer's heroic life.

I once owned, for example, one of Daniel's signed IOUs (bearing, regrettably, not his full signature, but his X since Daniel, as you must know, was not a writing man).

"Hmmm," said a disappointed Smoot, unaware of that fact.

For several years I had one of his eyeteeth (after the age of twenty-seven, Daniel retained none of his own, those being dentist-poor times, and brushing considered unmanly).

Smoot met that with mixed emotion. Although he always visualized Daniel with a mouthful of movie-perfect pearly whites, it made sense that Daniel would have avoided unmanly behavior.

I also owned a portion of the upper sleeve of one of Daniel's buckskin shirts, and, while the odor (those were not bathing times) was still offensive, inhaling a noseful of Daniel Boone, let me tell you, brought many a tear to these sentimental old eyes.

Smoot glanced at the leather shirts and breeches on his wall, uncertain if he had ever sniffed them.

As you may know, Daniel's wearing coonskin caps was a myth.

A dealer had once offered Smoot one of Daniel's coonskin caps. He was thankful, now, he had passed it by. That would have been five thousand dollars down the tubes.

What Daniel did wear were beaver fur hats, and would you believe I once had in my possession a small piece of felt from one of the very hats Daniel wore to cover his bald head?

"Bald?" Smoot said. He had always imagined Daniel with a full head of hair, perhaps with a bushy Colonial ponytail as well, hanging down a broad muscular back. He had a copy of a portrait showing long hair, he was certain.

> In the famous Thomas Harding oil sketch of Daniel, he was wearing a wig, as was often his wont. Other mementos have come my way as well from the grand pioneer himself or from close relatives. As I am sure you can appreciate, such historic artifacts have considerable monetary value beyond their nostalgic attraction.

"Hot damn," Smoot said. "Here's where she gets down to business. I bet the old gal's fallen on hard times, wants to sell something of Daniel's. Imagine, a poor schoolteacher getting hold of Boone-a-bilia!" He found his place, read on.

> At this point you are probably asking yourself, "I'll bet this Emily Boone wants to sell me one of her treasures." But you would be wrong. No, I want to *give* you something.

"Give?" said Smoot. "She's *giving* me something of Daniel's, Bolt."

Bolt gave Smoot another snort of oxygen.

> When I acquire a Boone memento, I hold it close, savoring its significance, and then pass it along to another of Daniel's descendants, thereby sharing my good fortune with others appreciative of their noble ancestry. As my pension and the Social Security provide adequately for my modest needs, the dollar value of these objects means little to me.
>
> So, I pass the enclosed item to you gratis. All I ask is that, when you have held my gift close to your bosom, learned its story, you pass it along freely to another of Daniel's descendants.

"Yeah, sure." Smoot read hurriedly, eager to get into the box.

What treasure, you are asking, is this old woman giving me? (Please, contain your curiosity and finish reading before opening the box. I delight in the suspense!) First, let me say, much as I wish it did, our mystery artifact did not belong to Daniel himself.

"Well, damn!"

Do not let that dismay you. It did belong to one of his many sons; his favorite, Israel, one of two sons who lost their lives to Indians.

"Hear that, Bolt? Near as good." Smoot was unfamiliar with such tedious details of Daniel's life as his lack of bathing, tooth-brushing and hair, and with the identities of his plentiful children other than Jesse Bryan, the man through whom Smoot traced his own ancestry. "Hmmm." Smoot reread the last lines. He always assumed Jesse Bryan had been Daniel's favorite. And, two sons lost to redskins? "Savages!"

Israel, as you may recall, had fiery red hair, and a fiery temper to match. He was a Yankee Doodle Dandy as they said back then, a showy man, popular with the frontier belles, and I can assure you he wore the enclosed . . .

"It's clothes, some badge or ribbon. Hot damn!"

. . . with great pride. Took it with him everywhere, wearing it to turkey shoots, church socials, courting, even on raids into Indian country before he met his untimely death at savage hands.

"Damn redskins!"

But here I am "stringing you along," as my grand-children might say, enjoying your anticipation. I hope my little surprise brings a smile to your worthy face. Proceed! Enjoy!

Yours sincerely,
(Miss) Emily Boone

Bolt held the box while Smoot tore at the paper. He ripped open the end, tilted the box in so doing, and out fell— Smoot scowled at the double handful of faded red hair. "What the hell is that, a wig? Daniel's son wore a wig, too?"

Bolt lifted it from the floor, handed the heavy end, the end with the stiff leathery stuff, pale hair attached, to his mentor. "I don't think so, sir."

"Holy shit!" Smoot dropped it. Actually, shot-putted the scalp a good ten feet. "That ain't from no old lady!"

Bolt picked up a four-by-six-inch gold-bordered, baby-blue card that had fallen from the box and held it for Smoot to see. Written in the same fine hand as the letter were two words above an inked death's head: *YOU'RE NEXT*.

28

Dressed in jeans and a plain gray sweatshirt, hair in a ponytail, no mascara, no lipstick, Nikki had barely spoken since Bo picked her up. She steamed at the thought of Amy Lou's words: first date. Who else had the old biddy told? And dear Uncle Digger, setting her up. And Bo with his insufferable politeness. He had even cleaned his pickup truck, inside and out. No man's car could be that spotless, she knew. The Glade Country Garden was overpowering, nearly masked the smell of dog, and the few hound hairs remaining in the cab's floor carpet all ran the same direction—proof he'd done his best to brush or vacuum them away.

Now, here he was, dressed western, fancy as Digger in his new cowboy outfit, introducing her with a colossal, embarrassing grin to—Save me!—*every one* of the waitresses and the owner, Fat Curly himself of Curly's Pork-a-Que. Nikki willed her lips into a grimace of a smile, cursing Digger a thousand times over.

Bo pulled out a chair, pointed out items on the menu. "If you're really hungry, I'd order the full rack. Beer's on the way. Leave room for Curly's apple pie. . . ."

Nikki mouthed a surly, "Whatever you say," barely audible over the restaurant clatter and the booming recording of the Charlie Daniels Band.

The waitress jotting down the order, lifted her pencil and cocked her head, no doubt thinking, Bo's got himself quite the little bitch on his hands tonight, don't he?

They sat at a center table surrounded by families, couples, all happy and gibbering. Nikki's only hope for revenge was the sequined snake carrier she had taken moments ago from her shoulder and placed at the center of the red-and-white checkered tablecloth beside the breadbasket. Despite her dark mood, she stifled a giggle. Wait till he sees the purse move! Maybe I'll scream myself. Chaos at Curly's. That'll give Amy Lou something to cluck about.

Bo took a pitcher of beer from the waitress, held it over his lap—perfect. He poured. Nothing from the purse. Coony II must be sleeping. Nikki reached for a slice of white bread, bumped the purse with the back of her hand. Nudge, nudge.

Bo froze in midpour, glass and pitcher suspended over his jeans, staring at the purse.

Beaming a genuine if malevolent smile, Nikki set the bread down, held her empty glass out for Bo to fill, ready to drop it, let it roll off the table, break on the floor for added effect.

"Excuse me, Nikki, ma'am," Bo said, "but I do believe your purse moved."

"Moved? Impossible." She pushed it toward him. "Although, I hung it on the back of my chair when I came in. It may have touched the floor. You know, in a place like this, maybe a cockroach crawled inside."

"I don't think that's too likely, but, darn! There it goes again. Am I seeing things?" He set the pitcher on the table edge. "Didn't you see it? The shiny part fluttered like."

"I didn't see a thing. All I've got in there is my wallet, some Kleenex and keys. You want to take a closer look, pick it up. Unzip it, feel around inside, because if a cockroach . . ."

Bo lifted it gingerly, hefted it in the palm of his hand. No movement. He held it close to his chest, slid open the zipper tab. Nikki leaned over the table, glass in hand, ready to squeal.

Bo poked two fingers inside. "Well, what do you know? It's a little milk snake. How do you suppose that got in there?" Annoyingly fast on the uptake, he spread the purse for her to see. "Sure enough must have snuck in there from the floor, just like you said. Let me get Curly over here, show him what he's got crawling around. Hey, Curly!" He yelled across the tables. "Don't you worry none, Curly'll take it out to the kitchen, they'll shake it out, hack its head off with a cleaver, no harm done to your purse. Maybe give us dinner on the house, to boot." He shouted again at the bar, "Curly!"

"Give me that." She snatched the purse, rezipped it, slung it over her shoulder. "You didn't even flinch."

"Over a little milk snake? Couldn't be more than a foot and a half." He waved to Curly: *Everything's fine.*

"How'd you know it was a milk snake? What if it was a coral snake?"

"Red to black, venom lack. Saddles not bands—I was a Cub Scout. Anyways, aren't no coral snakes around here. Now, rattlesnakes? Plenty of rattlesnakes, especially lately."

"What do you mean," she leaned closer, canting her head, "lately?"

"We've had a dozen calls about rattlesnakes in the last week. One turned up behind the altar in the Heaven's Haven Tabernacle, another in the Dairy Dip john—places you wouldn't expect. If folks called us for those, must have been, who knows how many, turn up elsewhere. I hear the Heaven's Haven snake inspired the preacher to sermonize last Sunday about God raining venomous serpents on Mc-Afee County for its sinning."

"Rattlesnakes." She crossed her arms on the table in thought, recalling the pair at LeCoup's, the snakes that Smoot had to have sent him, but which were unmistakably from the deep south, not Kentucky. She raised a condemning eyebrow. "I suppose you shoot them?"

"Naw. Can't say I love snakes, but I like animals. I tell the boys to call me or box 'em, put them in an empty trash drum we have behind the HQ. I take them up to the forest, turn 'em loose."

"That's good. Good for you." The image of LeCoup's snakes returned. "What did they look like?"

"Heck, just timbers. Fair size. Dark saddles. I didn't count, but I'd say they had seven to ten buttons."

"Ground color? Stripe color? Was it yellowish brown or pink gray?"

Bo laughed. "Nikki, ma'am, I have no idea. You're interested, there's two of them still at HQ. You can look them over tomorrow." He poured a glass of beer, handed it to her.

She took a sip. "Good. Yeah, I'd like that."

"You know," Bo filled his glass, "that's the first interest you showed in anything I've said."

"Ummm. I've just been kind of . . ."

"Ticked off?"

Nikki shrugged. "It's not you."

"Maybe a little? After that first day, I guess I had it coming. And I know you're not high on gentlemen lately."

"Oh?"

"You know, with your boyfriend dumping you."

"What? Dumping *me*? Who told you *that*?"

"Whoa!" Bo spread his fingers, waved them in front of his face for protection. "That's a box I shouldn't of opened. I heard it from Beth Ann at the Chez, who must have heard it from Rubella, who got it from Amy Lou, who heard it from Etta, who heard it from Coony, who—"

"Who heard the real, no-one's-business, and not one-hundred-and-eighty-degree-backward version from dear old Uncle Digger. Wait till I—"

The waitress, platter on her shoulder, cleared her throat at Nikki's ear.

The pungent scent of barbecue not only took Nikki's mind off the wrong-way jilting, but snuffed out her original plan to poke at her food and feign indifference. "No better than Pavlov's dog," she said, and fell to.

"Who's dog?" Bo asked, already intent on rib surgery.

Ten conversationless, gnawing minutes later, Nikki touched her cheek. Bo raised his eyebrows: *Huh?* Nikki tapped the spot again. Bo took the hint, wiped away the fleck of orange with the back of his hand, and lifted the pitcher to refill his glass. She studied his face for several seconds, and said, "What's it like to have a brother?"

Bo's face blanched. The pitcher slipped from his hands, beer sloshed onto his empty plate, across the table. Nikki jerked away, barely missed a drenching.

"Darn!" He blotted the tablecloth with napkins. "Get you home beer-soaked, your uncle will be—"

"You all right?"

"Fine." Bo rubbed his forehead and closed his eyes. He opened them again, leaned across the table. "Where did you hear about Judas Bob? Oh—from Coony, of course. He didn't say anything about him being back, did he?"

"No. Hey, I'm sorry I brought it up. It's just that I'm an only kid and—"

Bo cut her off. "I don't talk about Judas Bob. Or my sister. We took different paths. It's in the past, and Coony should keep his big mouth shut."

Nikki drew a round face in the condensation on the beer pitcher, added a hat and two eyes with long lashes, and then a baseball-size mouth. She spun it to face Bo. "It's a portrait of your boss."

"Yeah, I recognize the big trap."

"Tell me," she said, on another, exploratory, tack, "Does Coony still suspect Uncle Digger?"

Bo wiped away the face and pointed a wet finger at her. "Tell me this first—did your uncle put you up to coming to dinner with me? To pry me?"

She sucked her lip, gazed at the ceiling, and shrugged. "The truth? I wouldn't have gone out with you otherwise."

"I figured. Glad I didn't ask you out on my own, then."

"What do you mean 'on your own'?"

"Not that I wouldn't have wanted to. You're—" He looked at the checkered tablecloth, and then up. "—very, uh, attractive, but I knew it wasn't me or a free dinner made you say yes. Coony kind of pressed me, wanted to hear what you found out in Cincinnati, like, apart from your uncle. He's probably getting it all out of him tonight. Coony's a lot better at making people open up than me."

"Sly Coony." Nikki sipped beer, peered over her glass at Bo, calculating. "And I guess he's the one put you up to washing dishes in the kitchen, the night we had dinner at his house?"

"He wanted to talk with your uncle. Alone."

"Uh-huh. And your happening to be there, the eating with them three times a week?"

"Oh, that's straight arrow. I seldom miss an invite to Etta and Coony's. Etta's a great cook, and there's always plenty to eat."

"You didn't answer my first question," she said. "Is Unc still a suspect?"

Bo twisted his napkin, considering. "How's this? You tell me what you know, I'll tell you what I know—neither Coony or Digger knows their own spy spilled the beans. Deal?"

She nodded. "Unc's kind of got this thing about the police."

"He ought to. He's got a record."

"Uncle Digger?" She sat six inches taller.

"Got himself arrested twice back in the sixties for protest marches and—get this—was nearly expelled from the University of Michigan for running across the football field buck naked during a game with Ohio State. Sort of thing the old folks did back then. Bet your uncle didn't tell you that."

Nikki shook her head, decided spying appealed to her.

"He also got a citation in California a year ago for driving too *slow* on a freeway. How's that?" Bo leaned forward, elbows on the table and grinned. "But none of that's the best. Back around 1970 your uncle was a wanted man."

She set her glass down with a clunk. "Uncle Digger?"

"While he was teaching at the University of California, Berkeley, your uncle gave at least a hundred thousand dollars to law enforcement agencies and politicians—'To help in your courageous battle against the demon weed'—he always included that in a little note with his check."

"No! Not Uncle Digger, can't be."

Bo grinned even wider. "The answer to that is: yes and no. The notes weren't exactly sincere, since the checks were all rubber. He opened checking accounts in half a dozen banks in California, apparently wore a disguise, used an alias: Riccardo Nilhouse Mickson. Then he sent the Mickson checks with his notes all over the place. Cops in five states, feds, too, were after this Mickson. They had fliers up in post offices. They eventually suspected your uncle, tailed him, stopped his car whenever they saw it, searched his apartment twice. Hassled him pretty good, I guess. Coony spent an hour on the phone with some western lawman he met at this conference he attended in Washington, D.C. The guy knew all about it."

Wide-eyed, Nikki asked, "They caught him? Uncle Digger went to *prison*?"

"Your uncle was clever. They never found his stash of checks—or of pot. I guess from the notes he was a toker. He never left prints or anything to incriminate himself. Nobody at the banks could ID him as Mickson. The notes weren't typed on his typewriter and the signatures weren't enough to prove he wrote them. But they figured out it was him, somehow, and a bunch of law people were hot. A California prosecutor finally scared the heck out of him, got him arrested on a bogus charge, left him in a cell with the bad boys for three days to shake him up, got him to plead guilty to a misdemeanor with no admission of the fraud. They fined him a hundred bucks—cash—put him on probation with a promise he'd follow the straight and narrow thereafter. And, except for the too-slow ticket, I guess he has."

"He never said a word about it, only to watch out for cops."

"No wonder, huh? Coony also learned your uncle's dean is real ticked at him for something—told Coony to 'throw his ass in the clink, what the reprobate deserves.' My guess is, your uncle's scared Coony will find out about the Mickson business and, with drugs tied to your other uncle's murder, will put your uncle Digger at the top of our suspect list and pass his criminal past on to his dean who will—I don't know—screw up his job or embarrass him. That's why he's been so squirrelly."

"Will Coony tell him? The dean?"

"Nah. Coony thought it was a hoot. Stories are, back in high school, before Etta's daddy, the judge, set Coony straight, he was a real hell-raiser. Smoked his share of pot, too, I'll darn well venture. There's stories—but none I'd dare repeat.

"Anyway, Coony got your uncle's prints the day of the murder, ran his name through NCIC. We found no matches at the house or the murder scene. The dope we found was real enough. Your other uncle, the dead one, had no drugs in his body except alcohol—from their drinking at the County Line—that's where Coony's taking your Uncle Digger tonight, by the way."

The waitress came by with coffee. Bo ordered apple pie a la mode for both of them. "Your turn. What did you and your criminal uncle find in Cincinnati?"

Nikki was staring through him, still savoring the dirt on Digger. Bo snapped his fingers. "Hell-oh-oo?"

Nikki blinked. "Sorry."

"You were about to tell me what you two found up north."

Over thick slices of Curly's apple pie and cinnamon ice cream, Nikki told Bo everything she could remember about Alphonse LeCoup, the Frenchman, including the mysterious gift-wrapped rattlesnakes and the Folk Museum of Eastern Kentucky.

*   *   *

Smoot hung up the phone, removed the oxygen mask, and slumped in his desk chair. The conversation had left him winded. "You remember Rusty Moffet, Bolt? That sheep farmer over near Ebeneezer Road? Talkative bastard?"

"Yes, sir." Bolt replaced the mask on the nearby walker and tilted back a Bud.

"He confirmed what I remembered. He's still got a drum of that red dye in his barn he used to mark sheep. It stains awful, I recall, because seven years ago, two Golden Leaf High football players ran from Moffet's field into his barn to hide when Moffet and his shotgun caught them abusing one of his ewes. They ran smack into a drum of that dye, tipped it, tripped, and got dyed themselves. Went red for weeks."

"Abusing sheep's against the Bible," Bolt said.

Smoot nodded. "Used to put the scarlet *A* on their foreheads for it back in the Old Testament. But that ain't what I got in mind today. That map of Cincinnati?"

Bolt opened it.

"Here's what I been thinking. LeCoup tried to rile us with that scalp—you buried it proper, read the Good Book over it?"

Bolt acknowledged he had.

Smoot cackled, slapped the map. "If the Frenchman wants to bid on the Lords of Trade plate, he's got to come here—I got that assurance out of Rita Rae. With you and the Rangers, he'll be scared to death. And, fear may keep the bastard north of the Ohio River, leave the bidding to one— to me. Serve greedy Rita Rae right."

Bolt finished the Bud, set it aside for his collection, and cocked an ear.

"When I had that detective scout LeCoup's house a few months ago—where's that snapshot?" Bolt fished it from a drawer, set it on the desktop. "Looks like some damned froggie castle, don't it?" Smoot asked.

Not having seen many froggie castles, Bolt wasn't certain,

but trusting Smoot's judgment implicitly, agreed it was the spitting image of one.

"What I want you to see is how it's all virgin white. What if you was to visit old Rusty Moffet, fill up a few balloons with that red dye of his, drive to Cincinnati, sneak onto LeCoup's property, pitch those balloons against that snow-white castle of his and dye it bloodred? Hah!"

"Hah!" Bolt agreed, and popped the top on another Bud in advance celebration of the foray north.

29

Coony McCoy's Bonneville rattled over the washboard ruts in Edgar's drive, trailing a pigtail of pink dust. "I assume," the sheriff said to Digger, "you're not opposed to a shot or two of bourbon tonight? Thought we'd eat at the County Line, where you and your cousin drank the night of the murder. Maybe you'll see something to jog your memory, huh?" At the dubious look on Digger's face, he said, "Hey, they play good old-timey music, cook up some fine fried chicken and catfish. Might have me some myself, Etta having kept such a short leash on me all week."

Digger nodded, felt his stomach butterflies flex their brittle wings from riding in a cop car with the head cop, cop paraphernalia all around, going to a fight-fuck-or-dance bar for booze and a meal of greasy food—the very bar that may have gotten poor Edgar murdered. He squirmed in his seat, bathed in ominous red light from the setting sun, and wondered what Coony's real agenda was.

Information, for a start. Before they left McAfee County, Coony had the whole story of the Frenchman and the Folk Museum out of him.

It was dark when they pulled into a gravel lot crammed

with pickups and muscle cars stained orange by flashing DRINK/EAT neon. Coony parked his blue Bonneville far around the side so as not to spook the patrons. Down-home country western bled from a cavernous tin roof shed.

The butterflies launched a dance in Digger's gut as he followed his host. Coony was dressed bad-assed in black jeans and boots, a black western shirt and his black hat, Digger in his fancy Lucchese boots, stonewashed jeans, white Stetson, a bright yellow Saturday night shirt with maroon piping and pearl buttons, the horsehair belt with the flying eagle buckle and a rolled, hot magenta bandanna around his neck. He regretted allowing Nikki to dude him up, hoped no one would notice.

Near the entrance, a skinny drunk in a fishnet muscle shirt swung at a hefty woman twice his size. She dodged and took a poke back with what looked like a table leg. Coony danced between the combatants, arms raised, palms out. "Just mind your own business and stay close." The couple parted, surged back when he passed. "Ain't no one going to bother you, okay?"

Digger answered with an uncertain nod as a second swing of the table leg connected with the drunk's shoulder. He watched him go down, walked wide, hurried to catch up with Coony as he pushed through double steel doors into an interior ripe with booze, sweat, smoke, cologne, and frying food. He wondered if Coony had a weapon stashed somewhere.

They entered a noisy soup of bodies and blue haze, lit like a carny show with strings of bare bulbs and last season's Christmas lights. Tables with mismatched chairs surrounded a dance floor with whirlpooling couples, bobbing and swirling to Hank Williams singing the "Honky Tonk Blues." A forty-foot bar stretched along one wall. Women squealed, men guffawed, and couples shouted mouth to ear over music blaring from black speakers the size of telephone booths, cranked loud enough to shake spiders off their webs in the rafters. Beer bottles crashed against one cinder-block wall, adding to a yard-high pile of brown broken glass at its base.

"We'll just ease past the bar to the other side," Coony said. "See that empty table over there?"

Digger saw fewer western clothes than ball caps, worn work boots, and T-shirts. Damn, he thought, I feel like a frigging poodle, down to the ribbon around my neck. Brenda Lee warbled the first few plaintive notes of "I'm Sorry" as they neared the bar. Digger heard glasses clink, snatches of bar talk. He imagined conversations trailing off as they threaded through the crowd. Then saw three men set their bottles down and stare. Frigging poodle.

Why in the world did Edgar bring me here that night? Edgar barely drank. Then he remembered telling Edgar how great a cold beer would taste. This was the closest booze to Golden Leaf. Edgar had accommodated him.

He saw a woman gape at him slack-jawed, elbowing her companion, and imagined Edgar's murderer taking note of the two strangers that fateful night, following them back to the motel, and waylaying Edgar alone.

He swiped perspiration from his forehead, thinking, the son of a bitch who murdered Edgar could be here tonight, watching me.

Uh-oh. More passing profiles became full faces. Didn't Coony see it? Like a ripple of suspicion, the laughter, gibes, and bar talk faded in their wake. He felt the weight of hostile eyes, forced himself to look straight ahead. He stuck his chin out, affected a John Wayne swagger, but stumbled instead. That table had to be a mile away.

Coony reassured him, "Just walk. Don't start nothing."

"Right." Peripherally, he saw hands set glasses and bottles on tables, bodies straighten, people whisper. Damn Nikki. I should have dressed down, not up. They'll be throwing bottles at *me* soon enough.

At the table, Coony took a chair with his back to the wall. Digger followed suit. Both had a clear view of the bar and—

absolutely no question about it—150 staring eyes. The music cranked up again, Patsy Cline, belting out "Walkin' After Midnight," but dancers lost their rhythm, slowed, leaned against one another, facing the strangers. Several men at the long bar climbed their stools for a better look.

Digger kept his gaze on the crowd at large but avoided eye contact with individuals. He leaned to the side, toward Coony. "I knew I overdid it, dressing like this. They know I don't belong here, resent—"

"It ain't *you*," Coony snarled. "It's *me*. Was stupid, I guess, but I ain't never run into a problem here before. I get a mite enthusiastic with the citations, particularly with out-of-county speeders. Enough of them must've recognized me to set the other ones off, like one of your chain reactions. Either that, or it's ones I sent to the pokey wants to cause a fuss. Or the damned Daniel Boone Rangers. And me with only a blackjack in my boot.

"Look, Digger, if they come at us, deck the first one fast. Lay him flat. I'll do the same. Use a chair, whatever. That'll give the other ones enough pause for us to make a dash for the door. Got it?"

Digger muttered, "Deck the first one. Got it." He felt sand catch in his throat, his palms grow cold, sweat trickle down his chest.

Someone pulled the plug on Patsy Cline, and she whimpered to a cemetery silence, followed by rising murmurs, shifting feet and chairs—the stirring breeze before a mean storm.

Crack! Eyes flashed to the bar. A bartender, black-bearded, thick as a badger, wearing a sleeveless sweatshirt, climbed onto the bar brandishing a Louisville Slugger. He smacked the oak again. *Crack!*

Digger mouthed an "Oh, nooo."

Coony whispered, "No, that's good. He sees there's trouble brewing. If we got the bartender on our side, there's hope."

The bartender assumed a wide stance, bat held in both

hands high over his head. "Listen up, you rednecks," he shouted. "I guess you all seen who just walked in."

. Digger heard Coony muttering, "On the other hand, if that sumbitch turns on us, it won't be pretty. Can't be sure, but I think I sent him and his brother up for auto theft a couple years back."

The barman jumped to the floor, walked ten paces toward Digger and Coony, bat in hand, parting the brooding crowd. He grabbed a chair, stood on the seat, and swung the bat around his head for attention. "I got something to say." He said it loud enough for whoever was in the johns to hear, too. He pointed the business end of the bat at the intruders' table.

He took a deep breath, and shouted it out: "WILLIE? WE LOVE YOU, MAN!"

The crowd cheered, whistled, hooted. A dozen beer bottles shattered against the far wall.

Crack! The bat sent a chair skittering. Yelling to Digger: "I don't know what brings you and your friend to the County Line, Willie, but you're sure as hell welcome. Drinks, food, women—whatever—is on the house. And the rest of you?" He swung the bat around the room. "You let old Willie enjoy hisself in peace, hear? No autographs or bullshit, or you got me to deal with. Got it?

"Now let's hear a good old country *ya-hoo* for Willie!"

Rebel yells and *ya-hoos* rattled the tin roof. A rain of bottles hit the wall. Coony kicked Digger's ankle, doing his best to speak without moving his lips. "Better stand up or something."

Digger tried to clear his throat, and coughed instead. He pressed his palms to the tabletop and stood on quaking knees, raised the white hat a foot over his head by the crown, forced a smile, and nodded his head in three short, pontifical bows, left, right, and center.

Ya-hoo Willies sounded again, echoed in waves, and then gradually subsided into raucous normality. Someone restarted the music, and Tanya Tucker began to sing "I Believe the South Is Gonna Rise Again."

Digger leaned to Coony, a brittle smile still pasted to bloodless lips. "Be damned thankful," he said through clenched teeth, "they didn't ask me to sing."

30

J esus Bob opened his eyes, found he was staring into
those of Jesus himself, no longer a mere two-
dimensional portrait on the wall, but Jesus's floating,
disembodied head. His eyes not glowing green as at
night, but red, accusing.

"You are such a fuckup," Jesus said.

"I'm sorry, Lord." He tried to raise his hands in prayer,
found they were tied behind him. Feet, too, bound together.
He struggled, gave it up. "You punishing me, Lord? Gonna
throw me in the pit of hell for . . ." He couldn't remember
the particular transgression. Somebody he had maimed or
killed, no doubt. He tried to think back, but his acid-laced
world went fuzzy. The faded institutional green wall blurred
into jungle, began to burn, flames leapt, raptors screeched
above, and then it changed to angular concrete, a long line
of cells. He heard metallic clanking, smelled cigarette smoke.

". . . for drugging your ass blind, for a start," Jesus said.

He squinted at Jesus, wondered how he talked without
moving his lips. A miracle. That's what Jesus did, miracles.
"Let me loose, Jesus. I'll be good. Stay off the medicine."
Repentant, he felt his eyes well with goodness.

"You'll stay off the medicine, all right," Jesus said, "or I'll leave you tied up like a trussed pig. What are you high on, now, LSD?"

"Jussa little square of windowpane wonderland—"

"Look at me when I talk, dummy."

"Yes, Lord."

"Over *here*."

Sis! Red lips moving when she talked, so it was her, not Jesus on the wall. Whoa, Rita Rae shimmered, became a dragon puffing smoke, metallic scales covered her body. The dragon lengthened, became a coiled rattlesn—No!

Slap. "Stop the damned screaming. C'mon, baby." She sat beside him, cradled him in her arms, rocking. She turned his head, blew smoke in his face, and gave him a light kiss on the forehead. "Come back to the real world."

Jesus Bob blinked at her. "Hi, Sis."

"You know where you are?"

"In the cabin. What the hell? Somebody tied me up."

Rita Rae walked to the metal folding chair at the small desk, slid it three feet away from him. She sat, elbows on knees, lit another cigarette, leaned forward, nearly nose to nose with him. "Nod if you understand what I'm saying." Nod. "You know who I am?" Nod. "Say it."

"Sis."

"I don't know why I don't ditch you, but there's some things I can't do. Orlando's coming, and we'll need heavy muscle at our backs. Our auction? All set. Riling Alphonse against Smoot, Smoot against Alphonse? A breeze. Why? Because of their hormones. It's your balls get you men in trouble, you know."

Jesus Bob nodded.

"I wouldn't have expected you to write the Boone letter to Smoot or find that scalp, but catching and delivering rattlesnakes should be a man's work—stop that shaking, you wuss! Anyway, I took care of it myself, so it's behind us. Everything's on schedule."

She stared past him, running over it all aloud, seeking

flaws. "I want this auction to play out without a hitch. Smooth as switching the dummy plate with Clarence Fouts at the Folk Museum. Yes, indeed. A little grab ass, a little payola, and that old fool stumbled right into it. Keep him walking the line, hoping for another sweet taste of Rita Rae, afraid of a stretch in the slammer if he blabs. Twenty-five thousand from LeCoup over the top for me. All comes down to balls again. Is it more nookie for Clarence, or do they get chopped off? You afraid of having your balls cut off, little brother?" She snip-snipped with her fingers.

Nod.

"Okay. So here's the deal. I'm gonna set you loose, but from now until this deal's done, I hold on to This Side Up."

"My medicine?"

"Mine now. I'll give you enough to keep you on keel."

"No!"

"Few lines of coke, a few joints a day. Oughta be plenty. Other side of it has to do with those balls of yours. I thought you wanted to hold on to them."

Nod. His eyelids flickered as Rita Rae grew cat's fur and long canine teeth.

Slap. "Stay with me and listen up. This is the big score. I need you conscious, watching these camo clods to see none of them goes berserk before we're finished."

"What about the law, Sis? You promised me a payback."

"*After.* When the cash is in my hands, I'll pass along your cut, put This Side Up in your eager paws, and I'm off to the Caribbean with Orlando. You can go with us, or stay and have your set-to with little brother Bo and Coony—a matter of *balls* again, right? And these big-balled soldier boys can cut loose, wipe this miserable town off the face of the earth. I always hated McAfee County. It'll be satisfying to read about it going up in smoke while I'm sitting on the beach, counting my money, sipping a margarita, Orlando giving me a foot massage.

"But *now*? I want you out of trouble. Not too high. Nearby. Got that?"

Nod.

She jiggled her locket at this face. "Or it's snip-snip."

The offices of Coup de Grace Investments were situated in the eastern Cincinnati community of Mariemont, a convenient twelve minutes from Alphonse LeCoup's Indian Hill nouveau château, not more than twenty from Raven Buckhunter's Mount Adams riverview condo.

Raven, junior partner, sat cross-legged and barefoot on a soft leather sofa, sipping a Starbucks skim latte, rereading her analysis of a company they were considering buying.

Raised with five other adopted brothers and sisters in Paducah, Kentucky, as Ethyl Schultz, Raven hadn't a clue of her birth parents. Her thick black hair, flashing-dark eyes, high cheekbones, and perennial Coppertone tan, however, always set her apart from—and often got her into fights with—the freckle-faced, pale-skinned kids she grew up with. Not until her first John Wayne movie at the Oak Street Majestic Cinema at the age of seven, did little Ethyl Schultz realize who she really was: an American Indian, one of the bad guys.

Her thirty-four-year history was pretty much summed up by the five documents framed over the sofa: (1) A yellowing certificate in basket-making from primary school with a pencil-written A+ and "Despite disciplinary problems, Ethyl has good manual dexterity, shows aptitude for the domestic arts," (2) her high school diploma, and, matted below, a sophomore year counselor's note, "While rebellious, Ethyl is not unintelligent—with application, may be a suitable candidate for junior college," (3) her BA diploma certifying that Ethyl Schultz had graduated from the University of Kentucky, (4) a congratulatory letter affirming that (good-bye Ethyl Schultz) Raven Buckhunter had made it to the Olympic archery qualifying semifinals, and (5) an MBA diploma from the University of Chicago, Graduate School of Business, testifying that Raven Buckhunter had graduated with high honors.

Raven flicked an approving fingernail at the twelve-page report. The proposed acquisition was a combination aluminum siding contractor and microbrewery, an exploratory venture launched only nine months earlier by an eastern utility fat with cash from its regulated gas and electric business, eager to move adventurously into a freewheeling unregulated marketplace. Alas, it had failed to match the expectations of an impatient and profit-hungry board.

Raven rechecked her summary: (*a*) Acquire at no more than 70 percent of asking price—seller will jump at offer. (*b*) Purchase, manage and resell through our Bahamian shell corporation. (*c*) Liquidate microbrewery immediately, rightsizing employees from 41 to 0. (*d*) Ship fermentation vats (Appendix I) to Quebec, there replacing existing manufacturer's identification with stenciled "U.S. Army, Dugway Proving Grounds Bio Test Vats" and transship to Iraqi contacts via our established French connections. (*e*) Right-size the aluminum siding sales force from 23 to 0, and increase order and shipping department personnel from 3 to 15. (*f*) Eliminate all door-to-door, direct mail, and TV marketing, and sell siding exclusively through Internet do-it-yourself Ponzi plan per Appendix III. (*g*) Resell company one month before sales curve peaks per Appendix IV. SUMMARY: Net profit: $13.2 million. Net employee reduction: 52.

Report in hand, she walked to Alphonse LeCoup's office, stood silently at his back, savoring the moment, and tossed the report over his shoulder onto the desk.

LeCoup went to the bottom line. "Once again you come through, my sweet. *Trés bon.*"

Before he finished the first paragraph, however, Raven had pulled the red lacquer comb from waist-length hair coiled high on her head, shook it loose, flipped her head back, and then forward, to send a shimmering black cascade over LeCoup's face.

She kissed him on the center-part of his black hair. "Time out?"

His body stiffened. "At the stake, *peut-être?*"

"*Mais, oui.*"

Thirteen minutes later, Alphonse LeCoup worked the combination lock on the soundproof vault door to his collection room. He swung it open, bowed for Raven to pass, shut it with a heavy *ka-thunk*. Inside, replaying a familiar scene, he entered one small dressing room, Raven, another.

Forty-five seconds passed and LeCoup minced out barefoot, wearing an ankle-length cotton granny dress, a blond wig, and high sunbonnet. The lights from the dressing room cast long yellow streaks across the darkened floor. He traipsed past Raven—crouched in the shadows, nude except for a fringed buckskin G-string, a tomahawk slung through it, and streaks, zigzags and geometric dabs of red strawberry glaze war paint.

The pioneer woman in the bonnet began calling in falsetto, "Oh, children? Where are you?" Looking left, right. "Come quick. There's Indians in the woods. William? Judith? George? John? Benjamin? Margaret? Clara? Isaac? Eliz—"

Raven slipped behind LeCoup in the granny dress, threw a slip-knotted loop of rope over his shoulders, pulled it tight.

LeCoup screamed.

"It's fire for you, colonial bitch!" Raven led him to the stake. "Go ahead, yell if you want."—He did.—"Your husband is scalped and dying, your cabin's burning, your brats rounded up as slaves." Breasts bouncing, nipples circled with dripping strawberry glaze, she danced around the stake, hooting, binding LeCoup to the pole. For good measure she clamped his arms in the wrist restraints.

Victim secured, she ran away, to return with a five-foot bow and a quiver over her bare shoulder. *Zip, zip, zip* from thirty feet away. Three arrows in six seconds pierced Le-Coup's bonnet, pinned it to the stake.

The pioneer wife screeched, fainted. Raven slapped her face. "Wake up, bitch," she said. "I'm not done with you yet."

LeCoup's eyes popped open. "Mercy!"

"Hah!" Another slap. "You invaded our land, spilled over

the mountains like ants after honey. We lived with the land, you—"

"Heathens!" LeCoup jutted his chin out, ready for the next—*slap*. Cheeks showing a fine burn, now. "Go ahead, savage. That's it. Hit a poor defenseless woman."

She did: Slap. "Harder!" *Slap, SLAP!*

The last one did it, the lights came on.

"Damn." Raven clapped, returning them to dim, dressing-room-lit twilight. Ambience restored, she pinched a hunk of the pioneer woman's red cheek and twisted. "You felled the forest, killed our game, churned out your white babies like vermin, destroyed our way of life—our identity!"

Eyes teary, Alphonse wailed, "Yes, yes, it's true! All of it! Punish me! Give me the hatchet!"

She whacked it into the wood to the right of his ear, slipped to the floor, and tapped him on the big toenail with the blunt end, hard enough to make him dance on one leg, more or less, considering the rope and wrist restraints.

Authentic *ow!-ow!-ow!s* reverberated through the collection room. Through pain-clenched teeth, Alphonse hissed at her. "That the best you can do? Go ahead—*fire my ass!*"

So she did. She darted into the shadows, trotted back with three sets of plastic fire logs, the kind furniture stores use in living room mantel displays, and set them at his feet, extension cords snaking into the dark. She bent over, flipping switches. The logs glowed, red Cellophane wafted ceiling-ward from interior fans. LeCoup screeched, kicked, writhed.

Not enough for Raven. "What do you say we *turn up the heat?*" She dropped to her knees and scooted under his voluminous skirts.

Struggling. Bobbing gingham. Panting.

Raven emerged, untied the rope, unshackled LeCoup's wrists. In short order he shucked his dress, gnawed her leather G-string in two, and licked off her war paint. Grunts, groans, and shrieks—truly savage sounds—rebounded from the darkened walls as the mythic adversaries went at one another in their frontier passion play.

Forty feverish minutes later, LeCoup lay in Raven's arms, bathed in red Cellophane firelight, smoking a pipe of kinni-kinnick. "Was it good for you, too?" he said, with a touch of his inevitable *après-sexe* insecurity.

"No complaints." She tickled his scalp. "But I do have a question."

He stopped in midpuff, shifted uncomfortably. "It's about the dress, isn't it? I swear, I'm not really—"

"You look cute in the dress." She tugged his beard. "It's this damned auction. With all your goodies, does this hunk of metal mean that much to you? Smoot Mudd, threats, rattlesnakes? The bottom line is—it's getting in the way of business. I've checked last year's stats, we're down a hundred and six rightsizings, as of this date."

"*Ma petite sauvage*, this is a matter of honor. Mudd, this hillbilly bête noire, plagues me. All these years, he defames my character, picks, picks, picks. Now, he has a Céloron plate—the one he snatched from under my nose on the utility's property—and I have a Céloron plate—the one we tricked the Folk Museum out of. And, next, what should appear? The grand Lords of Trade plate, stolen from the valiant French, given to the thieving British—*ma chère*, it launched the French and Indian War! This is our chance to avenge the infamy done our ancestors, turn the—"

"I thought you'd say that." Raven waggled his chin, gave him an affectionate smooch on the ear. "So, I've thought of a little trick we might play on Monsieur Smoot, something I think you'll enjoy. The sooner we scare him off and you add this hunk of pot metal to your collection, the sooner we're back in business."

"*Merci* for your understanding." He twisted his head, looked up at her appreciatively. "As a matter of fact, I, too, have in mind a coup de main." His eyes clouded with dark anticipation. "*Diabolique*, if I do say so."

31

Digger heard the screen door slam, looked from his desk to see Nikki run by carrying three pillowcases at arm's length, bottoms bulging. He called to her back, "No way! That milk snake's enough. What's in those bags belongs outside. I'm not bending on this, Nikki. You know how—"

"Okay, okay." She left, returned ten minutes later empty-handed. "Should you hear rattling in the garage, pay it no mind."

He twirled a cut-crystal squirrel on the desktop. "It looks like you're in snake heaven, kiddo. Found a kindred spirit, too. He stopped by, incidentally, your kindred spirit, while you were rock-lifting."

She jabbed a stick-stiff finger at him. "Not a word about Bo."

"Kiddo, I like Bo. Even if he is a cop. In fact I'm glad to see—"

"Bo is okay. He hasn't put move one on me, I give him credit for that, and he's not afraid of snakes, but don't you or Amy Lou, or Coony, or anybody else start any rumors, because—"

Waving air. "No, no stories. I'm happy to see you busy, really. Even with rattlesnakes."

At mention of the *R* word, Nikki began to pace, explaining about the southern canebrake variant, and the northern timber color pattern. "It's the screwiest, how they both seem to be purebreds, living side by side." She lifted a book from one of Edgar's shelves, walked around the room without opening it. "And why so many? On the move? Bo says this is the first time he's seen rattlesnakes in town. I'm plotting distribution maps." She tossed Edgar's book on the desk, hard enough to make Digger jump. "And . . . and Bo is *helping*, all right?"

"All right, already."

She went to the kitchen, opened the refrigerator door. Calling, "Want a glass of lemonade? I can't remember if it's the canned stuff or Amy Lou's."

"Amy Lou's. She was by an hour ago." He lifted the crystal squirrel again, stared at its black plastic dots for eyes, and set it down. "Bet you didn't know there are over a hundred cut-glass gewgaws in here. Amy Lou checked every one— because the last time she was here she noticed the missing clowns. Those grotesque colored glass ones with the bug eyes I hid under the bathroom sink?"

Nikki came back with a glass of lemonade, set it on the desk. "Yeah. Spooky."

She fiddled with another of Edgar's books, flipped through the pages.

Digger held out the squirrel. "She gave me this. Housewarming gift. Amy Lou thought we might like to start a collection of our own."

"Tell her to bring a glass snake the next time. Or, better, an *Ophisaurus ventralis*." Laughing. "An eastern glass lizard— that's what they call *Ophisaurus*. They're legless, over half their bodies are tail and they shatter if they get whacked."

"Very cute. This book you threw at me?" He tapped the cover. "It's one of Edgar's histories of eighteenth-century North America. What Smoot said about the French explorer

Céloron's Lords of Trade plate starting the French and Indian War? If that was the first spark, guess who fired the first shot?"

Nikki shook her head.

"None other than George Washington."

"Cannot-tell-a-lie George?"

"The very one. In the early eighteenth century there wasn't much thought about all that land to the west. As far as the French were concerned, it was theirs, claimed by La Salle in the 1600s. They were content to leave it to French fur traders and the Indians."

Digger moved the see-through squirrel aside, slipped a pair of reading glasses on his nose and rustled through his notes. "Then British colonists began crossing the mountains, more interested in homesteading than fur trading. The governor-general of Canada sent Captain Pierre-Joseph Céloron de Blainville down from the Great Lakes in 1749 to reestablish the French claim.

"The next year the Ohio Company was organized in London to exploit the land west of Lord Fairfax's Virginia holdings. George's brother Lawrence was a principal. Young George, a surveyor, explored west. Then the French governor ordered the area cleared of British colonials."

"Uh-oh." Nikki clicked her tongue. "Trouble brewing."

"You bet. In 1752, the Ohio Company began a road over the mountains toward what they called the Forks of the Ohio, where the Allegheny and Monongehela rivers join at today's Pittsburgh. Same year, the French planned a series of protective forts running south from the Great Lakes, the anchor of which was to be at that very same spot. King George ordered the governor of Virginia to tell the intruders to vamoose, and if they didn't, throw their derrieres out.

"The next year, twenty-one-year-old Major George Washington, adjutant of the militia of the southern district of Virginia, led a party to the Forks of the Ohio, scouted for the British fort, and rode north to give the French their eviction notice.

"Now, get this . . . I researched George's diaries, and found an entry dated the twenty-fifth of November, 1753, in which he relates that a Seneca Indian Chief called Half-King said the Commander of the French forces on the Ohio frontier told him—and I quote: 'Lead was the man that went down and took possession.' In other words, citing Céloron's plates as proof of the French claim."

"So, George knew about the buried plates?"

"You betcha. The French sent a reply to the governor: Kiss off. In 1754, a large French force found British frontiersmen setting up a fort at the Forks and sent them packing. The French continued what the British began, called it Fort Duquesne.

"George, by now a colonel and commander-in-chief of the Virginia forces, and his militiamen encountered an outlying party of French soldiers, engaged them and killed eleven men—those first shots, I mentioned. The French claimed the dead were diplomats, branded George a murderer."

"George, a murderer!"

"So they said . . . and then the tables were turned. The French and Indians attacked George's troops at colonial Fort Necessity. Outnumbered, outprovisioned, they surrendered. George was released in anticipation of a prisoner exchange, and went home to Mount Vernon.

"Not for long. In 1755, he returned with an avenging British Army led by Edward Braddock, determined to oust the French from Fort Duquesne. *Au contraire.* Braddock, playing by European rules of war, was trounced—and by now we're thick into the French and Indian War, which ignited in 1756 to a general war with France—Europe, the far-flung colonies, everywhere.

"The British rebounded and the war was settled ultimately with the Treaty of Paris in 1763. France relinquished its North American claims."

"So," Nikki said, "the Fitzes speak English, instead of the

Perriers speaking French. Cool." She slipped the book she had been playing with onto the shelf, driving another out the other side. It hit the carpet, pages splayed, spine up. When she picked it up, several pieces of paper fluttered to the floor. Digger pointed. "What's that?"

"Bookmarks, I guess. A book on the Caribbean. Let's see . . . movie ticket stub from Hazard, a couple of register receipts, and, looks like a letter." It was folded in thirds. Nikki opened it. "Hmmm. It's a copy of a letter addressed to someone in Miami from a museum in Barbados."

She passed it to Digger and he read aloud.

Dear Mr. Sosa y Castro:

Per your request, this is to certify that the Queen's Maritime Museum has deaccessioned the following North American items deemed extraneous to our focus on the Caribbean Sea, and that said items have been transferred to you for valuable consideration received:

1. Klu Klux Klanswoman and daughter's matching robes and hoods. White cotton full-length. Both hoods and sleeves w. lace and attractive pink tasseling. Southern U.S. c. 1930.
2. Scrimshaw cribbage board portraying American sailor, smiling, and Eskimo (?) woman in fur trousers and boots, bare from the waist up. 12¾" Early 19th c.
3. Small glass vial sealed with red wax containing a desiccated finger, flesh missing from the proximal two digits. Label: From the Murphy Cabin of the Donner Party, discovered and preserved this 14th of August, 1849.
4. L'Isle de Terre Neuve, l'Acadie. (partial) map of Canadian maritime provinces prepared by M. Bonne, Ingénieur-Hydrographe de la Marine. Trimmed round (11" diam.) and much stained

from (?) bird droppings and encrusted feathers (English Budgie?) suggesting secondary, non-geographical, use.

5. Grain of rice carved in the form of the Cardiff Giant, a gypsum humanoid believed to be a fossilized prehistoric man exhumed in 1869 at Cardiff, New York, the original purchased and exhibited extensively by P. T. Barnum (U. S.).

6. 7½" × 11" base metal plaque (lead?) bearing French inscription, date 29 July 1749, and names, Céloron, et al.

"Whoa!" Digger stopped reading, scanned the following half dozen items cataloged, saw nothing more of interest, and stared again at item number six. He clapped his hands. "Kiddo, we just found where the Lords of Trade plate has been all these years, and who's got it now."

They paged through Edgar's other books. Forty minutes later, they had a small pile of bookmarks: sugar packets, strips of napkins, grocery receipts, sundry snippets of colored paper, a shoelace. A few had unintelligible squiggles and symbols, one, a quarter page of blue-lined notebook paper, had several of Edgar's cryptic initials: LW—>LON. LOT. LW PB—>VA. LW, GW, PB, VA—>BAR.

"Different letters than in the atlas," Nikki said. "Edgar's handwriting."

Digger slapped the desk. "My gosh, kiddo—*L-W, G-W:* Lawrence and George Washington! Lawrence visited the Lords of Trade—*L-O-T*—in London—*L-O-N*—to set up the Ohio Company. He had tuberculosis, left Virginia—*V-A*—for Caribbean Barbados—*B-A-R*—hoping the climate would effect a cure. George went with him—the only trip George took out of continental America. And, Pb is the symbol for lead!

"We know George knew about Céloron's lead plates. What if Lawrence, a prominent Virginian, saw the plate the

Indians recovered when he visited the Lords of Trade and brought it back to show the Virginia assembly and governor, to shake loose funding for militia defense of the Ohio Company's land holdings?"

"Cool!"

"Lawrence's health got worse, he went on to Bermuda, and back to Mt. Vernon to spend his final days. He might well have left the plate in Barbados. I can imagine how George's seeing the thing itself, running his hands over it, would have inflamed his anger at the French."

"And," Nikki said, "if Smoot and the Frenchman know George Washington had his hands on it, no wonder they're so crazed."

Digger lifted the letter. "Written by Horatio Wembly, Director of the Queen's Maritime Museum, Bridgetown, Barbados, sent to an Orlando Sosa y Castro, Pre-Columbian Antiquities, Ltd., Miami, Florida. The date on the lead plate, July twenty-ninth? That's Céloron's first plate all right, the one the Indians liberated. This Sosa y Castro must be the one who's auctioning it."

He snapped the sheet with a fingernail. "Let's call these folks."

He phoned Barbados first, spoke to the assistant director, a Gaylord Trill, who told him Director Wembly was on an extended cruise, a much-deserved vacation, but, yes, the museum had divested itself of a small number of extraneous artifacts, nothing of real value. Mr. Sosa y Castro? A well-regarded antiquities dealer and generous friend of the museum.

"Hah!" Digger said after he hung up. "Some friend. Probably told them he was doing them a favor, taking junk off their hands. Well, let's call this 'friend.' "

He got the number from information, dialed, got a voice mail recording that Mr. Sosa y Castro was out of town, please leave a message.

Digger did: "Important, please call Harmon Perrier." He left Edgar's number.

32

The rising sun peeked over a hilly horizon. Coony steered from the stern of his twelve-foot aluminum boat while Digger slouched on the middle seat, legs stretched into the V of the bow. He dangled his hand over the gunwale, fingertips hop-skipping the mirrored surface. Eyes closed, he tuned into the Evinrude mantra, *putta-putta-putta*, took a deep breath of crisp morning air, and exhaled with an audible sigh.

Coony sighed too. "Nothing like going fishing."

"Thanks for inviting me. Lake fishing . . . Kentucky . . . it brings back memories."

"Kentucky? You been to Kentucky before?"

"Oh, yeah. I was born here."

"Hold on. You was *born* in McAfee County?"

"Not here. Danville. Clean town in the Bluegrass, south of Lexington. Haven't been back for decades. One of the things Edgar and I were going to do."

"Sumbitch! Though you're right about Danville not being *here*. Fancy horses, mint juleps, high-toned. Bluegrass is practically another country."

"Funny you should say that. My aunt always said that

about this part of the state—'You stay clear of those hills, Harmon, if you know what's good for you—that's another country.' With her dire warnings, I always had a case of the jitters driving through here to the east.

"Far as your other observation goes, I can't remember ever drinking a mint julep, and I'm afraid the Fitzes didn't qualify for the thoroughbred set. I went north to college, University of Michigan. Then, 'Go West young man'—Berkeley for post grad. Instructor. West again to Hawaii."

"I come out here to think," Coony said. "Get away from the crooks and the paperwork." He cut the motor, drifted to a stop. "Shhh—watch your moving around—lunkers below." He opened his tackle box. "I know the structure of this lake like the palm of my hand."

"Structure?"

"Lay of the bottom. I walked it when I was a kid. Original stream channel runs from there," he pointed, "underneath us, to there. Back in those shallows are the skeletons of trees, riprap to our side. Don't need no depth finder, don't need no fancy bass boat. The lunkers, they hunt left and right of us, run to the deep water if they're scared. They're down there right now, eyeing this torpedo we're in, listening. After a while, if we're lucky, they'll decide we're no threat."

"Maybe it's Edgar's death," Digger said, "but, truth is, I'm not into taking any fish lives. I'll watch."

Coony handed him a rod and spinning reel. "Very rare I take a fish home anymore. Capture and release, the new ethic." He whipped his own rod in a dry cast. "You remember how to use one of these? Next," he tapped the top tray in his tackle box, "you need to get acquainted with these. McAfee County specialty."

Digger looked at clear plastic boxes of long, multicolored, jellied lures lined up like sex toys in a head shop showcase.

"Winky Worms," Coony explained, "and what I'm putting together here is a split shot rig. Weed-guard hook through the back here, shot on the line at the front like this to weight it down. I'll cast, let it drop to the bottom, jig it back easy-like, and *Pow!* You'll see." He lifted his light graphite rod, and with a practiced flick of wrist and arm, threw the bait toward the shore, let it settle, and stripped the line in by hand, a foot at a time before reeling in the slack.

Digger stared, saw not Winky Worms but a nest full of baby snakes like the thing hooked in Edgar's mouth. He shut his eyes and willed away the memory, forced himself to pick one up. It felt slimy, trembled in his hand, protesting.

"That's a Scarlet Devil," Coony said. "Not a bad choice. Offal flavored. Want me to rig it for you?"

"Offal?" Digger sniffed his hands, and wished he hadn't. "No, I'll do it myself." He found a hook with a clear leader, fumbled with the line, wound up with an ungainly approximation of Coony's rig.

"You got too big a hook there. Worm's all bent, hooked too close to the middle. Won't get no action."

"Suits me fine. Wouldn't know what to do with a fish if I caught one." He cast toward a point six boat lengths off the bow, and saw the lure plunk seven feet away.

"Maybe you should float-fish," Coony said, drawing in line. "Lest one of us gets a hook in the ear."

Digger let the bait sink to the bottom at the side of the boat.

"Nice action," Coony said. "Bass'll like that."

Digger lifted the tip of the rod ten inches, let it drop. "Action, see?"

"Some action! Twenty bucks on the first one to catch something? See whose action pays off?"

"Why not?" Digger lifted the rod tip again.

Coony cast. "Been wanting to ask you something,"

"Shoot."

"Your dean. I called, checking you out. You know what he said?"

Digger stared at the faint ripples radiating from his line. "I can guess."

" 'Throw the reprobate in the clink.' What'd you do to piss the man off like that?"

Profound silence. Then: "Not a word to Nikki, your wife, or anyone else?"

Coony watched his last cast drop the worm within a foot of where he aimed it. While the bait descended, he shifted the rod to his left hand, spread his right palm on his chest. "You got my oath."

"In Hawaii they call me the . . . uh . . . Sex Doctor."

"You old dog. You poked your dean's wife!"

"Hold on. The nickname's kind of a joke with colleagues, because of my academic specialty—oceanic sexual practices. I write papers like 'Sex and the single Samoan,' 'The Pacific paradox: which came first, the missionary or the missionary position?' 'Metaphysical implications of the Fijiian yam dildo.' Serious business, but I inject a little humor when I can. Get the idea?"

"I get the idea: you got the dean's wife."

"You're moving too fast. Not to say I don't have a certain reputation." Digger read Coony's leer. "It's not my, uh, hardware—although there have never been any complaints in that department, either. More like—software. Field research. I've acquired a certain knowledge, you might say."

"Like in carnal knowledge of the dean's wife?"

"Hear me out. The dean's a pedantic bore, wears suits and bow ties—in Hawaii. The wife, Millicent, is a pleasant enough woman. Lonely, no doubt."

"Sure. Lonely."

"She must have heard some of them calling me the Sex Doctor, probably hadn't had a good roll in the grass for years."

"Stored it up, huh?"

"She invited me over for tea. I expected Dean Hotchkiss, faculty, spouses, one of those deadly compulsory affairs. Note on the door: 'Come in.' I enter, she calls from the back, says to have a seat. Tahitian drumming on the stereo, pretty hot stuff if you're familiar with it—hip-shaking music. No one else there. I figure the faculty are fashionably late, the dean still dressing. So, I pour a Planter's Punch from a pitcher on the coffee table. I hear her again from somewhere in the back, 'Turn on the VCR, remote's on the table.' I do, and the TV lights up—a porno video!"

"No!"

"Yes. Thais. Six or seven of them doing really disgusting stuff with pythons—*snakes*! Ugh. About the time my lunch reaches my throat, I decide I'd underestimated the dean, that he'd left in the wrong tape, that it was supposed to be some cultural thing, a Japanese tea ceremony or Chinese opera. While I'm savoring that thought, Millicent scoots in, wiggling her hips, wearing a *grass skirt*. Nothing else. Millicent is not the kind of woman who ought to be dancing around topless, believe me."

"Hah! But you poke her anyway."

"I do *not*. In fact, I dropped the remote, spilled the Planter's Punch in my lap. I stand, brushing off ice. There's Millicent shaking her hips, winking, the rest of her jiggling, Tahitian drums pounding, Thais doing it to slinkies on the tube."

"This is too much!" Coony slapped his thigh, laughing.

"Then, Bang! I hear the front door slam, I turn around, confused, fanning my wet crotch, and there's the *dean*, adjusting his glasses. I find out later he was supposed to be on his way to Maui. He came back for his briefcase."

Coony was rocking the boat, laughing so hard he could barely speak. "And found the fox in the hen house."

"What could I do? What could I say? I got the hell out of there."

"Left the scene of the accident. You coward!"

"I stayed clear of the university and didn't answer the phone for the three days before I left. So, that's my little problem in Hawaii. I stop over to lose my shirt in Las Vegas, and then fly here to find Edgar murdered and me a suspect."

Coony wiped tears from his eyes, and said, matter of factly, "You're no longer a suspect."

Digger gave him a long, inquiring look. "Well, well. How

about that? Nikki promised my luck would change—next I'll be winning our bet."

Coony rummaged through the cooler for a beer. He tossed one to Digger, opened another for himself, took a long swallow, and returned to casting.

Digger set his pole across the seat and gunwale. "So far, I'm doing about as well as you with your fancy rig, intimate knowledge of the bottom, precision casting, and jiggle returns, huh?"

"Never know what'll work, when," Coony said, but when he retrieved his lure, he changed to a bright yellow popper, removed the split shot, and began to fish the surface.

Coony cast the line again. "I know I promised not to talk shop today, but Etta checked on the Folk Museum of Eastern Kentucky."

Digger jiggled his bait on or somewhere near the bottom. "And?"

"Your gift shop woman was right. A lot of stuff was stolen, the insurance company made a deal. The director inventoried it all when they got it back, signed off on it. He was probably embarrassed to admit how sloppy their security was."

"I didn't like the shifty bastard. He might have shown me the damned lead plate as a professional courtesy. Could have checked my credentials easily enough."

"Like I did." Coony winked and waved away the worried look. "Good thing I did, too, or you might be behind bars, instead of enjoying this glorious morning." He poked Digger in the shoulder, smiled big enough to show him he might not have dug as deeply as Digger feared, and was pleased at the outcome.

A tremor in his line caught Digger's eye. He watched the line move away from the boat. "Aha!" He grabbed the rod, jerked it fast in a high arc, but instead of following his motion, the pole bent and the tip stayed in place, pointing to the water.

"Damned if you don't have a fish!" Coony reeled in, set his own rig down, dispensing advice. "Bottom fishing with no action. Sloppy-assed rig like that. I don't believe it. The way you jerked the pole, it's a miracle you set the hook." He put his hands on Digger's shoulders, pushed down. "Damnit, man, stay in your seat." Another look at the bent pole. "Lord, you must have a big one."

"Largemouth," said Digger. "Lunker. Thirty-pounder at least."

"More like a catfish or a carp. I'd say a tire if it wasn't moving. Although sometimes the big smart ones go easy first, testing, and run like hell when you least expect it. Take line in while you can. Steady."

Whatever it was swam away from the boat. Then it reversed direction, moved back and under.

"He's trying to foul the line and throw the hook." Coony put his hands on Digger's shoulders again, guiding him. "Move around the other side. Keep the tension up. Easy."

Digger caught a glimpse of something large and dark five feet down. "Oh, he's big. Big!" He tried to stand again, but Coony held him down with one hand, lifted a net with the other.

Digger held the rod handle at forty-five degrees, but the tip dipped under the surface. Resisting, a sinister, dark, unidentifiable form rose from the hazy green depths. "What the hell is it?" With no more than three feet of line out, he bent over, watched a shaft of sunlight strike a brown fist-size head, saw its body, below, indistinct but large as a microwave oven, backpedaling. Hell of a fish. Please don't let it be a—quick chill—snake. No, wait!—one of those *giant salamanders* Nikki talked about.

As the head rose to the surface, he stared into beady brown, gold-flecked eyes the size of small marbles, saw a hard pointed prow, bird's beak jaws clamped on the shank of the hook, half the worm down its gullet. He grabbed the line with his hand, couldn't raise the body, but the squat, torpedo-shaped head broke the surface, trailing a ten-inch, stretched *E.T.* neck.

"Sumbitch," Coony said. "It's the grandaddy of all snapping turtles!"

Digger heaved, and the jagged anterior of the snapper's thick leathery carapace, slippery with clinging algae, glistened in the air. Digger—line cutting into his hand, muscles screaming—and the turtle—massive feet churning—locked eyes for five long seconds in a stand-off.

Coony leaned over the gunwale, knife in hand. Digger shouted, "No!" But before the blade sliced nylon, the turtle blinked, opened its jaws and dropped like a stone. Digger was left holding a bent hook and half the Scarlet Devil Winky Worm.

"Sumbitch!"

"My turtle! I wanted to show it to Nikki."

"Not in my boat. Not no mean-ass snapping turtle."

Digger returned to his dead bait on the bottom routine. Coony began casting a silver spoon. He changed to a plastic minnow and had one weak strike. That was it. When the boat grew too hot to touch, Coony gave it up, motored back to the dock, and winched the boat onto his trailer. He started the engine. "Sorry we didn't do no better. Fishing gods not smiling on us, huh?"

"Hell, it was relaxing. Couldn't have asked for more." Digger held his hand out, palm up, by the steering wheel. "Except for my twenty dollars."

"Say what?"

"Our bet. I caught the turtle. You caught zip."

"The bet was for fish."

"Nope. You said 'First one to catch something.' "

"A turtle? Hell, you didn't even get it over the side."

"Would of, if you hadn't waved that knife at it."

"Shee-it!" Coony drove for thirty seconds, silent. He felt in his fishing vest for his wallet, pulled out two tens, and passed them to Digger. Two minutes later, he pulled to the side of the road.

Unsure what was up, Digger said, "No hard feelings?"

"Nah. Served me right, bragging on how I knew the lake so good. Come here, I want to show you something." Coony left the car, pointed to an overgrown, roofed, but unfinished building, apparently intended to be a restaurant. The cinder-block walls were unpainted, the windows glazed but boarded up. Coony motioned to it with an opened palm. "Behold: my dream."

Digger read the sign, whited over but legible. "A Big Boy. You want to open a Big Boy?"

Coony shook his head. "Bradford County got the state to widen the highway on the other side of the lake, found investors, and—boom—that's where the tourist business went. They stopped work here, put the Big Boy over there.

"You could pick up this and all that land fronting the lake for a song. Maybe not a song, but for a lot less than it's worth. Then? Finish off the building, put in a dock over there, attract another restaurant, maybe a lodge. Damn. What a headquarters this would make."

"You want to move?"

Coony kneaded his chin before speaking. "Here's a confession. That first day at the murder scene? You know why I didn't take you into headquarters, question you there like I should of?" Digger shrugged. " 'Cause I was ashamed. We're lodged in a pissant, to-be-ashamed-of little shack which no one else wanted." He kicked at a cinder-block sprouting grass. "Nossir. I didn't want to take an educated man like you from Honolulu hula-hula Hawaii, to see that sorry building, and that's the damned truth. I love this county and the people in it, do my damndest to keep them safe, but we're a poor-assed place, never enough jobs, never enough money."

Digger wasn't sure how to respond, so he merely nodded.

"My dream," Coony said, "If I can hang on, is to get us installed here before I retire. I'd pass the mantle to Bo, be an adviser for a few years. Etta'd be happy with that. She might stay on for a while, keep the wheels running. I'd put in an hour or two a day, fish the rest. So there you have it: my dream."

Digger kicked a warped two-by-four in sympathy. "Money's always the problem, isn't it?"

"Here's another confession. Not one I'd want certain people to hear or they'd conclude I'd damn sure gone over the top federal, but I'm glad those environment folks keep their eye on this county. If the coal people had their way, every one of those hilltops you see up there would be planed off without a care on God's green earth as to what it would do to Boone Lake and the streams that feed it. And those coal sludge dams? Disaster waiting to happen."

Digger kicked the board again. "Wesvaky Coal. Smoot Mudd."

"If it ain't one thing, it's another." Coony stepped onto a small stack of bricks and scanned the hills. "There's big trouble's coming to McAfee County, my friend. I feel it in my bones."

Coony jumped to the ground, lifted a small flat rock, and skipped it across the surface of the lake. "Enough down talk," he said. "C'mon, we'll head to Bradford County's Big Boy, other side of the lake, and you can buy me lunch with my twenty dollars."

33

Coony and Digger had been fishing since before sunup. Nikki drove to the sheriff's headquarters at a more civilized ten o'clock, eager to see Bo's deputy-captured, town-terrorizing rattlesnakes.

The HQ building looked less like the law-and-order blockhouse she expected and more like a recycled ice cream stand, with an unpainted cinder-block wing appended T-fashion to the back. She squinted at the painted-over hieroglyphics on the tall, double-faced sheet-metal sign at the front, and made out, sure enough, DA RY QUE N, barely obscured by a gold star bolted to either side and SHERIFF block-printed below.

She leaned into the carry-out window at the front, lettered RECEPTION, and gave her name to an ancient and cranky clerk behind the plate glass. He pressed a button and shouted "Mickey Fits" into an intercom.

Etta opened a door to the right, led Nikki inside, gave her a hug and a mug of coffee, and explained that the two deputy-captured rattlesnakes had grown to five. Bo was tied up at the county high school giving a "Your Future in Law Enforcement" lecture to the senior class.

"He'll be right along," Etta assured, but wouldn't allow Nikki near the snake barrel. She gave her a tour instead, explaining how she had nearly computerized the whole operation, such as it was. She even ran Digger's name through NCIC again, explaining how, though rural, remote, and poor, through the miracles of fax, phone, and internet, McAfee County was "linked with the world."

Deputy Johnny pointed proudly to his sketch on the bulletin board: *Have you seen this man? Chews tobacco. Drives dark pickup truck with Confederate bumper sticker. Wanted for reckless operation of a motor vehicle and felonious expectoration.*

Nikki studied the outline torso and right arm, the absent left one, the blank oval for a face, the arrow pointing to the space where the left arm would have been and the word *Missing.* "Exactly what I remember," she said.

"With luck," Johnny said, "someone will recognize him."

He escorted Nikki to his small lab and smaller darkroom, and (at her insistence but with a cross-your-heart oath not to tell Etta, Coony, or Bo) let her see the photos he had taken of her murdered Uncle Edgar. Nikki stared at them silently, with a mix of anger, rising tears, and magnetic fascination. When Johnny showed her the glossy of the shed rattlesnake skin at the murder scene, she used his magnifying glass to count scales. "If snakes could talk, huh?" she said, making notes in a small spiral binder.

Nikki reciprocated by showing Johnny her pet milk snake, Coony II, in the sequined snake carrier. Johnny suggested it might be fun to substitute Coony II for the coffee in fat Gabe's mug while he was away at the candy machine, and subsequently got a great shot of Gabe's face when his spoon stirred snake, not coffee. With a fair amount of shoulder jabbing and "Lighten up," Gabe finally spoke, and even, since Bo was not expected for another thirty minutes, and it was nearly eleven, volunteered to make a cross-county pizza run and take Nikki along.

With another heart-crossing not to tell Etta, Coony, or

Bo, Gabe hit the siren on a straight stretch, took it to a hundred, and nearly left the pavement twice as the highway bumped and dipped before switchbacking into the hills above town along the rise toward the Daniel Boone Forest. He dropped to a cautious twenty-five when the real pretzel twisters set in, and at one turn pointed to a missing guardrail where "some poor sucker from West Kentucky got his sawed-off school bus burnt to a crisp and himself smashed flat as a cow pie." He offered to stop and show Nikki the charred spot and "the squish mark fifteen feet up in the crook of an Indian cigar tree," but she declined.

While they waited for the pizza, Gabe allowed her (another oath) to handle his .38 (unloaded) and shotgun (empty), and call Bo on the patrol car radio. By the time they got back, Nikki had memorized eight police ten-codes.

Five minutes after one-eye-wandering Ike walked in waving his citation book, bragging he'd win the weekly pool, Bo arrived. With the exception of the dispatcher and the clerk at the Dairy Queen order window, Etta's ninety-three-year-old uncle who "hates snakes more than spiders," the whole cadre moved to the rear of the building for pizza and snake-handling.

Nikki leaned over the rattlesnake drum. "This is so-ooo screwy. Two of these animals look like good northern timbers, what we'd expect. The other three? Ringers for snakes from southern Georgia or Alabama."

Ike prompted, "Don't you need to get ahold of them to be sure?"

Nikki slid her four-foot snake tongs into the drum, picking among the merchandise. "Not only hold them, but count their dorsal scales."

"Be careful, girl," Etta cautioned.

"Hold on, ran out of film," Johnny said, reloading his 35-millimeter SLR.

Nikki raised a slowly squirming but surprisingly tranquil rattlesnake, barely pinched, more balanced at midbody by the tongs. "Stand back." She set it on the asphalt, shaded by the overhanging flat roof. The snake coiled, buzzed for five seconds, and went still except for a waving, satiny tongue with a forked tip. "Her stereo smeller."

Johnny circled with his camera. *Ka-chick, ka-chick, ka-chick.*

Gabe stared, unmoving, a tangle of pizza cheese stretching from slice to lips.

"Well da-amm, darlin'," Ike said. "What now?"

"I pick him up. See this?" She lifted an inch-and-a-half-diameter, three-foot-long clear plastic tube and placed one of the open ends near the snake's head. With a guiding touch from the tongs, she encouraged the snake into the orifice. "Pinning them behind the head the old way is traumatic. This minimizes stress." Fifteen inches in, the thickening body stoppered the tube. Nikki gently gripped the body behind the opening with enough forward pressure to keep the head end inside. She lifted the tubed snake to the picnic table, a carry-over from the Dairy Queen days.

"Now, Bo, I want you to count its dorsal scales around its middle here." She nodded with her chin to the section at the end of the tube. "Start with the first scale up from the wide belly scutes, trace them diagonally right around the body. Use your pen for a pointer. You'll have to get close, but I've got a good grip."

"Yeah," Ike said, "get real close."

Etta wrung her hands. "I'm not sure about this."

"Goll-ee," from Gabe, chewing absently. "Goll-ee."

"I'll get these published in *The Lawman* for sure," Johnny said, click-winding. "Get real close to her and the snake, Bo, so you're all in the frame. Look worried."

"Like this?" Bo said, expression unchanged.

Nikki asked Etta to write down the results.

Thirty seconds later, Bo relayed the count: "Twenty-seven scale rows."

Nikki extracted the first snake from the tube, returned it to the barrel, and repeated the procedure with another. After the fifth had been counted, she announced the results: "The three that look like they're from the south have twenty-seven rows. The two that look local, have twenty five." She sat on the bench seat of the table, drew her knees to her chin, thinking.

A suspenseful minute later, she stood. "Decades ago, biologists thought there were two varieties or subspecies: the northern, upland timber rattlesnake, *Crotalus horridus horridus*, and a southern, lowland form living in the Gulf coastal plain, the canebrake, *Crotalus horridus atricaudatus*."

Johnny said, "I don't get it. You said two of the ones here looked like—"

"Timbers, I know. And three like the canebrake variant. Canebrakes are lighter, with a more distinct reddish stripe down the back, prominent dark bands on a pinkish ground, and a higher dorsal count. Three of our specimens here fit that bill. Timbers tend to be darker, with a yellowish brown background and a lower dorsal count—although there's a dark phase that's nearly black, too. Two of our specimens are unmistakably yellowish brown northern timbers."

"So you got a mixed bag, so what?" said Ike.

"So, it's a big deal. A paper came out in 1973 saying they were all the same animal, different only at the extremes of their ranges, blended together in between, the scale counts inconclusive. Biologists dropped the subspecies names and now call them all timbers, *Crotalus horridus*.

"But . . . if you were to find clean-cut populations of both northern and southern variants living *together*, not interbreeding, it would be reasonable to conclude you had two distinct *species* not mere varieties: *Crotalus horridus* and *Crotalus atricaudatus*. No mixing. Robins and thrushes. Bullfrogs and green frogs. White oaks and pin oaks. That would upset the herpetological apple cart.

"A few researchers have raised suspicions that canebrakes and timbers might be distinct species, although given the variation in scale counts, color, and pattern, that's not something you can prove without nuclear DNA analysis."

"Cut to the chase," Ike urged.

"All right. About the last thing you would expect to find

is two clear-cut populations this far north. If more timbers and canebrakes turn up side by side here, with no intermediates, that's a darned good sign you have two kinds of animals.

"Man," she screwed up her face, thinking. "I wonder if they live in separate ecological niches, breed at different times to maintain genetic isolation?"

Johnny was thinking ahead. "You want more? We're getting at least a call a day."

"All you can find." Rubbing her hands together. "Write down exactly where you find them—"

"You mean like at the corner of Main and Elm?" Ike asked.

"Whoa." Etta raised a hand. "If they're careful, I'll let the boys haul them in for you, sweetheart—there's dozens of ice cream tubs left in the storeroom to hold them, but there are limits. And, it won't do to have my men bit."

"I know," Nikki said. "I can show you how to handle them—okay?" She scowled at the drum. "This is weird. Rattlesnakes are shy, normally stay clear of people. Something's upset the natural order."

Bo interrupted. "You want to know where a slew of them live? When I was a kid, I counted thirty-two of them sunning at a den early one spring."

"A *den*? Wow! This early in the year, they could still be hanging around it."

"You know, it's not all that far from your house. The same family owns all that land. I guess the den's still there if the coal company hasn't moved in on it."

"You mean they'd mine it?"

"Strip is what they do. Maybe not today or tomorrow, but when the price of coal rises. They hold options on a good bit of land in the county."

"Oh, man. Timbers are threatened all over, what with habitat destruction and humans killing them left and right. You know, the mother snakes give birth near the den. Somehow the babies are imprinted with the site, so they return year after year to hibernate. If that den's destroyed they could all die."

"No kidding?"

"Man, a *den* . . . Show it to me!"

Etta drummed her fingers on the table. "Bo's on duty, Nikki. And so are the rest of you. Lunch is over." She hustled them inside.

Nikki apologized. Etta said, "No big deal," whispering, "Men are lazy, sweetheart, and a pretty young woman and rattlesnakes is plenty enough to make them play hooky. If I didn't keep a close watch, nothing would get done. You come back when Bo's shift ends, and he can take you hiking." She gave Nikki a hug and walked her to the car.

Nikki met Bo at three. She released the five headquarters' rattlesnakes on a remote rocky hillside in the north of the county, within the Daniel Boone National Forest. "After I record them," she said, "I'll turn loose any new ones you find in town here, so as not to screw up the rest of the county's population."

They hiked into the wilderness above and behind Edgar's house. They saw deer, a lumbering bear in the distance, several birds Nikki had never seen before, and, according to Bo, elk tracks. Nikki also caught an eastern racer and a half dozen lizards, although they crisscrossed the mountainside for forty-five frustrating minutes before Bo finally found the den itself.

Nikki spotted first one rattlesnake, eventually five, sunning, coiled on limestone rubble at the base of an escarpment on the south side of a ridge. She watched through binoculars. "Earlier in the spring, I'll bet we'd see dozens. These are all timbers—*horridus*. I'd put money on it. There's a mystery here, all right. Maybe there's a den of *atricaudatus* somewhere else."

She set the binoculars down, wheeled around and punched Bo in the shoulder. "Neat!" she said. "Really neat. We're on to something big."

34

B ig Butt found Jesus Bob at the far edge of camp, head jutted out, spitting on ants.

"Bombs away," Jesus Bob said, and then, "Flood!" When he missed the next one, he called to the ground, "Sky's fallin'" and flattened the tiny insect with a boot heel.

"Guess who that guy is over there?" Big Butt said, missing the double-time blinking, the clenching fists. "The one in brown camos, talking with general Ben?"

"Don't give a shit," Jesus Bob said, but he looked. "Can't make him out."

"Real important. A em-miss-ary, says Ben. Been here once or twice before. He's from the Bear Mountain Sentinels, a bad-assed bunch, and he may be the baddest assed they got. We're thinking of being allies, them and us being against the same stuff and all. Man, between the Sentinels and the Rangers—"

Jesus Bob cut him off. "Shut the hell up, huh? Always runnin' off at the mouth." He caught the hurt look, scowled, walked to Big Butt's side, and gave him a sharp, conciliatory knuckle punch. "Hey, pardner, no hard feelings. I'm a little edgy since Sis kidnapped my stash, okay? Three joints and a couple lines of coke a day is hardly enough to keep me up or down. Look at my hand."

Big Butt watched Jesus Bob's fingers vibrate, saw a quiver run wrist to shoulder, shoulder to neck and back, like a robotics dance move, noticed the recurrent twitch at the corner of his left eye, and remembered his own smacked nose. He took two steps back. "No problem."

"Yeah, it is. You're my pardner, and I'm being an ass-hole." He whipped his face left and right, as if to dislodge a recalcitrant fly, and then stuck a finger in each ear, reaming them out, fists spinning at the side of his head. "You got any whippits up the mess hall? Hell, anything with a little boost or knock-back? There's jimson weed growing here and it's calling my name, but if I get jimson-whacked, Sis'll—you know." He made slicing motions at his crotch and groped himself. "I can't get it up no more—whadaya think of that? Not something I'd tell no one but you, pardner, unnerstand?" The words were spilling out, clippety-clip-clip-clip. "Maybe couldn't get it up for the last few months or so, neither, but it weren't something I thought about. Now I do. Damn. I feel like *shit*. Pissed off!" He shouted it to the treetops. "*Pissed off!* Where was I? Oh, yeah, you was telling me about this new soldier."

"S'okay," said Big Butt, edging farther away.

"Go on, tell me. Take my mind off how crappy I feel."

"Well . . . they say he's a hell of a shot. Can flip a silver dollar in the air, quick draw, and shoot it out of the sky."

"Challenge the bastard, blow his head off. Give you my cutaway holster, you want." Jesus Bob pressed palms to his eyes. "Do us proud." His right hand shot from his face to his side, slapped open the holster, gripped his Ruger Blackhawk .357 Magnum, drew it fast, gave it a sloppy finger twirl, and dropped it back with a quick smile. "Swish. Pow!"

"No way," said Big Butt. "I can draw fair, but I can't hit a bottle at twenty feet. On a rail. They say this guy keeps a .30/06 in his truck cab, picks off farm cats in the field out'a the window going sixty miles an hour. Hey!" He pointed past Jesus Bob's shoulder. "He's coming our way."

Jesus Bob took a long squint at the man, fifty feet away. "Why hell, the bastard's got only one arm!"

"Yeah," said Big Butt. "I said he was good. Look how he keeps it gripped on his handgun—big .38. They say he never takes it off, either, except to drive or do his business. Watch what you say, huh?"

The man briefly raised his hand waist-high in casual greeting, and then replaced it on the butt of the revolver, reflexively curling his finger around the trigger. He strode straight to Jesus Bob with a confident swagger. Chewing tobacco, he stared for a long second at Jesus Bob rubbing his eyes, and, longer, at Jesus Bob's exposed knuckles.

"You some kind of fairy?" said the Sentinel, and spit a glop of tobacco juice two inches from Jesus Bob's boot. "Like, what the fuck's a *bith*?"

In a surprisingly fast move for a man with wandering attention, Jesus Bob's right hand departed his face in a wheeling blur, and the A B I T H knuckles connected with the Sentinel's left temple. As the Sentinel staggered, knees buckling, Jesus Bob kicked him in the chest, lifting him a foot in the air. In one continuous move, the pounding hand dropped to Jesus Bob's side, snatched the .357 from his hip, cocked the hammer . . .

Big Butt yelled, "No!"

Pointing the .357 muzzle at the stunned man's head, Jesus Bob held his trigger finger steady, looked quizzically at Big Butt. "What's that you say?"

"Lordy!"

"Lordy?"

"Jesus Bob, partner, you . . . you can't shoot a one-armed man."

"And why the hell not? I'd say he was about to draw on me. *Damn*, I'm fast—look, his hand's still on the handle of his .38. Never got it out of his holster. Fella's got a hell of a grip to hold on like that after I kicked him, I'll give him that."

"He's a Sentinel. Our ally. And . . . shooting a one-armed man is, like, against the Code."

"Code? What fucking Code?"

"You know. Like, the Duke wouldn't do it. Shoot a one-armed man. With him down like that. Please, partner, don't shoot him."

Jesus Bob shrugged. "Okay." He reset the hammer and holstered the weapon. He leaned over the now gasping, rocking, one-armed man trying to right himself with his elbow like a sea lion with a missing flipper, and studied him for a long second. Then, he grabbed the man's head, and with a mighty wrench, twisted it 180 degrees.

Big Butt heard a muffled pop and squeezed his eyes shut. When he opened them, the one-armed man was lying belly to the ground, face up. Big Butt saw a final spasm, and then nothing.

"Lordy!"

Jesus Bob winked, gave Big Butt a diabolical leer. "See? Guns don't kill people, people kill people."

"Oh, man! He's dead."

"I hope to hell that's the case with his head on backwards, or the poor bastard couldn't see where he was going, only where he'd been."

"Lordy. A Bear Mountain Sentinel. Our ally. Killed dead. This is trouble. Big trouble."

Big Butt's panic got through to Jesus Bob. "I'm sorry," he said, and poked Big Butt in the ribs to get a chuckle out of him.

Big Butt pulled away and paced, avoiding the glazing eyes of the one-armed Sentinel. "Man, sorry ain't good enough. Wait till General Ben hears about it, I'll be busted to private. He'll rip your corporal stripes off—bet on it. The commander'll be pissed good an proper. This could be *war*. With the Bear Mountain Sentinels."

Jesus Bob cared not a whit about the war part, he'd be long gone by the time they got around to that. As far as his much anticipated payback to the law, he would deal with that himself if he had to. The rank meant zip. But the commander part? The commander was at the heart of his sister's plan. Commander trouble meant sister trouble. "Pardner, I may have fucked up."

Big Butt wrung his hands. "Maybe we can say he fell."

"Somehow, I don't think they'll buy that one. Why don't we say he insulted you guys? Called you pussies and I, like, defended your honor. Maybe you'd get a medal for that, huh?"

"Still be war with the Sentinels."

"Okay, okay. The rest of them are up the hill and don't know he was with us. We'll ditch him, say he left. What happened once he left here's no skin off our tails. Where's his car?"

"Behind the tobacco barn. I showed him my new truck and the arsenal when he got here. Can't see either of 'em from camp. Maybe that'd work. Maybe."

"Unbelievable!"

Jesus Bob and Big Butt nearly stumbled, so fast did they spin to see the speaker. Rita Rae! Sneaked up on them. Jesus Bob tried to move between his sister and the body to hide the evidence. Ineffectually.

"Let me guess. Someone—" Rita Rae slapped Jesus Bob across the cheek. "—was a wittle grumpy? Got carried away?" She kicked him in the shins, kept talking while he danced, directed her questions at Big Butt. "The guy with the backwards head one of yours? One of Smoot's favorites, no doubt."

"No, ma'am," said Big Butt, ready to jump back if one of her pointy heels struck his way. "He was a Bear Mountain Sentinel. That's worse."

"Smoot doesn't know him?"

"No, ma'am. The commander don't come up here much."

"You said the other soldier boys don't know this one was with you?"

"No, ma'am."

"Nuh-uh." Jesus Bob rubbed his shin, hopeful she would buy into the ditching the body plan.

"Hmmm." She glared at the limp Sentinel, the backward head, the glazed, open eyes, the single hand still death-gripping the revolver. "Yuck! Roll him into the weeds. I don't want to look at him and I sure don't want the rest of them seeing him like that either."

Eager to comply, Jesus Bob took a shoulder, Big Butt a leg, and they log-rolled the dead Sentinel five feet into a thick patch of goldenrod.

"Now, you." She pointed to Big Butt. "Go through his pockets, find his keys. Run to his truck—wipe your prints off the keys and wheel, be sure no one sees you. Hide the truck somewhere where this one"—she nodded to Jesus Bob—"can find it. Then join the rest of them, say you saw the guy drive off. Hear?"

"Yes, ma'am."

"Well? Get your lard ass in gear."

Big Butt stooped in the goldenrod, shut his eyes to avoid meeting the Sentinel's fish-eye gaze, and felt through his pockets. "Got 'em."

"So why do I still see you?"

He trotted down the hill toward the barn.

"Why *do* I put up with you?"

From beyond kicking range, Jesus Bob said, "Sis, this is the first time I screwed up since we been here. If I'd of had my medicine . . ."

She raised a warning hand.

"Anyways, didn't I do exactly what you told me with the professor guy? With the lead sinkers? Shut him up, huh? Scared the crap out of old Smoot, made him think it was the Frenchman? You put the icing on the cake with the scalp and the snakes in the box. Doing in the professor scared the hell out of the old museum fart in Morehead at the same time—I done the fishhook to let him know to keep his mouth

shut about the switched slab of lead. I thought of the worm
to fuck the local yokels' and the law's minds."

He watched her nod, could see he was getting through.
"I even threw some of my medicine around, pills and pot, a
vial of crank. Made the law think it was a drug deal. Came
up with that myself."

Maybe not exactly, he considered, recalling how he had
bent down after killing the old man, opened his THIS SIDE UP
case to do a few lines, celebrate, jack up the high—and then
saw the ten-foot rattlesnake slithering across the linoleum at
him. He tipped the case, spilled five hundred bucks of fine
dope before he got the case in hand, still open, running out
of that lousy shack before the snake could block the door . . .

"Yeah," she was saying, "you surprised me. Didn't think
you were that clever, little brother." Actually smiling. "Now,
back to this mess . . ." She glanced over her shoulder at the
body in the trampled goldenrod. "There may be a way we
can turn this around. . . ."

35

*S*moot's map took Bolt straight to the beige crushed-limestone driveway of Alphonse Le-Coup's pristine white château. As soon as Bolt ascended the curvy road into the posh, rolling green Village of Indian Hill east of Cincinnati, however, and saw the lean, fortyish blondes commanding their battle tank SUVs, the kids in their starter Jeeps, and the movers and shakers driving their Mercedes, Porsches, and other high-toned wheels, he realized a muddy pickup with Kentucky plates was apt to raise eyebrows.

His first thought had been to hide his truck in the forest—Smoot assured him Indian Hill was half woods—but Bolt saw immediately that Smoot had overstated the woods part and failed to mention the lawn part. Years ago, when Smoot and LeCoup had been buddies, trees had indeed covered much of the Village, but today, most of the woods had given way to lawn, acres of it, as neatly trimmed and sterile as Astroturf.

Bolt drove past LeCoup's, cursing at the threadbare bands of trees separating neighbors, for Smoot had also failed to mention that, unlike McAfee County, there were no rutty pull-offs into concealing vegetation, and that no one parked at the side of the road but the occasional lawn man. The lawn men did drive pickups, but they invariably bore Ohio plates and fancy logos on their well-washed doors, with beds full of lawn mowers, bags of grass seed, or drums of Mole-Be-Gone.

Bolt may not have been the brightest, but he knew parking at the side of this ritzy road would, in short order, attract the scrutiny of the gentry's cops or some nosy jogger with a cell phone relaying license numbers while he was at his business.

His first thought had been to pull straight into the drive, leave the motor running, jump out with the red-dye-filled balloons—currently bumping shoulders with one another in the cardboard box at his side like three fat ladies on a love seat—charge the house, pitch them, and be off. Assuming there was no sign of occupants.

He turned around, cruised by the house again, and saw not merely an occupant, but a damned *guard*, a swarthy guy in sunglasses, not in uniform, but dressed in a black turtleneck, loose black trousers, and black athletic shoes, sitting on the edge of a fountain reading a newspaper. A guard all right, and not some cheap rent-a-cop either. Armed. And a butler, too! Like on the TV. Some guy in a black dress-up suit and bow tie, walking out the front door, carrying a tray with a pitcher and glass and a plate of something, no doubt home-baked chocolate chip cookies for the damned guard.

So . . . Bolt squealed away from the white castle and entirely out of Indian Hill, which, as far as he could tell, was all monster houses and lawns, and not enough woods, with nary a strip mall, convenience store, bar, or even gas station in the whole unnerving place.

He found concealing mall-sprawl twenty minutes away in neighboring Kenwood, bought a six-pack of Bud, drove into a big parking garage, popped a can, and reviewed his problem. With the first buzz came inspiration. He dismounted, snitched a set of Ohio plates from one car, exchanged them for another Ohio set on a truck of the same make and model as his (no easy find, that, in affluent suburbia), and switched those with his own tags, tucked temporarily under the front seat. Next, he found a Signs While You Wait shop and ordered two magnetic signs, Vengeance Lawn and Painting (heh, heh), necessitating a flourish of his skinning knife when the clerk told him to stop back for them the next day. Two hours later, signs stuck tight to the pickup's doors, he headed back to LeCoup's, having made one more stop at a hardware store for half a dozen bags of fertilizer.

He parked at the side of the road by the strip of woods separating the white castle from the neighboring thirty-room mock-Tudor, confusing inquisitive eyes as to exactly where he might be lawning and painting.

He propped an opened bag of Scott's Lawn Care against the roadside wheel well, left the tailgate down, the other bags plainly visible, and scooped the three balloons into his arms (more difficult than he thought—they were heavy and awkward, wanting to roll this way and that). With a glance up and down the road, and across the lawns for cops or jogging housewives, Bolt scooted into the woods.

No more than twenty feet in, he tripped on a wild grape vine, felt one of the dye balloons roll over his forearm, watched helplessly as it bounced once and broke with a sickening *glop* on an upturned stick. Red shoe. Damn.

More carefully—because he caught sight of the guard every now and then through the trees, which meant the guard could see him, too, if he looked up from his newspaper and lemonade and cookies—Bolt worked his way through the trunks and brush bordering the long lawn, past the side of the house to the back. Fully as extensive as the green expanse at the front, the rear lawn surrounded a swimming pool with a gazebo on one side and a changing cabana on the other. Trees trimmed into balls and pyramids and swans formed a staggered privacy fence around a hot tub sunk into the patio not fifty feet from Bolt's bushy hideout. And above?

One big-assed snow-white wall, tall and broad as a drive-in movie screen with only two tiny windows, high up. Perfect.

Bolt swished through the weeds, peered front and rear for signs of the butler or guard, and, seeing none, dashed onto the grass. Twenty feet from the patio, left arm hugging one balloon, Bolt stopped, palmed the other in his right hand, extended his arm back for a grand pitch, and heaved, fast.

Unfortunately, Newton's first law of motion, the one about inertia, contradicted Bolt's intentions. The rubbery part of the balloon in his grip followed his hand, but the liquid inside said *No, wait a second or two till I catch up*, and what had been a sphere became an ovoid. A lengthening ovoid. No! Bolt felt the red bomb leave his grasp, heard it burst on the ground at his back. *Splosh*.

One to go. One. Another quick look this way and that—clear—and Bolt moved to the very edge of the patio. Taking no chances with the remaining projectile, he cradled it below his waist with both hands, fingers interleaved. He bent forward, hands between knees, for a mighty underhand loft. *Whoosh*. It left his hands intact, sailed for the second story, hit the virginal wall—Yes!—and then—Sonofabitch!—bounced off, dropped into the hot tub with an audible splash.

Bolt's stomach sank with the balloon. What now? He heard a *wwrup, wrrrrr* from the front—lawn mower starting up. Heading his way! Back to the woods, thrash to the road, dash to the truck, a swift angry kick at the opened fertilizer, slam the tailgate, and leave the cursed place. He drove by LeCoup's house for one last bitter look, saw a pickup parked at the side of the road up front with a two-wheel trailer hitched behind, Villa Beauty Lawn on the door, bags of Scott's Lawn Care in the bed, one guy at the center of Le-Coup's lawn riding a mower, another by a spreader, taking a glass of lemonade from the butler.

Bolt did the only thing he could under the circumstances: he beat it back to McAfee County and lied to the commander.

*　　　*　　　*

"Nikki? It's Bo." Calling early. "Your uncle up yet? Wake him, okay? Could you two meet me at the intersection of Rose and Main? In the school parking lot. ASAP."

"You sound worried. Oh, man, it's not a rattlesnake bite, is it?"

"No . . . it looks like we found your one-armed man. I'd like you to identify him."

"Cool!"

Nikki roused Digger, chattering about a lineup, wondering where would they get that many one-armed men if there was only one they knew about in the county, and, even if they did, how could she identify him if she had only seen him from the back, and . . .

"Sheesh, Nikki, I'm still half asleep. You'll find out soon enough."

Gabe waved their car to a stop barely inside the school lot. Two patrol cars, lights flashing, sat beside a dark pickup by the playground fence. Yellow tape kept onlookers at bay. Beyond, tiny faces peered from school windows.

"It's not the spitting bastard himself," Nikki said. "Just his truck."

"Here comes Bo, kiddo. I'm sure he'll explain."

Bo led them on foot toward the rear of the truck. Forty feet away, he asked Nikki to look at its rear end.

"Oh, the bumper stickers. Yeah, Confederate flag, and the one to the right I couldn't make out before." She walked closer and read it aloud: "Armed With Pride."

"Maybe," Digger postulated, "it means, like, differently-abled—you know, with his one arm."

"I don't think so, sir." Bo moved between Nikki and the truck, shielding her view. "See, we found him behind the wheel . . . he had a .38 revolver in his hand, there was another one in the glove box, plus a Saturday night special holstered at his ankle, and there's a loaded .30/06 mounted in a rack at the back of the cab—"

"A rifle?" Nikki said. "I don't get it, with one arm, how could he . . ."

"Don't know," Bo said. "He must have been, what do they call it—unidextrous. He also had two semiautomatic pistols—how he used those I can't imagine. I'd say the guy just liked guns."

Nikki scanned the backseats of the cop cars, saw nothing. "Where is he, the bastard?"

"He's there all right." Digger pointed. "In the truck cab. Glare on the window, but you can make him out. Spooky, he's just staring at us over the backseat."

Nikki edged around Bo. "What's he doing, looking at us like that? You have him handcuffed, huh? Neato, I want to see him up close, tell him what I think of—"

Bo gripped her wrist, kept her from running to the door. "Hold on, Nikki . . . the guy is . . . dead."

"Dead? He's looking right at us, how—?"

"Dead. Take my word for it—Johnny needed a tire iron to pry his cold stiff fingers from that .38. His eyes are still open. Actually, he—his body, that is—is facing forward, his head's turned all around the other way, looking backwards. Someone twisted it. That's probably what killed him."

"A safe assumption," Digger concluded.

"Eeuuw!" Nikki tried to shake loose from Bo, doing her best to get a good look.

Bo held on, led her back to their car, explaining. "Fella was dressed in camos, wallet in his pocket, chained to his belt. He works at a lumberyard in Coal City, has been into trouble before, plenty of fights, has a reputation for having a strong right. He's suspected of shooting at Treasury agents, too. Belongs to a militia, the Bear Mountain Sentinels."

Digger huffed. "Militias."

"That's right. Gabe ran a check. The Stokes County sheriff knew him right off. We thought of your uncle's murder, but the guy was in their lockup that night.

"With those guns, we thought he might have been planning to take a shot at two federal—Health-Education-

Welfare—people visiting the school today. One of them dresses like Happy Tooth, the other like Mr. Decay. But that's not it."

"What is it?" Nikki said. "C'mon, tell us."

"We found poly bags of pot in the cab, sheets of stamped cartoon characters, probably laced with LSD, crack cocaine, lots of small bills and change, three boxes of melting ice cream he was going to pass out: Drum Sticks, Fudgesicles, Eskimo Pies." Bo slammed a fist into his open hand. "The no good was *selling drugs to kids!*"

"Bummer," said Nikki.

Digger agreed. "Shameful. To kids, yet."

"Yeah. We figure one of the fathers got wind of it, caught him here early this morning right after he arrived, twisted his neck like that when the guy reached for his gun and left him in the cab. School bus driver found him." Bo sighed. "Now we've got to go hunting for the one who did this. Probably a model citizen, never committed a violent act in his life before, was outraged at what drugs do to young minds.

"I'll tell you this," Bo said, with a doleful shake of his head, "a cop's job isn't always the fun it's made out to be."

36

Alphonse LeCoup put his computer to sleep, dropped his glasses on the desk and rubbed the bridge of his nose. Eyes closed, he called to Raven in the adjoining office. "*Chère,* it's late. How's the due diligence coming on that hospital consolidation?"

"Beaucoup personnel elimination. A real bloodbath. Nice piece of the pie for us."

"*Fantastique.* I've been staring at this screen all evening. What say we go back to my place and relax?"

She materialized behind him, began massaging his shoulders with strong hands.

Fifteen minutes later their cars crunched to a stop on the gravel turnaround at the front of LeCoup's house. LeCoup waved to the guard, an ex-Israeli secret agent, grossly overpaid for such routine duty, but LeCoup always bought the best, and he damned well didn't want any more rattlesnakes dumped on his doorstep. "You stay up front here for an hour or so, Levi. The lady and I wish some privacy out back."

The man stood, acknowledged the order with a minimal nod and slipped back into the shadows.

LeCoup unlocked the front door. "Jeeves is off tonight,

sweet," he said with a pat on her tight behind. "How about we slip in the hot tub, get loosey-goosey, and retire to the collection room for a little pioneer crime and punishment?" He had his tie off already, was helping Raven out of her silk jacket as they walked through the foyer, bumping hips.

"Leave the lights out," she said. "And no noise until we're back inside. I don't want Levi Strauss up there peeking through the topiary at us."

"Levi Levkovitz," he corrected, with a nibble at her neck. "The man's a former Mossad agent, a real professional, follows orders to the letter, don't worry."

Shed clothes marked a trail down the corridor leading to the collection room. They moved toward an unassuming door to the side patio and the hot tub.

LeCoup flipped the agitate switch, ran his hand through Raven's hair as she slipped past him into the dark, steaming, and now gurgling water. He followed. For five minutes they lay back on opposite sides, nude, unmoving.

"I can barely see you, *chère*." LeCoup ran a hand up her calf. "But you feel great."

She giggled, grabbed his ankle and jerked, pulling him, sputtering, under the roiling surface. LeCoup bobbed, sucked air, got a good grip on one of her legs and slid under again, dragging her with him.

Raven's head broke the surface. She shook her water-logged hair side to side, felt LeCoup's beard tickle her inner thigh. "Ummm," she purred, tugging his ears closer. Out of breath, he came to the top, gasped air.

He cupped her breasts, ran his lips up her neck to her ear, whispered, "A warming fire by the stake, *ma petite sauvage*?"

Porpoiselike, Raven jetted from the water, darted for the open door and ran down the darkened corridor to the vault, giggling. LeCoup took up the chase. He caught up with her as she worked the combination lock.

Raven slapped his hands away. "Wait till we're inside. I

don't want Levi Strauss making his house rounds while I'm
out here in the buff."

With the click of the last tumbler, LeCoup pushed open
the steel door with one hand, goosed Raven with the other.
She squealed, "Ye-eek! Cold hands!" reached behind to
grip his wrist, tugged him into the collection room, and
shoved the door closed. "We'll leave the lights out. No cos-
tumes tonight, straight to the stake. I'll get the fire."

"You want some fire?" LeCoup groped himself. "I'll give
you fire."

"Dirty old man." She pulled him to the stake, hurriedly
slung rope around his waist.

"Old woman," LeCoup corrected, then said, "Forget the
fire. Go straight to the punishment." He segued into falsetto:
"Hit me for my treachery. Do it!"

She did, a good one: *Slap!*

The lights came on. They blinked, blinked again, retinas
recovering, and saw: LeCoup, red as Cardinal Richelieu's
cloak, Raven, redder than Rudolph's nose.

They both screamed. LeCoup fainted. Raven, woozy herself, untied him and slipped to his side, fearing heart attack.
Recalling her high school Red Cross training, she thumped
his chest, blew in his mouth, pressed on his sternum.

Even at the front fountain, despite the thick walls of the collection room, Levi heard the screaming. He snatched the key
ring from his pocket, unlocked the front door, pushed it open
with a foot, stood to the side, and leapt in, crouching low,
Uzi in hand. Silence. He ran down the hall toward the rear
of the house where the muffled screams must have origi-
nated, where LeCoup had said they would be—fooling
around, Levi assumed, no doubt in a bedroom. Hastily, he
checked the master bedroom—nothing, bed still made—then
a guest room—same, same—and worked his way back, heart
pounding.

He flipped the light switch, saw the tossed clothing, and beyond, the bloody footprints leading from an outside door into the house, into the vault. Big vault, he remembered from the house plans. With no outside windows. Locked tight and Levi didn't have the combination. He followed the footprints the other way, outside to the hot tub. He turned on the lights. God! Blood everywhere, hot tub full of it.

His mind raced—they must have been attacked in the tub. Shot? Silencer? Stabbed? He flicked off the lights, dropped to the ground, mind racing. Attacker must have run off. Wounded, the old man and the woman stumbled to the security of LeCoup's safe room. Or, was the bastard inside with them?

Levi dialed the police—the Indian Hill Rangers—on his cell phone, and then his partner, brother Liev, and Jeeves who had the lock combination. Eye on the vault door, listening, gun in hand, Levi waited for the cops, for the life squad, for reinforcements.

37

The Daniel Boone Rangers had gathered in the tobacco barn after supper. Ben sat on a wooden crate
marked ARMAS DE ESPAÑA, inventory sheets spread
before him.

"It came to me over my Rice Krispies this morning," he
said to the assembled Rangers. "I was thinking, this dreadful
music, the disrespect? What's become of our children? Sex
education is partly to blame—it's no wonder kids know what
it is by the time they're doing it. But the big question is: who
is behind it all, stirring up our youth? The answer came from
a strange quarter—my cereal spoke to me."

Ben spoke to widening eyes. "Indeed. The *Antichrist* is
what it said. I put an ear to the bowl and it murmured over
and over: the Antichrist, the Antichrist, the Antichrist."

"Cool," said Purcell. "On the TV, there's lots of stuff that
talks to you. Raisins, cats and dogs, toilet bowls—"

"Not like *that*," said Ben. "Although," he gave Purcell a
conciliatory shoulder pat, "you are correct about the TV part.
That is where he lives now, the spawn of a degenerate Hol-
lywood. In a flash of insight, the name of the Antichrist came
to me."

He rose, looked to, and beyond, the rafters. "I recalled the warning in Revelation: 'And I beheld a beast rising up out of the earth; and the beast had two long ears; and he spake in tongues, in a grievous mocking voice'—or words to that effect. Is it not obvious?"

Apparently, to the assembled troops, it was not, so Ben told them: "The Antichrist is none other than *Bugs Bunny!*"

That got everyone's attention.

"Consider," said Ben. "This unrepentant trickster wears women's dresses and makeup. He impersonates angels and lasciviously kisses the unwary, harrows Elmer Fudd and other authority figures with that hideous voice. And, of course, 'Bugs' . . ." Ben cocked a knowing eyebrow at the startled Rangers, ". . . is one of those *Jewish* names, is it not?"

"Yes!" Ben lifted his riding crop and slapped his thigh with it. "Bugs Bunny, the Antichrist, inculcates our youth with wrongheadedness, subverts the grand plan, paves the path of human destruction."

Silence reigned for several pregnant seconds as the Rangers considered Ben's revelation. A Federal-Alien-Zionist conspiracy was one thing, but lovable Bugs, the Antichrist? And a Jew to boot? Men averted their eyes from the general, clutched their sidearms for security.

Big Butt, never one to challenge General Ben, was the first to respond, perhaps intuitively sensing the need for a change of subject. "Speaking of dresses, there's talk of girls wanting to join the Scooter Shooters and Junior Rangers."

"Preposterous!" Ben waved his crop. "You see? See where it's leading?"

"Kind of threw me for a loop," said Big Butt.

"Listen up, everyone." Ben was off on a new tack. "And I will tell you about the Afganistani Taliban." He took a deep breath and walked among them. "Though they are heathens, not a Christian bone in their brown bodies, and are thus doomed to burn in Hell everlasting, these Taliban do know a thing about family values. They keep their females in the home with the children where they belong, out of the schools and the workplace where we have so many of them taking honest men's jobs—I heard at the shop only yesterday, there are more women working at the Winky Worm plant now than men. What do you think of that?"

"Indeed," Ben said to the rising grumbling. He set down his crop and uncapped the lid of a tin of smokeless tobacco (smoking being frowned upon in the tobacco barn arsenal). To underscore his point, Ben repeated it: "Taliban women stay at home."

"Don't they even shop?" asked Purcell. "I mean, do the men got to buy the groceries and all?"

"I imagine, young Purcell, they allow the women to drive to the supermarket. But then it's straight home. And they must always cover their bodies in black robes, head to foot, faces, too, for modesty."

Purcell frowned at that. "What about the titty bars?"

The apogee of Purcell's life had been a trip to the Kentucky city of Newport, on the Ohio River across from Cincinnati, where he had been the enthusiastic recipient of a lap dance by an energetic young female dressed in no more than a shoelace and a one-by-three-inch strip of lacy red satin. Purcell imagined his Jeanie draped in formless black cloth, from her blond bangs to her pink bunny-nose nipples (conjuring a fleeting but disturbingly intrusive image of Bugs Bunny in drag), all the way down to her painted toenails. Purcell frowned again. He didn't want to dispute the wisdom of a superior officer, but Ben *was* an old fossil, probably couldn't remember the last time he got any, and . . .

Ben slammed the tobacco tin shut and returned it to his pocket. "You miss the point, young Purcell! You always do. Pay attention to counting that ammunition. When the day of the big firefight comes, I don't want to find we're ten rounds shy of victory, hear?"

Purcell gave an assenting nod, and added, "Beast. Call me Beast, sir."

"Beast," muttered Ben. "That is what they call the Antichrist. Beware, young Purcell, lest you and that cwazy wabbit—" Ben corrected himself immediately. "—that *crazy rabbit*, become linked in infamy."

Jesus Bob joined the debate. "Why don't you tell Sis about those Tal-i-ban women, Mr. Barber? Tell her how fine she'd look covered in black sheets?"

Ben cleared his throat. "This discussion comes under the heading of military intelligence, and as such is confidential. Since you are with us today, mind as well as body, how about helping young Purcell with the nine-millimeter inventory?"

Jesus Bob watched Purcell's lips form numbers as he counted. To assist, he said aloud, "Twenty-six, four, fifty-five, a hundred and twenty—"

"Well, damn," said Purcell, "that done it. One, Two—"

Jesus Bob assumed his squinty look. "Speaking of fire-fights, how soon you planning to shell the sheriff's head-quarters? I want to see some blood and guts and tin stars littering the highway before I leave this sorry place."

"Best ask your sister about that, corporal. She has the commander's ear, perhaps his privates in hand, as well, if I may speak candidly—albeit figuratively I hope."

Ben stared through the open barn doors at the setting sun and a bloodred sky, a faraway look in his eyes. "Signs," he muttered. "The Jewish Antichrist rising from the Pit. Women stealing men's jobs. Rattlesnakes in the streets, in gardens, like the Biblical plagues in Exodus. Sightings and abductions. Silver tanker trucks moving our way. There's a turncoat sheriff at our underbelly and the commander has put us on alert."

He unbuttoned the flap of his fatigue shirt pocket, re-moved a small Bible, and pressed it to his forehead, whis-pering, "Armageddon is nigh upon us."

38

The ignominy of it," LeCoup said, seething, staring at his red—*red*—reflection in the master bath's mirror. "The police insisting to see us to be sure we weren't in the clutches of terrorists. 'I'm sorry if we've *embarrassed* you, sir,' when they saw my skin."

Raven was scrubbing her face, without effect, for about the twentieth time, muttering. "Us in the buff, Jeeves opening the vault door, all of them scrambling to see, Jeeves blubbering, 'Dear me, dear me, dear me.' That screwup Levi Strauss and his men in their spy suits: 'Don't worry, area's secured, sir,' And that potato of a life squad woman trying to get us to lie down on stretchers.

"As far as I can tell, *nothing* will take it off. I've tried Lava, Comet, Mr. Clean, K2R, Clorox, gasoline, hydrogen peroxide, Woolite, nail polish remover and gin."

LeCoup scraped his forehead with a dry loofah. "It's even worse for me."

She wheeled to face him. "What the hell's that supposed to mean?"

"Well, you know, your skin's already—I mean—and mine is, uh, pale—"

She bounced a bar of Lava off his forehead. "You son of a bitch!" Snatched the nail polish remover off the counter, wound up.

"There, there, my dear," he said, edging away. "Meant nothing by it. Calm down, please."

With a screech and a sidearm pitch, she burned the bottle past his ear, shattering it on the marble wall. She reached for a Sterling soap dish.

LeCoup backstepped into the bedroom, mumbling apologies as shampoo, a toilet brush, Drāno, and his hair dye flew past, bounced off the bed, dinged the wallpaper, stained the Aubusson carpet.

An hour later, and even redder from the scrubbing and rubbing, they were plotting in the collection room. Raven had been somewhat mollified by LeCoup's hasty promise of a new Mercedes coupe which only yesterday she had hinted might make a suitable gift for her upcoming birthday, and which, only yesterday, he had dismissed as wantonly extravagant.

"Custom-painted, robin's-egg blue with the eagle feather pinstriping?"

"*Mais, oui*, sweet. See? You're feeling better already. I'm sure this horrible stuff will wear off eventually."

"Better red than dead," she said philosophically. "If his goons got to the hot tub, they could have done us in just as easily."

"You misunderstand," said LeCoup. "Mudd doesn't want me *dead*, he wants me out of the auction, embarrassed to show my face, but *alive* afterwards to hear how he got his hand on the Lords of Trade plate and I failed."

He slapped a fist into an open palm. "I'm going after the coontail midget myself."

"No, send the Israelis after him. That's what they're trained for."

"You think I'm not up to a sortie? Too old?"

"I'm a decathlete," she said. "The challenge appeals to

me. But if you think your exercise bike and that suck-up personal trainer qualify you for a run through the woods at Mudd's fortress, followed by a retreat with his barbarians and hound dogs at your heels, you're fooling yourself."

"Don't worry about me. I've got surveillance photos, a detailed map, and brains—which he lacks. I acknowledge he'll be guarded—that piebald monster Bolt, maybe his play soldiers—but Mudd's security is worthless, Levi assures me."

"Let's hope Mudd's security is no better than Levi's."

"The little runt is so paranoid, we'll have him peeing his pants. And if he stays home when the plate is auctioned? He forfeits." LeCoup stroked her shoulder. "Are you with me, sweet? A well-planned sortie?"

She shrugged. "It might be fun."

"I want to come at him as our ancestors would have, invisibly from the forest. We'll strike terror in the dwarf's black heart, and then—poof!—gone. We'll mask, wear war paint, dress in buckskins."

"I'll take a hunting bow," Raven said. "Silent."

LeCoup danced with anticipation. "Tomahawks for me."

"With our skin like this," said Raven. "Why don't we cover our faces with those Cherokee Booger masks?" She pointed to two nearly identical gray wood face masks hanging on the wall. Oversize, ominous in their simplicity, they had large eye-holes with no more than a slit for mouths.

"Perfect." LeCoup patted her cheek. "I outbid the little rat for those at a Sotheby's auction four years ago." He whooped. "A raid! *Fantastique!*"

Nikki was out driving with Bo, night cruising the highway for herps. Digger had put away the last dinner dish and was settling in with a jelly glass of Edgar's bourbon and a paperback detective mystery.

The phone rang. "Hello?" A gravelly female voice on the other line said, "Roscoe?"

"Sorry. Wrong number."

"Who's this?"

Digger laughed. "No one you know, I'm sure."

"Mmmm. Sexy voice. Not from around here, are you?"

"Hawaii, ma'am."

"Hawaii! The Aloha State."

He realized he hadn't thought about Honolulu for days, and felt a momentary but sharp pang of homesickness, despite his impending poverty. "Indeed. The land of palm trees and sunshine."

"And Polynesians, hmmm? Big, friendly, good-looking people. I loved *Mutiny on the Bounty*—actually, there were three film versions, did you know that?"

Digger did. Not only that, he told her he was an archaeologist, had lived in Tahiti where Captain Bligh assembled the breadfruit to transport to the Caribbean. He had even visited Pitcairn Island, seen Bounty Bay where Fletcher Christian burned the fateful ship.

That got the caller really interested. "I've always gotten the tingles over archaeology, digging up treasure and mummies."

"It's usually a tad more tame," he explained. She asked if he looked like Harrison Ford in *Raiders of the Lost Ark*. More like Sean Connery, in the third version, he said, meaning older. Lord, she said, I get the tingles from Sean Connery. Just love mature men. How old are you, you Hawaiian Sean Connery? Uhh, middle-aged, he said. Experienced, huh? Digger agreed he'd seen some times. She sighed. Most men in McAfee County were bores. Tell me—are you a married man? No, not me. You wouldn't lie to a girl? Digger adjusted himself in the chair, took a sip of bourbon, noticed how warm the air had become, assured her he was straight arrow.

"I'm almost embarrassed to ask," she said. "But I'm all alone tonight. I felt like dressing up and was going to ask Roscoe—he's a drag, works at the hardware store—out for a drink. Any chance you'd care to meet, tell me about the South Pacific?"

Digger wiped his forehead.

"I teach at Golden Leaf High," she was saying. "Not to toot my own horn, but I'm no dog, lest you wonder. Some of the seniors flirt with me, naughty boys, though I'm in my thirties."

"I don't know—"

"Be a sport. There's a little bar just outside the county—"

"The County Line." Memories surfaced of dueling drunks, smashing beer bottles, the beefy bartender with the Louisville Slugger.

"No way. County Line's a fight bar. I had in mind the Hideaway, other side, in Combs County. Quiet little place up in the hills. Fronts a small family motel, the Mountainview. Friendly, well-lit. What do you say?"

"Well . . ." Thinking, Nikki's having fun hunting slinkies and I've already guessed the ending to this lame who-done-it. So the woman turns out to be less than she alleges? Separate cars. I'll have a couple of beers, tell her my niece is sick. Good-byes. No harm done. "Why not?"

"You can call me Mary."

"Digger."

"Cute!"

Mary gave him directions, said she'd meet him in forty minutes.

"I'll be dressed western. Long hair, trimmed beard."

"Ooo, sexy. Me? I'll wear red. Long legs, no beard." Giggling.

Digger rubbed on deodorant for the second time, slipped into his baby blue western shirt. He pinched the last snap shut, wondering what the hell had gotten into him. He'd said he was middle-aged. She'd be expecting, what, a forty-year-old? How would she react when this going-to-gray, loose-at-the-seams aging guy in dude cowboy duds, looking nothing like Sean Connery, walked in? Maybe he should have let Amy Lou "rinse out that gray." Or . . . maybe Mary was a Willie fan. A man could hope.

It was a small bar, just off the road, placed, as Mary had said, in front of a modest, old-timey, eight-unit strip motel. Moths sparked in the light of a small, painted, sheet-tin HIDE-AWAY sign lit with bare-bulb photofloods.

Digger looked apprehensively at the plain block building with its two small windows lit with MILLER TIME and FALLS CITY neon, staring back at him like glowing eyes to either side of a solid black door.

He climbed the stairs and walked in. It had all the right smells: stale smoke, beer, peanuts, after shave. Dim pine and age-stained plywood, nothing fancy. The jukebox was playing country and western, new stuff he didn't recognize. He let his eyes adjust, saw half a dozen high-backed booths, five square Formica-topped tables, and a twenty-foot bar. There were a few single men at the bar, but mostly couples hunched over tables, talking softly, privately. Furtive glances dismissed him as unthreatening.

And there on a bar stool, alone, oh my! Long legs indeed. Short skirt hiked high enough to see half her thighs. No stockings. Spike heels, red. Tight white, short-sleeve cash-mere sweater, loosely buttoned, showing off smallish but enticingly rounded breasts boosted by some push-up contri-vance under the sweater, hair high in a beehive cone: just the package a single man in a country bar dreams of.

She patted a stool, called to him, "Hey, Sean, you're late." Tapping a cigarette out of a soft pack, she gave him an ap-praising, disturbingly practiced look-over as he approached.

Digger took the next stool, muttered a sorry.

She waved it away, laughed. Digger saw glossy red lips, even white teeth set off by a nurtured tan, and blue eyes. Crinkle lines at the eyes and little smoker's wrinkles over the lips suggested the thirties' claim was a stretch, but Mary was still a good twenty years younger than he.

She swung toward him, uncrossed her legs, spread her knees to frame his. Digger saw two inches more of taut tan thighs as the skirt hiked up, more cleavage as she leaned toward him, touching his nose with a long red fingernail.

"The man in the white hat rescues the lonely maiden, huh?"

At mention of the hat, Digger took it off, looked for a place on the bar for it, remembered Coony's saying it was okay to wear it inside, and set it back on his head.

"A gentleman, too. Most of the bums around here wouldn't think of tipping their hat to a lady. So, you're Digger." She leaned close, cigarette in pursed lips, waiting for a light.

The bartender saved him, struck a match, held it out. Mary sucked flame, her eyes locked on Digger's. The tip of the cigarette flared, smoke enveloped them. Digger coughed, heard the bartender ask what he wanted. A beer—whatever. A bottle appeared on the wood, an inverted glass over the top. Digger poured, searching for words.

Mary took a long drag. "You don't mind my smoking?"

Still pouring, Digger coughed again, said, "Uh, no. Not at all."

"An archaeologist, huh?"

"And you're a teacher. What do you teach?" Mouthing the words in his mind: You can teach me whatever you want, baby. He blushed and watched foam run over the lip of his beer glass, down his fingers.

"History."

Mind a blank. He saw a jeweled locket at her neck, a big gold heart. "Beautiful locket, an heirloom?"

"Keepsake, you could say." She lifted it, gave it a smooch, and let it drop. He saw a red tattoo below her neck: two split halves of a heart, their inside edges jagged. The locket bobbed on its chain, settled over the tattoo.

"Nice tattoo." First time in his life he'd complimented a woman for a tattoo. He wondered if it had some connection with the locket, whether it meant a broken heart or a heartbreaker. He didn't have the nerve to ask. C'mon man—conversation. Say something.

He blurted out, "What do you think of the French and Indian War?" Dumb ass. He stared at his beer, his wet fingers.

"History," she said. "You want to talk history? Okay." She drew on the cigarette, set it in the ashtray, blew a cloud of smoke to the side, picked a speck of tobacco from her lips, and spoke, fast: "Iroquois League armed with European weapons drives out their brothers to the west—no Peaceable Kingdom to begin with. French and English kings, big ego guys across the ocean, puffed up with expansionist fever. La Salle reaches the Mississippi, claims 'all the land these waters reach'—that sort of macho bullshit. Add French traders lusting for furs, English colonists horny for land. Everyone has the hots for the Ohio Valley. Let's put a fort at the forks of the Ohio, protect our interests, huh? Frontiersmen try, French do. Virginian George Washington draws the first French blood. War's on. Shoot, scalp, pillage, burn. War's over at the Treaty of Paris, 1763. British win. How's that?"

"Um, pretty good."

"Now, let's talk about you, cowboy. What brings you to this part of the world?"

"I came to visit my niece and cousin." He stared at his beer. "Edgar was murdered."

"No!"

"I'm afraid so."

"Wait. The man killed by the satanic doper fishermen witches?"

Digger nodded.

"Did they catch them yet? Maybe it's somebody I know, someone right here in Golden Leaf. Roscoe, even. He fishes. Wouldn't that be wild? C'mon, tell me."

"Not much to tell. Was pretty awful. And no, they didn't catch whoever did it. The sheriff's working on it. Nikki, my niece, and I are helping. More like poking around."

Mary tugged his sleeve. "C'mon, details. I love mysteries. Pul-eeze."

Digger felt deflated. An image of Edgar in the shed with the worm in his lips rose to confound him. Hell, he thought, this woman's no better than Amy Lou, after dirt she can pass on at the beauty parlor. Or at her school, chattering about the sinkers and fishhook and the plastic worm over coffee and smokes in the faculty lounge. All I need is for Coony or Bo to be asking questions at the school about the one-armed man and discover everybody there knows as much as the law does—courtesy of yours truly.

"What's the matter, honey, cat got your tongue?"

Mary's ash dropped from her cigarette, landed on Digger's knee. He brushed it away. "Sore subject." He faced the bar, refilled his glass, lifted the bottle, signaling the bartender for a backup.

Mary put her hand on his. "I was insensitive. Let's change the subject. Tell me about archaeology."

Digger chewed his lip, stared at his glass.

"Pu-leeze?" She tickled him in the ribs.

He drew away, tried to ignore her, but wiggled reflexively. Mary kept it up, blew in his ear, squeezed his leg above the knee. He couldn't help laughing. "All right, already, I give up." He raised his hands. "Archaeology. I'll talk about archaeology."

"Treasure," she said. "I want stories about maharajas' rubies and pirate gold."

Digger laughed. "Not from me!" Then he thought, If you want to impress the woman, don't bore her to death with obsidian rime dating, or island settlement patterns, or midden analysis. He drummed his fingers.

"Okay," he said, slapping the bar, "How'd you like to hear about the curious case of the Fijian yam dildo?"

39

love it! The Fijian yam dildo." Mary gripped Digger's knees, swung him to face her.

"We begin," Digger said, "with the sweet potato, of New World origin and a South American food staple. Centuries ago, indigenous women discovered in the sweet potato's provocative form and texture—what shall we say—a pleasurable companion. But more, for the sweet potato would have been rife with symbolic associations: an archetypal male form buried in the fertile womb of mother earth."

"Wild," said Mary. "This South American sweet potato, would it be, say, bigger or smaller than a cucumber?"

"Trying to visualize it, huh? Some are smaller than the modern cultivated cucumber, some larger. More irregular, certainly."

"With bumps and stuff?"

"Yes."

"Mmmm."

"Ethnobotanists know the sweet potato spread from South America throughout the Pacific islands of East Polynesia, but it did not reach the more western islands of Fiji, Tonga, and Samoa until after European contact.

"How, you ask, did the sweet potato cross empty ocean? It could not survive floating in saltwater. Thor Hyerdahl thought the plant was carried westward by rafting Inca Indians. Others believe the Polynesians sailed east to South America, recognized its value, and returned home with it. However it got there, the sweet potato *is* in Polynesia, people eat it, and women do, uh, dally with it.

"Next we move to Melanesia, big islands, other side of the Pacific, northeast of Australia. Racially different. There we find the yam, originally a Southeast Asian tuber. The Melanesian yam gets quite large—"

"Oooo, how large?"

Digger held his hands wide, a fisherman describing the one that got away.

"Wow."

"The Melanesians eat the yam, but with restrictions. In New Guinea, I've seen people dress them up and trade them ceremonially with neighboring villages. Quite the event. I own several yam masks. It's sort of an incest taboo—you can eat the neighboring village's yams but not your own.

"As far as we know, however, yams were never used in Melanesia for self-pleasuring."

"Too big, huh?"

"That, or—who knows?—maybe they never caught on to it. Anyway, yams were disseminated from Melanesia eastward into Polynesia. But, while Polynesians eat yams, we find no yam dildos . . . or none that anyone will admit to."

"Polynesian babes were loyal to their sweet potatoes, huh?"

"Indeed. Compared to sweet potatoes, yams are ugly tubers. My own hypothesis is that Polynesian woman simply went for the prettier root.

"Let me recap: in Melanesia we have yams, no yam dildos. Polynesia has yams and sweet potatoes, but only sweet potato dildos. But, here is the real mystery. Fiji, between Melanesia and Polynesia, had no prehistoric contact with the sweet potato and thus no knowledge of sweet potato dildos,

but they did have yams. And, unlike the other Pacific islanders, Fijian woman not only used yam dildos, they were ob-
sessive. Fawned over them. Dressed them up, gave them
names, competed to grow the largest and longest.

"We surmise," he added, "that the yam dildo is an independent Fijian invention. Further, it is conjectured that Fijian women, though lusty, were so enamored of their yams
they ignored their men—who assuredly could not compete
in the size department. And that is the reason, we believe,
for the notorious belligerence and rampant cannibalism of
the Fijian male."

Mary drummed her red nails on the bar, considering, and
summed it up. "The men couldn't get any from their women,
so they ate one another."

"Succinctly put."

She hugged him. "Professor, you are a trip. And I don't
mind telling you, with all this sex talk, you're giving me the
tingles." She slid a hand halfway up his inner thigh and
squeezed softly. "Know what I mean?"

He did indeed. "Not to brag," he said, "but I probably
know more about sex in the Pacific than any other re-
searcher. In Hawaii, they call me the Sex Doctor."

"Oooo, I like it." She leaned close to his ear, brushing his
cheek with her lips, purring. "How about a treatment, Sex
Doc?"

Digger coughed, only in part from Mary's heady perfume,
hair spray, and boozy cigarette-tainted breath—he had never
expected the evening to go so well.

She whispered, "Do you have thirty-five dollars?"

Huh? Did he hear that right? There you go, he thought,
it's not my island charm—my little Mary's a hooker! Not your
garden variety hooker, because she knows her history. A
moonlighting history teacher hooker, that's it.

Mary noticed the hesitation. "You don't expect me to pay
for the motel room myself? Don't tell me you're a backseat
lover. I hate cheapskates."

"The thirty-five dollars is for a motel room?"

"Next door. You need a loan?"

"No." Knees trembling again. "I've got the money." He paid the bar bill and walked out in a daze, Mary's arm around his waist, her hand tucked in his rear jeans pocket, massaging his left flank.

The motel clerk nodded to Mary, "Ma'am," took Digger's thirty-five dollars, and tossed him the key to number eight. "Last room on the end."

Mary had her hand in Digger's pants before he got the key in the door. Linked in a clumsy embrace, they stumbled inside. Digger kicked the door shut and flipped on the light-switch to scout the territory: a sway-backed bed with a threadbare cover, two sixties-modern tables with mis-matched lamps, a lime green carpet, once shag, long since matted flat, a small TV on a brass stand next to a pale wood dresser with attached mirror, and a tiny bathroom beyond a half-cocked flimsy wood door.

He shut the light off, pulled Mary toward the bed.

"Hold on, Sex Doc." Mary flipped the switch back on. "I like to see who I'm doing." She broke away, rummaged through her purse, slapped a strip of three prophylactics, onto his palm, and headed to the bathroom. "Close the shade," she said, "I'll be back in a jiff."

Digger stared at the trio of foil squares and muttered, "Three?"

Mary paused at john door and blew him a kiss. "Not to worry, cowboy, there's more where those came from."

Digger dutifully attended to the shade, disrobed, and sat on the edge of the bed, mumbling to his underpants draped over the chairback. "Damn it man, you're old enough to be her father. The woman'll laugh at you. If this gets back to Coony . . ."

The toilet flushed. Mary opened the door and stepped out, arms wide, wearing only her locket, a gold Piaget wrist-watch, and her towering, now toilet-paper-wrapped beehive cone. "Why the long face? Worried I'd say no to your Sex Doc tricks? Hey . . ." she jiggled her breasts and laughed, "anything you want, baby. Just don't muss the hair."She leapt on Digger's lap, locked her ankles around his back, and rocked him backward onto the mattress.

Mary had an encouraging way about her. Springs squeaked in protest as the archaeologist and the school-teacher got to know one another. Arms and legs tangled with twisting sheets, the bed bounced, the frame banged wall-board. Scratching, panting, groping, and groans led to a *thump-bump* as they took a double roll off the bed. Cursing, back up, reconnected. Elbows flew, fists pounded to the mu-sic of Mary's "Oh, baby, yes, yes *yes.*" "Do it to me Sex Doc-tor." "You are sooo fine."

His confidence reinflated, Digger shifted position. "Here's a little trick I picked up in the Tuamotus."

"Eeee, I have never, *ever* been done like this." Mary, be-neath, craned her neck past Digger's ribcage, raised her wrist behind his back and squinted at her watch, maintaining di-alogue, "Keep it up, keep it up, keep it up."

She rolled Digger over, straddled him, bounced, moaned. The moans turned to a screech when she caught her reflec-tion in the dresser mirror: streamers of toilet paper flapping at her shoulders, her beehive at ninety degrees, parallel with her left shoulder. *"Damn!"* She righted it with a crunch.

"That's what I say, too," said Digger, below, blinking at her well-toned belly. *"Damn!"*

Forty fervid minutes later, they lay on their backs, un-moving, side by side like disinterred mummies, strips of toi-let paper heaped beside them, clinging to cooling skin, wrapping an arm here, a leg there. Mary puffed on a ciga-rette. Digger, jelly-boned, tried to stay awake. Mary propped a damp pillow at the head of the bed, sat up, spouting smoke rings. She dragged her fingernails across Digger's chest, scraping away strips of drying tissue. "Now, baby, tell me about this murder investigation of yours. I simply love mys-teries, and I want to hear all about it."

"Later," Digger said, drifting.

"Now's good," she said. "Unless you want to go another

round. I'm up for it, whadaya say?" She bounced, slung a leg over his.

He groaned, began with Nikki, Coony and Bo, told her about the atlas, Smoot Mudd, the Frenchman, Céloron and his buried lead plates, the coming auction, LeCoup's duplicate of the Jacob Cuppy plate in the Folk Museum of Eastern Kentucky, the nervous museum director Fouts, the letter from the Queen's Maritime Museum in Barbados, his call to the duped assistant director, and the message he left for the antiquities dealer in Miami. All in considerable detail as commanded. Then he fell asleep.

When he awoke, Mary was gone, leaving him with welts and scratches, a pulled groin muscle, smoke- and perfume-reeking, room-strewn clothes, and a note scrawled in scarlet lipstick on the mirror: "Sex Doctor—you gave me exactly what I wanted."

It was signed with a broken heart.

40

*S*moot chewed on a thick new cigar, pacing, scooting the walker up and back along his front porch like an eighteenth-century sailing ship captain walking the quarterdeck of his frigate. General Ben, puffing small clouds of cherry-scented smoke from a thin cheroot, retracted the magazine from his assault rifle, slammed it home, and removed it again, as if the repetition would diminish his anger over news of the one-armed man.

"He was a viper in our midst, Commander. We thought he had come to forge an alliance between the Sentinels and the Rangers. But no. The man used us as an excuse to spend time in Golden Leaf, selling poison to children." Ben clacked the magazine on the porch rail for emphasis and spit, although, gentleman that he was, he made only a *pthhh* sound and emitted no unseemly saliva.

"He had on camos," Bolt said, a thick plug of tobacco in his mouth. "A loaded rifle and side arms in his cab. Some people is saying he was a Ranger." Unlike the General, Bolt spit a viscous brown stream over the porch rail at a young sunflower five feet away. "Bull's-eye," he said, and watched the flower dip with the weight, and then rebound, petals stained in testimony to his accuracy.

Ben made the spitting sound again, leaned his assault rifle against the porch rail, set the clip above it, and paced. "This rumor about him being a Ranger, I have reason to believe, is being spread by our turncoat sheriff. To think that people could believe a Ranger would pollute the minds of our youngsters by feeding them drugs! I warn the men constantly about setting a good example. Cigarettes and beer ought to be plenty enough for teens, and the wee ones should stay clear of those, as well."

Ben's voice took on a preacherly air. "Yes. The Daniel Boone Rangers believe in wholesome nurturing, filling young minds with right thinking: pride in their Aryan heritage, respect for family values, and vigilance against the menace of the New World Order and the Federal-Alien-Zionist conspiracy." He waved the cheroot, inadvertently knocking an inch of ash onto the commander's porch floor. "We do not believe in scrambling their brains, for God's sake!"

"Damn straight," said Bolt, spitting, and then working the wad of tobacco to one side of his mouth to facilitate draining half a can of Bud via the other.

Ben adjusted the aluminum foil lining his cap. "I called the Bear Mountain Sentinels on a safe line—that pay phone by Wilmer's Ashland station—and they deny any knowledge of their man's scurrilous activity. In fact, they are sending us a conciliatory case of C-4. But I fear it may be some time before we resume discussion of an alliance. We shall deal with our slandering sheriff—"

Smoot scrabbled toward them. "You steer clear of Coony McCoy until my auction's over, hear? Last thing I need is the sheriff poking his nose—"

"His Semitic nose," Ben interjected.

"Whatever kind of nose, I don't need it poking. What I need is for you boys to be on your toes if the Frenchman shows up on auction day."

"Yes, sir," Ben said, saluting. "The Rangers are ready and able. And, sir?"

"General?"

"A little surprise." Ben rested his cheroot near the ammo clip on the rail and reached into a long cardboard tube, retracting a four-foot roll of cloth. "A project upon which I have been working assiduously." He held it to the log wall, pressed thumbtacks through grommets, and unfurled a four-by-six-foot flag. "Our standard. Sewn by the Golden Leaf High tenth grade home ec class. Beautiful, isn't it? The red background symbolizes the final battle against the forces of oppression, the field of fire from which we shall emerge truly free. We were a bit uncertain whether the Republic of Boone letters should be green or yellow—"

"Yellow?" said Bolt.

"My reasoning exactly," Ben said. "Thus green, the color of the forest."

Smoot nodded approval. "I like that fist at the center holding the gold cross with the coonskin cap on it."

"The cross is Mylar, the cap, real raccoon fur," said Ben. "And the assault rifle at the bottom, crisscrossed by the swift sword of the Lord? Both embroidered. The golden leaf at the top left corner and the blue Winky Worm at the top right are appliqué."

"Very pretty," Smoot said and frowned. "I don't think I understand the curved white thing across the top, above the lettering."

"The inverted crescent? That is the white rainbow of hope—no coloreds, see?"

Smoot studied it, nibbling the cigar, nodding. "Hell of a piece of art. Damn fine job, General. Damn fine."

He turned from the wall to Bolt, spit-sniping sunflowers at the porch rail. "Bolt get over here. Tell Ben what you done."

Avoiding eye contact with his superiors, Bolt studied his feet as he spoke. "I, uh, drove to the Frenchman's house in

Cincinnati. Took these balloons of bloodred dye—Frenchman's got this castle, white as driven snow, see?"

Ben raised an eyebrow. "I believe I see where this is going."

Bolt shot him a fearful look, wondering how the man could have found out already how he had screwed up. But, with a commanding cigar wave from Smoot, he continued. "The Frenchman had guards. Tan-skinned monkeys in black outfits, carrying Uzis . . ."

"Men in black!" Ben grew agitated. "Did you see black helicopters, too?"

Apparently Ben's information wasn't all that good. "Nope. But they could of been there, well back in the woods. Anyways, I counted six of these guards—" He glanced at Ben's face, fearing a skeptical sneer, but saw none. "—so I snuck up on the house through the forest, disarmed their trip wires, avoided their cameras."

"Penetrated their perimeter. And—?"

"I took those monkeys out one by one. Then I threw one of those balloons high at the center of both of the side walls of that castle, and one on the back. Man, they made twenty foot splashes like bloody killshots—permanent. That Frenchman'll have to repaint his whole damned house. At least two coats if he uses good paint, three if he goes for the cheap stuff.

"I took one of these guard monkey's throwing knives—"

"Were they Japs?" Ben asked. "Ninjas?"

"Probably," said Bolt. "Didn't spend time making their acquaintance, if you know what I mean. Whap across the back of the head, and move on. Carried them two at a time and trussed them like kee-bobs along the swimming pool diving board. Stabbed that knife into the Frenchman's front door through a coon-tail I brung with me to set the fear, before he saw the walls and his took-out guards."

"Damn fine," said Smoot. "Bet the pansy will stay in his froggie bed, lace covers over his head, and never set foot in McAfee County after that."

Ben agreed. "Yes. Well done. You should train the men in insurgency."

"I have a reward for you, Bolt." Smoot smiled—a rare occurrence. "You're a major now? Well, I'm promoting you to colonel—with General Ben's approval."

"Any man who completed a mission like that by himself," said Ben, "deserves recognition."

Bolt stared modestly at his shifting feet. "Shucks, weren't nothing."

Smoot turned to the general. "And you, Ben. With this flag, your good work with the men, you're due for a promotion yourself. Howsoever, with me the commander-in-chief and you a general already, the chain of command at the top gets a mite crowded. Give me a bit to think on it."

Ben saluted.

Smoot stuck the unlit cigar between his lips. "What say we celebrate, Bolt? Fire this baby up."

Bolt held out his butane lighter, thumb-flicked it, held a high flame to the tip of Smoot's cigar.

Aware of past incendiary cigar lights, Ben kept a watchful eye on Bolt's Bic, and thus missed the arrow flying past his elbow. He did, however, hear the otherworldly metallic *ka-whang* as it struck and knocked off Smoot's oxygen bottle regulator. He heard the ominous loud hiss, saw blue, and then orange plasma materialize from nowhere, engulf the commander's head and Bolt's hand (squeezing the butane Bic trigger for all it was worth from the pain). Then, flame-thrower-like, the jet shot to the wall, setting his wonderful new Republic of Boone flag ablaze.

Ben understood at once. He shouted, *"Ray gun!"* and dived for the floor.

Charred, eyebrowless, disoriented, Smoot rocked from one foot to the other until Bolt pulled him down.

On hands and knees, with Smoot still smoldering, but safe below him, Bolt flapped his scorched hand back and forth, blowing on it, ineffectually. "Yee-ouch! Ouch!" Thus distracted, he missed the *thimp, thimp* of arrows hitting the wall above their heads, and the deeper *thunk* of tomahawks striking the front door.

Ben belly-crawled to the edge of the porch, snagged the strap of his assault rifle and pulled it toward him. He peered into the woods, made out two figures—yes!—visible from the shoulders up, twenty yards away. He saw clearly their large gray, featureless heads, the huge dead-black eyes. He shouted, *"Aliens!"* and raised himself on upraised elbows to a shooter's prone position. He squeezed the trigger a moment before the aliens disappeared into the bush.

Ben banged the silent rifle on the floor—"Well darn!"—as he remembered the clip resting impotently on the rail.

Still crouching over the commander, Bolt looked up at the wall, saw the twenty arrows embedded in the logs, forming the outline of a skull and crossbones. He unholstered his bandoliered Colt .45, took aim with his left, unburned hand, at, what? Nothing but trees, bushes, and weeds. He emptied the clip anyway, perforating foliage and frightening wildlife for half a mile.

Ben alone saw it through the leafy treetops, flying high: the silent black helicopter. Or, perhaps a crow. His vision wasn't what it used to be. But he damned well saw the aliens, no doubt of that.

The scorched commander crawled from beneath Bolt, saw not only the arrow death's head but the three tomahawks in his front door, perfectly aligned, one above the other, such that had he been standing there, door open, one would have split his forehead, one, his breastbone, and the third, his groin.

Smoot cupped his hands around his blackened lips and screeched a warning, a full minute late, but far more accurately than he knew: *"Redskins!"*

41

Digger lurched into the kitchen at eleven-fifteen. Nikki slung a wet, wadded-up dishtowel at him. "Reflexes off? Hot breakfast is over." She took a long look at the wall clock. "Oh, about an hour and a half ago. Cereal's on the counter." She watched him collect a bowl, spoon, and cup, move silently, unsteadily, from the refrigerator to the counter, pour a cup of coffee, tip the box of shredded wheat, add milk and sugar. "You look like you've been hit by a car."

He munched sheepishly.

"You two have fun last night?"

Digger nearly dropped his spoon. How could she know?

He thought it through. Road cruising for herps. She and Bo saw his car, checked the bar, the motel. Bo's badge would have gotten them the room number. Listen outside? Hell, yes. He blushed furiously, kept his eyes low, thinking I don't need this. He felt his pulled groin muscle spasm.

"The hallway still stinks of beer, cigarette smoke, and cologne."

A lecture yet.

"The two of you meet at a bar?"

"Something like that." He leaned even closer over the cereal, chewing, chewing.

"I heard you sneak in at two-thirty. You must have called Coony right after I left with Bo."

"Coony?"

"Hey, if you two wanted to go out, why didn't you just say so? It's none of my business if you want to do boy stuff. Oh—" She paused, "—I get it. It was Etta, huh? Coony had to give her the slip? Afraid I'd spill the beans."

"You're sharp, Nikki."

"How'd you get the perfume on you? Did you pick up ladies? Ha! I'll bet you did. Well, I want to hear about *that*. C'mon."

"No ladies," he said, recovering. "Was a bar Coony took me to. They had this cologne machine in the john. Fifty cents and you push a plunger—*whoosh!* The stuff sprayed all over me. Coony rode me about it all night."

"Shoot," she said. "I was hoping for dirt. In case you wondered, Bo and I road cruised till eleven. Roads were wet, we found a bunch of frogs and toads, a water snake, and a couple of salamanders, fun, but nothing special. That's it. No moves on Bo's part. Bo's a buddy, okay? He's really getting into herps."

"Good, honey. Glad to hear it."

She joined him at the kitchen table, spread out her rattlesnake notes and charts. Anxious to get his story straight with Coony but afraid to telephone with Nikki nearby, Digger told her he was meeting Coony for lunch and slipped out.

He called the sheriff's office from the first phone he found. Coony surprised him with, "Glad you called, how about lunch?"

The Dairy Queen headquarters was every bit as humble as Coony had warned. Digger didn't ask for a tour, and Coony didn't offer. They opted for Chez Pancakes. "Pain in the ass help, but the best coffee in town," Coony reminded him.

Rubella informed them the blue plate special was pig's feet crêpes. After small talk and coffee, no crepes, Digger told

Coony about the Maritime Museum letter, his speculation about Lawrence and George Washington and Barbados, and how the lead plate found its way to a dealer in Miami.

Later, Digger eased his way into the liaison with Mary.

"You red-blooded old fart! Way to go. Glad to cover—your niece won't say nothing if she thinks it'll get me in trouble with Etta. Done deal."

"This honey was pretty hot. Really took to my Sex Doctor stories. Showed her a few of the tricks I've picked up along the way, too." He made half a fist, blew on his fingernails and polished them on his shirt. "Truth is, I wouldn't mind seeing her again, but—you know how those things go—we never exchanged last names. All I know is, she teaches history at the high school here and there's this Roscoe she's been seeing at the hardware store."

"Don't know no Roscoe in Golden Leaf. Describe her—I guess I've noticed most of the county's pretty women."

"Mary's around forty, lots of blond hair stacked up high, probably bleached, uh . . ."—blushing—"definitely bleached."

Coony winked. "Bleached hair. Not perzactly a rarity hereabouts."

"Slim build, toned. Long legs, knows how to use them."

"Most of the good lookers I've known started to pack on the weight with their first bite of wedding cake, so the age and build narrows it down. The long legs and the using them part, that's a mite subjective, speaking from a detective's point of view."

"Wait . . . she had a tattoo about so big." Digger held his finger and thumb about an inch apart. "Red. At the base of her neck. Two halves of a heart, jagged in between. It was mostly hidden by a big gold heart-shaped locket. I was wondering if it meant a Broken Heart or a Heartbr-"

Coony sloshed coffee into his lap, snatched a napkin, dabbed at it.

"You *do* know her. Don't tell me she's someone *you* . . ."

Coony shook the coffee stained napkin. "Nothing like

that. Worse. Mary, she said her name was? Ha!" He took a gulp of ice water, choked trying to get it down.

Digger watched Coony grow red in the face, hacking, and wondered if he should slap him on the back or do—what was it?—the Heimlich maneuver. Maybe he had an ice cube stuck in his windpipe. By the time he remembered how the squeeze trick worked, though, the ice would probably be melted and Coony, instead of choked to death, would be embarrassed to death at Digger hugging him. He decided to watch the color of Coony's face, and unless it went purple, pretend nothing was amiss. He took a sip of water himself, ignored the dying sounds across the table. Coony's distress gave him a chance to think. So, Mary had used a pseudonym? Maybe she didn't want him to find her again if the date had gone sour.

Coony was gaining the upper hand on the ice. Digger continued the conversation as if nothing had happened. "I don't really care if she used a phony name . . . Ohhh, I *see*. She's married! Damn. I should have guessed."

Coony still wasn't up to speaking, but he shook his head.

Digger fished. "Engaged, or tied up with someone? Not one of your deputies?"

Coony managed to wheeze a name: "Bo."

"Ohmigosh. *Bo's girlfriend!*" No wonder Bo's been so platonic with Nikki! And clean-cut Bo doesn't know Mary fools around. Wait till Nikki finds out her uncle poked her "buddy's" girlfriend while she and Bo were out hunting frogs. Wait until big Bo does. This is bad. Worse than the business with the dean's wife. "Bo. I'd have never guessed. Mary's got to be older than him—not that there's anything wrong with that. Hey, Coony, I'm really sorry. If I'd known—"

"Bo's *sister*," Coony said, loud enough to turn heads, having regained his voice. "Actually," now almost whispering, "his half-sister. Rita Rae Deaver. Here in town. Sumbitch."

"The one you told me about? The delinquent? The one got sent to Pee Wee Valley for embezzling?"

"The very one." Coony gripped Digger's forearm. "Digger, old friend, I hate to tell you, but I don't think it was your Sex Doctor stories that got Rita Rae so turned on. It must of been information she wanted. About me and Bo, I'd guess." Coony's face blanched. "Lord. If Rita Rae's back, Bo's brother Judas Bob is probably with her. This is bad news. Bad for me, bad for Bo, bad for McAfee County. Tell me everything you know."

Digger screwed up his face, trying to recall. "I was drinking. She told me . . . her phony name, Roscoe at the hardware, and the history teacher bit. That's all . . . but she did know history. Gave me a tight synopsis of the French and Indian War without blinking an eye. You sure about this?"

Coony patted his arm. "Surer than I'd like. Rita Rae's no slouch; she may well know her history. What else did you tell her?"

"Just small talk, some of my Pacific stories, and . . ."

"And?"

Digger remembered the third degree when he was dozing off. "Uh, I guess a little about Edgar's death, about Nikki, you and Bo, about Smoot and the Frenchman, the feud and the auction." He covered his face with his hands. "Hell . . . just about everything."

Coony groaned, took another drink of ice water, more carefully this time. "Sumbitch. Rita Rae was in Miami, last I heard. You said that antiquities dealer lives there. Five'll get you ten she's involved up to her heart tattoo in this auction. No wonder she knew about the French and Indian War. Hell, it wouldn't surprise me if that auction was up here somewheres."

Digger spread his fingers, still covering his face, and peered through them at Coony. "What's with the heart tattoo?"

"Some story." He nodded, remembering. "There was this salesman at the Winky Worm plant when Rita Rae worked here. Older fella, fast talker, sharp dresser. A horndog and a con man. He was the first to make the Million Winky Club.

Covered seven states, made big bucks. Rita Rae's thumper went flippity flop for him. He swore she was the moon and stars and took her to Florida on a promotional tour. Rita Rae was the envy of everything in skirts hereabouts. Fella became her mentor, gave her a taste for the good life, showed her how to work people."

Digger squirmed, but Coony seemed not to notice. "Then he dumped her flat for some country western backup singer in Nashville. Rita Rae took it bad. He sure as hell wasn't her first, but he was the first she fell for. Right after that's when she got the tattoo, the broken heart. Back then, a tattoo like that on a woman created quite the hullabaloo. Wasn't long after, she got caught embezzling at the Winky Worm plant."

"Oh, my."

"Ah, but that ain't the end of it. The Million Winky man stayed on, star of the sales force. Six months after Rita Rae got out of Pee Wee Valley, her old beau turned up stabbed through the heart with his own scaling knife, lying in a pool of blood with the tip of his penis cut off."

"Unngh!" Digger crossed his legs.

"Yeah. No prints, no evidence of who done it. Most people thought it was a jealous husband and the Winky man got what he deserved. Of course, I thought of Rita Rae, but she had moved away, and there wasn't a shred to link her to the murder.

"Years later, I heard she took to wearing a gold locket at her neck—mayhaps the one you saw. And the rumor was, inside that locket was the tip of the Million Dollar Winky man's John Henry."

Digger thought of the locket bouncing on his chest while Mary—Rita Rae—was bouncing on him. He made the *unngh* sound again.

"The Winky man had no family, but the company sent him off in style: Viking funeral, motored him into the center of Boone Lake in a flaming bass boat. Glorious fire, lots of oily smoke. Had a humongous fish fry wake after, free Winky

Worms for all. Yessir, that company never let a good promotional opportunity pass by."

"I don't know what to say."

"Say a prayer of thanks you didn't piss her off, or that
locket of hers might weigh a mite heavier around her neck
today."

"Unngh!"

"Tell you what I'm gonna do . . ." Coony set his cup down
with a clank. "Soon as I warn Bo, I'm going to corner Smoot
Mudd, find out the when and where of this auction and
whether Judas Bob is back.

"Oh, Lord, this is bad."

42

Dressed in white short shorts, a white tank top and white heels, Rita Rae waved to the vintage maroon-and-beige, high-finned, 1961 Chrysler Crown Imperial convertible pluming dust as it climbed the hill toward Barracks #1. It rolled to a stop, and a slender, cafe-au-lait-skinned tango dancer with a mouse-tail mustache and waxed black hair vaulted over the door. He wore a loose, mango-toned silk shirt over linen trousers the color of French vanilla ice cream, and white espadrilles, no socks. Arms wide, he called to Rita Rae: *"Querida!"*

Rita Rae took three bounding steps, leapt, and landed high, arms around his neck, long legs wrapping his waist. "Lando!"

Swaying, trying to keep his balance—he outweighed her by only thirty pounds—Orlando slipped a hand behind her neck, drew her face to his and gave her the kind of kiss his Latin ancestry and a nonstop drive from Miami warranted.

Rita Rae purred, disentangled herself, and led him to Barracks #1. "We have some catching up to do." She saw Jesus Bob at the door. "Look who's come calling, baby brother."

Jesus Bob, a wide grin on his face, held a hand out for a shake. Orlando slapped it away and gave him a hug instead.

"Looking good, *hermano*! Better than the last time I saw you, yes?"

Rita Rae confirmed it. "Yes, indeed, Jesus Bob is on the wagon."

"*Un momento*," Orlando said, and ran back to the car. He opened the trunk, fished inside, and came back with a stocky, foot-high, jade-green figurine with a babylike body and a feline face. "For *mi hermano*, Hey-zoos Bobe. A gift for your collection."

He football passed it, high, but Rita Rae intercepted it.

"Mine!" said Jesus Bob.

"What did we just say about a wagon?" She held him back, tossed the statue six feet in the air. It landed on a rock with a muffled *thwap*, and shattered into a dozen pieces.

Orlando put his hand to his mouth and screeched. "*Por Dios!* A priceless Olmec jaguar god. How could you?"

Ignoring the theatrics, Rita Rae nudged the shards with the toe of her shoe. She bent, reached amid the plaster rubble and retrieved a double fist-size poly-bag of white powder, "I'll keep it safe for you, honey," she said to Jesus Bob. "Promise." She gave him a quick kiss on the forehead, "Hang on," and ran inside, returning without the bag, but with three joints from This Side Down. "You take these and go for a nature hike while Orlando and I get reacquainted, huh?"

Jesus Bob grumbled, but, joints in hand, wandered toward the tobacco barn. Rita Rae crooked a finger at Orlando. "Inside. Let's crank up the salsa and make some noise of our own."

An energetic hour later, Rita Rae propped open the door with a chair to let out the celebratory steam and smoke. She was greeted by three Rangers standing by Orlando's convertible, waiting. "Uh-oh. You stay here, baby," she said over her shoulder. "I'll check out the welcoming party."

"Yes?" Wobbling slightly from her recent exercise, her do off-kilter, loose hair hanging in wet wisps over her forehead, mascara sweat-streaked, she walked toward the Rangers.

"About your guest . . . ," said General Ben.

Purcell explained. "We seen him come in."

"We did," agreed Big Butt.

"If you saw him, then you're not the three blind mice, are you?"

"I am aware," said General Ben, "the commander ordered us to extend you hospitality. But the fact is, we, uh"—backing off a bit at sight of Rita Rae's stiffening lip—"we do not allow his kind on the Reserve."

An eyebrow arched, a fist found a hip, her lip tightened further. "His kind?"

Committed, Ben took a deep breath and continued. "Colored, ma'am."

Purcell clarified: "A spic-nigger."

"Thank you, Purcell," Ben said. "I believe she comprehends."

Noting the heat shimmering over Rita Rae's reddening face, Big Butt baby-stepped behind Ben.

Rita Rae jabbed a red fingernail into Ben's chest. "Orlando," she said, "is *not* colored. Orlando is *Cuban*."

"Cuban?" said Ben. "You mean he's a *Communist*?"

Purcell clarified: "He's a Commie *and* a spic-nigger *and* a foreigner."

"Orlando is not a Communist," said Rita Rae. "He lives in Miami."

Orlando had come to the door, a towel over his shoulder, running a comb through slicked-back hair. He stepped down, walked toward the group with a silky stride. He heard the Communist reference, noted the military garb, the side arms on Rita Rae's interlocutors. Although his left hand was in his ample pants pocket fingering a seven-inch switchblade, he flashed a croupier's grin. *"Encantado de conocerlos, amigos. Orlando Sosa y Castro, a sus ordenes."*

"English," Rita Rae said from the side of her mouth, "English."

"Ah, *lo sien*—I am sorry. *En el norte* here, I forget. Gentlemen, I am Orlando Sosa y Castro, at your service."

"Castro?" said Ben, incredulous. "He's *Cuban*, and his name is *Castro*?"

Orlando smiled. "A common name, my friends, although it causes me some, uh, *irritación*."

Rita Rae translated. "Annoyance."

"Exactly. I, Orlando Sosa y Castro, am not a *comunista*, I am a freedom fighter. In fact, I led the first assault at the Bay of Pigs against that dog Fidel—no relation. If only your President Johnson had not pulled his support fr—"

Rita Rae whispered: "Kennedy."

"Of course. Kennedy. We would have driven the braying dog into the sea."

Ben gave him a squint. "You look too young to have been in that engagement."

"Yes, I was but a *niño* fighting with my father, brothers, and old grandfather. Tell me, have you ever heard of Che Guevara?"

Purcell guessed. "In them old *I Love Lucy* shows? The bongo-bongo man?"

"A Communist revolutionary," Ben corrected.

"*Exactamente,*" said Orlando. "My father and I led the army to his hideout in Ecuador. Perhaps you know the photograph of his dead body, the proof we kill him? It is I, Orlando Sosa y Castro, standing there behind the brave soldiers who shot the revolutionary pig."

"I thought that was in Bolivia," said Ben.

"Yes, yes. Very close to the border," Orlando said, still smiling. "Yes, technically Bolivia. But, enough of the small talking, eh? Has Rita told you what I bring for you *amigos*?"

"She has not," Ben said. "In fact, we are seldom informed of her activities or intentions."

Rita Rae leaned close to Orlando's ear and whispered, "No drugs."

Orlando waved the warning aside with long, fluttering manicured fingers. He moved to the convertible with the high fins. Trunk open, he leaned inside. "I have a gift for these freedom fighters."

Purcell and Big Butt stepped closer, but Ben held them back with a warning: "Beware of Cubans bearing gifts."

Orlando emerged from the trunk holding a sleek machine pistol. "An HK," he said. "Fully automatic. My personal weapon. I have a dozen more in this crate, brand new. A gift for our brave *comunista*-fighting guerrillas." He handed his weapon to Big Butt.

"Wow!" said Purcell of the crate "Near enough for everybody."

"Real macho gun," said an impressed Big Butt.

Ben took the machine pistol from Big Butt, ran his fingers over the gunmetal, ratcheted the cocking mechanism, gave an affirmative nod. "Yes, a fine weapon, indeed. Perhaps I misspoke, Mr., uh . . ."

"My friends call me Orlando."

43

oony pulled into Smoot's drive, elbow out the window, chewing Juicy Fruit. He waved to a camo-clad Ranger thirty feet into the woods, half hidden by foliage. The guard waved back, sheepishly dropped his arm, and ducked behind a tree. Coony turned to Bo, "There's a lesson for you: Don't wear fall camo in the spring. Now, when we get up there, you keep an eye on Bolt, I'll handle Smoot."

"Yes, sir," Bo said, agitated, fiddling with his holster. "You don't think he's here do you?" He didn't need to say who *he* was.

"If Rita Rae is behind this auction, then I doubt she'd play favorites by living under Smoot's roof. And if she ain't here, Judas Bob won't be neither."

"Lord, I hope not. Eleven years, Coony."

"To be on the safe side, we all better start wearing our flak vests." The car shook loose on the gravel as they rounded the last curve, passing the YOUR ASS IS SHOT, IF YOU AIN'T BEEN INVITED sign. "Odds are, Rita Rae'll lie low until the auction, so chill out, son."

Coony hadn't mentioned the embarrassing details of Digger's liaison, only that Digger had seen a woman who asked too many questions and fit Rita Rae's description.

"I don't like it, Coony. Too much bad blood. Between Judas Bob and us, between the Rangers and you, between Smoot Mudd and this LeCoup."

Coony slapped him on the knee. "That's why we're gonna be on our toes, right boy?"

"Yessir." Bo didn't sound convinced.

Coony tooted the siren once, and got out of the car, taking note of another Ranger, this one in urban gray camos, peering between green bushes to the left.

Bolt appeared on the porch, a Colt .45 Peacemaker in his left hand. "You're trespassing, lawmen."

Coony whispered, "You keep an eye peeled. I'll do the talking." To Bolt: "I need to talk to Smoot, warn him of t[r]ouble coming his way."

"What kind of trouble?"

Coony spit his gum into the weeds. "That's for Smo[ot's] ears. Get him."

Smoot scrabbled out of the door to the head of the sta[irs.] "I heard you."

Coony saw the bandages on Bolt's right hand, ga[uze] wrapping Smoot's forehead. He climbed the stairs, Bo at [his] side. "What happened to you boys?"

"The Frenchman came after us with a flame-throw[er,]" Smoot said. "Fine protection our law gives us."

Coony elbowed Bo in the ribs. "Come down from Cincinnati with a flame-thrower, did he?"

"And shot my house full of arrows. But we're ready for him if he comes again, damned redskin."

"Just what I want to talk about," Coony said. "Bolt, you hang back at the end of the porch, tell Bo about your beer can collection. I want a heart-to-heart with your leader here."

Bolt stood his ground until Smoot gave him a small nod. Both of Smoot's already burnt eyebrows had been singed off.

One of his eyes was red and watery, swollen half shut. The other narrowed at Coony. "A warning? You got wind of the Frenchman making another pass at me?"

"Could be, what with this auction. When and where is it?"

"None of your business."

"If it's in Cincinnati or New York or Lexington, you can go there and get your head blowed off on somebody else's turf. But I want no more murders in McAfee County. I may have to put you in protective custody, keep these auctioneers away."

"You wouldn't dare!"

"I would, and that's how I see it. Here's the deal. You give me the details, promise to behave yourself, and I'll back off. If not . . ."

"You swear not to interfere?"

"Long as no laws are broken, I'll stand clear."

Smoot rattled the walker in a burst of frustration. "I swear, Coony McCoy, if you screw up my chances of getting the Lords of Trade plate, I'll turn the wrath of the Daniel Boone Rangers loose on you. Damned if I won't."

Coony whistled, played with his hat, noticed Bo and Bolt at the far end of the porch doing their best to ignore one another. "Well?"

"Remember what I said about the Rangers." Smoot glowered and spit it out. "Four days from now, E-Z Zees Motel, second floor, high noon. The Frenchman and his whore stay in one room at the far end, Bolt and me at the other. Auctioneer has a room at the center. Floor's empty except for us. It's done over the telephone. Winner walks off with Céloron's first plate, loser goes home to Cincinnati with his tail between his legs."

"I understand the auctioneer is an old friend."

"Where'd you hear that?"

"I got sources. When did Rita Rae get into town?"

"Who?"

"Come clean or I shut it down."

Smoot shrugged. "Some spic found it in the Caribbean. She got it from him."

"And you believe her? Rita Rae?"

"Oh, it's on the up and up." Smoot's eyes glazed with anticipation. "Edgar checked it out. It's the one the redskins stole, got passed to London and alerted the British. You'd never guess how it got to the Caribbean, to some pissant island—Barbados—from London, and who had his hands on it." Smoot got a faraway look in his good eye. "Actually held it."

Coony pursed his lips, chewed a lip, working up a guess. "Could it have been, ummm . . . George Washington?"

"You son of a bitch! How'd you—?"

"Lawrence Washington brought it from London to Virginia, and on to Barbados with brother George keeping him company . . . so, odds are, Georgie must have fondled it." Coony grinned. "Just a stab in the dark."

"Damn you, Coony McCoy. I guess you know about George's letter then?"

"Letter? Can't say I do."

"Hah! You wait here." Smoot scuttled inside, returned with a sheet of yellowing paper bearing flourishing handwriting, sandwiched in a stiff, clear protective plastic sleeve. "Sent to Lord Fairchild himself in 1751." He held it out for Coony to read.

Hon. Sir,

Law has returned from London with the very Lead Plate Gov Clinton forwarded to their Lordships, bearing the Claim of the French King to the Interior Dominions. Let us hope it may strike the Burgesses and Gov Dinwiddie from their lamentable Lethargy and Parsimony, and that They will soonest support Appropriate and Necessary Response to defend our Interests west of the Mountains.

Your ob'd'nt Servant,
Geo

Coony removed a pair of reading glasses from his upper pocket and read the letter. "That's the real thing?"

"Fully authenticated, handwriting experts, paper-and-ink people—you bet. She offered it to the two of us for a single blind bid. I beat the Frenchman, just like I'll beat him out of the plate itself." Smoot pulled it away, clutched it to his chest.

Coony whistled through his teeth. "I'm duly impressed, Smoot." He followed that with: "Tell me, is Judas Bob with Rita Rae?"

"Calls himself Jesus Bob now—must have found religion. 'Bout time, huh? Before you ask, I haven't seen him, only talked to her. Don't know where she is, only that she'll have another chunk of my money soon enough. Once I get the plate in my hands, I don't care what you do with her and Jesus Bob."

Coony raised a finger. "One more question to satisfy my detective's curiosity: If Edgar Fitz did all this checking, how come I couldn't find any credit card or phone records?"

"I gave him prepaid calling cards and cash, so there'd be no record the Frenchman could trace. Told him to destroy any receipts, 'cause you can be sure the Frenchman has spies. The only records Edgar kept was his research notes, the ones the Frenchman stole when he murdered the man."

Coony nodded, motioned to Bo it was time to go. At the car, he tipped his hat to the porch. "Good luck, Smoot. Keep it legal and peaceful is all I ask."

"Don't you screw it up!" Smoot shook a fist. "You keep your word, maybe I'll let you see the Lords of Trade plate. Touch it, even."

"That," said Coony, "and seeing Graceland before I die, is all I ask from the Good Lord above."

Nikki met Digger near the McAfee County Courthouse, a turn-of-the-century, three-story, redbrick structure commanding high ground at the center of Golden Leaf. Deputy

Johnny, armed with a box of black and white glossies of Nikki and the headquarters' rattlesnakes, had treated her to lunch a block away at a home-cooking café, sandwiched between the telephone company and the Golden Leaf *Clarion*. While Johnny did his show-and-tell over the meatloaf special, Digger met with Etta's brother the attorney, and then stopped by the funeral home, a block off the square, to pick up Edgar's remains.

Digger led Nikki to Edgar's VW, parked half a block from the courthouse. "I sweated blood for those ashes," he said, pointing to a metal-capped container on the back seat. "I went in with a Quaker Oats box. They were touting a cloisonné urn, a memorial service, and a perpetual niche. We compromised. I came out with a three-hundred-dollar stainless-steel jug charged to my overloaded American Express card and a promise we were taking Edgar back to the family plot in Michigan."

"What family plot?"

"I was mistaken? Uh-oh. I guess we go to Plan B: the ride in the country, a high hilltop, a stiff wind, and a private goodbye."

"I like Plan B." She looked through the rear window at the steel canister. "Don't you wonder what they look like? You know—the ashes?"

"I do not, and get that ghoulish expression off your face."

"If you don't think it's, like, sacrilegious, I could make use of that container—you know, after—for my DOR specimens. My mason jars are nearly full."

"Keep your mitts off Edgar, Nikki."

She shrugged. "So, what's with the estate?"

"Ah, the estate. Etta's brother—looks like her, only flatchested and with a bad toupee—straightened it all out with a firm in Michigan. I signed a few documents, have some for you, and that's it. The library goes to me, the car to you, a thousand dollars to the Old Archaeologist's Home, and we split the estate, such as it is."

"How much land do we own, besides the house?"

"I know what you're thinking—your rattlesnake den, huh?"

"It's not just the snakes. Bo and I saw all kinds of wildlife up there. A piliated woodpecker, elk tracks—even a bear!"

"Here's the bottom line, Nikki. We inherit the house and around three acres, although since Edgar made only a few mortgage payments, the real owner is the bank. The original property is two hundred and twenty-five acres. The family offered it all to Edgar, but he couldn't afford it. Bottom line, Edgar had the money Smoot paid him, insurance, a small savings account in Ann Arbor, and retirement funds, but was deep in debt over some risky investing. After the attorney fees, the taxes, and debts, his net worth is around eight thousand dollars, or four thousand for each of us."

"Oh," she said. "Not that I'm not grateful, it's just . . ."

"I know. You had your sights on the rest of that land."

"Yeah. Bo says sooner or later they'll timber it and the coal company will strip it." She kicked the curb. "Hell, they may as well pave it over in concrete."

"Exploiting the earth got humans where we are today, kiddo—and will probably do us in at the rate we're going." He got a faraway look in his eyes. "Easter Island, for instance, is a perfect example of overpopulation and resource deple—Hey! What's going on at the courthouse?"

"Must be thirty people, moving in on two guys on the steps. Maybe it's a lynch mob! Bo said they had cells on the top floor."

"Lynch mob—you wish. Probably some tax thing."

"Let's check it out." Nikki quick-stepped toward the action. Digger followed.

"Look, Unc. That's Johnny at the top of the stairs."

Deputy Johnny, arms raised, was doing his best to calm a noisy crowd. He stood beside a florid, corpulent man in a shiny blue suit, undoing his top shirt button, loosening his tie, wiping his forehead with a white kerchief. ". . . only heard about it an hour ago," the man was saying, barely audible over the shouting. "We called a joint emergency meeting of—"

"So what are you gonna do about it?" yelled a heavy-set woman in navy coveralls, shaking a beefy fist. Shouts of agreement rose from the crowd.

Onlookers surged. They gasped as a thrown pop bottle shattered against the revered Great Golden Leaf, a ten-foot, bronze tobacco leaf fronting the courthouse.

"Stay calm, folks," Johnny urged. "The mayor's doing everything he can."

Nikki and Digger moved to the back of the growing, shifting crowd as more people streamed across the lawn. Nikki tapped a skinny man wearing a John Deere cap, on the shoulder. "What's going on?"

He flipped his cigarette at the mayor, mouthed a satisfied, "Hah!" as it bounced off a bystander's back in a burst of sparks. Glaring over his shoulder, he gave her the bad news: "The bastards shut down the Winky Worm plant, that's what."

44

moot threw a frail but angry punch at Bolt's shoulder. "I thought when those toy people bought the Winky Worm plant, it was in safe hands. The bastards got into some fancy corporate swap with that damnable Frenchman, spun it off to him, and now the redskin frog closes it down. All to get at me!"

Bolt offered him a fresh cigar, a soothing Panatella Pacifica. Smoot slapped it away, but when Bolt retrieved it, Smoot stuck it in his mouth, waxing philosophical. "What kind of a fiend would hurt innocent people to get at an enemy, I ask you?" He worked the walker. "Meet me at my desk, Bolt. You get the tobacco papers. We'll see what power can do."

Bolt had the boxes arranged by the time Smoot shuffled to his office. Smoot patted the side pocket of his buckskin jacket. "You know what I got in here, Bolt?"

"No, sir."

"And here?" He patted his other pocket. "Politicians! Bought and paid for. And it's time for a payback. Give me them binders."

Smoot sat, scanned the covers of the confidential Global-smoke binders, some thick, some thin, muttering as he read the labels, " 'Honoraria to our friends in Sports'—No. 'Honoraria to our friends in Cinema'—No. 'Honoraria to our friends in Congress, Book One'—Here we go." Smoot tugged the heavy volume toward him and opened the cover. "Damned small type. Here, Bolt, you pick a good one. Mean. There's pictures of them, their voting records, how much we pay them. Find one somewhere around Cincinnati who'll know about the Frenchman."

"That would be Book Six," Bolt said. He opened the cover, paged through it.

"We got one near there, Bolt?"

"Only a matter of picking the best." Paging. "Here we go. Congressman Joe Jolley. A Globalsmoke five-leaf rating. Look at his picture, Commander."

Smoot squinted at the photo. "Whew! He don't look so jolly. Sour enough to freeze a mother's milk. Yeah, Jolley. I remember the name. Good man, knows what side his bread's buttered on. Get him on the phone."

Bolt dialed, passed the receiver to Smoot.

A warm female voice came on the line, "This is the office of Congressman Joe Jolley, friend of family and flag. Welcome . . ."

"Give me the man," Smoot said.

". . . press one if you wish to make a campaign contribution," continued the voice. "Press two if you wish to hear Congressman Jolley's stirring rendition of the Pledge of Allegiance. Press three if you wish to leave a message complimenting Congressman Jolley for his recent legislative activity in your behalf. For all other inquiries, please stay on the line."

"Damn!" Smoot thumped the receiver on the desk, put it back to his ear, waiting.

Ring. Ring. Ring. Ring. Ring. Ring. Ring. Ring. "Hello. Congressman Jolley's office."

Smoot waited for the recording to play out. Instead, the voice said, "Hello? Is anybody there?"

"Yes, damn it, woman. Let me talk to Jolley."

"I'm sorry, the congressman is in conference. If it's in regard to a contribution—"

"Look here, this is Smoot Mudd, Director Emeritus of Globalsmoke International." He let it sink in.

"Globalsmoke? Yes, *sir*."

"Get Jolley. I don't have all day." He heard the line click to limbo. On hold. "Now we're getting somewhere, Bolt. You'll see." Seconds passed. The voice returned. "One moment please, Mr. Mudd."

Ten seconds later he heard a deep, male, sugary, "Mr. Mudd! What an honor to hear from you, sir. If you're calling with regard to that invasive bill in committee let me assure you as I've assured your associates at Globalsmoke, I've always opposed government meddling with the prerogatives of free enterprise. Regulation is the Devil's handmaiden, as I often say. Tobacco is a big employer: growers, processors, the health care industry. You and this country's vital tobacco industry as well as the tobacco farmers of America, those stalwart tillers of the soil—"

"Yes, yes. This ain't about tobacco."

"Ahhh . . ." Jolley lowered his voice to a whisper. "You want to arrange a backdoor boost? Let me get your number and someone from outside the office will call you back within—"

"Globalsmoke handles the moolah, man. That ain't why I'm calling."

"Coal? My environmental record is flawless, sir. I've voted against every—"

"Not the damned environment."

Smoot heard whispering. Apparently someone had done a quick computer check, because Jolley came back even better informed. "Not tobacco, not soft money, not the environment. Of course: guns. I understand you are a supporter of one of America's fine militias. As I told my colleagues this very afternoon over drinks and cigars after lunch, if we put a gun in the hand of every sweet-faced child in this great nation of ours and gave them proper firearms instruction, we would wipe out this ungodly violence in our schools. Yessir, guns are the backbone of democracy, the noble legacy—"

"No, no, no."

"No? An expedited passport, then? VIP Congressional tour pass?"

"Have you ever heard of Alphonse LeCoup?"

"Alphonse LeCoup. Certainly. Another opponent of the federal regulatory behemoth. A model of enterprise, a true scion of Adam Smith. The economy wouldn't move without citizens like you and Mr. Le—"

"What can you do to him?"

"Why, I do my best for him as I do for you, sir, defending his right to—"

"*To* him."

"Excuse me?"

Smoot told him about the Winky Worm plant closing. "Man can't go around shutting down businesses like that, can he? I want you to shut *him* down."

Long pause. "Ummm. Sir, Mr. LeCoup is also, a, um, generous supporter, a local citizen, and—"

"And? And? I want *action*, man."

"Action. Of course. Uh, ummm . . . if I were you—and you didn't hear this from me—my first stop would be the FTC. Of course, you never know what the IRS can dig up with a little encouragement. If discrimination because of age, race, religion, or national origin was a factor in this plant closing, HEW will be interested. And if it was a lockout, the NLRB. If they shut down to avoid cleaning up toxic waste, the EPA's your ticket. Fishing lures, you say? Check with the Fish and Wildlife people. They use dyes and scents in their product, don't they? FDA may be able to help. You're in the heart of tobacco country—you may be able to get the ATF to lend a hand. Interstate chicanery? Certainly the FBI. And I've found there's seldom an industry where OSHA—"

Smoot hung up.

This was the first mobilization of the Daniel Boone Rangers since the rumors (foundless, as it turned out) of an impending ATF/FBI/McAfee County Sheriff's assault following the unmomentous declaration of the Independent and Sovereign Nation of Boone. Only four Rangers were missing from the muster: one who had to stay at home to watch the kids; two, still employed, who couldn't get off work; and Bolt, who never left the commander's side. Fifteen others—eight of whom had been Winky Worm employees, six fortunates on disability who spent most of their time at the Reserve, and Jesus Bob—stood at parade rest. The Scooter Shooters and Junior Rangers were all in school.

Field Marshal Ben field-stripped his cigarette, dusted off his dress khakis, tucked his riding crop under an arm, and stepped onto a modest dais, an RC crate. "Intelligence has revealed the scoundrel who closed the Winky Worm plant: a *Frenchman* from Cincinnati named Alphonse LeCoup, linked to Asians, men in black, and black helicopters."

The men's frustration and anger, building all day, erupted in jeer and hoots.

"Rangers," Ben said, "what do you say to *retribution?*"

With a flourish of his riding crop to quell the satisfying outburst, he continued. "Colonel Bolt informs us that this man's house is well guarded by a contingent of ninjas, no doubt on full alert since his sortie. To avoid a firefight on well-defended foreign soil, I propose a lightning strike by a small, elite force against the Frenchman's office—in a place called Mariemont on the outskirts of Cincinnati. According to reconnaissance by a detective in the employ of the commander, it appears to be undefended. I am looking for a few good men. Volunteers?"

To a man, they raised their hands high, waving *Me, Me, Me*—all but Jesus Bob, who left the line and retired to the concrete Ten Commandments, explaining, "Hell, pardners, I'm always in for fun, but Sis won't let me out of her sight."

Ben moved up and down the line. He touched the crop first to the shoulder of a long-haired, bearded tow-truck driver with feral eyes. "Private Strunk." Ben moved next to a wiry captain and Winky Worm skid man, who, Ben knew, owned a suitable assault vehicle, a camo-painted van. "Ned Daggett." The final blessing of the crop went to the Winky Worm scent inspector. "Young Purcell."

"Call me Beast, sir," said Purcell, as Ben moved back to the RC crate.

Big Butt's narrow shoulders sagged with disappointment.

Ben stepped onto his humble reviewing platform and raised the crop for attention. "And," he said as the cheering subsided, "to lead this assault, I can think of none better than," the crop moved slowly across the assembly to point with finality to one man. "—our illustrious Colonel B. G. Butz."

Big Butt stiffened, jumped to attention, tensing his prodigious buttock muscles so rigidly with excitement that he parted the seam in the seat of his fatigues. Ignoring the draft at the back door, he threw a snapping salute. "I'll do my best, sir!"

"Of course you will," said Ben. "You are a Daniel Boone Ranger."

Digger spoke from his desk to Nikki, making peanut butter sandwiches in the kitchen. "I called Hawaii again. There are three more messages from the dean asking me to phone."

"And?"

"And? Of course I ignored them. Calling me on the carpet won't be enough. He's got something dire planned, all right, suing me for alienation of affection—"

"What *are* you talking about?" She came from the kitchen, sandwiches on a plate, a cold glass of milk in her hand, and set them on his desk.

"I, uh. Oh. I guess I didn't tell you. I thought I, uh—I guess it was Coony."

"No doubt. Boy talk, hitting the booze." She pulled a chair close to his. "Sounds like good dirt. I want to hear it."

"It's nothing. Has to do with reporting grades late."

"Hah! Cat's out of the bag."

He gave her a sanitized version.

"Sure. How much nudity was involved? I *know* there was nudity." She spun his desk chair for a face-to-face interrogation, and wheedled it out of him, every detail, down to the Tahitian drums, the expression on the dean's face, and the length of the grass skirt.

Digger held the cold glass of milk to his temple, certain if she kept it up she would have him blabbing about the wrong number phone call, the Hideaway Bar, the Mountainview Motel, the broken-heart tattoo, the three prophylactics, and jumping the bones of Bo's felonious half sister.

Fortunately, he was saved by the bell. The telephone rang.

Digger snatched the receiver. "Hello?"

"Mr. Perrier? This is Orlando Sosa y Castro. You called."

Nikki began to ask, "Who is—?"

Digger shushed her. "Mr. Castro, thanks for returning my call."

"Sosa y Castro. But call me Orlando, *por favor.*"

"Very well. Orlando. You buy and sell pre-Columbian antiquities?"

"Yes. Authentic artifacts from Central and South America, and fine reproductions, which I import in large numbers. You are a collector? Interested in the real thing?"

"A, uh, collector, yes. You deal in looted artifacts?" He ground his teeth at thought of grave robbers ripping through pyramids and ancient cities, leaving them in shambles, snatching the showiest objects, stripped of scientific context to sell—

"No, no," Orlando said, velvet-voiced. "I sell only pieces collected *legalmente*, eh?—before they pass the patrimony laws. If you wish to buy, you have no worry about these difficulties. However . . . not to broadcast your purchases, either, hmmm? *Siempre*, the authorities they look to make trouble for dealers and collectors. Yes?"

Digger harrumphed. "Indeed."

Nikki had been listening in, her ear near Digger's. She wrote a note, held it before his reddening face: *Miami Dealer?* He nodded a yes. She scribbled, held up another: *Don't piss him off.* Digger nodded.

"I understand you acquired some U.S. artifacts from the Queen's Maritime Museum in Bridgetown, Barbados."

Pause. "Um. Perhaps. And how is it you know about this?"

Digger hadn't thought it through, wasn't even sure what he was after. Hell, he knew the man wouldn't admit cheating the museum. What if this Sosa y Castro hadn't realized the value of the plate, himself? Maybe—and this thought made his stomach churn—Rita Rae had screwed it out of him. Literally, of course, damn it to hell.

So he hung up.

45

Harmon Perrier, my sweet ass," said Rita Rae. "That was the same name he used with LeCoup. His real name is Digger Fitz, as in Edgar Fitz, Smoot's man." She arched an eyebrow at Orlando. "Didn't it strike you as odd that was a local telephone number?"

"I thought he was one of Smoot's *amigos*, a collector. Impoverished as I am, every sale helps." He ignored Rita Rae's violin playing motions. *"Es verdad*, the pay-offs in Barbados, and that six-week trip for the director cost me enough coca to float his cruise ship to the moon and back. And our *amigo*, Gaylord Trill, the cash, the coca for him when he gets to Cannes, for the *muchachas*."

"Up Frenchette noses," Rita Rae said with an exaggerated sniffle. She turned her rear end to Orlando, lifted her skirt, and wiggled her butt. "Only way our wussy assistant director will get any."

"Yes, possible," said Orlando, "but, do not underestimate Gaylord. The boy is cool, *inteligente*." And our plan is *perfecto*." He gave Rita Rae a lingering pat on the rear end. "Like this."

She batted his hand away. "Something's wrong. This Fitz knows something."

"*No hay problema.*" Orlando summarized it, as much to satisfy himself as Rita Rae, ticking off points on manicured fingers. "One. You do switch for LeCoup of Kentucky *museo folkorico* Céloron plate, learn your old *amigo* Smoot, who has one also, will give his dried-up *cojones* for another, *especialmente* the mother of them all.

"Two. We research. Orlando learns Barbados *museo* has mother plate, growing dust in glass case. We find, buy Washington letter, sell to Mudd, and triple our money.

"Three. I, Orlando, become the good friend of Gaylord, *pobre* assistant director of Barbados *museo*, introduce him to wonders of *muchachas*, show him how the coca brings them squealing to his bed. Offer him life of his dreams, hmmm? Then you and me, anonymous *amigos del museo*, send director away on long cruise.

"Four. Gaylord gives us plate and writes the selling-artifacts letter, signing director's name while *el jefe* is sunbathing his fat white body at sea. Gaylord answers questions for agents of LeCoup and Señor Smoot. They report everything is *bueno* at sleepy *museo*, believe *museo* is too *estupido* to know one of the *artefactos* they sell me has value, yes?

"Five. We counterfeit the *tesoro español*, the pirate gold, for Gaylord. He switches, will take real thing to Europe and sell to finance his new life.

"Six, *el más importante*. We auction mother plate, make big bundle, retire to life we deserve.

"Later, after auction, director will return—Where is Gaylord? He finds 'I quit' note, thinks No wonder Gaylord leave, *museo* pay the boy so little. Maybe it is months, maybe never, they miss the French plate or find the phony gold."

Frowning, Rita Rae shook her head. "Lando . . . how did Fitz get your name?"

A shrug. "From papers of Sr. Smoot's archaeologist, *sin duda.*"

"It's possible I missed some. What if Fitz called the museum?"

"So what? Gaylord is cool. You remember when Señor Smoot's man, Edgar Fitz called the cruise ship, left the message for director himself to call back? And director, calls not Edgar Fitz but assistant director Gaylord, tells him to please call this Fitz, not to allow anyone to bother him again on his holiday at sea?"

"Yeah. Damn good thing. That snoop Edgar Fitz would have ruined the whole plan. Couldn't leave well enough alone, could he?"

A call to Barbados confirmed Rita Rae's suspicions and Orlando's confidence: Gaylord Trill, assistant director of the Queen's Maritime Museum, had been shrewd. The man calling himself Perrier must have discovered the letter certifying the unauthorized transfer of artifacts to Orlando Sosa y Castro. When Perrier called, Gaylord referred him to Orlando in Miami, hence the "Please call" message.

"See?" said Orlando. *No hay problema.*"

"No—big problema. I'm think it's about time to say good-bye to Digger Fitz."

Levi and Liev Levkovitz, founders and sole proprietors of AAA Acme Security ("First in the Yellow Pages, first in corporate and personal security") were posing as tourists, deep in the heart of east Kentucky, reconnoitering for Alphonse LeCoup.

Poor but bright and ambitious boys from Tel Aviv, the brothers had emigrated to the United States following their requisite military hitch in the Israeli army, in search of a grand dream: L.A. PIs with a closetful of black leather jackets, a block-long American convertible, 007 Walther PPKs under their armpits, and bevies of fawning blond starlets attending their every whim.

They settled first for washing pots and pans in their grandfather's delicatessen in Washington, D.C., studying judo and kung fu via mail-order videos. Moving westward and upward, they bused tables in a cousin's deli in Pittsburgh, picking up correspondence-course PI diplomas. By the time they reached an uncle's deli in Cincinnati, the Levkovitz boys were wearing vinyl jackets and knock-off Ray Bans, driving a rusty old Buick ragtop, chasing if not always catching the blondes, and ready for their first assignment.

One slow Wednesday the flirtatious Levi chatted up a promising but plain and mousy-haired public relations account executive managing the regional promotion for a fast-food chain. Speaking in hushed tones, Levi explained how he and his brother were ex-Israeli Mossad agents working undercover as waiters. (A half-truth: the waiter part was straight-arrow.)

The account executive mentioned her firm was seeking security for an upcoming visit by her client's spokesclown, fearful of abduction by eco-activists intent on dyeing his orange Afro, rain forest green. Ex-Israeli secret agents seemed just the ticket.

And so they proved to be. The clown left town as carrot-topped as when he arrived. Word of the likable, but rumored-to-be-deadly, Levkovitz boys got around, and Levi and Liev made Cincinnati their home. Relentless in their quest for professional excellence, the black-clad duo seldom missed a gun show, a bounty-hunter convention, or spy-toy extravaganza.

This was the brothers' first trip south of the Ohio River. They stayed at the E-Z Zees Motel the previous night, posing as fishermen, making a great show of their Walmart fishing gear to the desk clerk, inquiring about sharks, tides, and other fishing stuff to cement their cover. Motel floor plan in hand, they checked out, and walked fifty paces to Chez Pancakes for breakfast.

With two tall stacks (no sausage, ham, or bacon, thank you) under their belts, the brothers moved to the register to pay. Levi fished money from a secret jacket pocket, while Liev proceeded to the car with the motel diagram.

Levi read the name tag of the cashier, Rubella, a blonde (of the bottle variety, but blond, nonetheless). A hoarse and chunky woman, older than him by fifteen years, but a babe, he decided, who would do in a pinch if times were hard and the hour late in the middle of nowhere. He slipped off his Ray Bans and looked her in the eye. "Rubella is a beautiful name. Call me Levi." He winked.

"Like in Levi Strauss?"

"My grandfather."

"Really?" She took a drag on a cigarette, appraising. "You're sure not from around here."

Levi gave her an enigmatic smile, prolonging the geographic mystery. Women, he knew, went weak at the knees from his accent. "You like the jacket? It is real leather. Go ahead, touch it." He held out his arm. "Soft like a baby's bottom, eh?"

Rubella looked at the convertible in the lot, his black-clad companion in the shotgun seat. "Tourists, huh?"

"Reconnaissance." The word never failed to impress them. "And we will be back." He winked again, hinting at possibilities. "Soon."

"Where you from? East somewheres, huh?"

"Israel." This always bowled them over. Next would be talk of Arab terrorists and the Holy Land, the parting of the Red Sea. Levi had stories.

"You mean you're—" She looked again at the other one, in the car, their black hair and eyes, rich tanning-bed tans. "—Jews?"

"Like Jesus," he said. That was always the killer for the Christian babes. He turned his face side-to-side, displaying a bold profile.

"Jews," Rubella repeated, paling in the face. She reached absently for her cigarette in the ashtray, pinched the lit end instead, and burnt her fingers. She sucked on them, cursing incoherently.

"Yes, Jews," said Levi, ignoring the display. "Israelis,

though practically Americans. Technically, of course, we are still aliens."

"*Aliens!*" Rubella stared, eyes wide. "What are you *doing* here?"

"Reconnaissance, as I said. An assignment. Checking things out." This one, he decided from her reaction, would be a pushover.

"Oh, Lord." She forgot the first cigarette struggling to re-light itself on the floor, and lit a second, drew smoke deep into her lungs.

Levi decided to have some fun. "We like it here, this part of your country. We may buy it. Money is no object." He fingered the thick gold chain at his neck. "Or annex it. You know, like the West Bank?"

"Take it *over*?"

"Yes. We have much money, much power." Levi found her vulnerability arousing. Hint at power and money, you could have any woman alive. He could have this one now.

Liev began blowing the horn.

Annoyed at the interruption, Levi leaned across the counter, brushed the stunned Rubella's cheek with the back of his hand. "No time now, my dove," he said. "But we'll be back. Soon. *Shalom.*" And he was out the door.

46

Few communities are as peaceful as the idyllic Village of Mariemont in suburban Cincinnati, a planned community built in the thirties. Stands of mature beech woods and elm-lined meandering streets intermingle with Tudor- and Federal-style public buildings, apartments, and shops. For homes, English cottages à la Mother Goose are favored. The high points of the community calendar are the Fourth of July parade and the summer art fair. Mariemont is, in a word, tranquil.

Not today. The Village had never witnessed such excitement, might never again. Twelve police cars, beacons blazing, bearing insignia of six communities lined Wooster Pike and Miami Road west of the town square. There was a SWAT van and an ominous bathyscaph-like sphere perched on a red carriage belonging to the Cincinnati Bomb Squad. The FBI and ATF people were on the way, along with local, and soon, national media.

Nearly a hundred spectators crowded the scene, mostly retirees and housewives at this time of day, many behind strollers or clutching the hands of preschoolers.

"Look, that's them, by those cop cars, handcuffed—Iraqis

or Iranians," said an octogenarian a hundred feet from the action, peering over the crime scene tape. "Dressed in camouflage long johns. I heard one of the cops say they was trying to bomb the Mariemont American Family Sculpture."

"Shameful," said a grandmother, squeezing a granddaughter to her side. "The American Family Sculpture. Who would do such a thing?"

"A-rabs," said another old-timer, "or Serbs or Cubans or Russians. Foreigners with no family values."

The Mariemont officer-in-charge was briefing the representatives of the responding forces. ". . . got a call from the school to investigate. Officer Schofield comes across this suspicious vehicle: van, blacked out windows, camo paint job—idling, two wheels over the curb on Plainfield near the intersection with Wooster. Schofield stops, calls in an 11-96, sees three men in camos desecrating the American Family Sculpture, standing by that low wall that connects the father, mother, and toddler with the grandparents and babies at the sides." The OIC huffed a snort of disgust. "Hell, they were *pissing* on it! Burns me to think about it."

"What the world's coming to," said the Cincinnati sergeant.

The OIC nodded and continued: "Schofield radios a 288, loosens his holster, hollers for them to stop. One of them bolts, his dingus flopping, runs right by Schofield, crosses Wooster and runs into the woods toward the Little Miami River—that way." He pointed. "Schofield didn't get a good look at him, but said he had a humongous ass, looked like a pear with legs. Search is on for him.

"The other two run back to the van, still dribbling. Was a driver, a fourth man, inside. He rolls down the window, points an automatic weapon at Schofield and fires a wild burst. He misses Schofield, but he pulverized the nose of the American Family grandfather. Schofield radios a Code 30. Driver fires another burst while the two pissers jump in. The van peels away.

"Schofield lets the running one go, pursues the van east.

It flies through the square and two lights, causing a three-car smash-up and a dogfight—standard poodle and a Yorkie, one of them little nippers.

"MacDougle, running radar base of Miami hill, hears the call, bottles up Miami. Two other officers block Wooster. The van sees the Wooster cruisers, swerves around the square onto Miami, sees MacDougle, and veers into that beech woods going at least fifty. Hundred feet in, he wedges tight between two big trunks."

"Good work," said the Fairfax man. "Then they gave themselves up, huh?"

"Hell no! Call for assistance was out to surrounding departments. Within minutes, units are surrounding the woods. Men behind cars, weapons drawn. I mean, hell, these fellas in the van have fully automatic weapons."

"And?"

"The rear doors open, one of them standing there, thickset guy with stringy hair and a beard, with a brown-paper package at his chest, yells it's a bomb, enough C-4 to blow up half the village. Says he's got his finger on the trigger, if his finger loosens—*ka-boom*."

"Uh-oh."

"Yeah, fast shuffling. About then, the SWAT people arrive. Orders are hold fire. Don't provoke him, see?"

"Oh, man, I guess."

"It gets worse."

"Worse?"

"Oh, yeah. Man with the bomb says he hates cops, that it's time to pull the plug on the whole rotten Federal-Alien-Zionist—"

"Alien, like in immigrants?"

"Yeah, hates foreigners. He's ready to blow himself, his compadres, and all of us off the face of the earth—what's needed to start the revolt, he says."

"Oh, man."

"Me and the SWAT guy try negotiation, but it's no go.

Everyone must be thinking: What kind of range does this bomb have? I know I was.

"Guy's screaming kamikaze stuff—when one of the ones inside yells, 'I don't wanna die!' and kicks the one with the bomb from behind, out of the van onto his face. Then the inside ones jump out, hands high. A good long second must of passed before we all realize the bomb had bounced two yards and wasn't going *blewie*. Two of the SWAT guys run hard for the crazy, subdue his ass.

"That's the three of them over there. The bomb people say the device is real, but on a timer, no deadman switch. Van's chock full of weapons, ammo, explosives."

The Indian Hill Ranger looked from the van to the Mariemont man. "What do you think they had in mind?"

"Pissing on the American Family statue was just an afterthought. They were really out to bomb the school."

"The school! Full of kids, this time of day."

The OIC slammed a fist into his palm. "Bastards! We're still piecing it together. One of the perps, the skinny young one with the half-shaved head and the pimples—the kicker— walked into the school carrying the bomb—plain-wrapped in brown paper. Of course no one knew it was a Code-10, then. Hall monitor asks what he wants. Says he has a delivery for the Frenchman, mumbles something about all the village buildings looking the same. The monitor directs him to a—" He consulted his notes. "—Mr. Douleur's room, the French teacher.

"Kid with the bomb walks into the class, angry-like, asks this Douleur if he's the Frenchman. Douleur says he is, but gets ticked, you know, at this kid breaking up the class without saying excuse me or whatever. Apparently, Douleur has quite the rep as an enforcer, a stickler for politeness. So he takes the kid by the ear, twists it—remember how they used to do?—and hauls him off to the principal's office, the kid holding the bomb all the while. When they pass the front door, the kid shakes loose and bolts with the bomb. The

French teacher yells he's going to put him on endless deten-
tion, and then goes back to his class and finishes the lesson.
The hall monitor sees the kid run, calls us, and that's why
Schofield was investigating."

The Indian Hill Ranger posed the question they were all
thinking. "You think the kid was someone this French
teacher flunked, or what?"

"Probably something like that, although the French
teacher didn't recognize him. None of them have ID. The
van's plates are registered to a Honda Civic. "They won't talk.
All we can get out of them is their rank and serial numbers."

The Newtown man, a vet, spoke up. "I thought it was
name, rank, and serial number."

"So did I, but they just shake their heads when we ask
who they are." He consulted his notebook and nodded at the
three perpetrators, each standing by a different car. "The
crazy one with the beard says he's a private, serial number
eleven. The old guy, a captain, serial number six. And the
one who's got it out for French, the kid, is a private, number
thirteen."

The OIC checked the notebook again. "Correct that. I see
we do have part of a name. When Abrams first asked the
pimply-faced kid who he was, he said, 'Call me Beast, sir.' "

47

igger thanked the smiling man in the dark brown shirt and Bermuda shorts for the long white box. He realized instantly what was going on when he saw the *Flowers from Hawaii* in red script.

"What is it, Unc?" Nikki set down her lemonade, reached for the box. "Flowers. Neat."

"Not so neat." He followed her to the kitchen table, watched her cut the tape, pry open the lid. "They're from the dean's wife. I hoped that was water over the dam. Millicent is apparently still paddling upstream."

Nikki tossed him a white envelope from inside the box and peeled back layers of wet Hawaiian newspaper. "Oh, wow. Anthuriums." She waved a waxy, scarlet heart, five inches across, by its stiff green stem. "Hard to believe it's not plastic, huh?" She set it aside and burrowed. Each layer revealed another flower, brilliant red, burgundy, orange, or pink, all large and perfect: two dozen, resting on tropical foliage.

Digger lifted a handwritten letter from the envelope and read silently for several seconds. "What *do* you know? Listen to this:

Dear Harmon:

Upon threat of transfer to student registration, Kalia, the department secretary, gave me your address. I tried unsuccessfully to reach you by telephone. Following your hasty departure, I moved into the faculty club, plotting vengeful scenarios. Millicent, of course, pleaded "It was all a mistake," but how could finding you and my wife of thirty-six years in flagrante delicto be a mere "mistake?" I am no man's fool.

Reflecting alone each night, resurrecting the image of Millicent in that grass skirt in primal splendor, dancing to the sound of Tahitian drums for another male, one with a reputation as a "man of the world" (the Sex Doctor, as they call you) caused me no small anguish. Truth be told, it had been some years since I had seen Millicent from a—how shall I say?—intimate perspective. Sexual. There.

To the point: Millicent has confessed her intended seduction was motivated by our waning ardor, that you came to the house unwittingly.

Harmon, I am so pleased I walked in before you succumbed to temptation. I realize I could not in good conscience have held you responsible for submitting to Millicent's allures. You are, after all, mere flesh and blood.

This painful episode rekindled long dormant passions. In the ensuing days (and nights!) Millicent and I have spent more time together (together!) than we have in decades.

My apologies and gratitude. I have always admired your tight lip when it came to others' affairs, and thank you in advance for your discretion in this delicate but satisfactorily concluded matter.

Yours sincerely,
Harris Hotchkiss III

P.S. You will be pleased to know a spacious corner

office with an ocean view has of late become available. I have taken the liberty of putting your name on the door.

"See?" Nikki said. "I knew your luck had changed." She began snipping anthurium stems, arranging the flowers and multicolored foliage in a water pitcher.

A voice sounded at the front door. "Yoo-hoo!"

"Oh-oh," said Digger. "Amy Lou alert."

Amy Lou let herself in, walked to the kitchen, and handed Digger a box. "Hope I'm not disturbing you. I baked a tea ring and thought—Oh, my! Aren't those just the most beautiful flowers you ever saw?" She ran a finger across one of the blossoms. "Land sakes, like something out of the Garden of Eden."

Digger was already picking at stray icing. He looked up to see Nikki's face strangely contorted, her nose twitching, head bobbing in a silent charade. Wha? She pursed her lips toward the flowers, bugged her eyes at Amy Lou, angled her forehead again in the direction of the flowers. Huh? Oohh. Flowers . . . Amy Lou. He tuned into the cryptic communication. "Uh, Amy Lou. The flowers . . ." He saw Nikki nodding. "They're from Hawaii. Just arrived. Your timing's perfect, because they're for you. From me and Nikki."

"For me?" Amy Lou sniffled, ran to Digger, threw a bear hug on him. She squeezed Nikki until her eyes bulged, and kissed her on the cheek. "Little boy lilies. From *Hawaii*. For me! Imagine."

"Gaylord called with a warning," Orlando said. "This Perrier—Fitz—he telephone the Barbados *museo* again, demands to speak with the director, but settles for Gaylord, hinting that the *museo* is cheated! He ask how Gaylord knows me. Gaylord tells him not to worry, I am good friend, give them many gifts. But Gaylord has concern this man will find the director."

"Fitz, the nosy bastard!" Rita Rae bounced her cigarette off the wall, threw it so hard her hair cracked. "Enough is enough. Where's Jesus Bob?"

"We met the auction woman code-named Salome, in Lexington," Levi said to Alphonse LeCoup, "and gave her the suitcase of money. Do you think that was wise, sir?"

"Necessary," LeCoup said. "That hundred and fifty thousand dollars was a good faith deposit. You think it's safe, our going down there?"

"No, sir," said Liev. "But if you insist, we have a plan."

Hands on hips, Raven said, "It had better be good."

"Two of our men will drive a bulletproof limo as a decoy all the way to a small forest at the edge of this Golden Leaf. We will fly you and the cash for the bidding by helicopter to rendezvous with the limo, and then drive you to the motel in another car.

"Only you two, besides Salome and the barbarian commander and his guard will be permitted on the upper floor. I have reserved a room on the first floor. We do not expect trouble if you lose the auction."

"Lose? You think I'm going there to *lose*?"

"We anticipated you would say that. So, if you win, you give her the cash, take the piece of metal and remaining money with you, leave by the side stairs. I will meet you in the parking lot and drive you to the helicopter. We exit by air. I will have armed men watching. If there is trouble, our men will fend off the barbarians and we will drive you to an alternate exit: a ship my brother has rented on their large sea."

"Lake," corrected Liev. "Large as the Dead Sea. Only it is fresh water."

"The ship has a cabin like a house, they are common on this sea," said Levi. "Very comfortable."

"A houseboat," Raven concluded, aloud.

"Yes," said Liev. "We cross the lake, disguised as tourists, take you to another car, return by a different route."

"Sounds like a good plan," said LeCoup. Raven agreed. Levi nodded. "The Mossad trained us well."

Ka-pow, pow, pow! The last shot of the three-gun salute echoed from the hills above the Reserve.

Making a rare appearance, but a necessary one to restore morale, Commander-in-Chief Smoot Mudd stood before General Ben. "In recognition of your good works with the men," Smoot said, "I promote you to the rank of field marshal. Congratulations."

"Thank *you*, sir." Ben clicked his heels. "While three brave men short, the Daniel Boone Rangers are battle-ready, eager to launch the counteroffensive that will initiate the revolt, secure recognition for the Republic of Boone, and initiate expulsion of the Federal-Alien-Zionist menace."

"No action until after the auction, hear?"

"Yes, sir."

Smoot scooted his walker along the line of men, halting before Big Butt. "And Colonel Butz, for your heroism during the assault on the Frenchman, I raise you to the rank of major general."

At a loss for words, Big Butt saluted.

"Let this man be an example to you," Smoot advised the Scooter Shooters and Junior Rangers. "Keep your noses and your weapons clean, and you'll grow up just like him."

Big Butt shuffled uneasily. When he arrived in camp yesterday, looking wan and frightened, he had explained how the local cops, the FBI, and the ATF were waiting for them in Cincinnati. He alone had escaped, waging a running firefight, shooting at least four of the bastards, scaring off the rest before he reached a wooded river and safety.

The preposterous reports of "an attempted school bombing" and the cover-up of the dead federal agents proved to Ben beyond a shadow of a doubt that Zionists had coopted the media.

Commander-in-Chief Smoot Mudd left five cases of Bud,

two boxes of Corona Bravada cigars for the Rangers, a carton of menthol cigarettes for the boys, and promise of an honest-to-God tank if the auction went well. Tabs were popping left and right. Celebratory smoke enveloped the parade ground as Ben led Big Butt aside.

"I see you are still shaken by the combat," Ben said. He patted Big Butt on the shoulder. "Perfectly normal psychological reaction."

"I don't know." Big Butt kicked at a clump of grass. "I mean, I appreciate the promotion, but a major general? I'm not sure I deserve it, sir."

"Nonsense. Your work with the Scooter Shooters and Junior Rangers? Let me tell you: a man never stands so tall as when he stoops to teach a child to shoot.

"Just look at you. Spit-shined brogans. The latest Glock at your side. Wash and dry polyester fatigues, always crisp and clean. Close-cropped hair, exemplary hygiene. You follow orders to a T and never succumb to independent thought. Bold and brave, you are an inspiration to the men.

"Why," Ben saluted, "you are the very model of a modern major general."

48

Big Butt motioned Jesus Bob to follow, leading him to his new pickup. Shielded by the truck, he looked past the silver flake, olive, not-so-drab custom paint at the encampment, concerned they may have been followed. Big Butt brushed dust from the hood, ran his handkerchief along the silver running board, and picked at a dried insect clinging to one of the chromed wheels.

"What the hell's this? You trying to sell me your truck?"

Big Butt muttered a no, and glanced back at camp. "We still partners?"

"Hell, yes, Major General." Jesus Bob laughed and gave him a sloppy salute, mellow, for the moment, having smoked a thick joint down to the nub. "Pardners in abduction." Jesus Bob leaned against the wheel well, extended to accommodate the pickup's oversize, double rear tires, and sucked the life out of the last few grains of pot, pinched in a roach clip. He flicked the dimming ash onto the ground. "Hey, man, I can tell you're worried. You still thinking all right, with hunks of your brains gone?"

"Yeah, sure." That wasn't the issue.

"Guess what's left of my liver's still churnin', too, though it's hard to tell with Sis cutting off my medicine—old liver hasn't had much of a job to do lately."

"My problem is . . ." Big Butt turned away and faced his new friend. "What I said about the firefight up north? Was all bullshit. I never killed no ATF, FBI, or even cops. I turned tail and ran. I was lucky to find a good old boy trucking south."

Big Butt buffed a speck of dust from the pickup's immaculate fender with his sleeve, avoiding eye contact. "I'm a liar, Jesus Bob."

Jesus Bob punched him lightly in the side. "Hey, man, you told 'em what they wanna hear—kinda like changing my name got me that cushy job with the prison chaplain. What's wrong with that?"

Spilling his guts, now, Big Butt told him the rest of it. "What really happened, was, we get to this place, looks like Disneyland, can't tell one building from the next, no addresses on them, neither. So we're cruising, putting away some beers. Finally we send Purcell, with the bomb, inside this big building, and damned if he don't find the Frenchman! But they run him out before he can hide the bomb. We drink some more, cruise, trying to figure out how to get back in there, then stop to water the grass, and that's when the cops close in. I ran. I guess the others got caught."

"You saved your ass. That was smart. See? Your brain's working fine."

"Yeah, but, hell, I blew my chance to take somebody out, make a man of myself. What kind of example am I to those kids?" Disgusted, he kicked at the yellow smiley-face on the tailgate of his beautiful new truck, missing it by six inches.

"Damn it to hell!" He kicked again, and smudged the happy-face's cheek. "I'm still a cherry."

Jesus Bob gave him another friendly jab. "Pardner, you are in luck. Because your good buddy Jesus Bob is about to take care of that. Sis gave me an assignment, and I'm inviting you in."

*   *   *

Digger turned the key and revved the engine of the VW. "Well, tomorrow's the big auction. I've had a sinking feeling we may never find who killed Edgar, so saying good-bye to him today will provide a measure of closure."

Nikki grumbled in the shotgun seat. "I think Uncle Edgar would have wanted me to drive. I'd get us there faster."

"This isn't a race, kiddo. There's no 'there' to get to. We'll enjoy the day, see where the road takes us. Somewhere up in the mountains. When it feels right, we'll send Edgar off with a fond farewell." He reached over the backseat and patted the stainless-steel urn, wedged between Nikki's collecting pack and the door. He stopped at the end of the drive. "Hold on, I want to check the mailbox."

Big Butt had carefully worked his truck into the bushes a hundred feet from the Fitz driveway so as not to scratch its paint. "Here they come. A VW, right?"

Jesus Bob snorted his second line off the dashboard to get himself into an adventurous frame of mind.

"Uh-oh," said Big Butt, "they're stopping. Maybe they see—no, it's okay, only looking for mail." He craned out the window. "Lordy! You see who that is?"

"Sis gave me the map, said a white VW, an old guy with long hair and a beard, and some girl." He rubbed his nose, squinted through the windshield. "Looks like we got it right."

"Man, oh, man, that's *Willie Nelson*! He's the one we're supposed to knock off? Willie Nelson and a babe?"

"I'll be damned. Sis didn't say. What the hell—make it more fun, huh? Lots of guys can say they offed some Jethro no one heard of. How many can say they did in Willie Nelson? Maybe we'll have fun with his babe, after. There's a story. Poked Willie Nelson's babe. I like it."

"I don't know."

Jesus Bob flashed his mean, squinty look. "You're not puss-ing out, are you? Telling me you're a yellow-ass chicken?" He flashed his knife. "Cause if you are, get out of the fucking truck and walk your yellow ass back up to your Boy Scout camp. I've got a job to do."

"No, no, it's just, I mean . . . Lordy, Willie Nelson. Man, Willie's the best. Seems like we oughta get his autograph first, or something."

"How about a hank of his hair, after? Move your ass, I'll drive. I don't want no yellow-ass chicken letting him get away."

Thirty minutes later, the VW wended into the cloud-shrouded green mountains of the Daniel Boone National Forest.

"I saw two DORs," Nikki said. "But I didn't say anything. You know, on account of Edgar."

"Good for you, kiddo." Digger stuck his arm out the win-dow. "With these low clouds, it's cooler up here. Take a breath of those pines." He turned on the wipers as a light mist speckled the windshield.

"On one of these tight turns," Nikki said, "right after a straightaway—" She unrolled her own window. "—fat Gabe showed me where some guy in a sawed-off bus peeled off and bit the big one. Right through the windshield—*kapow*! Bus burned up. Gabe said there was still a stain up in the tree where he hit and—"

"Okay, Nikki, I get the idea. Let's think happy thoughts. Look how pretty the valley is. It's still sunshiny down there. You can see almost all of Golden—"

Whump! The car lurched, swerved.

"What'd I hit?" Digger fought the wheel.

"That truck. Behind you. He hit *us*."

"Damn!" Digger steadied the wheel, glanced at the rear-view mirror. He punched the accelerator as the VW cleared a hairpin curve, leaving the truck momentarily out of view. "Drunks!"

"Yeah, where's a cop when you need one?" Neither of them laughed. "Watch out, he's trying to pass!"

Digger downshifted into another turn. The truck gained on the outside, crossed the center line, nearly made it around, and then edged to the right, well into the blind curve, crowding them to the shoulder. A camper barreled down the hill out of the clouds toward them. The pickup braked and dropped back.

"That idiot'll kill us both," Digger said. "If that camper had swerved, we'd all be dead. Road's gotta be slippery, too, with this drizzle."

"Slow down on the next straightaway, Unc. Let him go around."

They were well into a run of switchbacks rising to the ridge crest. Out of the next bend, Digger followed Nikki's advice, decelerated, worked the two right wheels onto the narrow shoulder.

Instead of passing to their left, however, the pickup sped up, headed directly for them. "What the hell?" Digger punched the pedal, swerved back onto the asphalt. Not fast enough. They heard the crunch of a taillight, felt the car bounce, but were away before the full force of the truck struck.

Digger mashed the horn. "Crazy bastards!"

Nikki raised her arm high out her window and flashed them her middle finger. She watched the truck roaring toward them. "He's not passing—he's trying to smash us!" She leaned over the backseat, peering through the mist-streaked rear window. "Driver and another guy. Here he *comes* again. C'mon, *move*. Faster."

Digger whipped the little bug left and right, barely missed another lunge. They rounded a sharp bend. Digger took it wide, felt the tires slip. He tapped the brakes, steered into the turn and regained control. The pickup worked to the inside, on a track to keep them in the oncoming lane or force them over the edge.

Digger veered in. The truck's front bumper brushed the bug's rear fender, jolting them enough to spin the wheel out of his hands. He overcorrected, went into a four-wheel slide on the damp pavement toward the guardrail. The valley loomed. Nikki screamed.

Three feet from the edge, the tires gripped, Digger reigned in the nose and accelerated. The bumper scraped the guardrail with a loud rasp, but they squirted from the curve barely wounded. The pickup followed seconds later, but caromed off the rail. It waggled and renewed the attack.

"Unc, maybe it's not drunks. Maybe it's whoever killed Edgar, trying to get us, too!"

"Not if I can help it—hold on." He worked the small car for all it was worth, putting distance between them and the truck.

They cat-and-moused to the mountain crest, the powerful pickup gaining on straight road and losing ground in the curves.

The road crossed a narrow foggy ridge and dropped into a four-hundred-foot shoot before the next bend. "This is bad," Digger said. He accelerated, the needle passed fifty, sixty. The truck roared out of the cloud and narrowed the gap. Digger made it to the bend well ahead, but entered too fast, crossed the yellow line. He braked hard. The rear end let loose, they slid into a 360-degree spin, barely missing the rail at the cliff side. He recovered, rode the double yellow line out of the curve. The road S-waggled. Digger kept his eyes front. "Where's the truck?"

Centrifugal force threw Nikki against the door. The VW bottomed out, and she bounced off the roof, despite the seat belt. "Can't see." She released the belt, climbed over the seat into the back for better vantage. She looked back. "Oh, man! He hit the guardrail hard, stripped the whole side of the truck. He's stopped in the curve."

A van coming up the mountain honked, swerved to miss

the VW, running two feet on the wrong side of the line. The driver kept his hand on the horn well past. They heard the Doppler shift in pitch as it whizzed by. Seconds later, they heard it hoot again when it saw the truck.

Eyes on the road behind, Nikki gave Digger the bad news. "He's on the move again."

With each curve, the truck fell farther behind. Digger felt an adrenaline rush as he found the rhythm of the mountain: brake and downshift before a curve, accelerate and up-shift out.

"Way to go, Unc, we're outrunning them." She regarded him wide-eyed. "You're a great driver!"

"Feel of the road's coming back."

"Coming back?"

"The year I spent on the Etruscan project, I owned an Alfa Romeo. Believe it or not, your old uncle—when he was a good bit younger—outran Italians."

Nikki reached over the seat and gave his shoulder a firm squeeze. "Mario Fitz! Keep it up."

She fumbled with the back seat belt, but couldn't get it together with the jerks and jolts. She braced herself instead, feet on the floor, arms to the roof.

Digger cursed. "Another straightaway." He slalomed through two shallow curves. The road rounded a spur. He caught snatches of forest to one side, sky to the other, saw the next ridge a half mile away. He tried not to think of the thousand feet to the stream below, working the gears instead, getting into the rhythm of the mountain.

Then he realized where they were headed: a gentle curve and a straightaway into a long valley, and knew that was where the powerful truck would catch them. He considered braking, pulling off the road, hiding, but saw only streaming foliage, rising cliff faces and guardrails.

"He's gaining on the straight stretches, Unc. Two more, and he'll be on our tail again."

"Afraid of that. Look down. When we're out of these curves, we don't stand a snowball's chance. Only a couple minutes away. Nikki . . . when we get below, I'm going to pull over fast. You run for cover, I'll waggle around the road to slow them, then drive into a cornfield and run myself."

"Leave you? No way!" She slammed a fist into her collecting pack in frustration. "Ouch!"

She rubbed her scraped knuckles and clapped. "My collecting jars! I've got three quart and four pint mason jars of formalin in my pack. They're heavy, four of them full of specimens. You slow up in a curve, I'll lean out and lob one of these babies at them. They get formaldehyde in their eyes, or if one breaks in front of their tires, it's all she wrote."

"If I slow down and you miss, they'll be right on our butts, and that truck has four times our mass."

"I pitch softball. Don't worry."

Digger downshifted, slowed. Nikki climbed into the front, rolled down the window, and lined her projectiles on the backseat, formalin-only jars first, specimen jars last. "I can get in a couple tosses each bend."

"There's no more than four turns left before the valley. Do good."

Digger glanced at the mirror, watched the truck grow in size. He slowed before a tight horseshoe, allowed the pickup to move within thirty feet.

Nikki leaned out with a pint jar and heaved. It sailed wide over the edge of the mountain. She grabbed another, pitched harder. This one went all the way over the cab, broke somewhere behind. "Missed. Move out, Unc."

Digger accelerated, scooted away. Between the curves, Nikki plucked her prized scarlet kingsnake out of the last small jar and flipped it on the floor. She got the jar recapped by the beginning of the next curve, pitched, and watched it break on the asphalt. Stiff coiled snakes rolled like hoops, and chunks of glass skittered into the path of the truck, but if glass met rubber, it had no effect. She cursed, grabbed another jar and shattered it in front of the pickup. She was sure she saw the front left tire roll over a shard, but the truck kept coming.

"Has those heavy tires," she said, wrapping her fingers around a quart. "I'm gonna zap them in the windshield." Barely out of the bend, she lobbed, watched it smash above the grille. Formaldehyde, glass, and snakes sloshed and thumped across the hood. They heard one of the men in the truck scream as a pilot blacksnake hoop-rolled up the windshield.

"Uh-oh," she said. "Passenger's got a gun."

"Great." Digger hit the gas. "Shot or run off the road. Maybe run off the road, then shot—"

"Quit whining and drive."

Two gunshots rang out, wide misses with Digger zigging and the pickup driver zagging to avoid Nikki's bombs.

Nikki readied another quart of snakes for the next bend. She heaved this one fast, saw it break in their grille. "That'll make their eyes smart," she said, fumbling for the last jar.

"Yes! The bastard dropped his gun." She watched it clatter on the pavement, bounce high and fly off the road. "They're rubbing their eyes." She saw the truck's wipers come on, and hefted the last jar. "C'mon baby, give 'em hell."

She sidearmed it hard, saw it catch the truck windshield high on one side. The man in the shotgun seat went silhouette behind a white spider web, but the driver, a wild look in his eyes, glared back, unscathed. She watched him lean over the wheel, extend a thick arm out the window, and shake a fist.

Concentrating on the road, Digger missed the action. "What happened?"

"Oops."

"Oops? What the hell's that mean? C'mon—get another jar ready. Valley's just ahead, one more bend before the straightaway. Two hundred feet, and I'll slow down again, give you a good shot."

"Better not. No. Speed up." She explained: "No more jars."

"Oh, damn."

"Yeah."

"Damn, damn, damn." He pressed the pedal to the floorboard.

"I've got an idea."

"Speak up."

"Edgar!" She was on the floor, scrambling for the urn.

"No!"

"Oh, yes. Uncle Edgar?" Speaking to the urn. "We need you, Uncle Edgar. Someone killed you and now someone's trying to kill Uncle Digger and me. Keep the Fitz name alive, Uncle Edgar. Show them what Fitzes are made of."

They were into the bend: a right that leveled off into the valley and straight road. Digger downshifted. The truck bore down. Nikki waited until Digger slowed. The truck was still in the bend, in a wavering skid but hot on their tail, determined. She leaned out the window, urn in both hands, lifted and kissed it fast, and then heaved, watched it arc high, land on the truck's hood. The lid spun off and Edgar, ten thousand, tiny, cindery bits of him, formed a vengeful gray cloud, enveloping the pickup's windshield.

Edgar stuck where he landed, bonded to glass and metal by the mountain mist and Nikki's formaldehyde.

Blinded, the driver held the wheel, followed the curve as he remembered it—but too long. He sheared off two guard posts—*craack, craack*—and sailed off an eight-foot embankment into the valley.

Digger hit the brakes, watched the pickup lurch from its initial bounce, roll over, right itself, and plow a hundred-foot swath through new corn. Ten seconds later, the doors opened, and two men stumbled to their knees in the field.

Nikki waited until they looked her way and gave them the finger. Raised it high and long. Then she waved.

"Say good-bye to Uncle Edgar," she said to Digger. "He did us proud."

Jesus Bob wrestled the crumpled hood. "Radiator's busted, but I think the fan's clear—oughta still drive. Long enough to get us back, anyways." He poked Big Butt in the ribs. "Ain't that the shits? Who'd a thought old Willie could drive like that? And what a feisty babe. One hell of a chase—shee-it! Bet he writes a song about that one, huh?" He caught the sour look on Big Butt's face, the . . . tears? "Hey, man. Don't let it get you down. There's always tomorrow for that kill. You stick with me, you'll get in it, don't you . . ."

Big Butt stared at the smashed front end of his formaldehyde-reeking pickup, the cracked grille, the missing running lights, the crumpled hood, the broken windshield, the custom metal-flake paint stripped to metal, the flattened top. Only the tailgate and his bumper sticker with the smiley face remained intact—and he himself had sullied those with his thoughtless kicks at the start of their adventure. Big Butt whimpered, "My shiny new truck!" He swiped the back of a hand across his teary cheek. "Made one payment on it. One payment. And look at it."

Jesus Bob swatted him hard across the temple. "Don't be a pussy. Shit happens. Now hop to. We get back, I'll buy you a new gun and a six pack. You want another truck, I'll steal you one. How's that?"

49

The next morning, Nikki drove to the sheriff's head-quarters, ostensibly to show Bo her charts of McAfee County rattlesnake distribution, but really to wish him luck on the potentially momentous day. The auction was to begin at noon.

"You nervous?" she asked.

"Nah. Coony has a plan, says everything will work out fine."

"I mean about your sister and brother." She couldn't ignore his misbuttoned shirt any longer. She touched the top, where it first went wrong, tensed when she felt the Kevlar vest.

Bo flushed, but set to rebuttoning the shirt with an anxious look around the office to see if anyone else was watching. "I wish Coony never told you two about them. They were out of my life. Forever, I hoped. And now, bang, they're back and stirring up trouble. Big trouble if I know Judas Bob." He checked the paraphernalia hanging from his belt, lingering at the gun. He unsnapped the holster, lifted the Colt .38 two inches, and slid it back. "Fact is, we don't really know if he's here at all. Maybe it's just Rita Rae. Coony wants me to hold the office down with the clerk and dispatcher while he and the others keep their eye on the motel and the auction—you know, so I won't have to see her."

"Good. That's good."

"I guess." He forced a smile. "Hey, you and your uncle okay? After yesterday?"

"Fine. Can't say as much for the bug, but we're fine, and it still drives."

"Still no sign of the truck. We put the word out in five counties: police, body shops, gas stations." He slammed a fist into his palm. "Some people are mean as snakes." He caught Nikki's raised eyebrow. "I, uh, you know . . . just an expression."

"Sure," she said, fake scowling. She poked him in the arm to let him know she was joking, and they laughed together.

Bo went serious again. "Judas Bob was like that. He'd hit the booze or drugs, and if it didn't knock him back, he'd be knocking someone else back. Mean." He got a distant look in his eyes. "Time passes, you magnify things. Who knows, maybe he dried out, or got religion."

"Hey, Bo?" Nikki stood on her toes, threw her arms around his shoulders, and gave him a long hug. "It'll work out," she said to his ear. "You'll see."

"This is it, men." Field Marshal Ben walked along the long line of militiamen, excluding Bolt, who seldom left Smoot's side, and Jesus Bob, whose allegiance today was with his sister, but including two Scooter Shooters and one Junior Ranger who had skipped school to join the grand campaign.

"Commander-in-Chief Mudd," Ben was saying, "needs our help to see that the Frenchman . . ." He saw their bodies go taut. "That's right, the Frenchman, the one who closed the Winky Worm plant—the Frenchman, who will be in Golden Leaf by twelve hundred hours with his squaw. There is a strong possibility the Frenchman may attempt to rob the commander of the treasure he has long sought, or assassinate him—possibly assisted by our turncoat sheriff and his minions."

Ben shook his crop in the air, spoke with uncommon vehemence. "My intelligence reveals alien-clone-packed *silver tanker trucks* McAfee County–bound from Wright Patterson Air Force Base in Ohio. There are rumors of *UN troop movements*. Bolt saw *black helicopters* at the Frenchman's. Two of our own men were *abducted*, fortunately returned with only insignificant parts missing, but abducted nonetheless. There were two more *UFO sightings* at the Pines Trailer Park only yesterday. Captain Grundy's wife Rubella spoke—*spoke* with a *man in black*, a self-professed *Jew*, who *bragged* he was an *alien* on reconnaissance, and planned to annex—*annex*— McAfee County into their satanic empire!"

The men broke ranks. Manly shouts and piercing whistles mixed with prepubescent and adolescent screams from the boys. Ragged gunfire erupted. Ben exhausted the clip of his .45 to regain their attention so as to deliver his carefully drafted summation. He took a deep breath, climbed onto a double RC crate dais, and began.

"We, the White Christian men of the Republic of Boone, the Lord's avenging angels, stand today on the edge of a new frontier. We hold these truths to be self-evident, that we are endowed by our Creator with certain un-alien rights, that among these are freedom from taxes and federal intervention, and the right to bear arms. Our new nation faces trial by blood and fire and vapor of smoke. Today, we shall fight the mother of all battles.

"Be assured, brave warriors, you have nothing to fear but fear itself, for we have plenty of guns and ammo. We shall not flag or fail. We shall go on to the end. We shall fight the Frenchman. We shall fight the federal and Zionist and interplanetary forces of evil. We shall fight with growing confidence and growing strength. We shall defend our land, whatever the cost. We shall fight in the cornfields and in the streets. We shall fight in the hills. We shall never surrender. We shall overcome!"

Men shouted, slapped palms, threw hats in the air. Automatic gunfire raked the clouds. Although, truth be told, it wasn't entirely Ben's words that drove the troops to frenzy, but the anticipation of finally unleashing their weapons on something other than targets or beer bottles or hapless animals. Soon, the Daniel Boone Rangers would have men in their sights.

"Disturbing news," Orlando said to Rita Rae. "I have a message from the *director* of the Barbados *museo*." He pressed buttons, put the phone to her ear.

"Mr. Castro? This is Horatio Wembly, Director of the Queen's Maritime Museum in Barbados. I have spoken with a Dr. Harmon Fitz in the United States who has made the most disturbing allegation. Had I not fallen hopelessly ill from rough seas and returned prematurely from an extended cruise, I would have missed his call. Dr. Fitz tells me he spoke with my assistant, Gaylord Trill, who, I find to my surprise, has left our employ without notice. Dr. Fitz says Mr. Trill confirmed that our institution deaccessioned various U.S. artifacts and sold them to *you*. He claims, moreover, that he has a copy of a letter, signed by *me*, confirming this transfer and that these artifacts may have substantial value.

"I know nothing of this, nor of you or your company. I neither wrote nor signed such a letter. And we most emphatically did *not* deaccession our material. My secretary is attempting to locate these items as well as Mr. Trill. Dr. Fitz is preparing to fax me this alleged document.

"Please, call me *immediately*."

Rita Rae hung up. "Fitz! That meddling old fool. If Jesus Bob had done his job, Fitz wouldn't have been alive to make that call. I don't want him or his niece talking to Smoot or

LeCoup or Coony McCoy. Where's Jesus Bob? Forget 'accidents'—what the hell are guns for, anyway?"

"*Cálmase, querida*." Orlando cradled her face in his palms, attempted to kiss her on the forehead, but she slapped his hands away. He grabbed her wrists. "Listen! Fitz says nothing yet or we would know it. LeCoup is on the road already. Smoot warned the law away. Those two, they don't care *how* we got the plate, only that it is *good* and they own it. Hear that gunfire? Smoot's army is ready. No interference, eh? I talk with their *jefe* Ben—after the auction, they fight the sheriff. And while they battle? We are gone."

"Not good enough for me. Where's Jesus Bob?"

"Jesus Bob is picking up Smoot's hundred and fifty thousand deposit—the tight old man waits for the last minute to part with it. Jesus Bob will be back soon. *Paciencia, por favor.* All is okay."

Levi prepared to stow LeCoup's auction cash, packed in a woman's handbag. Raven touched him on the arm, spoke loudly enough to be heard over the *whoomp, whoomp, whoomp* of the helicopter blades slashing the air over their heads. "I'll hold that on my lap, thank you."

He smiled a polite smile, but his thoughts, as always when he looked at this woman, were not polite. She's one to tie up, he thought, to show who is the master. Yes, she would enjoy that. He smiled again at his unfailing understanding of women, and passed her the handbag. "Of course, madam. I thought only of your comfort."

Jesus Bob loved the way Rita Rae's Mustang drove, decided he would buy one himself when he got his share of the loot. "I want you to go straight to Smoot's," she had said. "I want you to keep the top up and stay clear of the sheriff's office. Pick up Smoot's deposit and come straight back. I want you

with us when we go to the motel. I want to be there early.
And I want you clearheaded, too. One line of coke, and that's
it."

I want, I want, I want. Jesus Bob was sick of it. And
nervous as a rabbit in a ring full of pit bulls. He needed his
medicine. But no. "Not until after," she said. He thought of
Orlando's powdery gift and practically salivated. Actually, his
nose ran. He wiped it on his sleeve and accelerated. Maybe
he'd fly to South America with Orlando some time, see the
coke trees, buy all he wanted, cheap as dirt. Or go to Thai-
land or wherever it was they grew heroin.

He remembered the sour look on Bolt's face when he had
picked up the buckskin pouch with Smoot's deposit money,
ten minutes before. Old Smoot clutched it to his chest one
last time and told him to take it. "Soon as my money's in
their hands, Bolt," he had said, "the Céloron plate will be
mine. Mine." Jesus Bob could tell Bolt didn't give a damn
about the auction from the glare he got. Be fun to mix it up
with Bolt some time. But not as much as fun as with Bo, the
bastard—the bastard who ruined his life. Bo and his damned
boss, Sheriff Coony Fucking McCoy, the one who snuck up
behind him, coldcocked him, and sent him to do hard time.

Jesus Bob's knuckles went white on the wheel at the
thought of them, the bastards. Just wait, little brother. Just
wait. He looked back at the road, the once familiar road, and
realized he was driving, not back to the Reserve and Barracks
#1, but toward the sheriff's office. Hah! Whaddaya think of
that? Fine, he'd drive by, check it out, so when he returned
to finish his business, there'd be no surprises.

He wriggled in the seat, felt sweat running down his
chest. The dinky-ass building would be on the left, just
ahead. He slowed and—there it was. His face burned at the
memory of waking up in their holding cell, of Bo phoning
from the hospital, saying how *sorry* he was, but that they
were doing Jesus Bob a favor, giving him a chance to clean
the poison out of his system, that Jesus Bob had broken the

law and would have to pay his debt to fucking society. For what? Shooting a clown in the foot? Bo in the leg? Since when was shooting kin a crime, anyway?

If they hadn't sent him up for that, he wouldn't have had a record, wouldn't have gotten sent away the next time for beating that guy, or the time after that, for the robbery. Or the rest. It was that first time that nailed you, branded you "an enemy of the state" forever. Sonofabitchin bastards.

Ohmigod! There he was, standing out front. Bo! Fucking Bo.

Jesus Bob pulled into a Laundromat across the street and stared. Bo. And some broad. Wait. Not just some broad, but *Willie's* babe! The little bitch who threw that dirt on the truck and ran them off the road. What the hell? He watched her stand on her toes and hug him. Hug Bo. What the hell's going on? Two-timing Willie? From the way Bo hugged back he could tell Bo had a hard-on for her. Oh, man, *Bo's babe!*

Jesus Bob's mind went into overdrive. He hatched a plan, indefinite, but oh, so much sweeter than shooting Bo in the back. He waited, watched the babe get in her car—the same stinking VW bug that outran them—and drive away.

Jesus Bob followed, saw her pull into a tiny grocery on the edge of town. She went inside. He parked beside the VW and waited. No one else around. He ran a hand through his hair, practically on fire with nerves and anticipation.

Nikki set the bag of groceries on the hood and opened the door.

"Ma'am?"

She turned around, must have thought at first he was Bo. Even said his name, "Bo?" before she realized he was older, harder around the edges, thicker at the belly. Her mouth moved without speaking as he moved toward her like an old friend.

A hand over the mouth, an arm around her waist, and hoist. Light as a shot doe, though hardly as limp. A foot nudge to open the trunk of the Mustang, already ajar, and he tossed her in, slammed the lid. Muffled screams, thumps.

"Holler good, bitch." He tossed her pack and groceries in the backseat. "Hope you bought something tasty."

He stopped at the last phone booth on the way to his destination and called his sister.

"Where the hell are you?" she shouted, in a royal snit. "You got Smoot's deposit, didn't you?"

"Right here in a buckskin bag."

She noticed a hesitation. "You screwed up somehow. What's wrong?"

"Nothing. Listen, Sis, I got Willie's babe."

"Who?"

"The babe with Willie, yesterday."

She made him describe Willie, the babe, the driveway, the farmhouse, the VW. Satisfied he had the right babe, she said, "The name is Nikki. Wait, let me think." He heard a match strike, a long drag on a cigarette. "This is good," she said, finally.

Jesus Bob snorted. He knew that.

"Hold her, I'll call her uncle, warn him away from messing with us. Oh, yes, this is good. You bring her up here. No, not here. Some of these soldier boys may still—"

"There's this place," he said. "Other side of the ridge, their musket range.

"Good. Keep her till twelve-thirty. No later. Then tie her to a tree and drive to the motel, and we'll clear this burg. Got that?"

"Sure, Sis." Jesus Bob hung up, checked a number in the front of the thin phone book, and dialed again.

"Let me talk to Bo," he said.

50

evi and Liev Levkovitz's plan had gone without a hitch. The helicopter arrived uneventfully near a wooded area north of Golden Leaf. Raven and Le-Coup rode with Levi to the E-Z Zees in a rented white Taurus, while the dummy limo drove ahead as a diversion. The AAA Acme Security men moved to preassigned positions.

LeCoup and Raven followed Rita Rae's instructions to the letter—with the exception of Levi's presence on the first floor, the armed men posted nearby, the radios, and the matching .25 caliber Berettas tucked in their jacket pockets. They ascended the motel's external, western stairs at precisely 11:30 and, using the key Rita Rae had sent them, entered room 201, thus avoiding Smoot and Bolt's arrival at number 215 via the eastern stairs at 11:45. A tray of croissants and a carafe of coffee awaited them on the dresser.

Nervous, uneasy, Raven looked at the reproduction watercolors of big-eyed children romping with balloons and butterflies. "Nice art. And the carpet's a bold shade of orange. Bet that fiber never stains. Can't say as much for the bedspread, huh?"

"Cherie, we're not here for the ambience. When this is over, we'll do the Ritz in Paris, okay?"

Raven tossed a cheap red purse containing $400,000 for the cash-and-carry auction on the bed. Added to the $150,000 nonrefundable, good-faith money previously delivered to Rita Rae by the Levkovitz brothers, that made over half a million dollars available to snag the Céloron plate. LeCoup had intentionally bid a pittance for the George Washington letter to lull Smoot into failing to bring enough cash to the main event. Smoot, he knew, prided himself on paying no more for an artifact than he could resell it for, which meant a hundred thousand tops for the Lords of Trade plate. Even if Smoot brought double that today, he would go home empty-handed. Alphonse savored the thought of Smoot with the letter and he, LeCoup, with the plate itself.

At 11: 35 Levi called them on the radio to check channel clarity and assure them he and his men were ready.

Bolt checked his watch, 11:44. He climbed the motel's exterior, west stairs, set down the shopping bag containing the cash, took a careful look down the interior, fluorescent-lit, second-floor corridor—empty—raised his hand in an okay sign to the surveilling Rangers, and returned to carry up Smoot.

Based on LeCoup's naively low bid for the letter, Smoot was certain the tightwad Frenchman would bring no more than $200,000 to the auction; add the deposit, he would have $350,000 to bid. Smoot had $350,000 *with* him. Add that to the deposit, and he had half a million dollars to snag the plate. He hated to pay more for any collectible than it was worth, but this was war. Smoot was certain he had more than enough to beat the man fair and square. Although, in the unlikely event LeCoup pulled out all the stops and outbid him, fine, let him have the damned thing—for fifteen minutes tops. The Rangers were on standby for a recovery mission.

*   *   *

Chez Pancakes and the E-Z Zees Motel dominated the southeast quarter of the intersection of Golden Leaf's Main Street and the McAfee-Combs County Road. A four-way flashing stop light marked the crossroads.

A mom-and-pop gas station occupied the southwest corner, a half-completed strip mall ran diagonally across the northwest corner at the base of a low hill. To the northeast, backed against scraggly woods and brush, stood a fifty-foot cement block building housing Uncle Al's Bait and Winky Worm Outlet.

Six of Levi's black-clad security men armed with Uzis squatted on cement blocks behind the half-raised strip mall awaiting orders.

The Ranger Perimeter Defense Force, five men commanded by Major General B. G. Butz, hunkered in the trees across the highway, invisible in their camo fatigues except for the cigarette smoke storm clouds rising over their heads. Inside the bait shop, Field Marshal Ben stood by the galvanized red worm tank. Men lounged against the counter or sat on upturned barrels exchanging stories of weapons owned, animals slaughtered, and women conquered. In one corner, two Scooter Shooters, ages nine and eleven, and one Junior Ranger, twelve, shared a courage-bolstering, bourbon-laced can of Dr Pepper.

In the guise of plumbers, the Rangers had prepared a berm-protected trench outside the bait shop the day before. Early that morning they had sandbagged the entrance and windows, and Ben had distributed Orlando's pristine HK machine pistols as weapons of the day.

Bolt was to wave from the east stairway of the E-Z Zees: once if Smoot was successful, twice if he was outbid. In the latter case, Smoot had ordered the Rangers to immobilize traffic, capture the presumptuous foreigner and his corporate whore squaw, and recover the plate.

Ben planned to capture them anyway and put them before a firing squad for crimes against the honest wage earners of the Republic of Boone. The Rangers would next withdraw to the Reserve to lob recoilless rifle fire on the sheriff's office, the local nexus of the conspiracy, and on the highway, blocking advance of the alien tankers.

From the mountain reaches of the Daniel Boone National Forest, they would fend off the retaliatory invasion by the FBI, ATF, and NATO, until word of their noble battle spread like righteous wildfire among the nation's armed and long-suffering white Christian males. Thus would the Daniel Boone Rangers go down in the history books, igniting the revolt against the satanic axis of the Federal-Zionist-Alien-New World Order.

Ben, in the bait shop, was summing it up: "Four score and seven days ago—or pretty close to that—we brought forth upon this continent, a new nation, conceived in liberty, and dedicated to the proposition—"

"Excuse me, sir," said the comm center man, cell phone in hand, "but Silas across the way is on the line. He said two men in black pants and sweaters wearing black sunglasses arrived in a white Taurus. They filled the tank and bought some candy bars."

"What kind? The candy bars? Details are everything."

The Ranger checked with Silas and relayed the bad news: "Two Mars bars and a Milky Way."

"You see? They're homesick!" Ben began to mutter. "First, the sighting of a black helicopter, silent as a dragonfly, setting down north of town. Now, men in black turn up, driving a white federal car." He turned to the Ranger with the phone. "Tell Silas to leave the premises surreptitiously. It has begun."

Roy Lyle, the lookout at the bait shop window, binoculars to his eyes, spoke. "No sign of the law. No one was in that limo, but another white Taurus drove around the back of the motel half an hour ago."

"A white fed Taurus at the E-Z Zees, too?" said an ever more agitated Ben. "Lord! Why didn't you tell me? While we were waiting for the limousine, the Taurus must have deposited the Frenchman and his whore on the sly."

Ben's anxiety was contagious. Men scurried to check weapons, positions, mumble prayers.

Digger gripped the phone in two hands, so upset he could barely speak. "*Bo!* They've got Nikki! Kidnapped her. A woman called, muffled voice, warned me to stay here—"

"Rita Rae." Bo conveyed worse news: "I got a call, too . . . from Judas Bob. My brother. He's the one who has her."

"Your brother! What can we do?"

"Everyone but me, the dispatcher, and a clerk are near the auction. Coony says unless we know where Nikki is, there isn't much we can do now but keep our eyes and ears open. Rita Rae is at the motel—she must know where Judas Bob has her. Coony's keeping a watch on her."

Digger said, "She told me they'd *kill* her if we interfere with the auction, that she would call us when it was over, tell us where Nikki is. She promised they won't hurt her as long as I don't interfere and your people stay away.

"Bo—you have to know: the lead plate they're auctioning is stolen. They defrauded a museum on the island of Barbados in the Caribbean. I confirmed it with the director."

"Let me radio that to Coony. Hang on."

An eternal minute later, Bo came back on the line. "Coony says he'll stay clear of the auction, that the KSP and neighboring counties are on standby if he needs them. He's worried. Someone's going to lose, and there are Rangers and LeCoup's men all over the place."

There was a long pause and a click. A sixth sense told Digger that Judas Bob was nearby—at his house, had cut the line. He tensed, felt the hair at the back of his neck go stiff. He shouted into the receiver, "*Bo? Bo?*"

"I'm here. What's wrong?"

"Nothing. I thought the line—"

"Sir?" Bo said it in a weak, tentative voice.

Digger wiped his forehead, found himself crouching over the phone, scanning the windows, the door, the hallway. Nothing. "What?"

"Sir, I . . . I know where Nikki is."

"You *what? Where?* Is she all right?"

"I can only hope. Judas Bob said if he saw cops he'd kill her. Told me he was in the same place he and I fought the last time." Bo was talking more to himself than to Digger. "We'd get into it when we were kids. Judas Bob, my big brother, he'd usually whip me, but this one time, I got a lucky punch in, laid him flat. I got scared, ran away. He never hit me after that, just gave me this look. Scared the beejeesus out of me. All he had to do was give me that look, and I'd shake." He fell still for several seconds. "I think he liked that better than thumping on me. Wasn't long after, he ran off. The next time I saw him was at the car wash when he shot me." Another pause. "He wants me to come up there. Alone. It's me he's really after, not Nikki. He wants a rematch, just the two of us. Fight till one of us can't get up."

"I'll go with you."

"No. I know Judas Bob. He sees anyone else, it's all over for Nikki. He'd do it. I know him. It's him and me. There's no other way."

"Bo," Digger heard the panic in his own voice. "I can't sit on my hands here, knowing you're going after Judas Bob with Nikki as some kind of prize."

Bo began to speak, but Digger cut him off. "*Listen* to me. Before Nikki's father—my brother Warren—died, I swore to him I'd watch after her. With Edgar gone, she's all I have left. I'm an old man, Bo, I can't fight your brother. But I may be able to help. You can't take your men, but you can take *me. Please.* I've got to be there."

Bo didn't answer for five long seconds. Digger could hear him breathing. Finally, Bo said, "Walk to the end of the drive. I'll pick you up at the mailbox.

51

Our amigos are in their rooms." Orlando parted
the curtains, scrutinized the parking lot. "No
sign of *policía*. The back is clear, but I saw some
of LeCoup's men from the west doorway, in the
gas station. Camo Rangers across the street. Trouble."

"Of course," agreed Rita Rae. "But any mixing it up they
do after we close the deal will cover our exit. What about the
plane?"

"Four-seat Cessna behind a barn twelve miles south of
here. The Bahamian *piloto* flies for me before. We take off
from the road, then *poof*! Knoxville. Commercial flight to Miami. We disappear into sunset."

"Did you start that conversion van out back today? I want
to be sure it runs. We'll leave your Imperial in front, let them
think we're still here. The hilljacks can fight over it."

"Ah, my Imperial. A shame to leave her to these *bárbaros*.
The van, it runs *muy bien*. Don't worry, *querida*. All is well."
He arranged his HK assault pistol on the bed, lifted his loose
silk shirt to adjust the Browning Hi-Power at the small of his
back, and lined up their bags on the floor, including Jesus
Bob's This Side Up case, ready for a swift exit.

"One more inspection," he said. "Back in five minutes."

He looked up and down the hall: empty except for a maid with her cleaning cart, a graying, thick-set older woman. He passed her on the way to the west stairs, asked, "Is anyone else on our floor?"

"Folks with the sunburns at the end room just come in. You and the missus in 207 and 209. An old fella and his friend in 215. That's all, sir. Sir?"

"Yes?" What else had she seen?

"Check out's at one-thirty."

Orlando smiled, at the maid, at his own jitters. "Yes, *bonita*," he said. "Long gone by then."

"My name's not Bonita," said the maid. "It's Etta."

Orlando touched her chin with his forefinger, flashed his sparkling tango grin. "*Bonita* means 'pretty' in Spanish, my dear. A compliment, eh?"

"Oh." She put a hand to her mouth and giggled.

Orlando patted her on her kerchiefed head and trotted the other way, checked the east doorway, and then went down the central stairway. Only the desk clerk in the lobby, a slight young man in navy trousers and a cheap polyester, white, short sleeve shirt. "Boy?"

"Name's Johnny, sir."

"*Bueno*. Johnny." A hundred-dollar bill appeared between Orlando's first two fingers. He flourished it before the clerk's face and tucked it in the young man's shirt pocket. "Johnny, our floor is *privado*—no visitors, yes? Is why we rent all the rooms. You take this, buy yourself a good shirt, silk, eh? Give the señoritas weak knees." His smile evaporated, and he stared hard at the boy. "I want you to guard the stairway—no one goes up."

"Yes, *sir*," said the clerk, his hand already fondling the bill. "I'll watch good."

Orlando sprang back up the stairs, tap-a-tapped on the door, and rejoined Rita Rae.

"Five minutes till," she said. "Time to get the lead out." She pointed. "Take that briefcase, give them one last look."

As Orlando left the room, Rita Rae removed a compact Colt Pocket Nine from her Gucci shoulder bag, checked the clip, and slipped it back.

When Orlando returned, he said, "I see why they call them redskins."

Rita Rae gave him a quizzical look but didn't ask for an explanation. Orlando's English wasn't always the best. "You call LeCoup on the phone in the adjoining room," she said. "I'll call Smoot from here. Keep your eye on the lot and the hallway. I'd feel better with Jesus Bob here, but Smoot swore he'd keep the law away, and having that snip in little brother's hands is good insurance."

She dialed, cooed into the phone. "Smoot, dear, here's how it comes down. We'll start at one hundred fifty thousand—your deposit. You bid first. The Frenchman will counterbid on another line. The winner, with the prize, and the loser, with a sour face, will leave separately per my direction, to keep you lover boys from one another's throats. No need to pillow-fight. Is that clear?"

"Yeah, yeah. A hundred seventy-five thousand."

Rita Rae wrote 175 on a notepad for Orlando to see. She walked to the other room, and repeated the instructions. LeCoup bid $200,000. She told Smoot, who bid $225,000.

Rita Rae kicked off her Charles Jourdan pumps, massaged a foot while she let the suspense build. "The little guy says two-twenty-five," she told LeCoup. He raised it to $250,000. They bumped the bidding by twenty-five-thousand increments, but at LeCoup's $400,000, Smoot followed, grumbling, with a more modest jump: $410,000. Bids rose by ten thousand after that. At $440,000, the responses went slo-mo. Rita Rae began to cajole. "Alphonse, you came all this way to let that old man outbid you? I'd hoped the Lords of Trade plate would find a home in a truly A-class collection, but if . . ." "Smoot, I want to keep this polite, but I overheard LeCoup tell his woman 'no bastard offspring of frontier rabble' was going to best him. He offered four hundred sixty thousand."

Smoot repeated LeCoup's last bid aloud, incredulous. "Four hundred sixty thousand? Too high!"

"So, you'll let him have it? Going once," she drew it out, enjoying Smoot's anguish, "going tw—"

"No, no. Hell, no! Four-seventy. Give me a cigar, Bolt."

"This is going steeper than I thought," LeCoup said. "Smoot Mudd is a skinflint. I can't believe he bid over two hundred thousand, let alone four-seventy. Lucky to get a quarter of that at open auction." His voice took an accusatory edge. "How do I know you didn't just make that up, to get more out of me?"

"Then call my bluff, Alphonse." Rita Rae huffed, sounded offended. "Decline to bid. It's up to you."

"*Merde. Très bien*, I offer four-eighty."

Smoot returned, after much sputtering, with $485,000.

Rita Rae passed the news to LeCoup. She heard muffled back talk over the line. Apparently he had put his hand over the phone and was arguing with Raven. Rita Rae made out nearly every word: "A fortune for a dirty slab of lead. We could double that inside a year with shrewd investing." "Yes, but to let Mudd have it would be disaster. For me to own it, oh, such glory! To possess both the Lords of Trades plate *and* the most desirable woman in the world? The very thought gives me—" Silence. The pitch changed and Rita Rae realized LeCoup's hand was no longer over the receiver, but somewhere else. She heard rustling, recognized the sounds of husky foreplay, and then, "You did buy me that Mercedes coupe, and last quarter was superlative, I admit. Hell, the cash is in hand, go for it."

Panting, LeCoup mouthed the words Rita Rae wanted to hear: "Four hundred ninety thousand dollars."

Rita Rae smooched the phone, gave Orlando a thumbs-up, showed him the newly scribbled total on the pad, and ran to the other room to give Smoot the hard news. When he heard the Frenchman's bid, Smoot fell to coughing. She heard the hiss of oxygen, sucking sounds, wheezing. Finally, in a rasping voice, Smoot said, "Let's get this over with. Half a million dollars, and that's *it*." She heard Bolt in the background tell Smoot that, indeed, that *was* it. "That's all we brought, Commander."

LeCoup said he needed five minutes to think. Rita Rae blazed through three cigarettes listening to unintelligible whispers. Orlando squeezed her hand, kissed a medal keeping company with the gold chains at his neck, and crossed himself.

LeCoup came back on the line, none too happy. "My last bid. Five hundred and twenty-five thousand dollars. Let me tell you, if Smoot bids any more than that, he's a sucker, and I'll tell him that to his prune face."

Rita Rae sensed finality. "I shouldn't say this," she said, "but I think the old fella's fading. Give me a few minutes."

An interminable minute later, she lifted the phone linked to LeCoup and broke the news: "Alphonse? Congratulations! The Lords of Trade Céloron plate is yours."

"You're a mouthy bitch aren't you?" Fists on hips, Jesus Bob stood staring at Nikki, sitting with her legs extended on the plank floor of the single room log cabin, a loop of clothesline around her ankles, hands tied behind her back.

"All I said was, I have friends who will be looking for me. I don't have any money and I'm not just some tourist driving through. I know the sheriff and his deputies, too, so you better let me go."

"Bo. You know Bo, all right."

"You know Bo? Bo and I are—"

"I know what you are, you little bitch!" He swatted her cheek hard with the back of his hand. Nikki fell onto her side. Jesus Bob grabbed her ponytail, and righted her.

She blinked, stunned, eyes watering.

"That shut you up, huh? Bet you like the rough stuff, you and brother Bo." For a moment, Jesus Bob's eyes lost focus. He snatched at an invisible antagonist a foot before his face, and then scowled at Nikki. "What are you looking at, bitch?"

Bo's *brother*! Nikki sat silent, defiant, trying to keep the tears back.

"Ain't polite to stare."

Her eyes dropped from Jesus Bob's evil glint to his mouth, at the inch long fragment of green leaf and the sliver of pale purple petal clinging to spittle on his lip and chin, stuck there since he had come back inside.

He must have felt her gaze burn the side of his mouth, and he swiped at his chin, saw the leaf, now on the back of his hand. "That's right. I been eating bushes. Big jimsonweed outside. You know your psychedelics? Datura. Good shit, but hard to figure the dose. Ate some mushrooms, too. Maybe you'd like a nibble?"

She shook her head.

"Yeah. I don't suppose you and do-good Bo get high." He lost focus, his eyelids closed, and he slapped his cheek. "Visions gonna come on soon. You better pray they're good ones." He cocked his head, fear running over his face. "Huh? What's that? You hear rattling?"

Nikki shook her head again.

Jesus Bob pressed his temples with the pads of his thumbs. "Man, I got me a head-splitter! Damned mushrooms, you never know. Got any Midol, glue in that purse of yours?"

Shaking, trembling, saying, "No."

Jesus Bob clutched his stomach. "Woozy in the gut, too." He bent over, nearly lost his balance, snatched her black sequined purse, and unzipped it. "One thing I learned early. When a woman says no, she means yes. You got some diet pills in here? Valiums, I'll bet. But you're not the kind to share, are you?" He held the purse above his face and shook it.

Nikki squeezed her eyes shut.

Coony II, the milk snake, in expanding coils, dropped onto Jesus Bob's nose. Jesus Bob screamed, gave his head a powerful shake. Coony II flew off, hit the wall and dropped to the floor. Jesus Bob swatted his face. "Oh, Lord! Oh, shit! Did you see that? A fucking snake!"

He dropped to his knees, shaking, stared at the floor, and retched. He tumbled into the yellow green bile. Oblivious, he staggered to his feet and wiped his mouth with a sleeve.

Nikki wrinkled her nose, looked away.

"Fucking snake. Where'd it go?" He unholstered a huge revolver, scanned the ceiling, the walls, the floor.

Worried for her pet, Nikki said, "Wasn't a snake—it was a pencil."

Jesus Bob guffawed. "A pencil! No shit? I knew that weed had power."

He grinned. "The herbs are taking me down the midnight path, darlin'. Better watch out."

"Why don't you let me go? I promise I won't tell anyone."

"You're bait, little lady. Maybe I oughta put a hook through your lips, like they do with minnows, huh?"

Nikki stiffened.

Jesus Bob laughed, put his revolver back, and stretched. "Goddamn shit's giving me the droops. Can't have that with a guest on the way, can we?" He fumbled in his pocket, noticed the vomit on his jeans, on his palm, and wiped the hand on his shirt. He probed the pocket again, withdrew a small glass vial. "Near forgot. Got maybe two lines in here, all she'd allow me." He glowered at Nikki. "Fucking women. All alike, aren't you? Always hold back, never give a man what he needs."

He tapped half the contents of the vial onto the blade of a buck knife, snorted it though one pinched nostril, tapped out the rest, and snuffed it up the other. "Sorry, babe, not enough to share." He massaged his nose and lip. "Whoo-ee! I needed that." He sniffled a few times and punched an imaginary sparring partner, followed it around the room, and then winked at her.

"This must be your lucky day, babe, cause all of a sudden I'm feeling horny. About time, too." He groped himself and leered. "What say you and me get friendly before the Jimson or the mushrooms take hold again?"

He seized her ponytail, pulled her head back, and cupped one of her breasts. Nikki squirmed, fixed her eyes on the far wall, at the long bench with the muzzle-loading paraphernalia, and stifled a whimper.

Jesus Bob dropped her hair and fumbled with his zipper. He groped himself again. And again—trying to carry the ambitious plan forward, but his lower half wouldn't rise to the occasion. He went red in the face, furious. "You little bitch! You fucking tease, I'll teach you." He swung, but she swayed out of the way.

Jesus Bob stared at his hand, unsure whether it had connected and began to wander around the room. He lurched against a heavy wooden table, kicked a chair into the wall, and moved to the muzzle-loading bench. He lifted a long rod, set it down, gripped some kind of crimping pliers, menaced her with it, pinching the air by her face, and then threw it against a wall. Fumbling, scuffling, considering, rejecting.

"Hah!" he said at last, *"Lead,"* as a dim, dark memory surfaced. He held a metal funnel high over his head, thumped it on the bench.

Nikki watched his back as he lifted a fifteen-inch propane tank chest high. She heard the hiss of gas, a rasp, and a *snook* as a flame lit.

He pulled a stool to the bench. Nikki saw orange and blue flame; watched Jesus Bob drop a slab of silvery metal into a crucible. She heard mumbling, and clearly, "Mouthy tease, I'll give you a dose that'll shut you up good."

Then, from outside, she heard, "Judas Bob? Come out. It's me. Bo."

52

Bo had picked Digger up on the fly, no hellos. "Gonna run the siren. Hold on."

The car nearly bottomed out in a dip. Bo held the wheel in a racing grip, took it to ninety on a straight stretch, slowed on a sliding turnoff on a narrow road, and drove around the flank of a long green ridge. "I lied to Coony," Bo said.

Digger had trouble hearing him over the siren, wind, and road noise.

"Didn't tell him—you know—where Judas Bob has her, that I was going. I told the dispatcher—made her swear not to tell Coony unless I don't make it back."

Digger scowled, wondering if Bo had a plan. They took a curve at speed, and Digger thumped into the door. He rubbed his shoulder, thought of his and Nikki's escape from the men in the pickup, the first bump when the truck hit them. He pressed his feet to the floor and gripped the seat, remembering Nikki giving the stumbling men in the field the finger. Then, the day she caught the rattlesnake—fearless. And how she stood up to Bo and Coony when she thought her uncle was a suspect. How polished she had been during their lunch with Biffer. Spirited. Competent. And then his mind traveled forbidden ground. He thought of Edgar, that morning, and Nikki in the hands of Bo's criminal brother, of the horrible things people do to people.

Bo seemed to read his mind. "I don't think he's hurt her, sir. Judas Bob wants me, not Nikki." He cut the siren and turned onto a secondary road.

Minutes later, he took a turnoff into the hills. "Sir, I'm going to drop you off before I get there. I don't want Judas Bob seeing you. There should be clear open ground and an old log cabin set up on a fieldstone foundation with a rickety porch across the front. You watch from the trees. Stay put." He cut his eyes to Digger to make the point. "If anything happens to me, you work your way through the trees around the cabin. Just over the ridge top and through the woods, you'll see a bunch of church cabins. That's where the Rangers hang out. A good piece below, past a big barn, you'll find the highway to Golden Leaf. Flag someone down, get Coony."

Digger nodded.

"You're no match for Judas Bob, and you steer clear of any Rangers. And stay away from that tobacco barn with the billboard on it. Word is, that's their arsenal. It's probably full of explosives and may be booby-trapped. Don't worry about me. I'm not the kid I was when we fought the last time." He turned the wheel hard, pulling off onto a double-track dirt road rising through the forest. Near the crest, he stopped. "Here's where we part company."

Digger shook Bo's hand, jumped out, and hiked through the brush to the clearing. From the forest edge, he watched the cruiser stop beside a white Mustang convertible parked at the end of the dirt road, some sixty feet from the cabin. Bo climbed out and stared at the cabin for several seconds with no response. Then he released the Mustang's hood, bent over the engine, removed something, and threw it far into the weeds. He walked with his limping stride away from the cars to a small rise facing the cabin. Forty feet from the porch, he ran a hand across his forehead and shouted to his brother to come out.

Rita Rae heard muffled, metallic conversation from the hallway. LeCoup talking to someone on a radio, one of his Israelis no doubt, telling them the good news. No problem. She knocked. The conversation stopped. LeCoup opened the door, smiling. She did a double take at his red skin, but said nothing, concluding it was some trick to rile Smoot. She watched his eyes drop to the briefcase—zip right past her boosted cleavage and thigh-high royal blue miniskirt. His loss. She looked past him at Raven, whom she hadn't seen before. Rita Rae gave her a reflexive once-over. Young, inexperienced, Rita Rae decided, even redder than LeCoup—what the hell was the point? Dressed like a boy in running shoes, shorts and a warm-up jacket, too tanned to begin with for proper makeup, and too red at the present for it to matter, hips a little wide, legs too muscular. Tough to do anything with that straight hair. She supposed an old man like LeCoup might see the girl as exotic. Someone with style could stack that hair, put her in heels to lengthen the legs . . .

"The Céloron plate?" LeCoup was beside himself.

Rita Rae held the case behind her back. "The money?"

"Here." Raven handed Rita Rae a cheap red vinyl handbag. "Keep the bag. It looks great with your outfit."

Snippy, this one. Rita Rae fired back, "Shopped for the purse yourself, did you? Shooting for a match with the skin?" She saw Raven's jaw tighten, her right hand move to her jacket pocket—carrying a gun, no doubt. Rita Rae smiled, unconcerned. She knew LeCoup was too smart to risk trouble in the midst of Smoot Mudd country. Do the bitchy Indian girl good to get her juices up. She sat on one of the beds, opened the bag, saw stacks of strapped hundreds.

"It's all there," Raven said. When she saw Rita Rae

thumbing through it, she followed with, "I have a calculator if you can't count that high."

"Aren't you sweet?" Rita Rae said, with a cool smile. She fluffed each of the stacks at her ear, pretending to hear the count.

LeCoup opened the briefcase, the same one Orlando had shown him before the auction to fuel his greed.

Rita Rae closed the handbag. "Unlike your Kmart purse, the briefcase is Louis Vuitton. I thought *you* would appreciate that, Alphonse honey." Giving the *honey* just enough emphasis to needle his young companion.

LeCoup nodded, indifferent to the briefcase, or inflections, or female friction. He unwrapped the burgundy chamois, lifted the bare plate with the thin chalky-white patina, turned it over in his hands, and kissed the inscription. *"Magnifique."*

"Give me enough time to get back to my room," Rita Rae said, "and leave by the outside staircase. I'll hold Smoot up for another ten minutes, tell him you can't make up your mind, and then give him the bad news. If I were you, I'd be out of Golden Leaf by then."

LeCoup, eyes closed in near orgasmic reverie, pressed the plate to his forehead in a prayer of thanks.

"Understood," Raven said, right to the point. "We have a car waiting."

Stalling while LeCoup and Raven exited, Rita Rae told Smoot she thought LeCoup was getting cold feet, but she had to give him one last chance to raise the bid.

Smoot whined back, "Why the hell for? If he wanted it, he should of spoke up. I bid high, it's mine."

She checked her gold, malachite-faced Piaget wristwatch, squinting, trying to make out the tiny hands, irked that the bitchy Indian girl probably didn't need glasses yet. Orlando held up his fingers, five plus one. Six minutes had passed. "Okay baby," she said to Smoot, on the phone. "I'll go to the other line and give the Frenchman the going once, twice ultimatum." Instead, she set the phone down on the table, held her hands at arm's length and checked her nail polish. She blew Orlando an air kiss and lifted the receiver.

"Smootikins?"

"What? What?"

"You won."

"Hot damn! The Frenchman and the girl backed down." She listened to Smoot cough, the hiss of oxygen.

Bolt came on the line. "The commander can't talk. You bring his treasure here; I'll give you the money."

"You bet, Bolt, baby." Rita Rae hung up, flashed Orlando a thumbs-up and pointed to a briefcase identical to the one she had given LeCoup. "I hope I gave Alphonse the original. High bid and all that. Let me check, just to soothe my conscience." Twenty seconds later she turned the second plate over and ran a finger over a tiny nick at one corner, the only deviation from the original. "We're good, Lando. I swear, if I didn't know, I wouldn't be able to tell the difference."

"*Claro.*" Orlando blew on his buffed nails. "The mold, *perfecto*, the patina, *también*. Good for us that Señor Céloron's first plate was never buried. The oxidation was light, even, easy to match. If these two keep their mouths shut, they will never know. But soon, they will begin bragging, one to the other. Too bad we will not be around to see the confusion, the *espectacular* fireworks."

Digger heard Nikki shout inside the cabin. "Bo! Watch out, he's got a gun." Jesus Bob, wearing camouflage fatigues, appeared on the porch with a large revolver holstered at his waist, a pump shotgun cradled in his arms.

Bo took a deep breath. "Judas Bob, let Nikki go."

"Not likely. And times have changed, little brother. Call me Jesus Bob."

"*Jesus* Bob? Hah! I will not."

"Damn you, that's my name now!"

"Shame on you."

"Shame on *you*."

Let it go, thought Digger. This isn't the time for brotherly quarrels. Call him whatever he wants, just get Nikki out of there.

"Shame on *me*?" Bo said.

"For two-timing Willie."

"Who's Willie?"

"As if you don't know."

"Let her go, Judas Bob. I'm ready. Fistfight, man to man, like the last time."

"Yeah, sure. Can't say I blame you for screwing Willie's babe, though. She's a honey. Mouthy though, ain't she? But not for long, little brother. I'm cooking up something to shut that trap of hers for good."

From inside: "He's melting *lead* in here!"

Digger cringed, cursed his helplessness.

Bo shifted his stance, opened his palms, arms wide. "Okay, Judas Bob. Put the shotgun down, and we'll have it out, man to man. That's what you want, isn't it?"

"What I want?" Jesus Bob's voice rose half an octave. He kicked at the porch rail, looked wildly side to side. "What I want is you dead for ruining my life." He swung the shotgun from his waist and fired.

The blast knocked Bo three feet onto his back. Digger watched him writhe, try to right himself. He saw blood, heard Nikki scream from inside.

Jesus Bob jumped to the bottom of the stairs, ran to Bo, and whacked the stock of the shotgun across the side of his head. Bo fell back, still. Jesus Bob turned to the cabin. "That's it, honey," he shouted. "Scream while you can. Your porridge is almost ready, and Papa Bear is on the way."

53

Exiting via the west stairway, Raven and LeCoup skirted the maid's cart. Alphonse clutching the Louis Vuitton briefcase to his heart like his firstborn, Raven gripping the remaining twenty-five thousand in the inside pocket of her windbreaker. A maid opened the door, and they left the dark corridor, blinking at the sun. LeCoup moved to sidestep a small yardman on the stairs in bib overalls and a straw hat.

The yardman flashed a gold star. "Be pleased if you'd come with me downstairs," he said, preacher-polite.

LeCoup and Raven stumbled back, bumped into the maid at the top. "I have a .38 pointed at you under this towel," the maid said. "No sudden moves, hands out where we can see them. That's it, dearies. Now—down the stairs like the sheriff says."

LeCoup flushed. "What the hell is this?"

"Smoot's people," Raven said, disgusted. "It's a cross."

"You're stealing the plate?" LeCoup tightened his grip on the case. "No way. You may not know it, but we have armed men all around. You think I'm a fool?"

Etta took another step down, urged them forward.

"I'm not Smoot's man," Coony said. "Not in ten thousand years. Let's call this protective custody. Believe me, there's bad trouble if you two walk into that parking lot now. At least a dozen of Smoot's armed Rangers are across the street ready to pick you off. We're going into a room below until I sort things out. Bear with me a few minutes, huh?"

As soon as they were into the first floor hallway, Etta took their guns. In room 101, Ike cuffed them. "A precaution is all," Coony said. "Sit on the bed, make yourselves at home, and keep your mouths shut. All goes well, you'll be out of here before you know it."

The radio at LeCoup's waist squawked: "This is Alpha. Sir, are you all right? Did Salome make drop? You should be in back by now."

Coony lifted the radio. "Everything's peachy keen," he said, and switched it off.

"Move the damn cart, woman," Bolt said to the maid's back, negotiating Smoot around her. When he reached for the east door, Etta lifted a towel-covered shotgun from the mop rack, poked him once in the ribs, said, "Twelve gauge," drew back, and told him to shut his mouth.

Before Bolt could react, Coony, in yardman mufti, opened the door from the outside, training a .38 Police Special, hidden from bait shop view under a bandanna, on Bolt's torso. "Not a word, Bolt, or the next Bud you drink's gonna be leaking out of five holes through your belly."

Smoot cursed. "You sumbitch! You swore you wouldn't interfere."

"With the auction," Coony said. "The auction's over. And, as long as no law is broken is what I said. For now, consider this for your own protection. LeCoup's got armed men ready to do you in, believe me."

"The sore losing frog bastard. He don't know I've got Rangers armed to the teeth across the street. He messes with us, it's a blood bath!"

"Perzactly what I want to avoid," Coony said. "Now, you act like the help here is assisting you with your walker down the stairs. We'll hang out on the first floor until this situation cools off."

Two minutes later, Fat Gabe cuffed Bolt's hands behind his back. Shackled to his walker, Smoot was whining, coughing, threatening. Before he left Room 115, Coony made sure Gabe knew how to handle the oxygen. He winked. "Want you boys to be comfortable. With luck, you'll be home for supper."

"Sir? Ma'am?" Johnny, in his desk clerk outfit, knocked on the door of 207. "Your guests have left already. Not to rush you, but check-out's coming up, and we have a busload of Nazarene bass fishermen and their wives coming in soon, I was wondering—"

The door cracked open. Rita Rae hissed, "All the money we paid you and you give us the bum's rush?"

"Not at all, ma'am," Johnny stepped inside, "but I'd be glad to carry your bags if—"

"Get the hell out of here!"

But by then, Johnny had a .38 gripped in both hands, trained chest-high on Orlando, and Coony was inside pointing his handgun at Rita Rae.

"Lord," Coony said, as Etta cuffed them. "I never heard such language from a woman. And a damn good thing I don't *hablo* the *español*." He turned to his wife. "Dear, you secure their belongings, Johnny and me'll find them a nice quiet room downstairs." He heard Rita Rae's cursing shift gears to Jesus Bob, that if he had been back when expected, this wouldn't have happened. "Jesus Bob, huh?" Coony said. "That what you call him now? Well, your Jesus Bob kidnapped a young woman—I don't suppose neither of you knows nothing about that?"

Rita Rae and Orlando fell silent, considering the implication. Then they shook their heads. "I thought not," Coony said. "But it's good to know he's due. I give you my word on this: if he harms a hair on that girl's head, they'll be hell he never dreamt of to pay.

"Now, move out, and shut your mouths or I'll gag you. For your own safety, I don't want no one knowing where you two is hid."

Field Marshal Ben, wearing stars and gleaming gold epaulettes on his shoulders, stood tall beside the galvanized red worm tank. Minnows swam and crayfish scurried in gurgling aquariums to one side; to the other, crickets, mealworms, cockroaches, hellgrammites, leeches, and wax worms inched and rustled.

"I hope," Ben said, "there are no bugs in here. I vetted the building thoroughly last night. Has anyone checked today?"

The men exchanged uneasy glances at the aquariums and cages, at Ben.

Ben took the silence for *All clear.* "Captain Grundy," he said. "You, Private Aut, and Corporal Denny take positions in the trench, two facing the motel, one to the west."

Aut, a fastidious bank teller for Golden Leaf Savings, cast a wary eye at the muddy trench bottom. "It, uh, rained last night, sir."

Ben glared. "War is hell, man! No one said it would be easy. Put some newspapers down there. Improvise for God's sake—you are a Daniel Boone Ranger."

He noticed men plying admiring fingers over their new HK machine pistols, indeed, showing the weapons more attention than their CO. Ben slapped his riding crop on the side of the worm tank. *Whonk!* "Listen up. Major General Butz? Take Corporal Stinkbug"—neither Ben nor the others wanted the odoriferous Stinkbug indoors—"and join your men in the forest to protect the Humvee, Roy Lyle's pickup, and our flank. Roy Lyle is spotting. Where's Lieutenant Calley with the LAWs and the grenade launchers?"

A sergeant chewed his lip. "Uh, Calley's in back. We have the LAWs and grenades, but someone forgot the launchers."

Ben huffed. "Someone. Fine. Just fine. No way we'll be able to pitch grenades across that highway. What else did 'someone' forget?"

"Ear protection," said another man. "I had it all together back at the Reserve, but—"

A deep sigh. "Best cram some of that sphagnum moss from the newt tank in your ears, then."

"And flashlights. Only two here in the store."

Another sigh. "I see. Well, with luck, we should be back at the Reserve well before sundown. You have your side arms. Luther wants to stick with his AK-47, Major General Butz, his trusty .30/06 deer rifle. The rest of you are well-armed with Orlando's HK machine pistols. At least in the weapons department, we are prepared.

"Scooter Shooters? Junior Ranger?"

Three small boys, the rosy-cheeked Galvin brothers (Jene-Jene, seven, and Jerry, ten) and towheaded Heck Herkle, a skinny but mature-looking twelve, snapped to attention and saluted. The loyal youngsters had played hooky to join their elders in this, the great battle, with high hopes of promotion afterward.

"You two lads," Ben said to the brothers, concerned they would get underfoot, "stay behind that counter. You will reload the HK magazines. Every man has three preloaded clips. We have those, and plenty of 9-millimeter ammo and additional magazines, because"—he cast a jaundiced glare around the room—"I packed them myself. You boys keep full magazines at the ready. Yes, that's it, lads, begin loading— your small hands are made for the task.

"Heck?" he said to the twelve-year-old. "You stick with your .22 rifle. See what you can do with men in your sights instead of chipmunks."

Ben removed the small Bible from his shirt pocket, kissed the leatherette binding for inspiration, and rested it on the lid of the worm tank. He leaned his weapon against the side, took a last drag on his cigarette, balanced it on the corner of the Good Book, and raised his hands high. "Let us pray." Ben dropped his chin, but glanced around the room with not quite shut eyes to confirm the men had set aside their weapons and duly bowed their heads.

"The Lord is my commander," Ben began, "I shall not want for guns or ammo. He ordereth me to lie down in well-laid bunkers. He leadeth me besides these gentle waters of the minnow tanks. Yea, though I walk through the valley of the shadow of death, I will fear no fed, alien, Jew, or blighted son of Ham, for Thou art with me. Thy heavenly long gun and side arm give me courage. Thou preparest a battlefield before me—"

"Sir?" Roy Lyle, the one man with his head up, cut in, his hand on a spotting scope. "I think you should see this. About four hundred yards toward town. There's a silver tanker truck coming our way."

"Good Lord! So soon." Ben looked ceilingward. "Excuse me, Lord, for that interruption. "Amen." He shot a worried glance at the E-Z Zees. "Where, oh, where are Colonel Bolt and the commander?"

Roy Lyle shook his head. "No sign of them yet. But Orlando's convertible is still in the lot. The white Taurus hasn't left." Within a minute, binoculars to his eyes, he had news: "Top of the stairs. Bolt just come out. A maid and a workman are helping the commander down the stairs. Hmmm."

"What is this 'hmmm'?"

"Was no high sign from Bolt." Roy Lyle leaned closer to the scope. "Whoa, what's this? They went inside downstairs. I swear Bolt made a face at me before he disappeared, although with Bolt's face, it's hard to tell."

"Something is amiss," said Ben. "Everyone take their positions. We must be at the ready."

With no further sign of Bolt or the commander-in-chief, apprehension spread among the Rangers like an infectious fog. They waited. Nothing.

Ben paced. With a start, he snatched the smoldering cigarette from his Bible. Burned nearly to the filter, it had left an ugly, inch-long, brown worm track across the baby blue leatherette. Ben blew away the offending ash, scrubbed the cover with the butt of his hand, clutched the Good Book to his chest, and muttered, "Signs . . . Armageddon . . . the Antichrist uncovered."

One of the Rangers took a stab at levity: "Ehhh . . . What's up, doc?"

A few chuckled nervously, but Ben silenced them with a murderous squint.

At the window, Roy Lyle had more bad news. "A camper's broke down at the west side of the light, backing up traffic. There's a pale blue panel truck with a olive branch decal on the window waiting to get around it, a chink and a nigger inside wearing light blue helmets."

Ben spit out the bad news: "UN!"

"The silver tanker's right behind."

"Of course. The UN vehicle is its escort. Bring Lieutenant Calley and the LAWs forward." Ben tucked the sullied Bible in his pocket. "Spread the word: Prepare for action."

After the cryptic "peachy" message, Levi ran from his room, up the central stairs in time to see a maid and a workman helping an old man with a walker out the east doorway. But where were his clients? He worked the radio feverishly, speaking Hebrew and English, *"Hayesh mishehu she ra'a Adom Ehad o Adom Shneyim?* Has anyone seen Red One or Red Two?" He put his men at the gas station and those behind the strip mall on alert, warned those at the helicopter and limo, and brother Liev at the houseboat, to be at the ready. Back to his room, he grabbed a soft weapons bag, slung it over his shoulder, and climbed the west stairway past the second floor to the maintenance ladder and the roof.

*   *   *

Spooked with prebattle jitters, Corporal Denny in the muddy west trench confused Ben's "prepare for action" with "open fire." He stood up—contrary to all training—gave a rebel yell, and squeezed the trigger of the fully automatic HK for all he was worth. The first slugs hit the dirt at his feet, sending his companions scattering. As the recoil ratcheted up the barrel, bullets shattered the bait shop's new, internally lit Superplastics Supersign, peppered the shrubbery, the road, the front end of a Trans Am, the bed of a Dodge pickup, construction debris in the strip mall across the highway, the mall's unfinished cinder-block walls, the hillside beyond, and finally, the brilliant blue sky, before he exhausted the magazine.

"Always me," said flush-faced, eight-months-pregnant Elsie Esterhaus as she cranked the slow-clicking ignition once more. "And right at the light." She shot a worried look at the rearview mirror and saw the long line of traffic trying to get around her camper, stranded half into the roadway because of the narrow shoulder. If Woody was along, this wouldn't happen. One turn of the key, and the damned thing would start for him. But, oh, no—Woody wouldn't have anything to do with a kids' masquerade party. The Golden Leaf Volunteer Fire Brigade couldn't get by without him. "What if there's a disaster, and I miss it, Elsie?" he had whined, and she let him get by with it. Again. Well, the hell with Woody, the hell with the camper. Leave it here. She scooted out the passenger door and around to the back, forgetting entirely the pink foam plastic hair curlers she had planned to remove before she got to the Ringleys and the muumuu that she would have exchanged in the back for a clean white jumper. At the rear of the camper, she gathered the kids—Molly in her bunny costume with the long ears, Will in his Frankenstein getup, Tilly in his big-headed Bart Simpson mask, Mary Sue dressed as Humpty Dumpty, and little Peanut in his Mickey Mouse ears—and led them, hand-in-hand, back toward town. In fifteen minutes they would reach her sister's house and a car that ran.

They were abreast of the pale blue panel truck when she heard the gunfire behind. No, not firecrackers this time of year. *Gunfire*, like in the schools, in the churches, on the TV. A frightful, long burst of it, and then screams from the highway, and more gunfire. She gathered tiny Peanut in her arms and hustled the others before her. "Run!" she urged, and the motley masqueraders trotted as fast as their little legs would carry them, past the panel truck and alongside a long silver tanker.

54

The first unanticipated staccato burst from the bait shop raked a pickup and fatally wounded a Pontiac Trans Am, left it steaming barely north of the intersection. Ensuing gunfire blew out three tires of a lumbering Buick and scattered fragments of the week's groceries throughout its interior, but, miraculously, left the driver unhurt. Those who saw clear road ahead put pedals to the floor and, stoplight be damned, squealed out. The exodus led to a messy five-car smashup at the flashing light. Able drivers of disabled vehicles abandoned their wheels and ran, tumbled, got up, ran faster. Some, including the men in the blue panel truck, Mike Fong and Odell Hatcher from Laurel Electrical Contracting, on a call to check Generator 3 at Boone Lake Dam, threw themselves in drainage ditches, where they would tremble in the mud and cattails while the battle played out.

The five men of AAA Acme Security forces secreted behind the strip mall, mean hombres who had blown away the hearts of myriad paper targets, breezed through the roughest simulations and toughest field courses, had—alas—never taken live fire, never fired in return at flesh and blood of the human persuasion. At Denny's unexpected overture, joined within seconds by his fellow Rangers, Levi's men threw themselves to the ground, unaware that most of the 9-millimeter bait shop fusillade was strafing not their redoubt, but the hillside far over their heads.

Fearful of being overrun should they not respond, however, and aware—thankful—that their mission was not engaging the enemy but ensuring the safe return of Red One and Red Two, they soon rose to their feet and opened fire with their Uzis—now and then actually shooting through the strip mall's unfinished windows at the bait shop, but mostly firing into the air from behind the cinder-block walls.

Levi commanded from the E-Z Zees rooftop, convinced Red One and Two had been taken prisoner and were still somewhere in the motel. But where? Short of a risky room-by-room assault, he saw no easy solution. He directed the two men in the gas station to move to sheltered positions and surveil the motel.

He had previously identified the barbarian leader from the stars and epaulettes on his shoulders and the riding crop in his hand. Periodically, the man left the bait shop to confer with his troops in the woods. Levi hatched a plan: he would cross the highway well to the east, sneak through the trees, wait for his opposite number, capture and hold him hostage, and then effect an exchange for Red One and Two. He gave visual cues to a compatriot in the strip mall, directed him to cross the highway to the north, beyond sight of the barbarians, and work his way south where they would rendezvous and carry off the barbarian leader.

Big Butt crouched behind a thick oak, quaking, listening to the gunfire. A slug whipped through the foliage, cut a sapling in two, and thudded into a maple trunk six feet away. Though armed with a .30/06 deer rifle, two combat knives, one of Orlando's new assault pistols, and a Glock holstered at his side, he had a bad case of first battle terrors. Big Butt knew in his heart, once again, he would fail to prove his manhood and take a life.

With the notable exception of the veteran, old Luther, who fired his AK-47 in short, controlled, three-round bursts at probable targets, most of the Rangers fired their HKs on full automatic, chewing up the landscape but coming nowhere near hitting their adversaries. Not to discount twelve-year-old Heck with his .22 rifle, who, his aim honed from shooting small mammals and songbirds in the Daniel Boone National Forest, would score an early, if minor, hit: a bullet through the upper arm of one of the strip mall defenders.

"Where's Lieutenant Calley?" Ben shouted. "I want those LAWs up here pronto. The alien tanker is stalled at the intersection and now is the opportune moment to take it out."

"I want my mama!" cried ten-year-old Jerry, whimpering from the smoke and noise, eyes tearing, though his tiny fingers still pushed 9-millimeter cartridges into empty magazines at a feverish pace from behind the lure counter.

"Don't be a pussy," said his seven-year-old brother, Jene-Jene tossing a full magazine to a waiting Ranger.

"I got one! I got one! I know I did," said young Heck, war dancing around the worm tank with his .22 rifle. "Man, oh, man, this is better than video games! Give me a real gun. C'mon. I wanna blow some fed's head off. Pow!"

"Try this on for size, son," said a captain, slamming another magazine into his already hot-to-the-touch HK machine pistol. He handed Heck a prodigious .50 caliber Magnum, Desert Eagle semiautomatic pistol. "See what you can do with a man's gun."

The heavy weapon sank nearly to the floor in Heck's slight hands, although, ignoring the captain's "Whoa, just kidding," Heck flicked off the safety. "Hold on," said the owner, but Heck was already at a sandbagged window. He seized the grip in two hands as he had been instructed in Major General Butz's Junior Rangers firearm's class, lifted the weapon with difficulty, aimed through the narrow aperture, and—most significantly—pulled the trigger.

The recoil sent Heck for a triple back somersault into the worm tank. The stupendous report deafened men to either side. Sphagnum moss, the Rangers learned early in the engagement, was a poor substitute for proper ear protection.

Ben screamed again for Calley, but while the Rangers saw his mouth moving, few heard him.

"In the trench," a lip reader shouted. "Calley's waiting in the trench."

Ben nodded, crouched at the door, and crawled along the sandbagged redoubt. He saw Calley with five stout tubes, the LAWs: preloaded, disposable, light antitank weapons. Ben pointed to the silver tanker. Calley gave him a thumbs-up, popped the protective caps from the ends of one of the LAWs, extended the retracted tube, set it on his shoulder, and put his eye to the pop-up sight. Private Aut crept behind to watch.

Ben tapped Calley on the shoulder, and with a *whoosh*, the LAW rocket streaked to its target, missed it by six feet— high. Half a mile away the steeple of the May Street Community Church was no more.

Aut, injudiciously crouched behind Calley, was caught in the LAW's back-blast. He stood bolt upright, screaming, his fatigue shirt burned from his body, his torso smoking like charred sirloin on a backyard grill. Before he could be cut in two by Uzi fire, his companions wrestled him to the ground and, in short order, doused him with minnow water in lieu of medical attention.

First-aid kit. Something else they had forgotten.

Undismayed, Calley had the second LAW primed, the area behind him well clear this time. Ben tapped again. *Whoosh*, and . . . direct hit! Or nearly. The rocket raked the top of the tanker, exploded near the back. Ben saw flames, a tsunami of white liquid sloshing from the ruptured hull. He held binoculars to his eyes, scanning for cloned alien embryos.

*   *   *

Trotting around a pale blue panel truck and alongside the tanker, curler-haired, oh-so-pregnant Elsie Esterhaus hustled her five children before her like baby chicks. "Hurry, please hurry."

Elsie and the young masqueraders were knocked to the ground by the shock wave seconds before being enveloped by a breaker of whole milk. The wave swept by, leaving them gasping, flopping amidst cream and curds. Coated head-to-foot in glutinous yellow-white milk fat, Elsie struggled to her feet, saw her chicks, some on hands and knees, some already standing, sputtering, but, Thank God, still alive.

Ben, with the binoculars, gave the men the blow-by-blow. "Oh, Lord, it's disgusting. It must have been full of, like, yolk. I count six aliens, still alive, but dying, I am certain, as soon as they get a whiff of this good green Earth's oxygen. The big one is shaped like a gourd, has knobs all over its head. Some of the little ones have humongous heads, one is as round as an egg, two have twin antennae . . ."

Big Butt finally got a grip on the fear that had immobilized him, perhaps shocked into action by the thrill of firing Orlando's machine pistol on full automatic, raining 9-millimeter hail at the Zionists—yes, *Zionists*: the elusive word popped into his head with the clarity born of battle.

A Ranger, blood drenching his forehead (a consequence not of enemy fire but of a low-lying tree branch) jogged to Big Butt's side. "Roy Lyle thinks he saw a man in black infiltrate the woods, sir. Circling around this way. What should we do?"

"Shoot his ass!" said a newly spirited Big Butt. "Ask Ben to secure our flank. I'll cover the north perimeter. Have the men keep their eyes peeled on the road to be sure no more of the bastards cross the highway."

"Yessir." The man disappeared into the brush.

Big Butt dropped to his hands and knees, crab-crawled north, scanning the woods for the infiltrator. Less than a minute later, beyond the Rangers' perimeter, he saw the . . . Zionist! The word came easily now. He said it again and again, a battle mantra: Zionist, Zionist, Zionist. "You're one dead Zionist," he said to the weeds, " 'cause Major General B. G. Butz is on to you."

Another flutter of movement in a stand of poison ivy. Too far, Big Butt decided, to trust the sloppy machine pistol or his handgun. He worked the .30/06 off his shoulder, moved to a shooter's prone position, moved his eye to the scope. Now he saw it: the glint of gunmetal, the head and shoulders through the wavering trilobed foliage. He moved the crosshairs to the upper torso, took a deep breath, exhaled, forced his tense muscles to relax, and fired.

The Zionist jerked, went down. Heart shot. Big Butt had his first kill.

Rangers cheered as Calley's third LAW took a magnificent chunk out of the Zionists' strip mall redoubt. Unfortunately, as the smoke cleared, they saw no body parts, no white flag.

Calley had the fourth LAW ready. "See that fed Taurus over at the station?"

Whoosh. The rocket missed the Taurus by thirty feet but sent a gas pump to gas pump heaven. An enormous crackling fireball rose over the general store like an incendiary grand opening blimp. Tongues of flame licked the pavement, lapped the second pump, set it off with an audible *Whoomp!* and rolled on to the store. The burning building was anticlimactic, but the collective fire and smoke were visible from four counties. Gunfire ceased for nearly a minute while adversaries set their arms aside and gawked.

No sooner had hostilities resumed than a Ranger

touched Field Marshal Ben on his epaulette. "Sir, we got a bad problem. Fire six or eight magazines with these machine pistols and you can barely touch them. They're misfiring and locking up. Casper's hand is all tore up from when his blew apart on him."

"Find Luther," Ben said, still entranced by the conflagration catty-corner to the bait shop. "Luther knows firearms."

"Sir?" Another man, another problem. He relayed his conversation with Big Butt, explained about the infiltrator.

"Soon as I deal with these malfunctioning weapons, I'll join Major General Butz in the woods," Ben said, wishing for a moment he was a mere NCO and could enjoy the fireworks free of the burden of command.

Luther entered the rear door in a crouch. "I heard slack fire, even before the gas pumps went up, what's wrong?"

A man explained about the weapons, passed his own machine pistol, nearly too hot to handle.

Luther examined it. "I'll be damned. This is no Heckler and Koch, it's a cheap-ass knock off." He pointed. "Milled parts? These are stampings. Steel? Hell, it looks like pot metal. Look here. You ever see an HK with Chinese on it? You're lucky it fired at all. Where'd you get this piece of crap?"

Three of the men answered in unison: "Orlando!"

"Let me see another one." Ben passed his. "All crap," Luther said. "Eighty-six these bastards now, before anyone else gets hurt."

"Got no rifles," said one of the men. "Hell, we won't hit nothing this far away with pistols. There must be a hundred feds and Zionists over there. What if they close in?"

Angry muttering rounded the room: "Orlando, that damn greaseball." "Never trust a spic." "HKs, my ass. No wonder we didn't hit nothing."

"With a name like Castro," Ben said, "I should have known."

Roy Lyle raised a possibility. "Orlando's Imperial, the blue convertible with the fins, is still in the motel lot."

"Aha," Ben said. "Lieutenant Calley, I'm going to check the northern perimeter. You have one more LAW there, why don't we repay our south-of-the-border amigo for cursing us with these worthless weapons?"

55

Big Butt belly-crawled to his victim, scanning the woods for more Zionists. He approached the poison ivy with caution, itching with even a thought of the fierce allergic festering he got from a brush with the noxious weed. He looked both ways. Dense vegetation separated him from the strip mall and gunfire. He rose to a crouch, parted the vines with a long stick, and saw the bloody hole in the back of the—not black clad Zionist, but—*No!*—camo-shirted Ranger.

Lordy, I shot a Ranger. A Ranger! And in the back to boot.

Poison ivy forgotten, Big Butt bent to roll the man over. He smelled him before he saw his face: little Stinkbug.

Big Butt flushed with rage. What the hell was the man doing this far forward? Didn't he know there was a Zionist afoot? Stinkbug was under orders to stick close to the others, but, oh, no, he was never one for orders, and now look what he had done. The dumb bastard.

His anger gave way to fear with the thought he may have been seen. Fine thing for a Major General to shoot one of his own men. In the back. Even if he did ask for it. He dropped to his hands and knees, scanned the forest. No one. He got to his feet and ran for all he was worth, crashing through the brush, all the way to the bait shop.

Coony opened a slit in the closed, double curtains of Room 105 and peered outside. Behind him, Rita Rae and Orlando were cuffed to the bed frame. Smoot and Bolt, secure with Gabe, were in 115, and LeCoup and Raven, with Ike, in 101. Etta and Johnny were guarding Rita Rae's and Orlando's possessions in the motel office.

"Looks like D-day," Coony said in soliloquy. "I hoped with the principals in custody we could negotiate, but them boys wasn't into waiting. I called in the Marines—Bradford and Combs county sheriffs and the KSP are on the way. You'd think they'd of run out of ammunition, firing like that. So far, thank the Good Lord, the shooting's kept north of the road. I just hope there's no civilian casualties." He took his hat off and rubbed his forehead. "Be suicide to go out there."

Rita Rae spoke to his back. "Then stay inside. Let us go. Give us our money, and we'll take our chances. You've got no reason to hold us."

"Ho. Ho. Ho." The three words came out slowly, dripping with sarcasm. "As a start, the Céloron plate was stolen." Coony turned from the window, faced them. "Which one did you sell it to, anyway?"

Neither answered, so he said, "We'll sort it out. What I really want to know, is, where's your brother Judas Bob? If you know where he's got that girl, I'd advise telling me right out if you don't want to add kidnapping to whatever else I got against you. I swear, if he hurts—"

A deafening explosion ripped the parking lot, breaking windows in a third of the rooms fronting the E-Z Zees. The curtains behind Coony blew inward with tornado force. A piece of Imperial tail fin slapped Coony's back, throwing him hard to the carpet. Only the heavy, rubberized drapery saved him from shattering glass. Coony lay on the floor, gasping, lungs emptied of air, blood seeping across his upper back.

Uninjured, Rita Rae and Orlando moved fast. Orlando pointed. "The keys are in that pocket under his belt."

"Heave," Rita Rae said, and they jerked the bed in small jumps toward the prone lawman. "The other cops may be here any second." She grabbed the frame and tugged. "Harder! Once more. Yes!" She worked a finger through Coony's belt loop, pulled him toward her, fished the keys from his watch pocket, and shucked the cuffs.

Coony struggled to rise, but Orlando wrestled his hands behind him, cuffed them, stuffed a washcloth in his mouth and secured the gag by tying a twisted pillowcase around Coony's head. Orlando lifted Coony's .38 from its holster, pressed it to the back of Coony's head.

Rita Rae grabbed his wrist. "Are you crazy? You think that won't bring the rest of them running? You kill a sheriff, they'll hound us to the ends of the earth. C'mon, let's find our money."

A quick look in the hall revealed half a dozen frightened guests, but no men with stars. Rita Rae hustled Orlando toward the central stairs, up to their rooms.

At the auction suite they found one door ajar, both rooms empty.

"What now?" She swiped a sweaty hank of hair from her forehead, paced in a tight circle. Outside, the gunfire rose and fell like rolling thunder. "There have to be more cops here. They've got our money. Jesus Bob will be here soon. Maybe we can catch one off-guard, make him tell us . . ."

Orlando took a quick look out the window at the remains of his convertible in flames, the tanker, its rear third gone, the smoke drifting over Chez Pancakes from the once-gas station, the abandoned cars, people in ditches, huddled behind the restaurant, under parked cars.

He took Rita Rae by the shoulders. "Listen, with this war, if the *policía* catch us again, we'll never walk another beach.

Those are Smoot's and LeCoup's guerrillas out there. What do you think they will do to us when they discover the con? We leave, *querida*. *Now*, with our skins."

"All that money." Rita Rae rubbed her eyes. "We can't just leave it. It's here. In one of these rooms. I know—"

Orlando shook her. "*Now!*"

She put a hand over her mouth and drew a sharp breath, blinked several times, and nodded.

Orlando gave her a consoling squeeze, then checked the hallway, saw the back of the phony maid through the door to the outer stairs. He took Rita Rae's hand and ran with her down the central stairs to the lobby, the rear door, and the conversion van.

Levi spoke softly into his radio to the man who would rendezvous with him. "Barbarian leader is moving north of the battle. He is alone. I should have him in minutes." He repeated it in Hebrew to Liev at the houseboat, *"Ha nagid ha akzar holech tsafona min ha milchama. Hu levad. Adbig be dakot."*

He bent to his Cordura weapons case, selected a CO_2 rifle, a veterinary dart, and an ampoule of a potent synthetic opiate designed to anesthetize large four-legged mammals. In the dilution recommended by his Superspy correspondence course manual, Levi surmised it would have the desired effect on the two-footed variety as well. He assembled the charge and crept forward.

Minutes later, Field Marshal Ben slapped at a biting sting at his upper back. With a curse, he knocked away what he imagined to be a fat hornet, a cicada killer. He shuddered at the horrific sensation of a predatory insect piercing his flesh, and kneaded the fire at the back of his shoulder. Despite the pain, Ben smiled at the irony of escaping the deadly 9-millimeter hail raking the woods and being stung instead by a lowly arthropod indifferent to the affairs of men.

A minute or two later—whoa—Ben felt a twinge of vertigo. He steadied himself with a hand against a tree trunk. He felt another disorienting rush, dropped his weapon, rocked on his feet. Allergic reaction? A psychologi . . . Ben's vision shimmered in starry bursts, then flickered, dimmed, and a purple tide surged through his skull and drowned all thought. Knees buckling, he fell to the ground.

With Ben slumped at his feet, Levi chattered over the radio in Hebrew—*"Nagid tahat raglai . . ."*—with brother Liev, who informed him he couldn't get the damnable houseboat started. Levi promised to send Ari, "the prince of motors." He waved to his approaching cohort who would help him carry away Ben, switched to English and channel two, directed the men across from the E-Z Zees to keep a watch for Red One and Two. On channel three, he learned from the men at the strip mall the only casualty was a minor shoulder wound. Back to Liev, more Hebrew—*"Hakol beseder . . ."*— then English to the strip mall, "Return to base. This is Alpha. Send Ari to my brother's ship. We have abducted barbarian leader and conclude operation. Will fly him out in helicopter. I will probe enemy lawmen myself to arrange exchange of barbarian leader for Red One and Two. If anyone runs into Red One or his woman, call immediately."

Like a broken wire making intermittent contact, snippets of Ben's senses reactivated. He believed his hands were bound behind his back, but he had no sensation, no feeling at all. His eyelids were too heavy to open. But he did hear fragments of conversation, enough to fill him with terror. First, a run of horrific, guttural *alien*, then English: "Return to base, Alpha Centauri . . . mother ship . . . have abducted Aryan leader . . . operation in helicopter . . . I will probe enemy myself to . . . change Aryan leader . . . into . . . woman . . . immediately."

In his mind, Ben screamed, a long, piercing, pitiable cry. But his slack throat wouldn't respond. He managed only to part his lips and drool onto Levi's black boot.

56

Digger's heart thumped under his ribs like a bird in a box, his mouth went to chalk, and he sank to his knees. Bo: shot, clubbed, maybe dead. Nikki: in the hands of Bo's demented brother, melting *lead*. An image rose of Edgar, lead fishing sinkers rammed down his throat.

In the distance Digger heard dull pops and *ratta-tats*, and concluded Coony and his men were under siege by the Rangers. He gripped a sapling and raised himself.

He watched Bo's brother move to Bo's cruiser, heft his shotgun, and blast the grille, then the front tire. The car settled to the right. Another blast, and it sank forward, the left tire gone, as well. He fired another round into the dash, then walked to Bo and nudged him with his boot toe. Bo didn't move. Jesus Bob laughed and spoke to Bo's supine body: "So much for the righteous fucking law." He bent over, took Bo's gun, stuck it in his waistband, and reloaded the shotgun. He ripped Bo's radio and a canister of Mace from Bo's belt, pitched both high in a trap shooter's arc, and fired twice.

His targets fell to the ground unscathed. Hot with fury, Jesus Bob stomped to the radio and blasted it, then turned his gun on the Mace, twenty feet away. The cylinder exploded in an angry white cloud. He stumbled back, rubbing his eyes, and then shambled to the cabin. From the base of the stairs, he called, "Yoo-hoo! Papa Bear's got some porridge for you, babe."

Digger saw him disappear inside, then heard a muffled, mocking, "Bo? Why Bo's dead, babe."

Nikki wailed a long "Nooo!"

Digger cursed his inadequacy. Bo probably had a shotgun in the cruiser's trunk, but the keys would be in his pocket. To go to Bo and then to the car in plain view of the house would be suicidal. He looked around for a club, wondering if he could make it to the porch, tempt the man outside and knock him out. A long shot. Bo had said to run, but by the time he got help, it would be too late for both Nikki and Bo.

Even as he ran over unproductive scenarios, Digger found himself working his way through the thin woods lying to the right of the cabin, thinking he might be able sneak to the porch or a window, unseen. And then what?

Wary of giving himself away by snapping a brittle branch, he glanced at the ground and froze, terrified, in an awkward, half-completed stride. His foot was within six inches of the back of a four-foot *rattlesnake*, lying camouflaged against the forest litter. It was thick-bodied, dark as coal dust, unmoving.

The childhood Bible image of the satanic black serpent in the Garden of Eden loomed before his eyes. He gasped, barely recovered his balance. In the slowest of slow motion, he eased back three steps, imagining the snake pinned under his foot, thrashing, the heavy, arrow-shaped head whipping back, embedding inch-long fangs in his calf. He nearly bolted.

Instead, he willed himself to immobility. Transfixed, he counted ten silent rattles, watched the muscular body slowly expand and contract in a patch of sunlight as the reptile breathed. In a disturbing insight he realized that his worst fear and a possible solution to his dilemma co-mingled at his feet.

Here was his weapon.

Sure. Now what? Lure Bo's brother out here, hope he steps on it? Pick it up by the tail, carry it to the door, and toss it to him? Sheesh!

The rattler lay in a long S, facing a rocky ledge three feet away, presumably its den. Still, except for the slow breathing, it seemed unaware of Digger's presence.

Unsure why, possibly merely procrastinating, Digger found himself scanning the forest floor, the clearing, the trash at the fieldstone foundation. He spotted a dirty, pale yellow, five-gallon plastic bucket, its wire handle missing, and hatched a plan. He cat-stepped backward, edged out of the vegetation, and ran in a low crouch to the cabin wall. He returned, nerves afire, perspiring, holding the empty bucket at his stomach. The snake still hadn't moved—was apparently sunning or sleeping. How could they sleep without closing their eyes? The rattler raised its chin perceptibly, its satiny tongue tasting air. A cold worm skittered up Digger's spine, a bead of sweat dropped from his chin with an audible *pwock* into the bucket. Could snakes smell fear?

The cabin had been silent. Now he heard, "Where the hell's that damn funnel?" and Nikki, indistinct, pleading.

Focus! He reran a mental film of Nikki handling the rattlesnake she had found in the forest above Edgar's house. Digger knew what to do, but his limbs went rigid at the thought. He heard a loud curse—apparently Bo's brother had burnt himself. Nothing from Nikki. Digger squeezed his eyes shut and groaned.

Another curse galvanized him to action. Stalking-slow, so as not to spook the snake, he lowered the bucket to the forest floor. He backed away, found a sturdy five-foot branch with a crook at the end, and edged back to within three feet of the snake's tail. Ever so slowly, from a low crouch, he extended the branch with both hands, worked the crook into the leaf litter beneath the midpoint of the long body, and lifted gently. The rattle buzzed, the serpent swung its neck toward him and flicked its forked tongue, but made no attempt to strike. Arms trembling, Digger hoisted higher, leveraged the long body so it now hung from the stick in a long, upsidedown U.

The scientific corner of his brain commented on how heavy the reptile felt, how subdued its response. The worrying corner wondered if something was wrong with it.

Before he completed the thought, the snake began to crawl from the branch. Digger felt the weight shift, watched it throw a whip-like coil to shake free. The head and neck stretched, slid down toward the rocky ledge and freedom. The chin touched ground. Another two seconds and the trunk would flop to the forest floor from the branch, the head would nose its way into the rocks, and the rattlesnake would be gone.

A screech from the cabin and Digger acted. Without thought or pause, he gripped the branch solidly in his right hand, extended his left, wrapped his fingers around the snake's tail above the rattles and held on. He felt rough scales, yielding skin over straining muscles. The snake's head and neck lashed side-to-side, but Digger tightened his grip and held the bulk of the body on the branch.

In a swift move, he swung the reptile over the bucket, nosed the snub head inside, slowly loosened the tail, and watched the trunk follow the head. The buzzing rattle hung on the pail edge for a long second, then slithered inside.

Digger stared in disbelief at the hand that had touched the snake's skin and its bone-dry rattles. With a shiver, he shook his fingers, then rubbed them against his pant leg over and over until the skin chafed.

A thump from the cabin brought him back to the moment. He leaned forward, and peered into the pail. Perhaps sensing safety in the opaque bucket, the snake had coiled at the bottom. Although its tongue flickered, it no longer rattled. Digger watched it for several seconds, then lifted a dried leaf, let it slide from his palm onto the snake, as if it had fallen from a tree. No reaction. He dropped another, then tossed a handful, covering the thick scaly coils at the bottom.

Gut churning, he kneeled, pressed his palms to either side of the bucket, and lifted. What was it Nikki had said? They could strike half their length? That meant well past the top. He rose to his feet, held the container at arm's length, and walked from the forest to the ragged lawn in front of the cabin. Ten feet from the base of the stairs, he cradled the pail at his roiling stomach.

Did Nikki say they were deaf? Or simply had poor hearing? How would it react if he shouted? With the rim of bucket no more than ten inches from his chin, Digger willed himself to yell. "Hey, you in the house!"

"Stay away!" Nikki. Still alive.

Jesus Bob materialized at the doorway, stepped onto the porch, head wavering like a wobble-headed plastic dog on the dash of a float-boat car. His left arm cradled the shotgun. He had a holstered revolver and Bo's gun tucked in his belt, and in his right hand, some kind of laboratory tongs. He saw Digger, forced his eyes to focus. "Willie?"

Humor him. "That's right." Digger wondered if he had been at the County Line the night he went out with Coony. He glanced down: leaves. No climbing snake.

"I got your babe, Willie."

Digger decided the man was drunk or high. Don't plead. Keep him off guard. He shook his head. "Not my babe."

"Gonna give her a dose of hot lead. And I don't mean like my loving brother Bo got. Or the old man."

Digger nearly dropped the bucket. "Edgar Fitz?"

"That's the one. Smoot's scientist. Lead," he repeated. "Get my drift?" Jesus Bob waved the tongs in the air. "Soup's on, Willie."

Digger bit his lip. Act calm. Improvise, keep him off guard. "The hell with her."

"Huh?"

"I said the hell with her. She's fooling with some cop."

"Damn straight," Jesus Bob lifted his head, angled his chin, eyes following an invisible demon. Without warning he lifted the shotgun and fired in the direction of his gaze. *Blam!* From inside: "No!"

"Got it," Jesus Bob said. "Fat-assed snake."

Digger nearly stumbled from the noise. He felt motion in the bucket, panic in his gut. A quick look revealed shifting leaves but no rising snake. He forced himself to speak, loud enough to be heard in the cabin: "You got it, all right."

Jesus Bob dropped the tongs at his feet, pumped the shotgun, and pointed the barrel at Digger. "Sorry, Willie, but Sis wants you out of the way. What'd you do to piss her off, anyway?"

Digger swallowed, resisted the urge to drop the bucket and run. Say something, anything. "It was, uh, music. This new arrangement of Dixie. The Tahitian drum rhythm, those black chicks singing the doo-wahs. She got all worked up over it. Bitch! They're *all* bitches."

The gun barrel lowered six inches. "You got that right, pardner." Jesus Bob's eyes wandered, focused again on Digger. "What are you doing here, Willie?"

Digger remembered what Coony had said about Bo's brother being a druggie. "Picking psychedelic mushrooms. Woods is full of them. Got some morning glory seeds here, too, and jimsonweed." He fast-checked the snake: still leaf covered.

"You're into good shit, pardner."

"Wouldn't be where I am today without mother nature's help."

"Whoa!" Jesus Bob backed up, looked high over Digger's head. He wiped his forehead with the back of a wrist and stared.

Digger considered a charge, but as fast as Jesus Bob had looked up, he refocused on Digger. "All of a sudden, you was fifty feet tall. How'd you do that?"

"Mushrooms," Digger said, trying to remember his psychedelics.

"Had me a bite or two before," said Jesus Bob. "Weird shit. Yellow with bumps and flies crawling on 'em. I ate some of that jimson, too."

"Want some more?" Digger edged forward with the bucket. "Take your pick. Any flavor you want."

Jesus Bob took two steps down the stairs, leaned over to see, then stopped. "No, man. Gotta stay sharp. Shut up the babe inside. Do the sheriff, get back to Sis." He raised the shotgun. "Hey, man, I hate to do this, but Sis—"

Digger upended the pail, fast, flipping the snake at Jesus Bob's head. The toss would have been wide, but the long writhing body caught the slick barrel of the gun and slid along it to the big man's chest.

Digger dropped the pail and ran. Twenty paces away, with screams at his back, he looked over his shoulder.

Jesus Bob had seized the snake's body with his left hand to brush it away, and the terrorized reptile struck him between the eye and temple. Wild with fright, Jesus Bob tugged at its body, snagging fangs and teeth in his flesh. Reflexively, his finger squeezed the trigger of the shotgun.

The blast snapped Digger's head back. He saw white, felt searing pain, and stumbled to the ground.

Jesus Bob fell backward and the shotgun clattered to the floor. When he hit the porch, still gripping but no longer stretching the snake, its fangs dislodged, and it struck him twice more, once on the chest, once on the forearm. Jesus Bob flung it away, got to his feet wild-eyed, slapping his bloodstained face. Wailing, he spun full circle, flapping his arms at demons, then bounded inside.

On his knees, stunned by pain, Digger steadied himself with one hand on the grass, and palmed his eyes with the other. He dropped the hand, realized he was blind in his right eye.

He swiped his face in panic. Blurry vision returned—the eye was awash with blood. He nearly retched when he saw his crimson-soaked hand.

Digger probed his face, felt flowing blood at his forehead,

torn skin over his swelling eyebrow, at his hairline. He touched his lid, blinked, and determined both eyes were intact. The searing pain ebbed to a sufferable, stinging throb as he sat. Aware he could see and think, he stripped off his shirt, rolled and tied it around his forehead, stanching the bleeding.

Digger rose to his feet, sucked air at a surging pain, and nearly fainted. He wobbled, confused.

Loud thumps, shrieks, and curses from the cabin brought it all back in a fearful rush: Bo's brother, the rattlesnake, Nikki, hot lead.

Energized, Digger bounded up the stairs, saw Jesus Bob writhing inside, tearing at his face, and then Nikki, face wet with tears, sitting on the floor. Her back was against a table, her ankles and hands tied, her forehead bound to the table leg. Digger released the ropes, scooped her in his arms, and carried her outside.

"How bad are you hurt?" she said as he untied her. The look on her face told him it wasn't pretty.

"I'm okay," he said, wondering if his skull was fractured.

Nikki caught sight of Bo, his thigh, side, and head bloody, too. Dead still. She got to her feet, took two steps toward him, and fell, wincing. She held her knee and rocked. "The bastard kicked me in the knee when I tried to get away. Help me to Bo."

They found him alive, moaning softly, the side of his face puffed and discolored, his eyes half-open but unfocused, one pupil half the size of the other. His thigh was pocked with punctures, bleeding freely, but with no arterial spouting. Part of his shirt had been blown away, but the Kevlar vest had protected his groin, stomach and chest.

Nikki ran her fingertips across his forehead. She spoke at his ear. "Bo? Can you hear me? We'll get help. Your brother—"

Jesus Bob freight-trained from the cabin, cursing. He stumbled down the stairs, one eye shut tight, the skin around it swollen, shiny, the other wide with fright. He swept the air with his arms, punching, swiping. "Fucking snakes! Get 'em away from me!" He ran a jagged course across the musket range, falling, rolling, standing, shouting, then disappeared into the woods.

Bo spoke a coherent sentence. "You . . . you all right?"

"Uncle Digger saved me."

"Get help. Coony . . ." Bo fell to mumbling.

Nikki squeezed Digger's arm. "We'll carry him to Bo's cruiser . . ."

Digger explained how Bo had immobilzed the Mustang, how Bo's brother had shotgunned the cruiser. "You can't walk anywhere with that knee. Bo told me how to get out. Stay with him. I'll find help."

"You sure you're all right? It must hurt. . . ."

"I'm okay. Take care of Bo." He gave her a short hug and moved for the far woods and the crest of the ridge, the direction Bo had told him to go, feeling rocky, in agony, but doing his best not to show it, aware Nikki was watching.

Moments after her uncle disappeared, Nikki saw a tendril of smoke curling from the cabin doorway, a flicker of flame through one window.

She spoke to Bo's battered face, explaining, "Judas Bob had a fire going, melting lead, was gonna do bad stuff to me. Digger threw a rattlesnake at him, Judas Bob was bit—must have knocked his torch over." She went rigid. "Coony—my milk snake! He scared your brother. He's still inside."

"Go on, find him," Bo said in a weak whisper.

Nikki touched his cheek and limped to the cabin.

57

Digger, head throbbing, slumped onto a tree stump at the ridge-top. Fearful he would pass out if he kept up the pace, he rested for half a minute, listening to his breathing, to songbirds, celebrating life.

He noticed smoke rising from where he had left Nikki and Bo. Nikki must have torched Judas Bob's cabin.

Time to move. Get help.

He rose to his feet. Below, he saw the Rangers' outbuildings and empty pickups, but no Rangers. Hoping to find a telephone, he entered three structures, unlocked, smelling of mold and cigarette smoke. No luck. Apparently they used cell phones or radios. He found no keys in the trucks, so he headed for the dirt road leading down the mountain past a large tobacco barn. A plume of oily black smoke rose over the valley in the direction of Golden Leaf. He heard muffled gunfire, and, more distantly, sirens.

He was halfway across the campground lawn when he saw the big gun, the recoilless rifle, pointed at the town, an ominous eleven-foot tube with a thickened base, mounted on a heavy tripod. Fearful, yet curious, he approached it, extended a finger to touch the barrel. Nearby were crates of ammunition, and below, lying ominously on a wood pallet, he saw five bare shells with names crudely painted on them in red: Bo Deaver, Etta McCoy, Johnny Shirey, Gabe Clark, and Ike Wilson. He looked again at the barrel. The breech was ajar and one shell had been loaded, undoubtedly bearing the name Coony McCoy.

"I think not," Digger said, pondering sabotage. Then another, more potent, idea came to mind. He took long look at the barn—their arsenal, Bo had said—and studied the weapon.

He had never seen anything like it, but the lanyard trigger mechanism was simple enough to fathom. He closed the breech, removed a dust cap from the front, wrestled the tripod—the assembly was unwieldy for one man but maneuverable—roughly ninety degrees to the right, toward the barn, two hundred yards away.

He placed his eye to the telescopic sight, his hand on a wheel at the side, the traversing mechanism. He rotated the gun to the center of the barn and with a few turns of the second wheel, adjusted the elevation, aiming it beneath a painted TOBACCO IS IN YOUR FUTURE message and a pair of rosy-cheeked teenagers. A smaller rifle assembly was mounted on the larger barrel, apparently for test firing to center in the larger weapon. At such close range it was superfluous. If Coony's round missed the target, the deputies would follow through.

Standing to the side, a finger in his left ear, his right hand on the lanyard, Digger shut his eyes tight in anticipation. He pulled the lanyard.

Whoomp! In synch with the loud, if muffled, report, jets of flame shot from ports at the rear. Digger felt searing heat, but sensed no jumping carriage. In fact, the barrel barely moved. Had it misfired?

In the microsecond of his doubt, the barn went up.

He saw a flash, heard a loud *Blap*, watched pulverized barn siding, earth, and smoke explode into a small, fierce supernova. He dropped to his knees as a secondary explosion, then a continuous concussive series, like the booming climax of a fireworks show, lifted the whole barn from its foundation and shattered it over five long seconds. The ground rocked. Digger put his hands to his ears, too late. He threw himself belly-to-earth. The bone-jarring noise left him dazed, ears stinging, whistling with white static. Flame flared like a struck match and rose as an expanding ball of fire. Smaller explosions crackled like strings of Chinese firecrackers. Shells and shrapnel sliced the air in straight-line incendiary streaks leaving contrails of braided white smoke, while hot burning debris arced in lazy parabolas, cascading like flaming hail onto the hillside, lighting small brush fires and setting two of the cabins afire.

Awed with the destruction, Digger chewed a knuckle at what he had done, and shot a guilty look left and right. Then he broke into a boyish grin and laughed.

He jammed rocks into the barrel, knocked over the big gun, and ran. Halfway down the hill, he stopped to catch his breath. Over his shoulder he saw smoke and flame from the campground fires spiraling hundreds of feet into the air. Above, a small airplane droned. He watched it gain altitude, fly in a wide curve around the smoke, then head south, away from danger.

Minutes later, Digger reached the highway, sweaty, winded, paying the price of his exertion with a splitting headache. He sat on a guardrail awaiting the approaching sirens, feeling bone-tired but surprisingly good about himself.

A sergeant spoke to Major General B. G. Butz. "Sir? Field Marshal Ben went into the woods fifteen minutes ago. He ain't been back. Men are searching, but no one's seen him."

"Sir?" A corporal raised his hand. "Most of us have plenty of ammo since the HKs jammed up, but we're running out of cigarettes and change for the machine here. Okay if we bust it open?"

"Sir?" Yet another Ranger besieged the new officer in

charge. "Not only Field Marshal Ben is missing. No one has seen Stinkbug neither."

Big Butt shifted uncomfortably. The men looked at him for instruction. He knuckled his forehead, coughed—and was saved by Captain Grundy: "The little bastard probably run off when the going got tough."

"I'll bet he did," said the relieved Major General. "Stinkbug was never much of a soldier."

Roy Lyle: "Sir? Hard to tell with our men afiring, but the Zionists and feds may not be shooting back no more."

Big Butt made his first command decision: "Hold your fire!"

The reports trickled off as men got the order. Indeed, they heard nary a pop from across the highway.

"We run 'em off!" said Calley, standing tall in the trench, waving his pistol in celebration. That no one picked him off testified to their adversaries' departure.

Men began to cheer, clap one another on the back. An exuberant sergeant put a round through the drop ceiling in celebration.

Roy Lyle tempered their jubilation: "I hear sirens."

"Hmmm," said Big Butt, his shoulders slumping from the ever-weightier mantle of command. What now? Where *was* Ben?

He felt a tug at his trouser leg: "What about us, sir?" asked young Heck the Junior Ranger, a nasty bruise blooming under a walnut-size knot on his forehead from his gymnastic encounter with the red worm tank. Behind Heck, faces smudged, tiny fingers bleeding from loading magazines, Jerry and Jene-Jene, the Scooter Shooters, rose on spindly knee-scuffed legs.

Big Butt drove the siren worry from his troubled mind and patted the youngsters on their heads, all three. "You boys take off now, scurry out the back. That's it, brave lads," he said, much as he thought Ben would have phrased it. "Run along." He shooed them with his hands. "Get your rest. It's a school night."

As the sirens rose in pitch and the Rangers' cheers diminished, pragmatic Luther asked, "What now, sir?"

Big Butt covered his ears with his palms, quenching the still-distant wailing. He took a heady breath of victory while it still hovered in the air and gave the command he knew Ben would want him to: "Pack up the Humvee and Roy Lyle's pickup. We'll return to the Reserve and rain holy hell on the sheriff's headquarters with the recoilless rifle."

No sooner had he spoken, than the building shook. An ominous, subsonic tremor rattled the foundation, the remaining windows, cages, Rangers' bones.

Calley shouted "Mortar attack!" and dove for cover, followed by the others. One man tripped and fell into the newt tank. Big Butt tumbled gracelessly to the floor.

Imperturbable Luther, still on his feet at the front door, put binoculars to his eyes. Thirty seconds later, he gave them the bad news. "Big explosion. Black smoke over the Reserve. Had to be our arsenal. Must be the ATF come up from the south, or a NATO air attack."

Men rose, looked to their new leader, still sprawled on the concrete, for direction.

The vehicle guard, standing over Major General B. G. Butz, shifted his stance sheepishly, and responded to the late "return to the Reserve" order. "Sir, uh . . . see . . . Roy Lyle's truck got shot to hell and we, uh, left the Humvee run to be sure it'd be ready, and it, like, run out of gas. And with Silas's station burnt up . . ."

Big Butt rubbed watering eyes. He looked up, around, at worried, expectant faces. "Hell," he said. "We won the battle didn't we? Let's just go home."

58

*S*moot and Bolt, LeCoup and Raven, had been in custody in the county courthouse jail since yesterday. Now they were in the headquarters holding cells, two by two, the antagonists in view of one another for the first time.

"Bitch!" Bolt threw a French fry through the bars at Raven in the next cell.

Raven caught it on the fly and whipped it back, catching Bolt on the ear. "Piebald cretin!"

"Squaw!"

"Reddest redskins I ever seen," Smoot said with a hacking laugh that trailed off into silent goldfish gasps.

"Enough of that." Coony sat on a rolling desk chair, his back straight, wearing a neck collar and a loosened shirt over his bandaged back. When he spoke, rather than turning his head, he rotated the chair. He unwrapped a stick of Juicy Fruit and slid it into his mouth. Etta, fat Gabe, and Johnny with a tape recorder, sat in folding chairs at a long table behind him, sipping coffee and eating doughnuts.

Perched on a fold-down steel bench, Smoot said, "Damn you, Coony McCoy. You let us out of here."

Alphonse LeCoup agreed with Smoot for the first time in over twenty years. "Absolutely." Red-faced with indignation (or sheep dye, it was hard to tell), he fumed. "This is preposterous. I've never been in jail in my life."

With a wicked smile, Coony said, "Consider this a mere taste of what may come."

"He's toying with us," said Raven. "He's got no grounds to hold us. He's opening himself up for a class one libel suit."

Smoot seconded the thought. "Bet your ass."

LeCoup leaned into the bars. "You told us you were taking us into protective custody. That was yesterday."

"Indeed I did. Smoot's Rangers would of shot you full of holes if they'd got hold of you. And Smoot, LeCoup's men would of returned the favor."

"Then why are we still here?" Raven asked.

"I like the sound of criminal mischief. Mayhaps we'll think of something with a tad more bite. Johnny read you your rights?"

"Yes, yes," said LeCoup. "Look, our attorney is on the way—"

"From Cincinnati?" Coony's lips curled into a sly grin.

"The main judge and the McAfee County prosecutor is Coony's wife's kin," Smoot explained. "But," he faced Coony, "*my* lawyer's from Kentucky, you sumbitch. He's chief counsel for Wesvaky coal, coming down from Ashland, and he won't fart around with you. So you'd best let Bolt and me go. Now."

"Let me recap," Coony said. "Your Rangers blew up a gas station, a store, and a tanker full of milk, they half destroyed a construction project, shot up six vehicles—plus exploded a classic Chrysler Crown Imperial convertible, the tail fin of which did this here to my back. Lord knows how many windows was broke, or how many sleepless nights the good folks of this county will have as a result of your damned war. Lest I forget, the May Street Community Church presently lacks a steeple.

"Your men," he jabbed a finger LeCoup's way, "had a hand in that as well, plus they did Lord knows how much damage to Uncle Al's Bait Shop and Winky Worm Outlet. You're all accessories."

"I might add," Coony turned and blew his wife a kiss, "Etta sings in the choir of the May Street church, and I take crimes against fishin' damn serious."

"Hell," said Smoot. "Insurance'll cover it all."

"Of course," agreed LeCoup. "That's what people buy it for."

"I believe I told you," Coony added, "there was a man shot to death."

Smoot shook a fist at LeCoup. "A Ranger! A martyr! Done in by his Zionists!"

"Mayhaps, mayhaps not. Most of the fire yesterday was 9-millimeter. Johnny found what he believes to be a .30/06 slug in a tree trunk just past the body. The KSP forensics fella says the through and through wound profile supports that as the type of slug that did the deed. This tree is north of the victim, which puts the shooter not west, across the highway, but south, toward the bait shop. A search is on for the casing. Johnny also found a gunmetal finish cigarette lighter with a fine set of fingerprints beside the body—and whoever dropped it ought to be itching real good from poison ivy. So, let's hold back on those accusations till all the evidence is in, what say?

"Johnny read you your rights, and I guess your lawyers told you all to keep mum before they got here? That's good counsel. I advise you to say nothing."

A silent minute passed before Smoot asked, "Where's my Céloron plate?"

"*Your* Céloron plate?" said an outraged LeCoup. "*My* Céloron plate. I bid high. If you think this pint-size backwoods marshal is giving it to *you*—"

"*You* bid high? I bid high. Won it far and square."

Coony's eyes moved from one cell to the other as they spoke, like a net judge at a tennis match, enjoying the volleys.

"There's two Céloron plates," Coony interjected, matter-of-factly, savoring the expressions on their faces.

"*Two?*"

"What are you talking about, *two?*"

"Two lead plates." Coony sniffed the air. "I do believe I smell a counterfeit."

"No way!" said Smoot. "Edgar checked it out. Real good."

"As did my man," said LeCoup. We even did a lead isotope analysis, a comparison with a known Céloron plate. Same composition. No question. The documentation is irrefutable. And I examined it myself, before the auction."

"Safe to say," said Coony, "one was good—she probably showed you both that one. How close did you look—after? If it makes you feel any better, the copy's so good, we, even Digger Fitz, and he's an archaeologist, can't tell them apart. I guess she figured whenever you two got to bragging and discovered you'd been had, it wouldn't matter which one was good. Rita Rae would of been long gone."

Smoot shook his fist. "You're lying, you sumbitch."

"Safe assumption," agreed Raven. "It's some kind of trick."

Coony crooked a finger. "Johnny?"

Johnny lifted a thin slab of drab gray metal from a cotton-lined box, a familiar inscription clearly visible. He held it high in his right hand, and then raised another in his left with a "Ta-daa!" He put his hands behind his back and held them out again, an identical plate in each hand.

Smoot nearly burst. "Where is she, that conniving, thieving bitch? I'll damn well bet she can tell them apart."

LeCoup's eyes bulged. "Wait till my Israelis get done with Rita Rae and her smarmy friend."

"She's gone," Coony said. "They're both gone. Flew the coop, thanks to Smoot's boys' convertible-eating rocket. Bulletins are out, surrounding counties put out road blocks, but so far, zip."

Smoot cut to the quick: "What about my money?"

"They left empty-handed—we impounded near a million dollars from their room."

"Thank the good Lord," said Smoot. "Most of that's mine."

"No, mine," said LeCoup.

"You're sure?" said Coony. "That somewheres around half the near million dollars we found in the possession of Rita Rae Deaver and Orlando Sosa y Castro in rooms 206 and 207 in the E-Z Zees Motel, at approximately twelve-forty-five P.M. yesterday, the day we took you into custody on the same floor, belonged to each of you?"

"Damn straight," Smoot said. "Gave it to her in a shopping bag."

LeCoup concurred. "Indeed. Mine. We gave it to her in a cheap purse."

Grinning at his cleverness, Smoot said, "Tell you what, Sheriff. Give us our money back, and we'll flip for the plates and leave with no hard feelings. What say, LeCoup? Let a toss of the coin settle it?"

Raven nudged LeCoup. "*Certainement.* We'll leave with our cash and one of the plates, and the lawyers and the insurance people can sort out the rest. Done deal."

Coony waved the thought away. "Not perzactly. First, the Céloron plate in question was stolen from the Queen's Maritime Museum in Barbados."

LeCoup huffed. "Nonsense. We checked that out thoroughly. My man went down there, spoke at length with the assistant director. We have a signed letter from the director. All aboveboard."

"The director's signature was forged," Coony said. "As you may well have known. I suspect all you boys really care about is an artifact's authenticity."

"Not true," said LeCoup.

"So, the plate—both of them actually, since we can't tell them apart—will be returned to the museum."

"No!" Smoot began to pant. "Bolt, I need a cigar. Now."

"All gone, Commander. How about some oxygen?"

Smoot kicked at him, banged his walker against the bars.

"Mine! The plate is mine. You send it back to that museum, after all this, Coony McCoy, so help me . . ."

"You can't do that," said LeCoup. "I have documentation . . ."

"If I was to buy your stories about this alleged artifact auction," Coony continued, "I must conclude you were negotiating for stolen property."

LeCoup gave him a double take. "What in the world are you talking about—*alleged* auction?"

"Here's what bothered me," Coony continued. "We arrested Rita Rae Deaver and Orlando Sosa y Castro for possession of stolen property. Lord, what a surprise it was to find so much money in there. And you're telling me it was *your* money—both of yours—and you gave them near a half million each for a hunk of lead?"

"Of course," said LeCoup. "But I don't see where this is leading. It was a perfectly legitimate transaction."

"You're trying to put one over on us, you bastard," added Smoot.

"How much," Coony asked, "would one of these thingies bring at a public auction? Half a million?" No one spoke. "Four hundred thousand? Three? Etta did some checking with the New York auction houses. A small fraction of the money we recovered, you may be sure." He chewed his Juicy Fruit, let the silence build.

"It was only . . ." he winked at Etta and his deputies, "when we found the drugs that it all came together."

"Drugs?"

"What drugs?"

"Sure," Coony waggled a finger at them. " 'What drugs?' That's what they all say. A metal suitcase full of dope. Gabe?"

Gabe, powdered sugar coating his mouth and cheeks, left the room, returned with Jesus Bob's This Side Up. He opened it, turned it to face the cells.

"I've never seen so many different kinds of drugs together in all the years I've been sheriffing," Coony said. "A fair amount of pot. A kilo of cocaine." Gabe pointed as Coony spoke. "The KSP will work with us to confirm this, but—give me that list, Johnny." Coony took a pair of reading glasses from his top pocket, slipped them on. "Most of it is labeled. Hashish, opium, heroin, LSD, PCP, Darvocets, arsenic, strychnine, codeine, ether, nitrous oxide whippets, amyl nitrate, ecstasy, crack cocaine, methamphetamine, mescal beans, desiccated lotus, dried toads, blister beetles, and some unidentified pills, powders, leaves, and a truly nasty-looking fungus."

He removed the glasses. "A salesman's sample case, right? With plenty to pass along for the first order. Rita Rae and this Castro was high-end dealers—and that's what all the money was for. The auction business was only a cover."

Smoot was sputtering, coughing. LeCoup tried to shake the bars, ineffectually, shouting. *"Merde!* This is a frame-up. Preposterous! I'm a businessman!"

"Ain't they all?" Coony jabbed his reading glasses at him. "Yes, drugs *is* business, big business, and McAfee County don't tolerate it. Why, my blood fairly boils to think you people was trying to set us up as a drug supermarket, bringing in gangs of armed thugs. We found one of them only days ago, trying to sell your poison to children."

Smoot stomped, kicked, swore. LeCoup and Raven mouthed outrage and perfidy. Bolt took advantage of the confusion to whip a chicken leg at Raven, hitting her in the forehead. She picked it up, waved it at him, and returned the pitch, missing Bolt but knocking Smoot off balance. Bolt caught him by the shoulder and glared.

Coony turned to Johnny. "I think we better turn off the tape recorder, with all this cursing and blasphemy. My, my."

He let the furor taper off, and recapitulated: "You was financing a drug deal. Considering, too, what your men did to the people of McAfee County, I'd say a jury is fair certain to not only convict but recommend a prompt lynching."

Coony let it sink in. He went to the table, spit his exhausted gum into a napkin, ate a doughnut, drank half a cup of coffee. "Unless—"

"Unless what?" said LeCoup.

"Here it comes," Smoot said.

"Get it in your heads that the plates *will* be returned to the museum, that the confiscated drug money, including the twenty-five thousand you were carrying, Miss Buckhunter, *will* become the property of McAfee County." He raised a silencing palm. "Done deal. What's not yet carved in stone is the charges. The Commonwealth of Kentucky takes a dim view of drug dealers. Smoot, and you Mr. LeCoup, might never see the light of a free day again. Bolt and Miss Buckhunter will be lucky to collect Social Security on the outside with good behavior—if Bolt was capable of good behavior. You all understand the *grav*-i-ty of this?"

Everyone but Bolt nodded. LeCoup sat on the bunk and wiped his forehead with a silk kerchief. Raven sat beside him, holding his hand. Smoot leaned on his walker, still angry, but deflated. Bolt hefted a half-empty can of Dr Pepper, an eye cocked at Raven.

Coony pointed at him. "Put it down, Bolt." He waited a long half-minute before speaking. "Now, we may be convinced to hold off on the drug charges against you upstanding citizens if certain terms is met. This is off the record, understand? Nonnegotiable. Hear me out. If you agree, nod.

"First, I don't want no more feuding that endangers the people of this county."

They all nodded to that, except Bolt. Coony waited. Smoot kicked Bolt, and Bolt tipped his head in a yes.

"Smoot, I will be compensated for this tail fin injury— we'll work something out with the judge. A damn miracle no civilians was hurt bad, though, Lord knows, enough property was destroyed. Instinct tells me the insurance people are less apt to see this business as accidental than as one of their 'acts of war,' so you folks will make good on damages personally, and pronto. To make it simple, the motel and the

Chez repairs, and anything west of the highway—that would include the Ranger-exploded gas station and the milk tanker—falls on Smoot's shoulders—" He waited for the banging of the walker to settle down. "—and anything east, on Mr. LeCoup's.

"Mr. LeCoup, Miss Buckhunter? I want to see the Winky Worm plant reopened inside of two weeks."

Raven jumped to the bars. "Impossible! To renegotiate would wipe out—"

Coony cut her off. "Sad for a woman to waste her youth in prison."

She looked to LeCoup for reasurrance, found none, and sat, wilting.

"You two *will* cooperate with our investigation. I'm sure you're fishin' fans, so I'm guessing you will jump at the chance to endow an annual McAfee County bass fishing contest with a healthy cash prize. Help our tourism, see? Run it the weekend before election day, call it the McCoy fish-off."

LeCoup and Raven communicated through eye gestures. LeCoup shrugged.

"Smoot? The Reserve—you'll find there's been some changes in the architecture up there—is to be closed to the Rangers. After all this trouble comes to roost, I don't know how many will be running around loose, or dare show their faces to the people of this fair county, but you're no longer their sugar daddy. Good-bye Republic of Boone."

Huffing oxygen, Smoot refused to make eye contact.

"You will repair the May Street church steeple, and add that gold cross at the top they been wanting, too. And, I want to see you set up an archaeological museum here in McAfee County. That's right. Kentucky pre-history, see? Small building by the lake, I got a spot in mind. That'll boost tourism, give kids respect for our heritage. Stock it from your collection. That way, maybe you'll take some pride in it, huh? Sure—call it the Mudd Museum, make it your legacy."

Smoot sucked on his lip, bounced his walker a few times on the concrete, and nodded without looking up.

"And Bolt? You're to give up beer."

Bolt lunged at the bars.

Coony kicked his chair back on its rollers, hands raised, chuckling. "Just kidding about that last part."

He gripped the arms of the chair and pushed himself to his feet, wincing, and then walked the length of the cells, giving each of them a curt smile. "Good. Judge'll be by shortly. There's a few papers to sign, spelling out details. This is voluntary, see? You'll tell the lawyers it was your idea, and we went for it. You renege or we start getting calls from those legal birds, we file the drug charges and you take the hard road to the Graybar Motel.

"Howsomever . . . if we're all agreed, we can say our good-byes within the hour."

59

ikki raised the back of Bo's hospital bed so he could see everyone without moving. The shades and door were closed and most of the lights off. The top of Bo's head was swathed in white bandages, as was Digger's forehead. Bo had multiple dressings on his right thigh and half a dozen bristly sutures rising from scab-crusted lacerations across his discolored cheek and temple. Although out of intensive care since the previous midnight, he had spoken his first coherent sentence only an hour ago. Nikki had given him a summary of recent events, but was unsure it registered.

Coony entered the room in his neck brace, looking nearly as pale and haggard as Bo. He sat on the edge of the bed and patted Bo on the knee. "Damned if you don't look like some Egyptian mummy, boy."

Nikki screwed her face into a Medusa glare.

"I'm funnin', darlin'. Bo knows how I feel about him."

"Shot me in the same leg," Bo mumbled.

"You're too goodhearted." Coony gave him another affectionate pat. "Soon as you saw that shotgun, you shoulda blowed him away. See what you get, running off like the lone Mountie? Good thing you took your snake-charming artilleryman here, or you and this young woman would be dead as Judas Bob. Damned if Digger didn't put the final nail in the coffin of the Daniel Boone Rangers to boot."

Nikki beamed at Digger, but gave Coony a "careful with the death talk" look.

"Yeah, who am I to lecture? I nearly lost my head, too. I hoped to take hold of Smoot and the Frenchman after their auction, put them on the bullhorn, and cool down those idjits across the road, but some jackass let loose shooting for no good reason and all hell broke loose. It was a damned if you do, damned if you don't see-nar-ee-o. Rangers had a lit fuse. If I'd of called in help earlier, they'd of gone nutso right off."

Coony lifted a plastic vial from his shirt pocket and clacked it on the movable tray at Bo's chest. "Lookee here, boy." Coony lifted the vial and rattled it. "A memento. Eleven pieces of shot they took out of your leg."

Digger shook a similar vial. "I only got two."

"If that shotgun blast had been about six inches closer, Digger, you'd have got the whole load, and damn well lost your head. You was both lucky."

Bo opened his eyes and attempted a smile, but it didn't go far.

"He keeps asking about his brother," Nikki said.

"The sumbitch who shot him. Guess he didn't hear me before. Well, Judas Bob is stone cold dead, and about time. He admitted to Digger it was him who killed Edgar Fitz. The dogs found him just before sundown, snakebit—Digger here throwed a rattlesnake on him. Nailed him three times. What do you think of that?

"And the rattlesnake?" Nikki asked.

"Well, don't you have the big heart, too?" Coony said. "No sign of the snake, so Judas Bob must not of poisoned it."

"And your snake?" Bo asked, in a hoarse whisper.

Nikki lifted her sequined snake purse. "Coony?"

The sheriff answered her. "Yeah?"

"Not you," Digger said. "That's what she calls her pet milk snake."

"Do tell? And should I take that as a compliment, darlin'?"

"You should. He's a beauty." Within seconds she had Coony II out and weaving through her fingers. "After the cabin caught fire, I went back, found him crawling against the far cabin wall. Got my collecting pack and my pickled scarlet kingsnake out in time, too."

Bo's lids had closed. Coony patted Bo's uninjured leg, unsure whether he was conscious. "Son?"

"Yeah, I'm here," Bo said, eyes still closed. "Some gimp I'll be. I can't believe he shot me in the same leg. And I let him do it. Again."

"Water over the dam, boy."

"Your brother kicked me in the knee," Nikki said. "I'm limping, too. And on the same side as you. We're like twins. What do you think of that?"

Bo mumbled incoherently. Coony leaned closer to hear. He spoke at Bo's ear. "Listen up, son.

"First . . ." He set a shoe box on the shelf over the bed, opened it, and tilted it for Nikki and Digger, and then Bo, to see.

"Oh, yuck," Nikki said. "A scalp."

"No," Coony said. "It's only hair."

"Hair," Bo's eyes opened. "Cut up in pieces."

"That's right. You all right, boy? You up for this? For news?"

Bo's eyes opened, focused on Coony, shifted to the box. "I'm fine." His lids fluttered but remained open. "Whose is it—the hair?"

"Listen up, you'll like this. Boy hand-delivers the box to HQ at five last night, see? It says 'Sheriff' on top. They'd just put out the fire—Rangers blew up Silas's gas station, Bo. A milk tanker, too. Fine mess. So, I didn't have much time for the box. An hour later, a call for me comes in. Matter of life

and death, they say. I take it. One of LeCoup's boys—not that
he said, but it had to be—told me he had 'abducted the barbarian leader.' This voice goes on to say he had cut the hair
in the box off this leader's head as proof. I'm thinking, I have
Smoot, and Smoot's already shaved off his own hair, so who
the hell is this voice talking about? I look in the box, and
realize when I see the white Brylcream wave still stuck together, and the mustache, they have old Ben the barber, the
Ranger's head honcho, who started this damnable war.

" 'So what?' I say. He says if I don't release LeCoup and
the woman, right now, that isn't all he's going to cut off,
starting with a little party for Ben. He says this word—it's
spelled *B-R-I-T*." Coony noted the confused looks. "Yeah, I
didn't know it neither, so I looked it up. Sounds sort of like
priss. It's this Jewish ceremony. Apparently, old Ben was
never circumsized. . . ." He acknowledged the groans, Digger's tightly crossed legs. "Hell, I figured Ben might enjoy
some festivity after this serious business he got us all involved in, so I say, 'Do tell? Well, I'm thinking of holding on
to the Frenchman and his friend for at least ten years,' and
I hang up."

Bo's lips curled into a small smile.

Coony adjusted his hat. "Yep, I may have spoken rashly,
son. We may be driving to Bradford County for our haircuts
henceforth."

Bo chuckled. "Worth the drive."

"Thought you'd like that. Here's more news. You'll like
this even better. You know the Big Boy they never finished
down by the lake?"

"The one you showed me," Digger said.

"That's it. You with me, Bo?"

"I hear you." Bo's eyes had closed.

"All is not doom and gloom. Etta and me kind of figured
with Judas Bob in the picture, there ought to be drugs about.
When we arrested Rita Rae and her friend after the auction,
sure enough, we impounded dope. Scads of it, along with
LeCoup's and Smoot's money. Drug money, see? Enough not

only to buy that Big Boy and all the land around it, but fix up that building first rate. New headquarters, a proper comm system. What do you think of that, boy?"

"Rita Rae," Bo said, following the wrong trail. "Custody?"

"Still looking for her, though she damn well may have got away scot-free. I had Rita Rae and her slick friend handcuffed to a bed in the E-Z Zees when one of Smoot's Rangers blew up her friend's car in the lot. Knocked me on my ass. I woke up hurt, in my own cuffs, my gun stole, and a ruby red lip print on my forehead. Ain't that just like Rita Rae?"

"You're hurt?"

"No big deal. But you didn't hear me. We impounded near a million dollars. Besides our new headquarters, if the county offers that lakefront land as bait, I'm damn sure we'll be able to attract a marina. Maybe the E-Z Zees will put up a lodge.

"Was we to prosecute Smoot and the Frenchman, with their high-powered lawyers, they'd of flown free sooner or later. The big fish always get away, don't they? But those gentlemen kindly agreed to make it square. Smoot's gonna build a museum on that land and LeCoup wants to sponsor a first-class bass contest. Museum, marina? Hell, we'll have a real Big Boy there soon enough, and more. That means jobs here in McAfee County, Bo. And fishin', right off the back porch."

"That's good," Bo said, and then, "I never got to see her."

"I think Digger here may have got a good look at her. Ain't that right, Digger?" Coony gave Digger an exaggerated grin. "When Bo's feeling up to it, you can give him a blow-by-blow of your encounter."

Digger looked at the floor, blushing. "I ran across her by accident—didn't know it was her until Coony told me."

Nikki gave her uncle an inquiring look, but Digger didn't elaborate.

"New headquarters," Bo said. It finally registered. "How about that."

"Yep. Next time our friends visit us, we'll be in new quarters on Boone Lake."

"Oh, yeah," Bo said, with a sinking voice. "They'll be leaving."

"Not me," Nikki said.

Heads turned to her. Bo opened his eyes.

"Not right in the middle of my rattlesnake study and with you in a hospital bed." She touched Bo on the nose and turned to Digger. "Unc, the weird timbers here will be my dissertation! Population dynamics, defining microranges and habitats, maybe resurrecting the canebrake variant as a distinct species. It's perfect."

"Sounds like a fine subject, kiddo. I've got to head home, but—why not? You stay. We'll manage to hold on to Edgar's house for a while."

"I'll collect through the summer, go back to Ann Arbor and analyze data over the winter, travel to look at comparative material, but make this my base. I'll get back into fieldwork in the spring. Bo can help, huh, Bo?"

"I will," Bo said, raising himself on an elbow. "I'll help."

"Etta and the boys will be real pleased you're staying with us, young woman," Coony said. "And Digger? You'll come back to visit? Check up on your niece and do some serious fishin'?"

"You bet," Digger said. His face sagged with the thought of leaving, and the realization that between his stolen car and the Las Vegas debt dooming his mortgage, it would be a long time indeed before he could afford another trip. He tried to console himself with the prospect of the new corner office at the university, but the equation didn't balance.

"Why the long face?" Coony poked Digger in the shoulder. "Here's something to cheer you up." He passed him a long, gilt-edged plastic box. "A Millennium Special, Winky Worm Collector's Kit. See the number on the lid? Only two digits. That's a limited edition. But that ain't all." Another poke and an affectionate slap on the chin. "I called the director of that museum in Barbados, told him we recovered the Céloron plate, and how important it was. About knocked him off his proper butt. He had no idea what that hunk of lead represented. The irony is, he himself would of traded it and most of that other stuff to Rita Rae and her friend Orlando for a rusty ship's anchor back at the beginning. Anyways, when I told him how you and your niece was responsible for getting it back, as well as a fine reproduction, guess what?"

Nikki and Digger shook their heads. Bo managed a "What?"

"He said he was going to see you two got a cash reward."

Nikki clapped. "Way to go!"

Digger cocked his head. "No kidding?"

"You betcha. Five hundred English pounds. That's somewheres around three hundred dollars apiece."

"Oh," Nikki said.

A bitter smile crossed Digger's lips. "Three hundred dollars?" He pointed to Nikki's pet. "I guess that *is* a lucky milk snake."

"It ain't a fortune," Coony acknowledged. "But it'll help pay the airfare back next spring. Anyways, the reward ain't the best."

Digger raised an eyebrow. "And that would be?"

"You spend money, it's gone." Coony squeezed Digger's shoulder, patted Nikki's hand, clasped Bo's knee. "But good friendships are forever, huh?"

"You're right," Digger said. The gloom lifted, and he laughed. Hell, he thought, I'll sell the house, get an apartment near the university and walk to campus. I always hated yardwork, anyway. He took Coony's hand in both of his and shook it.

60

Nikki and Digger left Edgar's house for the Greater Cincinnati International Airport. Digger had dressed western, his boots, shirt and jeans by now comfortably broken in. Nikki had a tape of Willie Nelson playing. She cranked it up when Willie sang the opening chorus of "My heroes have always been cowboys," and gave her uncle a poke in the ribs.

Digger forced a smile and returned to watching the landscape, chin on forearm, elbow out the open window.

"You'll be on the plane inside of six hours."

A mile down the road, he said, "I'm going to miss them, kiddo. Coony, Bo, Etta, the rest." He laughed, but it sounded brittle and caught in this throat. "Who'd ever think I'd say that about a bunch of cops? Life plays strange tricks, huh? Hell, I even invited Coony over to go deep sea fishing—and meant it."

"You'll see him again. And I'll come over at Christmas to check up on you."

Minutes later, they slowed for a familiar intersection, the site of the McAfee County War, as the locals were already calling it. Traffic was backed up with slow-moving gawkers.

Tow trucks had removed the disabled vehicles, although the ruptured tanker still lay at the side of the road as a reminder of the violence. The pockmarked bait shop was CLOSED FOR RENOVATION. Two teenagers, ignoring the yellow tape, poked through the ruins of the gas station and general store. An entrepreneur had opened a roadside souvenir stand on one corner, selling spent 9-millimeter cartridges and bits of twisted and charred debris with hastily printed certificates of authenticity. The blackened chassis of Orlando's convertible still sat in the E-Z Zees lot, although the loose wreckage had been hauled off.

Digger looked at the boarded-up window of the Chez, the WE ARE STILL OPEN! banner. "Hey, look. Amy Lou's pink Caddy is in the lot. She must be inside."

Nikki slowed, pulled in. "I know," she said. "I thought you'd want to say good-bye."

"You know, kiddo—I'd like that."

Nikki parked, left the car unlocked out of local habit. She slung her snake purse and collecting pack over her arm but ignored Digger's bag in the back.

Digger muttered "priorities" to himself and shrugged. "Only Hawaiian clothes in my suitcase. Serve some local kid right to run off with it."

Nikki stopped ten feet from the door. "What did you say?"

He chuckled. "Nothing. We going inside or not?"

"We are. And when you see her, you give Amy Lou a hug, shake her hand, or whatever, and thank her, but don't get into a conversation, okay? You and I have time for a short cup of Chez coffee as a last memory for you, but if she stays, we'll never get out of Golden Leaf."

"What do you mean, 'thank her'?"

"Just do it, okay? And be sincere about it. I'll explain later."

Amy Lou was at the counter, discussing the Rangers' Last Stand with Rubella. Rubella was lamenting how empty the house was with her husband visiting relatives in Texas. Amy

Lou set her cigarette alongside Rubella's on the edge of the counter, patted Rubella's hand, and turned to Nikki and Digger. She cast a worried scowl at the bandages on Digger's forehead, and spread her arms. "Lord, I can't stand long good-byes," she said, and hugged first Nikki, and then Digger.

Pressed against her fleshy chest, Digger smelled hair spray, stale cigarette smoke, and strong perfume. He had a momentary flashback of an aunt's smothering hugs, but resisted pulling away. He patted Amy Lou's back instead, found himself, to his surprise, resting his chin on her shoulder and squeezing back.

"I'm going to miss you," he said. "You've been kind."

"Pish-tosh." She pushed him away. "Now don't you worry about this child. I'll keep a close watch on her."

"I'm sure you will." He saw Nikki over Amy Lou's shoulder, raising her eyebrows, a silent *Well?* on her lips. He acknowledged it with a short nod. "Uh, thanks, Amy Lou. We really appreciate it," he said, with another glance at Nikki.

She gave him a pantomimed *Good.*

"Was nothing." Amy Lou handed him a shopping bag. "Homemade oatmeal cookies inside for the flight. And"—she lifted a pink box and returned it to the bag—"some Mary Kay samples—for men. I'm sure they have representatives in Hawaii, too, to reorder. And if they don't, you write." She took his hand again. "Write anyway. I want a postcard with surfer boys and big curling waves." Her eyes were tearing up. "Like I said, I just fall to pieces with good-byes. God bless." And Amy Lou was out the door, trotting to her pink Caddy.

"We'll take our usual place at the back," Nikki said to Rubella.

At the table, Digger asked, "What was that 'Thank you' stuff all about?"

Nikki was all smiles, but wouldn't say a word until they had coffee in their cups and the waitress returned to the kitchen. Digger removed the bag of cookies from the shopping bag, set it on the table, and began to nibble.

"Amy Lou and I worked it out," Nikki said. "About Edgar's property. Not the part with the house, but the rest of it, the two hundred and twenty-five acres with the rattlesnake den that backs up onto the Daniel Boone National Forest. You know—how we could save it."

"From strip-mining, logging? I don't understand, there's no way we can—"

Nikki pressed a fingertip to her lips to silence him. "Listen. The family who owns it wasn't anxious to see it raped, because of their granny living there all those years. But they weren't about to give it away, either. No one turns their back on easy money, do they?"

Digger had a disturbing recollection of a green baize craps table, eager faces urging him on, a small fortune in stacked chips, the winning streak, and then, disaster. He shook it off. "I don't understand, kiddo. Wait! Don't tell me you got Biffer to—"

"Biffer saving rattlesnakes? Ha! That'll be the day." Nikki nudged her pack across the floor with her foot, to Digger's side of the table. "Go ahead, open it."

He slid the pack to his feet and unbuckled it.

"That thick folder—pick it up, see what's inside."

He removed a brown cardboard expandable file with a tie-down flap, set it on the table, untied the cloth ribbon closure and began to shuffle out the contents.

"*Jeezle*, don't dump it. Just *look*."

Digger peered inside, saw banded stacks of currency. He whistled. "Holy moly, kiddo, these are bundles of fifty- and hundred-dollar-bills!"

"That's right. Count it—under the table."

He did a rough count at lap level, looked at her, wide-eyed. "It must be . . . at least sixty or seventy thousand dollars!" He spent more time with it. "Seventy-five thousand."

"Cool, huh?"

He cast a guarded look around the restaurant. "Nikki. Where—?"

"When I went back inside that log cabin where Judas Bob

had me—you know, looking for Coony II when the fire started? I found Coony II, grabbed my pack, and saw Judas Bob's buckskin pouch on the floor. The flames were picking up by then, but I took a quick look inside the bag, saw all this money. I stuffed it in my pack, didn't say anything, figured it was Judas Bob's, and after what he did to us, I sure as heck wasn't giving it back, right? Then at the hospital, when Coony said Judas Bob was dead, and started bragging about how he outsmarted Smoot and the Frenchman, and got all their drug money? I figured this had to be some of it left over.

"Anyway, I kept it. I called Amy Lou and asked how much was the land worth? She said it depended on when, to whom, and for what. It's not farmable, although it has plenty of old timber the loggers would love to get their axes into. The family owns the mineral rights. And with a seam of coal under it, the coal company would be making offers sooner or later. But she didn't see a long line clamoring to buy it right off, either." Nikki spoke fast, anxious now to let him in on it. "Somehow Amy Lou got it in her head you had big bucks and were interested. She said if the family heard a cash offer, even a lot less than they expected, they might jump on it.

"I told her you had seventy-five thousand dollars, that you didn't believe in banks, kept your savings in cash, and that you might be willing to part with it if you could keep the land the way it is.

"She said that wasn't enough to buy all of it. But the two hundred twenty-five acres is divided into five parcels—and we could probably pick up the two largest ones, including the den and mineral rights, with a cash offer for seventy-five thousand, even though the land's worth a lot more. Sad to say, that wouldn't save all the den's snakes when they spread out during the summer, but it would protect the den itself and preserve close to half the habitat for the timbers and the other critters.

"Biffer's always telling me, 'You can't save the whole world, Nikki'—and I guess that's true—but I'll darned well do what I can."

"Nikki, I'm proud of you."

She responded with an *Aw, shucks* grin. "So—Amy Lou's been on the phone nonstop, and she put the deal together. The money goes anonymously to the Nature Conservancy with the proviso they buy the two parcels from the family. The family gets a fast seventy-five thousand dollars, and the Nature Conservancy keeps the land in trust—pristine, forever, lying right next to the Daniel Boone National Forest. It'll be called the Fitz Forest Preserve—after Edgar, see?"

"Wonderful! Aren't you and Amy Lou the business-women? I'll bet Biffer would be proud, too, of the way you put it together—although I wouldn't mention the slinky philanthropy part." He pushed the file across the table. "I can't think of a better way to spend your windfall."

"You don't understand." She pushed it back, grinning. "This is your money."

Digger's mouth fell open. *"Mine?"*

"I found a *hundred and fifty* thousand in the cabin. I already gave Amy Lou my half. This is yours. For your debts."

Digger stared at the cardboard file, letting it sink in. He set it on his lap, opened the flap again, poked inside, looked up, and shook his head. "I don't know what to say."

"Say you'll fly straight home—no stopovers in Las Vegas."

He crossed his heart. "Promise!"

"Good. Then drink up, stow your cookies, and grab my pack. We've got to hit the road to stay on schedule."

Digger looked again at the fat file in his lap, at Nikki's pack, and at Nikki, sipping the last of her Chez coffee. He hefted the file once more, and then, with an imperceptible shrug, and out of Nikki's view, emptied the cash into her open pack at his feet. He took Amy Lou's bag of cookies from the table and stuffed it in the empty file for bulk.

After casually rebuckling the pack and retying the file

flap, he hoisted Amy Lou's shopping bag and Nikki's pack onto the table, and stood, the cookie-stuffed file in his hand. "Nikki Fitz," he said, with a bow. "You are the greatest."

Her face reddened. "Whatever you say, Unc."

He moved around the table, pulled Nikki from her chair and clamped an Amy Lou death grip hug on her.

She wriggled away, held him at arm's length.

"What?" he said. "My deodorant failed? You don't like hugs?"

"No, hugs are nice." She leaned close, gave him a peck on the cheek, dangled her sequined purse at his nose. "Only . . . don't squash the milk snake."

AUTHOR'S NOTE

The French expedition led by Captain Pierre-Joseph
Céloron de Blainville and the buried lead plates are
factual, as are the activities and travels of George
and Lawrence Washington, the Madame Montour
anecdote, and the George Washington diary quote (*Diaries of
George Washington*, vol. 1, 1748–65, University Press of Virginia, 1976).

There is some question as to whether Céloron buried six
or seven plates. In his journal, Céloron states six, and his
cartographer, Father Bonnecamps, plots six on his map. The
first plate described by Céloron, however, bears a different
place name from the one received by George Clinton (1686–
1761), Governor of New York Colony, and forwarded to London in 1751, though both are dated 29 July 1749. It appears
that when the Lords of Trade plate (as I refer to it) was recovered by the Indians, Céloron may have buried another
bearing the same date but a different locality and failed to
mention the first.

I am unaware of any record of this first plate after it
reached London. While plausible, there is no evidence that
Lawrence or George Washington saw or handled it, although
they likely knew about it, and were aware of the lead plates
and the Céloron expedition as a basis for the French claims.

The locations of the buried plates are as related in the
text. Of the seven original plates, it appears four have been
exhumed: (1) the Lords of Trade Plate, present location unknown; (2) a partial plate (portions melted by its discoverers
to make bullets) in the collection of the American Antiquarian Society, Worcester, Massachusetts; (3) the only complete
plate, at the Virginia Historical Society, Richmond, and (4)
Céloron's second plate buried near today's Franklin, Pennsylvania, that an entry in the eighteenth-century journal of

Christopher Gist (published in 1893) suggests may have been recovered at that time (present location unknown).

The Cuppy story, the Washington letter, the Folk Museum of Eastern Kentucky, various Kentucky place names, and the Queen's Maritime Museum in Barbados are fictional.

No rattlesnakes were harmed in the writing of this novel. Excepting the occasional exaggeration, the snake lore is authentic.

Digger's explanation of the curious distribution of the yam and sweet potato is correct. Although the yam has mystical significance in Melanesia, if either tuber was used recreationally as he suggests, it has yet to be reported in the scientific literature.

ACKNOWLEDGMENTS

A deep bow to Stod Rowe for introducing me to Monsieur Céloron and his lead plates. I am grateful to my agent, Eleanor Wood, and my editor, Bob Gleason for their enthusiasm and insights. The Fiction Critique Group of the Cincinnati Writers Project provided valuable advice—thanks, guys—and Ryck Neube has been a font of information and bent humor.

A belated thank-you to my mother for putting up with the critters: the bugs in the jelly glasses, the alligator in the bathtub, the snakes in the pillow cases.

I appreciate the generous assistance of the American Antiquarian Society; Craig J. Boreiko, International Lead Zinc Research Organization; Claire Brinker; Joseph T. Collins; C. Wesley Cowan Historic Americana; Sheriff Lee Davidson; Will Eckstein; Martha Goodway, Smithsonian Center for Materials Research & Education; Isabel Jimenez; Peter Obermark; Lisa Odum, Mt. Vernon Ladies Association Library; Sherri Kempf; and the Virginia Historical Society.

Any interpretation of information others may have provided to me is my own.